THE SHADOW ACADEMY

ADRIAN COLE

EDGE SCIENCE FICTION AND FANTASY PUBLISHING
AN IMPRINT OF HADES PUBLICATIONS, INC.

CALGARY

The Shadow Academy
Copyright © 2014 by Adrian Cole

Edge Science Fiction and Fantasy Publishing
An Imprint of Hades Publications Inc.
P.O. Box 1714, Calgary, Alberta, T2P 2L7, Canada

Editing by Robyn Read
Interior design by Janice Blaine
Cover Illustration and Design by Neil Jackson

ISBN: 978-1-77053-064-5

EDGE Science Fiction and Fantasy Publishing and Hades Publications, Inc. acknowledges the ongoing support of the Alberta Foundation for the Arts and the Canada Council for the Arts for our publishing programme.

Alberta   Conseil des arts du Canada   Canada Council for the Arts

Library and Archives Canada Cataloguing in Publication

Cole, Adrian, author
The shadow academy / Adrian Cole. -- First edition.

ISBN: 978-1-77053-064-5
(e-book ISBN: 978-1-77053-065-2)

I. Title.
PR6053.O388S53 2014   823'.914   C2014-903411-3
                                       C2014-903412-1

FIRST EDITION
(H-20140618)
Printed in Canada
www.edgewebsite.com

Dedication

To my Jude

AFTER THE
PLAGUE WARS

~ Extract from the Secret Journals ~
of the Historical Society

It would be impossible to compose a definitive history of Grand Britannia, not only because a significant number of details have been lost, but also because the remaining facts have been obfuscated, one has to assume deliberately; so much of the truth, we are told, is not in the interests of the populace and would serve only to hinder progress towards the redevelopment and renaissance of the Islands.

The Plague Wars, responsible for the worldwide collapse of civilization as it must once have been, are today variously regarded as natural conflicts between nations; supernatural debacles engendered by irresponsible fanatics; and acts of a god or gods who have since the Wars had little more than mythic status with the populace. Clearly the Wars were as dreadful and as horrifically destructive to humanity as they are painted, and undoubtedly this has done much to foster an attitude of reticence and refusal to share information amongst the authorities who now control us.

There are a small number of people who need to know, we are told, while for the rest of us there is a thick curtain drawn over those remote days. Our Historical Society is therefore necessarily a secret order. Our recorded history is a labor of many minds, many researchers, people who seek the truth in the honest belief that only in truth can we move forward, both as individuals and as a nation in what may one day become a new world.

What the Society can conclude is that before the Plague Wars the world was thickly populated. Although this seems outrageous and even laughable today, Grand Britannia had a population numbering in the millions. (See appendices 2 and 7.) There were many cities and they were all linked by a very complex and highly sophisticated transport system that extended from what we know today as the very north of Caledon down to Londonborough and across to Dumnonia in the southwest and Cumra in the west— even across the sea to High Burnam. It is difficult today, with the Islands almost completely covered in forest, when even moors and uplands are succumbing to the spread of the trees, to visualize the terrain as it must have once existed.

Londonborough has always been the administrative heart of the nation, and although it survived the Plague Wars, it did not do so intact. So much of its original infrastructure has collapsed. The energy that Man once harnessed is now elusive, the sources of power either dried up or corrupted, fallen into disrepair. And, as stated at the outset of this work, knowledge has been lost. This has been exacerbated by a policy of deliberate suppression. The Central Authority that rules us from Londonborough today remains fiercely protective of its power and is afraid of releasing too much knowledge. To some extent this is understandable, but there is a growing feeling among scholars and intellectuals that the new power base is self-seeking, elitist, and ironically promoting a Dark Age.

The position of our Society is therefore a tenuous one. Our reasons for absolute discretion and secrecy we believe to be fully vindicated. The truth may come at a high price.

PROLOGUE

APRIL

SKELLBOW MOVED THROUGH the corridors of the old building uneasily, pausing occasionally to listen for any sounds in the night. Outside, the moon was high overhead, near full but obscured by passing clouds. Skellbow had finished the nightly lockup, jangling his keys and stomping his feet as he made his way back down to the entrance foyer. The sounds he made were deliberate. He hated the silence of the ancient Academy at night. He much preferred the place in the daytime when it was teeming with kids, even though their rowdiness and cheek roused his anger. After nightfall the place was empty and echoing, dead. Colleagues mocked his fear of spirits and supernatural agents, but they weren't the only reason he loathed this shift.

Security! The Prime, Miss Vine, had an almost obsessive regard for it, especially with another Inspection due. She ruled her Academy with a remorseless will to succeed in all things. Getting anything wrong was not a good idea.

"Security!" Skellbow muttered repeatedly, as if the word alone would ward off any consequences of error. "Not my fucking job. I'm just covering for Jordan. Not my fault if he's ill." He fiddled with the huge bunch of keys as though by doing so he would spot any that he hadn't used to secure the building.

There was a small overnight staff, and everyone would bed down in the Academy when they had finished their paperwork. The threat of the Inspection meant more work for all of them and some were frantically preparing for it. Rather them than him. At least, for once, the Prime wasn't here. Skellbow never felt anything but highly nervous in her presence.

His keys had their own secure cupboard near the tall double doors to the outside. Skellbow was about to lock them away when he was cut short by an insistent knock on the doors. He almost dropped the keys, turning to stare at the source of the sound in horror. *The Prime! It's her, for certain.* The knock came again and he went to the door, pressing up against it. Very slowly he unlocked it, easing it open no more than an inch, prepared to slam it shut and relock it if need be. Light from the thick candle in the niche just over his shoulder slanted out into the darkness. By its flickering glow he could discern a face. No one he recognized.

"Mr. Skellbow?" a gruff voice asked.

"What do you want? This place is shut for the night."

"We're the contractors. Working on the sea wall."

"It's the middle of the fucking night," Skellbow growled, readying to slam the door and bolt it.

"I know. But we need our tools. We left them, thinking we'd be back in the morning to finish the job. But we've been called to do another down in the barracks. Early start. We need those tools. Only take us a minute."

Skellbow was trying to think of a good reason to argue, when he became aware that someone was behind him. He swung around, even more on edge.

It was Carl Trencher, one of the senior staff. "Barry. What's the problem?"

"Builders, sir. They want their tools."

"At this time of night?"

"Shall I tell them to... come back in the morning?"

"I better have a word with them."

Trencher wore a long outdoor coat and was evidently about to go home for the night. He went to the door and eased it open a little further. Skellbow heard him speak to the men outside, not catching the words, but after a brief, polite exchange Trencher turned back to him.

"It'll be okay, Barry. Can't be helped. Just let them get their stuff and they'll be away again."

Skellbow nodded reluctantly.

Trencher allowed the three men into the foyer. They were all thickset, muscular navvies, used to hard labor by the look of them.

"Wouldn't have bothered you, mate," their leader told Skellbow. "We'd have stayed in the pub. But we need those tools." It was clear to Skellbow from the man's accent that he was no local man.

"I'll see you tomorrow, Barry," said Trencher. He gave the caretaker a last nod and slipped out into the darkness.

Skellbow grunted and led the three men further into the building. "Sea wall, you say?"

"Yeah, north wall," said the spokesman. The other two were silent, eyes taking in their surroundings, but they were otherwise apparently indifferent.

Skellbow masked his disapproval with difficulty. He hadn't wanted these contractors here in the first place. Dunstan Fullacombe, the Master of the Watch, was a first-rate stone-mason and he certainly hadn't wanted contractors in to fix a wall, sea wall or otherwise. But Trencher was in charge of the premises and he had insisted.

"Quiet in here at this time, mate," said the spokesman. He had an angular, unshaven face and eyes that lacked any kind of warmth.

Skellbow nodded. "Keep the noise down. Couple of staff, probably asleep by now."

They walked wordlessly down several echoing corridors until Skellbow opened a door to a narrow courtyard. Directly opposite them the high sea wall loomed like the threat of an avalanche. Moonlight picked out the curved line of its parapet and the stone steps that led steeply up to its wide, unprotected top.

"I'll be in the foyer," said Skellbow, eager to be free of them.

"It'll take no time, mate. Wait for us there."

As the three men crossed the yard, Skellbow closed the door and returned through the building. Once back in the foyer, he slid a bolt across the main doors to keep anyone — or anything else — out.

He waited, slumped against one of the stone columns beside the doors, cursing his fellow caretaker, Jordan Creech, whose shift this should have been. Still, he could get off to the pub in time for a pint, as soon as these three goons had gone. They were military men, typical of the types that the Central Authority in distant Londonborough was sending out more and more these days. Seemed the Authority wanted its own people to swell the ranks of the forces in the barracks here in Petra. Skellbow, like many of his fellows from the area, resented the influx into their southwestern province of Dumnonia.

His morose thoughts were interrupted by a flickering of the candle that told him its life expectancy was fading. At the bottom of the key cupboard there was a box of fresh, fat candles. He took one out, lit it with the last of the existing one, and slid it into its holder. The exercise prompted him to consider, impatiently, *Where the fuck are they? Shouldn't take them this long to find their tools.*

Skellbow made his way back down the corridors, and as he approached the door to the courtyard, he saw movement through a window. Instinctively he ducked, though he was probably invisible from outside. What he saw made his breath catch in his throat.

Two of the men were carrying something through another doorway into the courtyard — a door he'd locked earlier. It led to an internal stairway up to some offices and a private staff area. He knew he'd locked it because he'd been up there a short time ago, talking to Drew Vasillius, one of the teachers. Vasillius, one of the staff working late that night, had been happy for Skellbow to lock the lower door because he was going to bed down in the back room once he had finished his work.

How in buggery did they get a key to that door? Skellbow asked himself, his whole body growing cold. The men were carrying some kind of large sack. *Sack?* Transfixed, the caretaker watched them manhandle it through the courtyard and up the first of the narrow steps ascending the fifty-foot-high sea wall.

He had no choice but to respond. He moved to the door to his right, threw it open, and crossed the courtyard. The spokesman for the three contractors stepped out of the shadows at the foot of the steps to the sea wall, limned in a pale wash of moonlight. He looked like a spectre.

"What the fuck is going on?" said Skellbow, conscious that he was shouting.

"Nothing to worry about, mate. One of your colleagues is a bit under the weather."

"Who is it? Mr. Vasillius?"

"He's had a fainting fit."

Skellbow pulled up just short of the man, whose hands were in shadow. "That's bollocks—"

The man shook his head. He looked very alert, body tensed. "Overworking. Needed some air."

Skellbow looked upwards. The two others had got their burden onto the sea wall and now disappeared from sight. Skellbow was a biggish man, the nature of his work making him fitter than most men of his age, close on fifty, and he had never shirked a fight when he was younger. Instinct took over now, brushing away all his earlier fears — this was no supernatural threat he was facing — and he abruptly pushed the spokesman aside.

Though he was taken unawares, he made a grab for Skellbow. Skellbow, deceptively nimble, escaped the contractor's grip on his forearm and scaled the steps. It was a treacherous, awkward climb, but he clambered upwards with purpose. Behind him the contractor snarled an angry warning to the two men who were on top of the wall. Beyond its low parapet, which was no more than two feet high, was a drop of over a hundred feet to the churning sea below.

In front of him, Skellbow saw the two other men. They were alone. There was no sign of what they had been carrying.

"What's happened?" he gasped, dragging in ragged breaths.

"He went nuts!" said the first of them. "We were trying to help him. Get him some air. He just hit out at us. Started swearing. Next thing, he was up on the parapet." The man pointed to it.

His companion joined in. "Yeah. Lost his head, mate. Jumped off."

Skellbow, aghast, walked to the parapet and looked over its edge, but below the incessant crashing of waves and the explosive rise of spume obscured any sign of a body. No one could possibly have survived a plunge into that. Beneath that white maelstrom there were rocks, jagged and merciless. Vasillius would have been smashed to pieces.

"Nothing we could do, mate."

Skellbow turned around. The spokesman had joined them on the wall. He and his two fellow contractors were staring pointedly at the caretaker, and they shifted with practiced ease into a formation that penned him in, up against the parapet. *God, are they going to fling me off, too?*

"Why would he do it?" said Skellbow. He was too afraid now to ask them about the sack.

"Stressed out." The spokesman's right hand moved into a shaft of moonlight and Skellbow saw with rising horror that it held a long bladed knife. The caretaker's shoulders tensed, his fists balling.

"You'd better go down and give the alarm, Mr. Skellbow. Let people know what's happened. But get it right, you hear me?" The knife swung slowly up, its point levelled at Skellbow's chest.

"Suicide," he breathed.

"In a minute, the three of us will be gone. We were never up here. We just picked up our tools down below and were out in a couple of seconds. Okay?"

Skellbow said nothing. His skin crawled as though something in the darkness was uncoiling, only inches away from touching him, polluting him.

The spokesman delicately touched the edge of his blade. "You're a family man, Mr. Skellbow. You've a fine wife, Myra, right?"

Skellbow felt his gorge rising. "What do you mean?"

"Young son, doing well here at the Academy. Davie, is it? Yeah, Davie."

"You leave them out of it!" Skellbow hissed.

"Whatever you say, Mr. Skellbow. Barry. But I need to hear you say what I want you to say. We came, picked up our tools, and left. Then, when you came out here to lock up, you saw Vasillius fling himself off the wall. You agree that you'll stick to that no matter who asks you what and we won't need to pay a visit to Myra and Davie, when you're not around."

Skellbow felt something briefly touch his arm, but his eyes remained fixed on the knife.

"Shit, why don't we just heave him over?" said one of the other men.

The spokesman scowled. "No, no. We've done our job. No need to queer the pitch by dumping Mr. Skellbow. That right, Barry?"

Reluctantly the caretaker grunted his assent.

"Good. We're going now. Lock up after us and then raise the alarm."

Skellbow's resistance drained. He could hardly move. The spokesman waved his two companions along the wall and they descended the steps as quickly as the incline would allow.

"Now you," the spokesman said to Skellbow, pointing to the stone steps with his knife. The caretaker managed to find the will to move and went down after the others.

A few minutes later they were back in the foyer. Skellbow unlocked the main doors and two of the men slipped outside. Their spokesman turned for a last word.

"Do the sensible thing, Barry. By the morning, we three will be long gone on the road back to the city. No one will know you're not telling the truth."

"What about the wall, your work?"

"All finished earlier today. And we put a little something into the stones. This place is marked now, Barry."

Skellbow hardly moved, his teeth clamped, holding back the fury within him. *Marked? What does he mean by that? Marked for who— or what?*

"If I find out you've let me down, someone will be back. And I promise you, it will be very bad, Barry." Something evil in the spokesman's eyes reinforced the threat.

"Okay, okay. Just leave my family alone."

Beyond the door, a sudden gust of wind swept across the playground and the spokesman cocked an ear as if listening to it. "Hear that, Barry? Keep your ears and eyes open. Every breath of wind, every bird that flies by, every wave that breaks on the wall, you can be sure that we'll be watching, listening."

Skellbow shuddered. God alone knew what agents these men could call upon. "I hear you."

The spokesman gave a curt nod, as if he had just concluded a routine business transaction, and he was gone, swift as thought.

Skellbow shut the door, locked it, and bolted it. He made his way quickly along the ground level corridors, back into the courtyard, and crossed to the doorway that led to the stairs to Drew Vasillius's office. He quickly ascended the tower's winding staircase, only to find Vasillius's office empty, with nothing indicating there had been a struggle. It struck him as strange, given what he had seen. The room was tidy, papers put away, the chair tucked under the desk. As though Vasillius had put things in order before leaving. Skellbow left the room, closing the door behind him.

Re-crossing the courtyard, he studied the numerous angled roofs high overhead, half expecting to see something up there staring back at him.

He made his way, deeply disturbed, through the building to the Academy's bell tower and let himself in to its relative sanctuary. A few moments later he was tugging hard on the bell ropes, waking the town to the story he would fabricate for its startled people.

PART ONE
A SEED OF DOUBT

I

PETRA: MIDSUMMER

CHAD MUNDY HAD his first view of Petra Dumnoniorum from the crest of the last of a number of hills after his long and arduous journey from distant Londonborough along the Great West Way, the arterial route from west to east of the country. The forest, which pressed up to the very walls of Londonborough, had seemed interminable, as though the world was no more than a matted tangle of trees. Here at the northern edge of Dumnonia the trees had at last given way to the open hills, which undulated towards the coast and the lonely city that Mundy now studied sleepily out of the aperture in the side of the horse-drawn carriage. He could see through the haze of the waning summer afternoon the broad river valley unfolding to where the fortress city clung to the steep incline of its far side, secure behind high walls. Several spires formed part of its skyline, one spiking the dropping sun as it fell towards the western sea beyond the city. The late sunlight bled across the roofs and parapets, coating them in shades of rusted red and crimson.

Mundy grimaced at the morbid thoughts prompted by the image. *Been on this damned road too long,* he thought. *I should be relieved to be here.* Somehow he felt the reverse, as though he was about to cross shifting sands.

The baggage train had been traveling for a week, its several carriages and carts drawn by teams of horses bred for the purpose, their progress necessarily slow and ponderous. Two hundred miles of being bumped and buffeted. A human cargo amongst so much other provender: medical supplies, fuel, a few additional weapons, and, although nothing was said, Mundy was certain there was a chest of coins. A lot of trade was through barter, but coinage in Londonborough was growing— *bound to seep out to the extremities in time,* Mundy thought. And then there were the soldiers. Fifty strong, under the command of the weather-beaten Sergeant

Crammon, whose barking tones cut through the still forest air from the early hours deep into the evening, every day. *Does the man ever sleep?* Mundy wondered. He'd read about machines, those semi-mythical things, and Crammon must be the human equivalent. He was, of course, precisely what the Authority required. His soldiers, mostly young men fresh out of Londonborough's military bases, were pliant to him, obedient to the strict codes that governed their profession. Their eagerness to reach Petra manifested itself as a murmur of excitement which even the rigid Crammon tolerated.

Mundy was the sole occupant of the passenger coach— another trial on the everlasting journey. The coach trundled down the last slope towards a narrow stone bridge. Mundy saw the small naval dockyards across the river, forming the eastern boundary of the fortress, a dozen or more ships of varying types berthed there. He had no idea what sort of craft they were. Warships, he assumed, or at least ships geared up in some way for the defense of the realm. The fortress city itself was more of a town, he thought, although it was far larger than any of the way stations he had passed through on his journey here. They had been isolated stockades, staffed by no more than a score of hardened military men, armed and alert as if expecting imminent attack. Their weapons had been unique to their posting— guns of one kind or another. Even at the military academy where he had trained, Mundy had rarely seen guns. The all-encompassing forest lands were dangerous places and defense against encroachment required extreme measures.

Guards patrolled Petra's boundary wall, built of stone and at least twenty feet high, light glinting on their javelins, pikes, and other weapons. They seemed primed for war. This remotest of Grand Britannia's provinces seemed on first glance to be as obsessed with the possibility of hostile invasion as Londonborough was.

As the baggage train drew to a halt, Mundy heard Crammon and one of his corporals talking just beyond the window.

"Good turnout," said the corporal.

Crammon snorted. "That's for our benefit, son. This bloody lot spend most of their working day on their arses, from what I hear. They're no more prepared for the Invasion than the fucking sheep out in their farms. They've been ordered to sharpen up for us. Come back tomorrow. The wall will be deserted." His voice was instantly recognisable to Mundy as a Londonborough voice. Like most of the soldiery traveling down here, he was from the city.

The corporal laughed appropriately. Mundy sensed the unease in it. His voice had a different inflection, which Mundy guessed to be of this area. It explained the youth's discomfort.

The Invasion, Mundy thought. *The threat that hangs over us all, a sword of Damocles.* How real was it? Across the southern sea was the massive central continent of Evropa: the received wisdom was that the Plague Wars had been started there. Now the continent was even more overgrown than Grand Britannia, choked with weed and tree, almost devoid of human life. The huge losses of population had led to the deterioration and collapse of the urban network and, indeed, the towns and cities themselves, allowing the return of a forest wilderness on an unprecedented scale. But whoever was there, word had it, would be set on conquest. They would covet the Islands. Everyone's duty was to prepare for the Invasion. The coastal fortress cities were manned as early warning stations, their lookouts' eyes seaward, ever watching for the first signs of enemy action. After all these years — no one really knew how long ago the Plague Wars had ended for the Authority had, as far as Mundy could determine, always done its best to obfuscate the records — the Authority still demanded this preparation, the training of soldiery, a navy, everyone a cog in the defensive machine.

We're all of us getting more and more indifferent. It'll never happen, we say. Can anyone remember when there was even a real hint of an Invasion? The transport moved on across the bridge. *What's this place going to be like, so far from Londonborough and the extremes of military control? What drives Petra?*

He had spent the last three years of his life in a combined college and military academy in Londonborough, training to teach and undergoing the military preparation that all citizens were required to go through. He had majored in English, and because of a natural aptitude his military expertise was in hand-to-hand combat, though he had no idea how he had inherited such an inborn talent, if talent was the word for it. He had needed that skill, though; more than once it had saved his hide in a tough scrape, and, he thought, *doubtless I am going to need it in this remote neck of the woods.*

Beyond the bridge the baggage train slowly moved under
a massive stone arch as two tall wooden doors, which were
a good foot or more thick, hewn from arboreal forest giants,
opened for them to pass through. Once inside the town, the
bulk of the train headed off for the barracks somewhere behind
the docks, while the passenger coach pulled up in an open
square fronted by a white-walled building. A flaking sign
above its main door proclaimed it to be The Coach House.
Several men came outside to meet the coach, exchanging
pleasantries with the driver and his two colleagues.

Mundy got out, stretching cramped muscles and blinking
in the light of day. Even though it was early evening it was
noticeably bright. An unfamiliar cackle above him made him
duck instinctively, but he realized immediately, with some
irritation, that it was a clutch of large white gulls that had
come to investigate the new arrival and the chance of a late
meal. They dropped insolently to the pub roof and stared
fixedly at him.

"Mr. Mundy?" One of the men stepped forward. He was
younger than Mundy's twenty-two years, thin and bright-
eyed, dressed in a rumpled light jacket, the suggestion of a
moustache across his upper lip. He held his hand out almost
apologetically.

Mundy shook it, not reacting visibly to the hot, weak grip.
"Yes, I'm Chad Mundy."

"Very pleased to meet you. You're very welcome." The young
man grinned awkwardly, putting his hands in his pockets as if
they were a source of embarrassment. "I'm Andrew Wilkinson.
I'm the helper." He made it sound like an official post.

"Pleased to meet you, Andrew."

"Have you got some bags?"

One of the coachmen had dumped Mundy's three cases
down behind him as if glad to be rid of them. The man was
already back up on the coach. Within a few moments it moved
off, disappearing under the far eaves of THE COACH HOUSE
into the shadows.

Wilkinson nodded. "I've told one of the boys to get Mr.
Skellbow to bring up the cart. He's one of our caretakers.
We've got two at the Academy. The Master of the Watch is in
charge of them. There's a cart to take us up to the Academy.
Have you been there? Oh, of course, you must have. When
you came for your interview—"

Mundy gently interrupted, "Yes, this is my second visit. Though I didn't get to see much of the place when I was here before."

"Mr. Goldsworthy will be your mentor. Everyone calls him Brin. He teaches English." He said it as if teaching English carried with it a certain distinction, and Mundy was hard pressed not to grin. "He couldn't meet you this evening. Staff Meeting with the Senior Magisters. And the Prime, Miss Vine. Have you met her? Oh, yes. At your interview. Sorry."

His waffling was cut short by the arrival of a horse-drawn cart, driven by a bushy-haired giant, a scowl of concentration pasted to his face as he pulled up short. A thin cloud of dust eddied about them.

"I'm to take you up to the Academy," Wilkinson said. "Brin Goldsworthy will meet you later." He started loading Mundy's cases.

Mundy offered his hand to the burly caretaker. "I'm Chad Mundy."

"Skellbow, caretaker," said the man as he shook hands uneasily, as if unaccustomed to doing so, grunting his own hello through a rather fixed scowl.

Moments later they were on their way through the narrow streets. Petra was built on the steep side of a hill. Mundy recalled from his first trip that all roads seemed to lead up, often precariously, to the Academy above the town.

"Are you replacing Mr. Vasillius?" said Wilkinson, sitting between Mundy and Skellbow in the front of the cart, eyes watching the side streets as though he expected something to emerge and challenge their passage.

Skellbow looked briefly across at the young teacher, almost reprovingly, but then his eyes again fixed on the winding slope ahead. He gave a curt call of encouragement to the horse.

"Mr. Vasillius died," said Wilkinson. "Did they tell you? Nice man. We miss him." He clammed up for a moment, as if Skellbow's glance had hit a nerve.

Dead man's shoes, Mundy mused, not for the first time. He'd been told discreetly that his predecessor had died, though he'd not attached anything to it.

"Someone has to do his job," said Wilkinson, as if he felt the need to qualify his earlier remarks. Mundy concluded that Wilkinson's nervousness and odd way of expressing himself was probably due to the fact that he was a little slow.

They traveled in silence to the main gates of the Academy. These were set in another wall, which was far lower than the immense outer wall to the city. Unlike that huge granite city wall, this one was made from red brick. The wrought-iron gates looked to Mundy, from their uniquely ornate style, to be unusually old. Well preserved and painted black. *They're not that behind the times here.*

"Interesting gates," he said.

Skellbow reacted as if he had been poked. He nodded, though there was still no breaching the scowl. "Creech's pride and joy, these gates."

"Jordan Creech is our other caretaker," Wilkinson explained. "In charge of security. Mr. Skellbow is maintenance."

Mundy nodded. "Where on earth did you get them?"

The caretaker shrugged. "Been part of the Academy since long before any of us was around."

"How old is the Academy?" said Mundy, looking up at the sprawling building before them. It was constructed mainly from red brick, its high windows of a style and shape that suggested the building belonged to another world. The glass in the windows was leaded, the lintels of sandstone, slightly darkened by exposure. Granite steps led up to the main doors, which were black with age. Towers and spires rose from the main body of the building, their ancient slates seemingly in a creditable state of repair.

"Hundreds of years, I'd say," said Skellbow, swinging down from the cart and stroking the nose of his horse. He appeared to have ended his contribution to the discussion, ready to get on with whatever other chores his role demanded.

Wilkinson had deliberately kept out of the conversation, instead unloading Mundy's cases. "I'll take you to your rooms," he said eventually. "You'll be in the east wing. Until you find somewhere of your own in the town. All in good time. Food's not bad here."

Mundy inserted the occasional word of thanks into Wilkinson's endless chatter as they entered the old building and made their way through numerous corridors and up stairwells. At this time of day the building was unusually quiet, almost eerie. Mundy was too tired to take in the sur- roundings. He was familiar with them to some extent from being shown around earlier in the year. He could explore later. Right now all he wanted was to soak in a bath to ease his battered muscles. Afterwards, he told himself, he would visit the canteen and eat an entire side of beef.

Wilkinson must have read his mind. "Mrs. Bazeley knows you're here. She's our chief cook. She doesn't usually cook after the end of the school day, but she always does something for new staff." He had stopped outside a suite of rooms and gestured for Mundy to go in.

"Thanks be for Mrs. Bazeley." Mundy smiled as they entered.

"Brin Goldsworthy will be here soon. He'll sort out your grub."

Mundy could see that Wilkinson was anxious to leave, as if he had overstayed his welcome. Mundy shook his head. "Thanks, Andrew. Much appreciated. You must let me buy you a drink some time soon."

Wilkinson coloured slightly. "That's very kind." He scurried off. Mundy closed the door and began unpacking.

· ✳ ·

Mundy was surprised to find he had a bathroom, equipped with a steel tub that was fed by twin taps set in the stone wall behind it. Amazingly, one of the taps provided *hot* water. He would have to get hold of Skellbow again to ask him how the system worked. *How the hell do they power it? And heat it? A lot of places in Londonborough are crying out for something this sophisticated.* The pleasures of a hot bath took over and he dozed on and off while soaking. Soon the rigors of the journey were forgotten. He was here. Petra Dumnoniorum.

Well, Mundy, this is what you wanted. A break from Londonborough. A fresh start, out in the new world. A challenge. It will be that, all right.

Shortly after he had toweled down and dressed there was a firm knock on the door. He opened it to face a man of medium height, once muscular but now a little overweight, his eyes unusually bright, his complexion ruddy.

"Chad Mundy?" he said, hand out like a piston.

"You must be Brin Goldsworthy," Mundy nodded, shaking hands and having his own almost pulped.

"Brin. Sorry to miss you in the town. Special meeting with management. Nothing but meetings at the moment, after the Inspection. Settling in okay?"

Mundy let him in and Goldsworthy looked around the room as if he might find someone lurking within. He was dressed in smart slacks and a stiff shirt, the top buttons undone, the plain tie loosened. He looked as if he had been engaged in strenuous exercise.

"Yes, fine," said Mundy. "I had a bath. Hot water. Amazing."

Goldsworthy chuckled. "You can thank Dunstan for that. Master of the Watch. He's a dab hand at technical stuff. Done more to eradicate draughts and run the heating through the Academy than anyone would have a right to expect. You hungry?"

"Famished."

"Mrs. Bazeley makes pies to die for. She's fattening all of us up, bless her." Goldsworthy ushered Mundy out into the airless corridor. The Academy had an ethereal quality, as though it had been long abandoned.

"It's unusually quiet in here. Bit like another world," Mundy commented.

"No boarders. All the kids are local. Some come in from the farms. Furthest away is about ten miles. After that it's all forest, right up to Southmoor. Same across the river, over to Northmoor. Nearest ones walk in. Others ride."

"Yes, I saw the stables when I first visited."

They made their way down through the labyrinthine passages and stairs to a large hall that Mundy assumed must have been beneath ground level, as there were no windows. The silence was slightly unsettling and Mundy imagined the place heaving with youngsters, the air thick with the sound of clattering plates. Tables and chairs were spread out in neat rows, washed and gleaming. Beyond them was a long shutter behind a worktop. Goldsworthy tapped loudly on it: Mundy couldn't imagine him doing anything quietly.

A section swung aside to reveal the beaming face of the cook. "Pleased to meet you, Chad. Call me Emily."

The two men sat at a table, the air filled with a delicious aroma that made Mundy's mouth water. Goldsworthy leaned back, puffing out his chest, although it seemed an unconscious movement. "So I'm your mentor. Always look after the new recruits. You a married man?"

"Me? No. Not even close."

"My wife works in the town. Does a bit of restoration."

Mrs. Bazeley delivered two plates, swimming with gravy, huge pies and enough vegetables to feed a family. "Plates are *hot*." She set cutlery down with another beaming smile. "Leave some room for the apple tart."

"You are a queen among cooks," Goldsworthy told her, attacking the steaming pie.

"Just as well, with all these funny hours you staff work."

"Blame it on the Inspection, Mrs. B. You know what it's like."

"I do. Everyone's running around like headless chickens," she laughed.

Goldsworthy snorted with amusement. "Don't let our Prime hear you say that, girl. She'll have you on the next baggage train out of here."

"Miss Vine knows a good cook when she sees one. And them Enforcers didn't complain about my cooking either." She laughed again and left them to their meals.

Mundy had never tasted a pie like it. The meat, which Goldsworthy declared to be pheasant, was unbelievable. "I gather the Inspection was less than satisfactory," Mundy said between mouthfuls.

Goldsworthy's food was disappearing rapidly, as if he had not eaten for days. He grunted assent. "Not good. You'll hear more about that at the morning gathering when Miss Vine addresses the troops. We've got four months to get our act together before the Enforcers return. If they're not happy then, well, it won't be good."

"Sounds like I've picked a bad time to start a career here," Mundy said with a wry grin. What little he had learned about the recent Inspection made him uneasy.

Goldsworthy pushed his plate away and wiped his mouth. "You'll be fine. It's us that need to toe the line. Well, according to the Enforcers anyway. You've been drafted in to bring fresh ideas, new tricks. Ideal for a youngster like you. Your speciality is the same as mine, teaching English, I gather?"

"And unarmed combat."

"Useful skill to have. I'm staves, pikes, spears, all that. Plus I like using the bow, but we're a bit short on top bowmen. Drew Vasillius was our expert. He'd been here a long time. Only had another couple of years to go to retirement."

Mundy let him talk, sensing a note of distinct sorrow.

"He hadn't been well for a few months. When you're like that, the Academy can be a pretty stressful place. Took its toll."

"Was he a popular man?"

"Very much so. Local chap, like most of us. Oh, no offense, Chad." The apology was obviously genuine. "We're not the least averse to new blood. Hell, we need it. Everywhere does. You'll be very welcome, I promise you."

"That's a relief."

"Drew had his own views." Goldsworthy seemed about to embellish this comment, but sat back again as Mrs. Bazeley presented them with two more plates, this time loaded with slices of apple pie drenched in thick, yellow custard. When the cook had again disappeared, Goldsworthy prodded at the food as if he had lost interest in it. "Did they tell you how he died?"

"I didn't like to ask."

"Suicide." Goldsworthy spoke the word as if it were foreign to him.

"I don't quite know what to say—"

"This place certainly got to Drew. One night he went up on to the north wall. Runs along the seaward side of the Academy. Doubles as the city wall and drops sheer down to the sea, a good hundred feet or more. Drew threw himself off. God knows why, but people do strange things when they lose it."

Suddenly Mundy no longer felt hungry. "That's too bad."

"Well, all in the past. We move on. Speaking of which, let's get you down to the local hostelry. After that feast, I could do with a drink. I'll introduce you to some of the staff."

II

LONDONBOROUGH: MIDSUMMER

ALTHOUGH IT WAS midsummer, clouds curdled over the colossal urban sprawl of Londonborough, blotting out most of the light as though a vast, lumpy blanket had been draped over the city. For as long as anyone could remember it had always been so: the days were as grey as twilight, the city air dense and oppressive. Whether this was something to do with the ancient wars or with localised freak meteorological conditions, the phenomenon was something that the limited science of the city could not explain. Indeed, its inhabitants had long since given up attempting to fathom the mystery. There were more important things to pursue in the metropolis. The city itself, dismal and foreboding by day, funereal by night, stirred fitfully, whole areas of its buildings silent and empty, succumbing to weed and rot. Somewhere amongst those redundant edifices people existed in slowly growing numbers, but where they had once swarmed, they now existed in isolated pockets. What was once the hub of the world had become a mausoleum, its silence broken sporadically, its darkness a restless, flowing tide, eager to close in and claim the last of the defiant structures.

Near the centre of the city, where a number of tall buildings resisted the decline, a solitary tower poked up at the swirling elements overhead, a monument to Man's persistence. High inside it, in rooms that were kept pristine, maintained immaculately, and serviced by dedicated, determined staff, the offices of the Central Authority were like something from a bygone, more dynamic age. Outside its long windows, the crippled city spread out, a defeated giant organism. But within, life pulsed, vibrant, inexorable.

The conference room boasted a long central table, polished and gleaming. Every morning the room was cleaned and dusted with an almost obsessive attention to detail. Chairs were set precisely. Crystal jugs were filled with the freshest water available and glasses set in readiness. Ancillary staff made their many checks and then ghosted back into anonymity. The room fell silent but for the steady ticking of an ancient wall clock. Reputedly it had never been allowed to stop, as if it were the vital heartbeat of the building.

All meetings here began traditionally at 9:00 a.m. Just as punctually, at five to nine, Luther Sunderman arrived and sat at the head of the table. This morning he carried a thick dossier, which he opened and began to peruse. It was labeled "Petra Dumnoniorum Academy." Sunderman had read it a number of times and knew its contents intimately. He and his team of Enforcers had compiled it, having spent two weeks at the remote southwestern Academy, assessing its performance and achievements. The door opened and the first of that team arrived.

By nine o'clock, the expected company had assembled. Nash, Eversley, Stanton, Culverton— all dressed as Sunderman was, in immaculate, light suits. They were well groomed, smooth shaven, bright and alert. Their own papers were set neatly before them.

"Good morning, gentlemen," said Sunderman in a relaxed, cool voice. He appeared to be in good humour. Sunderman in one of his frosty moods always made for an uneasy morning and an atmosphere that usually fermented errors.

"I think we are satisfied that this report is complete. It seems to capture the details of what we all found at Petra. Very comprehensive." Sunderman paused briefly to see if any of the team wanted to challenge him. No one did.

They were joined shortly thereafter by an older man, wearing an even more immaculate suit. He wore several gold rings and had a habit of tapping on the tabletop, not to draw attention to these priceless objects, more in distraction, as if not altogether comfortable. He was, however, a senior member of the Authority, outranking even Sunderman.

"Well, Luther— the last of the fortress city Inspections. I do hope it's an improvement on the others." Lionel Canderville was a well-preserved man in his late sixties, his eyes sharp as a hawk's, his white hair combed back in a thick mane that ran down over his collar. He looked like a man who would never lack for anything, whatever the economic, social, or political vicissitudes of the world.

Sunderman indicated the wall beneath the clock, where a framed map decorated a large area. All eyes turned to it. The map bore the legend Grand Britannia, and although it had clearly been drawn by a cartographer of some skill, it seemed a very simple affair, its coastlines and islands sketched in, lacking detail. The southeastern corner of the main island contained Londonborough, shown by a red circle. In the context of the Islands, this circle was relatively small, highlighting the vast green expanses that covered almost everywhere else. Around the coast were a number of smaller circles, each set near the mouth of a river.

"We inspected the northern fortress cities of Northcastle, Liverton, and Hullborough over a year ago. Since then we have been in the east to inspect Coldchester, to Sevenmouth in the west, Southerhampton in the south. Our conclusions in all cases were that the degree of alertness and preparation for any potential invasion by our enemies is barely satisfactory. The fortresses are essentially an early warning system, remote, strung out along a considerable area of coastline. They should, if properly attended and managed, alert Londonborough expeditiously in the event of sightings."

"We receive regular reports, but all negative?" said Canderville blandly.

"Yes, sir, discounting occasional shipping— traders and fishing fleets, all of whom operate out of these city ports."

"So for a hundred years or more, there's been no sign of the Invasion. Not so much as a hostile rowing boat." Canderville sipped his water and watched Sunderman with the bland confidence of a superior enjoying his rank.

Sunderman smiled uncomfortably "Indeed, sir. Sadly this tends to make for complacency. We found in all six fortress cities a lack of focus."

"And we can't have that," Canderville smiled, tapping the table.

"The problem is twofold as I see it," Sunderman continued. "The apathy— and I think that the Primes and their military commanders in each academy have woken up to our concerns, as all six fortress cities have extended their watches along their sections of the coastline. Improvement is slow, achieved against a general trend of indifference to the Invasion."

"Secondly?"

"Attitude to the Authority, sir. Independence for the fortress cities would not benefit Grand Britannia. They need to contribute fully to the holistic needs of the Islands. The Authority must maintain control. These six fortress cities demonstrate a distinct decline in respect for it. In their early days, they were almost completely dependent on Londonborough for survival. They now flex their muscles— a good thing, of course, in terms of progress. But our coastline must be policed adequately. If they were independent, they would be picked off easily by any invading forces."

Canderville leaned back. "How confident are you that the six cities remain dependent on us?"

"I'm certain a little more work will bring them into line."

"And this latest Inspection? Petra Dumnoniorum. It's pretty damn remote."

Sunderman pursed his lips as if something had irritated him. "I'm more concerned about Petra than the others. It evidences the same apathy, lack of respect, willful resistance to the requirements. But it's more entrenched. The Dumnonians are tough and resilient, which is good. But they do like their own way."

"Who's the military chief down there? Storm Gunnerson, isn't it?"

"Commander Ian Gunnerson, yes."

"I know the man. Used to be tough as old boots. Not gone soft, has he? Time was when he'd have a man flayed just for a creased collar."

"Gunnerson is not the problem. He may not be as strict as he was, but his soldiers are as good a regiment as any other. Same with their naval presence. When it comes to the crunch, they do buckle down to it. We've sent several units to Petra over the last year. So the regiment is not just made up of locals. Nearly fifty percent of it consists of trained men from Londonborough academies. Gunnerson will conform."

Canderville was taking it in attentively. Ultimately all this would reflect on him with his own committees and councils. If the fortress cities were in a mess, his superiors would call him to account. "And Petra's Prime?"

"Miss Cora Vine. If anything, she's tougher than Gunnerson."

Canderville drummed his fingers, his rings glinting. "So we have perfectly adequate staff at the right level. Then what's the problem?"

"I have had long discussions with Miss Vine. There's no doubt that she is dedicated to her work, absolutely an Authority person. Our ideals, our vision for the revival of the Islands — she's fully committed. The students in the Academy are almost entirely local. Their families likewise, going back as many generations as are known. So do local customs and traditions. They make good soldiers, provided they are integrated with our own. Hence our sending more external troops.

"I think we need to make an example of Petra. It needs to understand that the Authority will not tolerate deviation from its rules, ideals, and values. The students who leave the Academy and join the military are not necessarily meeting those requirements. Worse, they don't seem to care. The Prime has been told to exercise whatever powers needed to turn this around. Gunnerson has enough muscle within his regiment now to do the same.

"Our Inspection also revealed deep-seated problems with some staff. This is the heart of the matter. It's hardly a revolution, but there is certainly a hard core — again local men and women — who resist the demands of the Authority."

Canderville nodded. "Well, you'd better weed them out."

"This business calls for a specialist. I'd like to bring in a new member of my team. Michel Deadspike. Very experienced, exceptionally skilled in many of the military specialisms and a credit to the Authority. I've appended his record to your report."

"I've heard the name," said Canderville, his expression implying that any information he had was not necessarily positive. "You'd stake your reputation on him?" Canderville smiled, his perfect teeth very white. "But then— you are."

"I'm sure that Deadspike is what the problem at Petra calls for."

Canderville rose, taking a proffered copy of the report from one of the suited men. "Petra," he said, as if trying to tug something out of the file. "Have I read some other report about that place? A death or something?" He made it sound as though there had been a fresh outbreak of plague.

Sunderman masked his emotions. A thin smile pasted itself across his features. "Indeed. One of the teaching staff. Rather tragic."

"Suicide, wasn't it?"

"Yes. Wretched man flung himself from the sea wall. He was never found. We replaced him with someone from one of our institutions rather than another local man. An Authority man. Chad Mundy. Young chap, shows a lot of promise."

"Not an agent?"

"I thought perhaps someone more subtle, sir. Someone who can settle in and share confidences. Mundy's demonstrated himself to be reliable. He's from the city. Trained here and always delivers according to Authority requirements. No family. Orphaned, like so many of them. I'm sure we can rely on him. As for a more stringent approach— well, we have Mr. Deadspike."

· ✳ ·

Deadspike was a tall, thin creature who walked in a deliberate manner as if treading on glass. His face was very pale, pinched, framed by thin, almost jet-black hair. His eyes were an unusual grey, narrow, their gaze always calm. Sunderman met that gaze now, not quite immune to the faint suggestion of arrogance.

"I should imagine Canderville will tire of his position before long," Deadspike said insouciantly.

"He'll move up on to one of the committees by the end of the year." Sunderman nodded. "An opportunity for one of us lesser mortals."

Deadspike's gaze was steady. He was used to sharing confidences with his superior. At least when it suited him. It gave Sunderman the impression that they were an effective team. *If you want to progress*, Deadspike could have said to his superior, *you need to toughen up, my friend. Too much negotiation, not enough muscle.* Instead he opened his file, his long white fingers flipping the pages. "All the more reason to solve the problem of Petra."

"You're to lead the follow-up in October. Canderville agreed."

Deadspike nodded thoughtfully. "I see that our contact within the staff at the Academy is one of the Senior Magisters. Carl Trencher. A reliable Authority man?"

"A man after your own heart, Michel."

"You flatter me, sir. People say I have no heart."

Sunderman's laugh was a short bark. "They do indeed. But there's no room for sentiment in this business."

Deadspike smiled, reminding Sunderman that if he had enemies, this clinical machine of a man would be the last person he would want as their ally.

"Petra is an unusual proposition," Sunderman went on. "The Academy is unique, not the least in its history and its, shall we say, intrigues. To be frank, Michel, it could be quite a treacherous place. Stubborn."

"The Prime is strong?"

"Yes. I'm sure she's as ambitious as the rest of us. But the success of the Academy is her principal goal. She believes in the discipline and commitment of the Authority. I had many discussions with her while I was there. She's very cooperative. She won't challenge you. Well, not unless you propose something that she really objects to. Then you'll see that's she has a mind of her own."

"I would enjoy that."

Deadspike seemed to be lost in thought for a moment, but Sunderman knew his colleague to be inordinately astute. He sifted information for details that would have escaped the scrutiny of many another meticulous observer.

"The man who died," Deadspike said at last, "has he been replaced?"

"Yes, by a man called Chad Mundy. I was in two minds about putting a candidate forward. The vacancy occurred midterm, limiting the choice. If it had happened during the summer break, we would have had a whole new batch of qualified staff to interview. As it was, we needed someone who was immediately available. I certainly didn't want someone who had been out of teaching for any length of time and transferring even a willing person from one of the Londonborough Academies would have been a bit hit and miss."

"Forgive me, but do we not have any of our privately groomed staff available?" *Surely such a move was obvious. This is no time to be soft.*

"I didn't want to put an agent in. I just have the feeling that if the staff at Petra sensed in any way that new staff going in are agents of the Authority, they'd clam up and be even more difficult to monitor and control. Besides, we already have some good contacts in the Academy and in the town. And with you there, we're well represented. There will be no need for the good people of Petra to think that every new member of staff is an agent."

"How was Mundy chosen?"

"Throughout his training, he's shown himself to be reliable, trustworthy, and loyal. Ironically, he would almost certainly have been approached by us at the end of his training. He's good agent material."

Deadspike nodded slowly; he evaluated every word as painstakingly as an archivist perusing an old manuscript. *But he's not our agent. Surely an oversight.*

"We were satisfied that his potential as a teacher was excellent. Arranging him to complete his studies a month or so early was easy enough."

"Did he produce a thesis?"

"Yes, on dialects. A pet subject of his. He saw his appointment to Petra as an opportunity to study a local dialect in situ. He has no family and has tended to be something of a loner. Shortly after he accepted the post, I had him watched carefully. My conclusion is that he, like many of the new breed of citizens, sees the Authority as vital to the regeneration of the Islands. He is very self-disciplined. I should have said, he excelled at his military discipline, unarmed combat, which calls for a particular dedication to rules."

"Interesting," said Deadspike. "So local politics are not likely to woo his affections. He doesn't sound like the rebellious type." *But, my dear Sunderman, I would like to probe that little detail for myself. Not the sort of thing to be taken for granted.*

III

PETRA: MIDSUMMER

SKELLBOW FINISHED UNHARNESSING the horse and eased it into its stable for the night, talking to it softly. As he slid home the bolts, a shadow fell across the doorway. For a moment Skellbow felt cold. Since the night on the wall he lived in perpetual dread, forever waiting for something shapeless and malign to form itself out of the night. But it was Jordan Creech, his fellow caretaker. He helped Skellbow roll the cart into its booth, padlocking it into place. Creech was tall and rangy and moved in an unhurried way. Little ever seemed to phase him, Skellbow knew. He envied him his philosophical attitude to life.

"New teacher all right?" said Creech.

"Seems OK. Another outsider."

"Those Inspectors like their own types in."

"Fucking Authority," Skellbow growled, spitting into the straw.

"Speaking of which," Creech said, "we're to go and see Dunstan." He laughed.

Skellbow shot him a suspicious glare. "Why? I'm done for the day."

"The beer'll keep for a few minutes, boy."

Skellbow muttered something unintelligible under his breath, but followed his wiry companion out into the courtyard, pointing to the iron gates in the boundary wall. "New man liked your gates, Jordan."

Creech turned to respond, but Skellbow was already heading for the tall bulk of the Academy. "Can't beat iron." Creech smiled to himself, knowing Skellbow's credulous nature only too well. "Demon bane."

Together they wound their way through the corridors to a set of ancient stairs lunging down into oppressive shadows. Oil lamps, lit earlier, had been set in niches in the wall at regular intervals, and as the two men descended, their shadows flickered on the mouldering walls in a bizarre parody of a dance. They went deep below the cellars cut into the bedrock on which the sprawling buildings were built. Creech pushed aside a creaking door, scraping its base along a slab of slate. Skellbow scowled at it, making a mental note to add it to his list of pending repairs.

The room opened out into a large, vaulted chamber. It smelled strongly of damp and earth: there were mushrooms and lichen on the walls. The place resembled a huge cave. At the far end, a jumble of steel tanks and rusting pipes seemed to have been welded to the walls, lengths of the pipe disappearing into the stone like the entrails of some hybrid beast.

Bent down before this grotesque conglomerate, Dunstan Fullacombe, the Master of the Watch, was wrestling with a section of the pipe, like a supplicant before a shadowy god. He heard the two caretakers coming across the stone floor and got to his feet, wiping a smear of muck from his forehead. Well over six feet tall, he weighed in the region of two hundred and fifty pounds. He described himself as a big eater and no one who knew him would have argued with that.

"Don't know why you bother," grunted Skellbow. "Rusted up to hell. Fuck knows how old it is. I got the water working well enough. Roof tanks are full. Last us all summer."

Fullacombe pointed to a pile of bulging sacks, tied up with string. "The staff are producing more rubbish than ever. All these sacks are full of waste paper. Ideal way to fuel the boiler, together with a pile of logs." The huge Master of the Watch wiped his hands on a torn strip of rag and tossed it aside. "I had a visit earlier."

"Not the Carnivore?" grinned Creech. "Moaning about something again."

"Not Miss Vine, no." Dunstan Fullacombe could not bring himself to use the Prime's nickname, though he never prevented anyone else from doing so. "Wroxton."

Sebastian Wroxton was one of the three Senior Magisters.

"And?" said Creech. He was smiling, but evidently irritated.

"Usual thing," said Fullacombe. "Security reports."

Creech swore. "I check and double check everything. Nighttimes, every door, window. Cleaners know the drill. Don't leave as much as a mouse hole unblocked."

"Have you written a weekly report?" asked Fullacombe patiently.

"I haven't had time to write a fucking report—"

"They want weekly reports. Miss Vine wants to see them. I have to sign them off. Wroxton told me that she's getting het up over it. If she don't get her reports, Jordan, she'll be on our backs."

"Spend so much time writing reports, there's none left to do the job!"

"Since the Inspection," said Skellbow, "the boss has been like a cat on a hot tin roof."

"The Enforcers will be back in October. You've seen the list of things we've got to have done by then," said Fullacombe.

Creech shrugged and for once seemed resigned. "Okay. I'll get it done."

"List everything you can think of. Especially any repairs or making good. And don't go sending in a written report with anything on it that hasn't been done. You do that and it'll be the one thing that the boss will pick out. You know what she's like."

"All this fucking fuss just because some twat threw himself off the sea wall!"

Skellbow stiffened. "That's no way to speak of Drew Vasillius, Jordan! Fuck me, he was a decent bloke—"

Creech clapped an arm across his shoulders. "I know, I know. I didn't mean any harm. No disrespect to him. But he was a sick man. Comes to something when a man like that flips and kills himself. But in this place, we could all lose our grip, chasing our tails all the time. Any more bollocks from these Inspectors and we'll all be jumping off the wall."

But there was no trace of a smile on Skellbow's face. Talk of the dead man renewed his cold sweat. He could feel the thick shadows around him pressing in, listening. *Marked*, the killers had said. *This place is marked.*

Back up in the dwindling daylight, Skellbow nodded his farewell and was gone without another word.

Fullacombe came up from the cellars to see Creech looking at the retreating Skellbow. "Is he going to be all right?"

Creech shrugged. "Trouble is, he blames himself."

"No one could have known what Drew Vasillius was going to do. He was a troubled man—"

"Even if I'd been on the night shift, there's nothing to say that it wouldn't have happened anyway. You know as well as I do that if someone had wanted to get up on the wall, they'd have done it. You can't secure a wall like that. And Drew Vasillius was obviously determined. Barry seems to think that he could have prevented it. But I don't see how."

"Nor me," said Fullacombe. "All we can do now is check and double check. Make sure everything's locked and double locked."

"Can't do any more than we are. I'll sort out the reports, Dunstan. You'll have them in the morning."

"If they want to take us to task, they will. Wroxton told me they look at everything, not just the kids and what they achieve. Once they see you as failing, whether it's academically or what, they start pulling everything to pieces. So if we keep our end up, the boss will leave us alone and get on with other things."

· ✳ ·

Goldsworthy had taken Mundy into another local inn, the Fox and Feathers, the favoured gathering place of many of the Academy's staff. As promised he'd introduced Mundy to several of his new colleagues, and once he felt that the newcomer was comfortable, he'd left him to it. While Goldsworthy was organizing their next round of drinks, Mundy was embroiled in a lively debate. Most of these younger teachers had originated in Londonborough, as it turned out. Like Mundy, they had trained in its various Academies. For a while it was enjoyable to exchange banter with them and news of the city.

"So how did your interview go?" asked one of the young women, Penn Ranzer, brushing back a thick mop of curly brunette hair from her face. She had a deep suntan and a smile that Mundy tried not to stare at. He had noticed her almost as soon as he had sat down. She was obviously more than capable of holding her own in a battle of words with the group here, delighting in the verbal ripostes, most of which she won.

"It was all a bit rushed. I was told about the job a few weeks ago and when I said I was up for it, they sent me down almost overnight."

"So you met the *Carnivore*?" The girl's eyes, a deep, penetrating blue, were brimming with mischief. He couldn't be sure if she was inviting him to play along or not.

He bought a few moments of time by sipping at his beer, amazed at how delicious it was. Not at all like the

Londonborough treacle brew he was familiar with. He would have to be careful with this stuff.

"Our beloved leader," someone said from the group, Mundy wasn't sure who. "Cora Vine, Regina." There was general laughter around the table.

Mundy smiled, deciphering the anagram. "Your Carnivore gave me a bit of a grilling."

"You got off lightly, then," said a youth called Zak.

"Trencher, the Senior Magister, did a lot of the talking. Anyway, they must have been happy enough with what I said. By the end they offered me the job."

"Did they tell you about Drew?" said another of the young men, his eyes slightly clouded, his face made ruddy by the beer.

"Melvin!" said Penn sharply. "Give the poor man a chance to settle in."

"It's okay," said Mundy. "I heard about what happened."

"What did they tell you?" said another of them, Dane Elland, a tall, lugubrious man who seemed a little nervous, hands clasping his pint glass tightly.

Mundy realised they were all watching his face for his reaction.

"For goodness' sake," said Penn. "Get some more beer in and let's have a bit of music. Tonight we celebrate our new arrival."

To Mundy's intense relief the group took up the suggestion as one, and within a few moments someone had produced a battered old guitar, struck the first chords, and launched into song, joined by more and more of the swelling company. Penn smiled at him, and he was glad she had had the presence of mind to rescue him from potential embarrassment. *She didn't have to do that*, he thought. *Intelligent as well as attractive.*

While this was gathering momentum, Mundy noticed another figure sitting to one side of the barroom, quietly sipping his own tankard of beer. It was Skellbow the caretaker.

Making his brief apologies, Mundy worked his way through a press of bodies to where Skellbow sat. The caretaker took a moment to recognise him but nodded, looking slightly embarrassed.

"Mr. Skellbow. I just wanted to say — can I sit here a moment? — that I was amazed by the hot water in my room. Are you responsible for it?" Mundy sat awkwardly on a stool across from the caretaker. "It's so much better than anything we ever had in Londonborough! I'm sure the top brass had it, but we never got better than lukewarm water." Mundy knew that the beer had loosened his tongue, but the pub's atmosphere had mellowed him.

"I spent a lot of time on that old pipe system," said Skellbow. "There are loads of water tanks up in the roof spaces. Fed with rainwater. I've set in a lot of new pipes. Made here in the town. Got fires in different parts of the school. You just got to know where everything is."

"Well, it's brilliant!"

"Dunstan's trying to do something with the original boiler, but I reckon it's buggered. Been rusted up and clotted with muck for— bloody years."

"Original boiler? From when the Academy was first built?"

"Guess so. What's it to you?" Skellbow abruptly pushed his tankard aside, as if he had said too much and was about to lurch to his feet and go. He was looking around nervously, his eyes avoiding Mundy's.

"Must be very old. Since what, before the Plague Wars?"

"I don't know nothing about the Plague Wars, Mr. Mundy."

"No. Well, not many of us do."

Skellbow emptied the tankard and banged it down. "You sound like one of them Inspectors. They asked a lot of questions, too."

"No. I'm not an Inspector. They'll be inspecting *me* when they come back. I'm just interested in old things."

"You speak to Dunstan, then. Maybe he'll show you the boiler. I'll stick to the pipes and the fires." Skellbow did get up. "I don't think *management* would like us wasting time on some old boiler," he said scathingly. "You'll excuse me, Mr. Mundy. Time I was off home."

Mundy watched the caretaker nudge his way through the packed crowd. He was either uncomfortable talking to newcomers, or he was a naturally very nervous guy, Mundy concluded.

· ✳ ·

Skellbow pulled up the collar of his jacket as he stepped outside into the night air, although it was very warm. Instinctively he glanced at the roofs. Nothing there. The side street he took to was narrow, rows of cottages on either side hemming it in, their windows lightless. The street was empty.

It had been two months since the death of Vasillius. Skellbow had done what that so-called contractor bastard had asked him. Said he'd seen Vasillius up on the wall. Gone up to see what was up. Told them that Vasillius had said that he couldn't take any more. Then jumped.

Once the lies had started, they had flowed swiftly. Skellbow had hated it. He told the story repeatedly to those who questioned him. It got easier, but he felt more and more oppressed. The killers had gone, as promised. No one knew a thing about their visit. And Skellbow never said a word to Trencher. But one thing kept coming back to rake the caretaker's nerves.

This place is marked now, Barry. That voice, that warning.

Something shifted in the gloom ahead. Several shapes materialised out of the night and it was all Skellbow could do to stifle a groan of horror. He put a hand over his mouth, standing stock still in the middle of the street, frozen like a hare caught in sudden torchlight.

"Evening, Barry," said a voice. It must have come from one of the figures. They stepped forward, men, not phantoms. But he took little comfort from the fact. They all wore scruffy trousers and rough shirts, as if they had come straight from a tour of work on a renovation project or something equally as physically demanding. *Contractors.*

"I don't know you," said Skellbow as they closed on him, no more than a few steps away. This street was not far from the dockside, where the pubs were stuffed with seamen of one kind or another: Petra's naval detachment, traders from up and down the coastal hamlets, and other, less recognizable crews. This ragged bunch had the look of privateers.

"But we know you, Barry. And we know yours."

"What the fuck do you want?" Skellbow's fists clenched. It was all he could do not to launch himself at the glib leader. "I've kept my part of the bargain."

"We know, Barry. We just want to be reassured. Just wanted to let you know that we're always watching."

Skellbow wanted to hit out, to swear, to unleash all the suppressed anger and frustration these people had poured into him, but something restrained him. There was a movement behind him and he swung round, arm raised to strike.

To his amazement he saw Mundy, the new teacher, standing there.

"You okay, Barry?"

"Piss off, mate," one of the pack called out. "Barry's with us."

Mundy made no move. His face was expressionless. "Barry?" he said again.

Skellbow took a deep breath. "I'm okay."

"You sure?"

"He said he was okay, pal. Now fuck off out of it," snarled the man who had spoken. He pushed forward and made to grip Mundy by the throat, but Mundy easily slipped aside, caught the man's arm, and in a blur of movement yanked it up behind him. The others moved forward as one, coiled like springs.

"I'll break his arm," said Mundy, and something in his tone struck home with the man's companions. They went very still.

"Don't be a twat," said their leader. "There's no need for that. There are six of us. We'll break every fucking bone you've got and feed you to the otters."

Mundy ignored the taunt, tightening his grip so that the man he was holding gritted his teeth on a gasp of pain.

Skellbow had stepped back a little, now almost beside Mundy. "I just want to get off home," he said. It seemed to diffuse the situation.

"You do that, Barry. Remember what we said."

"I said okay."

Mundy released his captive, thrusting him towards his fellows. He swung round, his face a livid mask, but the one who appeared to be the leader put an arm on his shoulder. "Take it easy. Barry's fine. We'll find better company down at the dockside." He gave a jerk of his head and, morosely, the men turned away, moving off down the street.

"I'll remember your fucking face," said the man Mundy had held, rubbing at his arm. But he was pushed back down the street by his leader.

"Good night, gents," said the latter. "We'll be seeing you." He laughed softly, turned, and in a moment the six men had melted into the darkness.

"God, Barry, who the hell were they?" said Mundy.

"Just some roughs from the docks. There are places in Petra that you don't want to go on your own. Were you following me?" he added, his face suddenly creased with suspicion.

"No, I was looking for the toilet. I just happened to see you. It looked as if you were in trouble. Were you?"

"No. Just a bunch of bully boys. They usually stick to their own haunts. Riverside scum. Sometimes they come up here, spoiling for a fight. If it hadn't been me, some other bugger would've copped it."

"You'll get home okay?"

"Sure. They'll have forgotten us by now. Let them break a few heads on the wharf. They'll get some of the same."

"Okay. I'll see you."

"And thanks, Mr. Mundy. You look like you can handle yourself."

Mundy grinned. "I don't court trouble. But I was trained by some very hard men. And I don't scare easily."

"I can see that, Mr. Mundy."

"It's Chad." He gave a brief wave and went back towards the pub.

Skellbow waited until he was gone, turned to look down the street, then made his way down another side street, heading for home. He shook his head, cursing under his breath. Mundy was okay. But it had been a mistake. Now he would also be marked.

IV

LONDONBOROUGH: TWO WEEKS EARLIER

BY HIS FINAL year at Wellington Military Academy in Londonborough, Chad Mundy had become close friends with Erroll Detroyd, himself an English teacher highly skilled in hand-to-hand combat. As two outstanding students of the martial arts, they were often paired, and ironically it was their fierce but cool rivalry that welded their friendship. Not only that, but they also shared a keen interest in the riddles of history: during their period of training, their competitiveness and debating skills had increased their understanding and mastery of both fields. They shared each other's highs and lows, teased each other over girlfriends, although Mundy wouldn't claim to have had much success with the fairer sex (unlike Detroyd, who attracted girls like honey attracted bees) and supported each other in disputes with colleagues. They were like brothers, with no secrets from each other. But there was one private area of Detroyd's life.

He claimed to have an old aunt who lived in a rundown part of the city. He said he visited her occasionally, more from a sense of familial duty than great affection. He never divulged much detail, but Mundy respected his privacy and never questioned his friend's periodic absences. He wondered at one point if it was in reality a girlfriend, imagining that it might even be an illicit affair with a married woman. The academy would have frowned upon such a thing. But in time, Mundy thought maybe this intrigue was mere imagination on his part. After all, there was no reason for his friend to lie about it.

So it was a pleasant surprise when Detroyd one day announced that it was time for Mundy to meet his aunt. "She's very secretive," he said. "And eccentric. Trusts no one. I'm honoured in that respect!" He laughed.

Mundy frowned. "And you want *me* to meet her? Why?"

"Two reasons. First, I trust you, Chad." Detroyd had a steady gaze and when he fixed anyone with it, it was unflinching, as though he would skewer anything dark buried in a person's psyche. "Secondly, she's a fountain of knowledge about history, especially about developments since the Plague Wars. I've told her about our mutual interests. But we'll have to be very careful. Some things are off limits. Rules of the Authority. But she wants to pass something on. I don't want her compromised. But she says that people like us, who genuinely want to learn from the past, should be told."

Mundy was happy to agree and shortly afterwards, on a night of drizzling rain that seeped in from the east and added to the obscurity of the streets, the two young men crossed part of the old city. It took them over an hour on foot. A few voices hailed them, vagrants shambling about the area like lost souls, isolated and forever restless, but the two men came to no harm. Detroyd was familiar with the journey and the few people that lived about these semi-derelict parts of Londonborough were used to seeing him. They kept to themselves, rarely meeting in daylight, never at night.

They stopped outside a tall building in a reasonable state of repair. It had several storeys and a few of its many windows were dimly lit, but most of that bleak façade was in shadow, like so many of the city's abandoned structures. The two men climbed weed-choked steps. It looked to Mundy as if no one had been here for many years. It probably suited the inhabitants of the building to give that impression. Detroyd had a key and let them in, locking the tall door behind him.

An oil lamp barely illuminated the dusty hallway, old curtains hanging in tatters, the floor tiles cracked. Several pieces of furniture were strewn about, looking as though they would fall apart at a touch. Crossing the gloomy area, they came to another door. Again Detroyd used a key.

Beyond, he flicked a switch on the wall. To Mundy's utter amazement, a light came on overhead. He gaped at it, but had to tear his eyes away, it was so fierce.

"Shit, Erroll, is that an *electric* light?"

Detroyd laughed. "Not the only surprise."

Mundy cleared his eyes of the bright after-image of the bulb. They were in a small room, the walls freshly painted, the floor polished. There was another door opposite them. Detroyd grinned and flicked another switch. Amazingly, the door slid aside, as if it, too, was operated by electricity. *How can an old building like this have electricity in it?* Mundy pondered, still bemused. Such things were practically unique in Londonborough.

Framed in the doorway was a woman of about fifty, her hair neatly tied back in a bun, an encouraging smile on her slightly lined features. She kissed Detroyd on the cheek. "Erroll, my dear. Lovely to see you." She spoke in a cultured voice, turning to Mundy and offering a hand. "And this must be Chad."

Mundy shook her hand carefully, but her grip was surprisingly strong.

"You must call me Amelia," she said. "You must forgive us, Chad. We have misled you a little. Please don't be alarmed. It's just that we have to be very careful."

There was an awkward pause before she said, "Have you heard of the Historical Society?"

"Vaguely. I thought it was a myth." Mundy studied her face for a few moments, but detected no duplicity there.

"I assure you, we're real, Chad," Amelia said, again with her disarming smile.

"Not something the Authority would condone," said Detroyd.

Mundy felt his pulse racing. On the one hand he felt trapped here: he was at their mercy and it was even possible that this was all an elaborate test *by* the Authority, an evaluation of his loyalty. But if this really was the legendary Historical Society— how would it be to share *their* knowledge?

"This is about trust, Chad," said Detroyd. "If you want, you can leave. But I don't believe you're a devout Authority man."

"No. I'm not an extremist, one way or the other."

Amelia nodded. "We believe in individual freedom of choice. We need to be governed, but government should be fair and even-handed. In Grand Britannia we live, sadly, in a totalitarian society. We're not revolutionaries, but we do fight for what we see as our rights."

There was a long pause, but slowly Mundy grinned. "If I went back now, I'd never sleep again thinking about what I might have missed."

Amelia stepped forward and gave Mundy an unexpected hug, kissing him on the cheek. "I am so pleased, Chad. You won't regret it. Now, we have to be circumspect. Always assume that you are being watched, monitored. Erroll has been followed here before now. But we have a set-up that deals with that sort of thing. Someone from the Authority did come once, nosing around. All they found were some dusty apartments and Erroll's decrepit aunt, hard of hearing and daft as a bat."

"The Society," said Detroyd "is not high on the list of the Authority's targets for investigation. They know it exists, but we're not seen as a threat."

They went into another room that was old-fashioned, decorated with some taste: an elegant mirror, a set of deep chairs, settee, and a polished, antique table.

"The Society isn't based here. We're hidden a few miles away in a secret location. Only a few of our members know its exact location, for obvious reasons."

Amelia then questioned Mundy about his background, health, and interests, all the time scribbling away in a pad as he answered. He found it easy to talk about his interest in history, and doing so convinced himself he was not actually party to any controversial knowledge that could bring reprisals from the Authority. He told himself that he was exhibiting no more than a reasonably healthy interest in something that would fascinate anyone living in these times. The Authority might restrict certain avenues of exploration and research, but it would have no real cause to persecute him.

"Tell me," said Detroyd. "You and I have never spoken about it, but have you ever heard of something called 'Daybreak'?"

"Can't say I have."

"The Society is very interested in it," said Amelia. "It's of great importance to us."

Mundy thought she would enlarge on this, but she turned to other matters. "Chad, there's a meeting of the Society to-night. We'd like you to be there."

And so it began, his absorption by the Society.

· ✳ ·

Amelia had been correct in her assumption that the building was being watched. As the horse-drawn carriage pulled up outside the front door that Mundy and Detroyd had recently entered, a pair of men studied it from across the street. In a terrace of disused houses, on an attic floor, they crouched behind filthy curtains, looking out through the cracked window. They saw the carriage and nodded silently to each other.

Obviously it had come to fetch someone. And that had to be the two students from the Academy they had seen enter earlier.

"They're on the coach," said the first. "You know what to do." His companion nodded and left the room silently.

Within minutes he had gone below, where he traversed a claustrophobic corridor choked with rubble and rotting furniture to an outside courtyard that was no better maintained. Two other men were waiting, both on horseback.

"They're in the coach," said the first. "Wait till they reach their destination. Soon as they get out, interrogate. Make a note of the address."

The two men on horseback saluted, turned their steeds, and eased out towards the street. They waited, giving the carriage across the way time to take on board its passengers, who were hidden behind curtains of some dark material. Moments later the driver flicked his long whip gently and the single horse moved forward at a steady pace. The two riders followed like ghosts, silent and perfectly merged with the night.

Half an hour later the carriage stopped in a wide square, fronted on three sides by dilapidated warehouses with collapsed roofs and shattered windows. The final side of the square was taken up by a sprawling building, topped with a huge, sealed dome. It looked incongruous in the debris and destruction around it. The two horsemen slowed and moved their horses forward very slowly, glancing nervously at one another. This was the last place they would have wanted to come.

The domed building was one of the ancient Plague Pits. Under normal circumstances, no one had entered such a forbidding construction for years. Surely the Society they were watching did not have its secret base *in* there?

They came under its intimidating shadow, drawing their cloaks tighter about them as if to ward off the miasma surrounding it. The driver of the carriage did not appear to have noticed them. He sat stiffly up on his seat, holding a tight rein on the horse. It waited, patient as a statue, unmoved by its surroundings. After a few minutes, no one had emerged from the carriage: the two horsemen exchanged puzzled glances.

The first edged up to the driver's line of sight. "We're on watch in this part of the city," he said, holding up a badge of office. The driver turned his head, nodding indifferently. The fact that the rider had a rifle strapped to his horse's flank didn't seem to disturb him. "Hold still, driver. My companion would like to talk to your passengers."

"Fine by me, guvnor." The driver stifled a yawn.

The other rider had swung down from his horse and now stood beside the carriage. He held the reins to his horse loosely in one hand and with the other opened the carriage door. Two faces peered out from the poorly lit interior.

"Have we arrived?" said one of the occupants, a large man dressed in a colourful suit that was a couple of sizes too small for his portly form.

The rider was taken aback. For one thing, it was obvious that these two men were not the ones who had originally entered the Society's building. For another, they looked perplexed at being here. "Why have we stopped again?"

The rider masked his own confusion. "Sorry to trouble you, sirs. Night watch. We have to check everyone in this area. There's been some trouble. It's for your safety."

The two passengers were leaning almost out of its door. "Very well, officer. I'm Julian Farsley and this is Humbert Barradol. We work for the Central Authority. Procurements. We're on a social visit." Both men waved passes.

The rider nodded uncomfortably. "Has anyone shared the coach with you?"

"No. We stopped a while ago and thought for a moment someone might try and hitch a lift with us. But no one appeared. We did wonder what the driver was playing at. Can we get on soon? Pressing engagement, if you see what I mean."

The rider managed a weak smile. He could imagine what sort of sordid assignation these two were referring to. "Just give us a moment or two with the driver." He closed the door and walked his horse to his companion, shaking his head.

The first rider scowled across at the driver. "When you stopped, half an hour back, why was that? Did you pick up?"

"Nope. I was paid to call at the old building and wait for a few minutes. Then drive on to here and stop again."

"Paid by whom?"

"Didn't give a name. His coin's good enough, though. S'all I need."

"So why did you stop here? Who are you expecting?"

"No one, guvnor. I didn't ask no questions, just took the money. Stopping ain't no skin off my nose. Now, if you're done, I'll get these other two gents to their destination. They paid separately."

Both riders swore under their breath. They'd been taken
for a pair of monkeys. The two men they had been expecting
to challenge in the coach never got into it and by now they'd
be long gone. The Society's real base would remain a mystery
this night. Sunderman would not take very kindly to this.

· ✱ ·

Mundy and Detroyd had been taken on a devious route through
some very old underground passages, emerging well over a
mile from the building where they had met Amelia. Followers
of the Society had used this device a number of times: the eyes
of the Authority had yet to uncover the deceit. Mundy found
himself in another, comfortable building where members of
the Society were pleased to embrace him. It was to be the
beginning of a fascinating phase of his education.

Thereafter he had enjoyed the Society's company many
times, sometimes with Detroyd, his own standing with the
members growing with each trip. Mundy had visited the Society
for the last time a few days before he left Londonborough
for Petra. The Society Chairman, Hewitt Marlmaster, was an
elderly but remarkably shrewd and perceptive man. Although
Mundy never knew what he did in the working world, he
imagined him as an executive or even councillor.

"Chad," he beamed. "Only Amelia and myself here tonight.
We just wanted to wish you luck. We're going to miss you
and your razor-sharp mind."

"I'll certainly miss these gatherings," Mundy said, with
some feeling. "They've come to mean a lot to me."

"Time you went further afield. We've had a few chaps like
you who've gone out there into the wilderness. Because it
is a wilderness, Chad. Once you leave Londonborough, it's
empty— so few people out there since the Wars. The Authority
is trying to hold things together and communities are fighting
to stand on their own two feet. And independence may not
be in their best interests. But we are simply historians. What
we learn about the past should be available to everyone in
this brave new world of ours."

"In my case, slightly nervous new world."

"I envy you. God, I say that to all of you that go out
there! Anyway, you help the people. Learn what you can
from them, too."

"You won't be entirely cut off from us," said Amelia. "You'll be contacted when you get there. We have someone at the Academy. They may not make themselves known to you immediately. But they know about your connections with us."

Mundy nodded. He respected the Society's obsession with discretion. Its members were convinced, Marlmaster in particular, that secrecy protected lives. There was even a suggestion that lives had been lost in the past, or at least, members of the Society had *disappeared*, as the chairman put it. He had always been at pains not to speak ill of the Authority, but other members of the Society, Detroyd included, went as far as to vilify it.

"You're too trusting," Amelia had told Marlmaster in front of Mundy once. "You sometimes see the world as you want to see it, Hewitt."

Marlmaster had simply shrugged. Now, his face suddenly more serious, he said, "Chad, do you recall us once asking you about something called 'Daybreak?'"

"I've heard that expression used a couple of times during our gatherings. But only as part of someone else's conversation. I've never pried. There's an air of mystique attached to it."

"It's something the Society is investigating," said Amelia. "We know it was extremely important, historically. But it's sensitive. More so than anything else we have learned about the past. Don't ever mention it."

"Your contact," added Marlmaster, "will use it as the password by which you'll recognise them. And they may have learned something."

"Be patient," Amelia said. "In the meantime, there's a rhyme you need to learn and commit to memory. We don't really understand its significance, but it's one of the few things relating to Daybreak." She handed Mundy a sheet of paper on which the rhyme was written in a neat, legible hand in the Old Tongue.

Mundy read it to himself, translating it as:

> *Speak to me of daybreak*
> *One midsummer's morning.*
> *Whisper all its secrets;*
> *Cry their fearful warning.*

"Can you learn it by heart and destroy the paper before you go?" said Marlmaster. His face suddenly appeared haggard.

"Yes, of course." Mundy read the words again. Somewhere in the depths of his mind, something seemed to stir, although reluctant to surface. An elusive memory perhaps, hidden away as if his subconscious had smothered it, afraid of what it might mean.

V

PETRA: MIDSUMMER

MUNDY ROSE EARLY, washed, dressed, and shaved. He looked out of his window: it was another cloudless day and the bizarre events of the previous evening seemed little more than a bad dream. Last night's almost supernatural view of the Academy's skyline with its sinister sea wall looked quaint in the light of day.

Goldsworthy arrived punctually and took him down to the canteen, where he boomed out more introductions: Mundy shook a few hands. Breakfast itself consisted of a bowl of steaming porridge followed by eggs and mushrooms and the fresh water that seemed to be the house speciality.

The hall was filled with staff by the time they had finished eating, the noise level of numerous conversations rising steadily until it was only possible to hold one by shouting across the table. Goldsworthy was in his element. As the clock ticked away until the appointed hour of the assembly, the noise died down, as though everyone here was preparing for something formal rather than a mundane assembly. The air was appreciably stiff with tension.

Goldsworthy guided Mundy through the sudden torrent of staff exiting the food hall. "After we're done, I'll introduce you to Sebastian. Senior Magister."

Mundy nodded. "Yes, he wasn't at my interview."

"He has a special responsibility for the Academy connections with the military. Bellona has for the navy and Carl Trencher's links are with the church. He must have got the short straw."

Mundy didn't comment. He was ambivalent about religion.

Everyone funneled into a tall assembly hall, almost as though entering a church, their whole manner changing to one of reverence and respect. Mundy felt it ripple through the crowd, a curiously unsettling experience that reminded him of his days at the military academy, when such gatherings

were conducted under the stern gaze of the sergeants. You did
not want their eyes to fall upon you. There were no sergeants
here and there seemed to be no reason why people should
not chatter. Those who did talk did so quietly, leaning across
to each other as if exchanging conspiratorial information.

At the front of the hall there was a dais, with seating that
overlooked the entire company. Mundy recognised both of
the people who stood in front of their chairs up there. One
was Senior Magister Bellona Haveris, a reserved woman in
her late forties, hair pulled back in a tight bun, neat suit immaculate. She looked down on her colleagues with a vague
smile on her lips— Mundy recalled that she had been pleasant
and relaxed with him at his interview, warming up when she
enthused about her work. The other figure, in direct contrast,
was the second of the Senior Magisters, Carl Trencher. He was
of medium build, stocky, with a chiseled face, eyes that were
always alert but cool, his black hair swept back tidily from
his unusually white forehead. Whatever emotions moved him
this morning, they were inscrutable. He looked to Mundy as
though he would not blink if a gun had gone off. His bland
gaze took in every detail in the hall as if seeing everyone for
the first time, that, or he was counting heads.

When all the staff were in, with the large clock above the
dais indicating 8:15 a.m., a third figure ascended the wooden
steps to the dais, taking up a central position. The Prime had
arrived. The silence had become almost eerie.

Cora Vine was a tall woman in her fifties, her equine face
pale, as if she were a stranger to sunlight. Her eyes were
bright, sparkling with a slightly unnerving interest as she
gazed upon her congregation. When she spoke, her long,
slender fingers moved through the air like the hands of a
conductor, punctuating her words, weaving a kind of spell
over those herded below. She wore a dark trouser suit, with
a leather belt and buckle that almost drew the eye away from
those mesmerizing hands. Her long, cascading hair was an
unusual shade of white, and it shone as the rising sun behind
her slanted down through the tall windows.

"Good morning," she said, and there was an immediate,
none-too-enthusiastic chorus of "Good Morning" in response.
"There are a few notices," said the Prime in a sharp, clear
voice that every ear in the hall picked up.

Mundy listened, the words washing over him as he studied the woman he had heard so much about. At his interview he had not spent much time in her company; he recalled the day as being very fast-paced, as if it had been something of an inconvenience, a necessary obstacle that had to be negotiated during an agenda of far more important processes for the Prime and her senior colleagues. Once he had been able to demonstrate that he had the qualifications and qualities that were needed to fill the vacant post, the rest of the business became something of a formality. And there had been no other candidates, so no time needed by management to be spent agonizing over a choice of appointee.

"Now I want to say something about the Inspection," the Prime was saying, her eyes narrowing, hawk-like, as she warmed to her task.

"Here we go," muttered Goldsworthy, giving Mundy a gentle nudge. One or two heads in the rows of seated staff in front of them turned to each other, but no one spoke. The atmosphere grew palpably tenser.

"As you all know, the Enforcers were not able to award a pass to the Academy when they visited us three months ago. I need to remind you of the process that we are now in as a consequence of their findings."

"We're all crap," Mundy heard someone murmur behind him, but nowhere near loud enough to be heard at the front.

"Generally our standards are good, or at least satisfactory, but we must improve in a number of areas. *All* of us need to raise our game. Whatever we do, we need to re-examine and look at how we can improve. We will be revisited in October. That's four months away and for nearly half of that time, we have our summer break."

"She's done her maths," another voice whispered.

"Not long, staff. Not many weeks to lift ourselves. The Enforcers remarked quite pointedly on the quality of student that we are preparing for the military and naval bases attached to Petra and beyond. They have used expressions like 'too independent,' 'insufficiently disciplined,' and 'lacking in respect for the Authority' time and time again in their report. Academic levels are below par— in some areas, *and you know well enough which they are*, levels are failing. Now, I know that work has already begun to address the issues specifically raised in the report. My senior colleagues and I

receive progress reports from every area on a regular basis. We
see signs of improvement, but none of us can be complacent.

"You need to question each other and yourselves, every
day if necessary. Ask yourself, Am I delivering? Am I doing
all that I can possibly do to ensure that the Academy achieves
its goals? Am I giving enough to the students? Because if not,
if *any of us* fall short of that aim, then we will be held to account when the Enforcers return in October. They have made
it very clear that the Authority will act if we fail. I cannot
contemplate what that will mean. But it would be disastrous
for you, for the Academy, and for the students.

"For the next four months, we will run our own internal
inspections. Every lesson, every training session, must be
rigorously prepared and executed. We may exist on the very
edge of a struggling civilization, but we are not barbarians.
Our future — the future of our youth — must not be compromised by this dogged, negative attitude. We are not just
a team here in Petra; we are part of a bigger picture. Some
of us seem to have lost sight of that.

"Let's be clear, staff. If anyone has any doubts about that,
or is not signed up to the way forward, then it's time to move
on. Petra Academy is no place for you if you think you can
get by on the old ways. It will be hard, very hard. But if we
don't get it right, it will be much harder." She drew herself
upright, as if to launch into a final blast of admonition. But
she simply nodded.

"Right," she said abruptly, as if the entire matter was forgotten. "Mr. Trencher, you wanted to say something about
the training schedule?"

Mundy could sense the claustrophobic air of disquiet. Voices
were not raised above a whisper, but a current of something like
anger flowed among the staff now. Mundy was not surprised.
They had received a verbal caning. He was used to this at the
military academy, where the sledgehammer-to-crack-a-nut
approach proliferated. He'd got used to it and even expected
it, responding automatically. But here? In a school? Were the
staff that bad? The Prime evidently thought so.

Once the remaining business of the assembly was completed
— there was no further contribution from the Prime, who
had assumed an attitude of attentive silence while Trencher
spoke — Mundy was bustled away by Goldsworthy. Beyond
the hall they were again pressed into a steady flow of staff

and now the noise level was significantly up. There were few smiles.

"There we are," said Goldsworthy. "Get on top of our game or find something else to do." He laughed, but this time his grin was fixed.

"She doesn't take any prisoners," said Mundy.

"You should hear her on a bad day."

"I've read the Inspection report," said Mundy. "It was less than brilliant, but I would have thought the staff would be up to straightening out the problems."

"Yes, sure." Goldsworthy nodded. "They're a bloody good lot here. There's not a soul who hasn't been working his or her socks off. The boss is just a very hard taskmaster. And if the ship goes down, she's finished. No one wants to fail, Chad. No one gains anything."

"What exactly would it mean?"

"The Authority would step in and run the place. Probably use the military. The locals would hate it. It would mean even more of a rebellion. Bad enough trying to keep the kids on the right track. Their parents are a lot bloody tougher! I've taught a good few of them." He stopped outside a classroom and from within came the unmistakable din of students, as though at least a hundred of them were packed in there. "Speaking of which, come and be introduced!"

Goldsworthy opened the door and strode into the wall of teenage angst and sound, Mundy a step or two behind him, closing the door. Their entry dampened the sound, not quite muting it. Thirty mixed fourteen to fifteen-year-olds simultaneously focused their butterfly attention on the two teachers.

Goldsworthy faced them, hands on hips, shaking his head. "All right!" The noise dropped a few decibels. "Good morning, rabble."

"Good morning, Mr. Goldsworthy," the students blasted back at him as they shuffled to their feet, or at least swung round on their creaking wooden chairs.

Goldsworthy perched on the edge of the teacher's desk. "Listen up, you horrible lot!"

Mundy veiled his amusement. He could see that Goldsworthy and this particular group obviously shared a mutual respect. His apparent insults were part of the way he had shaped that respect from them: they enjoyed and doubtless expected it.

"Listen, listen. Thank you. I want to introduce you to our new teacher, Mr. Mundy. Mr. Mundy, this is Ten B2. I've told them you can get planks of wood measuring ten by two."

"You're sick, sir," someone said and then laughed.

"And anyway, you shouldn't take the piss out of us. We'll tell Mr. Wroxton. He'll get you the sack."

"Will he?" Goldsworthy laughed. "See what we have to put up with, Mr. Mundy? A lovely little bunch, aren't you?"

Heads nodded and there were more than a few howls of agreement.

"Good morning, Ten B2," said Mundy.

"Good morning, Mr. Mundy," chorused the reply.

"Is there a Mr. Tuesday?"

"Enough of that, Robinton! I'll do the jokes," said Goldsworthy.

"Your jokes are crap, sir!" someone else called.

"Now, listen! Mr. Mundy teaches English. He is also a man you'd better be nice to, because he specializes in hand-to-hand. Any of you tough guys step out of line and your physical training will get a whole lot tougher."

Several of the boys started weaving their hands about in vague karate motions, but the sound level had dropped again.

"So, look after Mr. Mundy, understand? If I hear any bad reports, you'll be in *my* bad books. Okay? I said, *okay* Ten B2?"

"Yes, sir," they sang out, for the most part grinning like demons.

"All yours," Goldsworthy said quietly to Mundy, and moments later he withdrew from the classroom.

Mundy looked around the room, his gaze meeting the eyes of many of the thirty assembled youngsters. "So what have you been doing in English?"

There was no immediate response. Some of the group exchanged glances or a few muttered words.

"I can't believe you're all shy," Mundy said with a mock scowl. "What were you doing with Mr. Vasillius?"

"Are you the new Mr. Vasillius?" one of the girls asked, leaning back in her chair with a hint of impudence.

"Your name is?"

"Maggie, sir. Maggie Hunderly."

"Thank you, Maggie. I'd like you all to give me your names when you speak to me, okay? That way I'll get to know who you all are. Now, I'm not the new Mr. Vasillius. I'm the new

Mr. Mundy. But I am teaching English and I will probably pick up from where you left off."

Several of them started to speak at once, but Mundy silenced them. "Just to make things easy, if you want to say something, or ask a question, put your hand up."

"Mr. Vasillius didn't—" Maggie began.

"Hand up, Maggie!" Mundy said sharply, so much so that she swung her hand up almost without realizing it.

"Thank you," said Mundy. "Go on."

"Well, Mr. Vasillius went ill, so Mrs. Darnley was teaching us."

"Okay, so what did Mrs. Darnley teach you?"

"Some poxy book," grumbled a thick-set lad three rows back. He was leaning on his elbows, face screwed up with boredom, lips pursed in defiance.

"Hand up!" said Mundy.

The boy made a half-hearted gesture of compliance, grinning at the equally bored boy across the aisle from him.

"Stand up," Mundy said to him, calmly.

"Why? I ain't done nothing."

"That's part of the problem. Come on, stand up. We want you to give us the benefit of your wisdom." Mundy's gaze locked on the boy's resentful smirk, but the boy turned away. He did, however, shuffle to his feet, as if proud to show that he was tall and broad-shouldered. *Likes to perform for his mates*, Mundy thought.

"Thank you. And your name is?"

"Darren Hacker, sir."

"You sound like a fighting man, Darren. I can see I'll have to watch you."

Hacker smirked again.

"So, what is this poxy book you have been reading?"

There were a few sniggers. "Dunno," said Hacker, hand rubbing his mouth as if he were trying to think of something amusing to say to impress the class. "Something about a policeman interviewing a load of toffs about a ghost."

"The policeman *is* the ghost, Hacker, you tosser!" another boy called.

"He's not a policeman," said one of the girls at the front, turning a look of fierce disapproval on the boy who had called out.

"Hold on, hold on!" said Mundy, interrupting the brief spell of laughter to regain the initiative. "Remember to put your hands up. Now, Darren has identified the book, maybe not its name, but I know the one. So— you, young man." He nodded towards the boy who had derided Hacker.

"Riley, sir. Maele Riley."

"Hand up!"

Riley's hand went up slowly.

"You said the policeman was a ghost. And this young lady," Mundy went on, indicating the girl who had spoken up, "who is?"

She put her hand up, smiled thinly, and said, "Tara Bendle, sir. He's not a policeman, sir. He's an Inspector."

"And the difference, Tara?"

"He's a detective. Policemen aren't detectives."

Mundy nodded again and began to tease out of them what they knew about Priestley's *An Inspector Calls*. He found that the way to get this group thinking was to have them bounce things off each other, even the toughs, using their oblique way of coming at things to liven up the discussion. It turned out that they all knew more about the play than he had expected and far more than they thought they understood.

At the end of the lesson, as the group barged and bustled their way out through the door to their next session, Hacker paused in front of Mundy, their eyes level.

"What can I do for you, Darren?"

"Sir, are you taking us for hand-to-hand?"

"I am indeed. First lesson tomorrow. Are you any good?" Mundy smiled.

"Pretty good. I beat Mr. Gunster. He's a prat."

"Now, come on. I don't want to hear that kind of talk. I haven't met Mr. Gunster, but I'd like you to show a bit of respect."

"Are you better than him?"

"I don't know. But let's find out tomorrow, shall we?"

"I'll be there, sir." Hacker nodded with another of his smirks. He made for the door, but Mundy called him back.

"Listen, Darren. It's not about winning or beating people. What's the number one rule?"

Hacker looked at him as if he'd asked him to recite the works of Keats.

Mundy broke into the glazed look. "Defend yourself. Don't be an aggressor."

Hacker grunted and turned to go. Riley and two other boys were waiting for him in the corridor. "Kick the other fucker first!" Hacker said, making sure that Mundy heard him, but Mundy let it go. As he closed the classroom door and prepared to go to the next lesson, he found Maggie Hunderly waiting for him.

"What's the matter, Maggie?" he said, starting to walk down the corridor.

"Mr. Vasillius, sir," she said, obviously uncomfortable. "I don't think he was ill, sir."

"He probably didn't seem ill, Maggie. Stress isn't quite like a dose of the flu or a bad cough. You don't always know you've got it. And not everyone else realizes you've got it either."

"My mum knows Mrs. Vasillius, sir. She says he wasn't ill. He wasn't very happy. But my mum says Mrs. Vasillius thinks that Miss Vine didn't like him. Didn't want him."

Mundy felt himself tensing. "Okay, Maggie. I'll keep that in mind. Have you said anything to anyone else about this?"

"Everyone knows about it. We liked Mr. Vasillius. But I didn't say anything to the Inspector."

"The Inspector?"

"Mr. Barrazelli. He asked us all the questions. Like Tara said, sir, he wasn't a policeman— well, he was sort of. But a detective is a bit different, isn't he?"

"Yes, that's right. Did you tell him what your mum said?"

"No."

"Okay. Let's just keep it to ourselves. Be very careful who you speak to, eh?"

She nodded, and then she was gone before he could say anything else. In her wake she left a strange atmosphere. It was like a part of something he had already sensed, something almost imperceptible at the core of this Academy, in a place that seemed crowded with silent shapes, secrets waiting to be uncovered.

More secrets. All revolving around the dead teacher, Mundy thought. It was easy to imagine the shade of Vasillius still drifting through these corridors.

VI

PETRA: MIDSUMMER

MUNDY MET CLASS Ten B2 the following morning out on one of the small fields within the Academy boundary wall, the sunshine as remorselessly bright as ever. He was still trying to keep Goldsworthy's amusing insult out of his mind as he spoke to them, but they were obviously not very academically minded. They lined up for him in rows, girls over to the right, boys on the left, all in gym kit. Mundy had been surprised to learn that some of these lessons were conducted with the whole class and not single sex. But Goldsworthy had said that when it came to training, everyone was expected to be prepared for all eventualities.

"Put it this way, Chad: if the Invasion does come, the Evropans won't bother to segregate anybody. They'll just come in and fire away, or whatever."

"Do you think there'll ever be an invasion?"

"Probably not. Whoever is over there is likely trying to rebuild the mess left behind by the Wars, like us. Wouldn't have time to invade us. Nor the need, I shouldn't suppose. But the Enforcers would have me boiled in oil for saying such a thing. So we carry on. I tell you what, though, Chad. If we were attacked, Petra would give the buggers a hard time of it."

Those words came to mind now as Mundy took stock of his class. "Exercise," he told them. "Exercise and more exercise. Over and over again. Fitness. Readiness. All things that the military drill into you, day in, day out. Why's that, Darren?"

"So we can beat the shit out of the invaders, sir."

"Language, Darren. On my shift, you all mind your language."

"Oh, sir," someone groaned. "Why does it matter?"

"Discipline. Do you know what it is?"

Maggie put her hand up. "Sir, it's how you keep order."

"How who keeps order?"

Several hands went up, accompanied by calls of "the teachers!"

"What about you?" Mundy asked them.

They looked puzzled.

"What about *you* keeping order of yourselves? Mr. Goldsworthy told me we've got some very good football, hockey, and netball teams in the Academy. *Teams*. Playing together. Playing together is like fighting together— I don't mean fighting each other. I mean fighting as a team. And good discipline means a good team. So, first things first: discipline. If you can all understand it and how important it is, then we can think about the next step."

"So no swearing," said a skinny youth with a lopsided grin.

"No swearing." Mundy nodded. "If you want to swear, stop, think, and don't. You do that and you've exercised *self*-discipline. I can discipline you, but in the first place, it's better if you do it."

"How you going to discipline us, sir?" said Hacker. "Cane us?"

"No. I've got something *much worse* than that in mind."

There was a chorus of howls and catcalls, but most of the students looked slightly dubious, not sure whether Mundy was joking. "And I don't need to report you to Mr. Goldsworthy. This is between us. You are my team now. We work together. But I lead."

"Mr. Vasillius said we were a team," said Tara.

"That's good, Tara. You all liked Mr. Vasillius, didn't you?"

There was an immediate silence, but most heads were nodding.

"Then let's respect him and what he taught you." After another pause, he started circling his arms. "Okay, team, get those arms swinging. Slowly, slowly. A little faster. That's it. Don't poke anyone's eye out. Just keep circling."

For the next ten minutes or so, Mundy had them doing basic exercises, ignoring their moans and groans. Then he had them running on the spot for another five minutes until they were all gasping like geriatrics. He could see who was taking it in their stride and who was struggling. Generally, he thought, they weren't bad. The girls were especially strong.

"Okay, and… stop. Take a breather. No slouching!"

He called Hacker to him. "Darren. You were telling me yesterday that you're pretty good at hand-to-hand. Let's see what you've got."

Hacker looked at his cronies and they exchanged knowing glances as he strutted out to the front. He stood before
Mundy in an attitude of mild defiance.

"Just use your hands. No feet yet," said Mundy. "Okay?"

Hacker bent into a crouch, hands out before him. He was
muscular, his jaw set, his eyes hardening.

"You go for it, Darren," said Mundy. "Put me down, if
you can."

Hacker was silent, frowning with concentration. The kid-
ding was over. His own brand of discipline had slipped into
place. He moved closer into Mundy, a hand snaking out,
testing the water. Mundy watched closely, his eyes fixed on
the boy's hands: they had become twin blades, the thick fingers spread. A chop from either hand would be painful if it
landed properly.

Then Hacker made his move, feinting a right-hand thrust,
watching Mundy evade it, then following up with a chop
that was intended to break bone. But it never landed. Mundy
had moved out of his reach, slick and easy, like a shadow.
Hacker's chop sliced down through air. Mundy made no
effort to counterattack. The boy stepped in again, trying a
different approach, but as he drove in, or chopped, he found
himself almost stumbling as he struck at thin air again. Several
futile attempts later, with Hacker starting to show signs of
real exasperation, the boy rushed in, this time intending to
grip Mundy, pull him in, and lock the grip. Mundy was like
an eel. One minute Hacker had him, the next he was holding
emptiness.

Hacker's chest was rising and falling more rapidly and his
eyes narrowed. Anger was rising in him like bile.

"Discipline, Darren," Mundy said quietly. "Stay cool. Anger
saps strength and concentration."

Hacker swept in again and this time he managed to close
with Mundy, locking an arm around him and up over his
shoulder. The boy leaned into the throw and used his not
insubstantial strength to swing Mundy from his feet. Mundy
went with the throw, knowing that if he had not done so,
he would have had a dislocated shoulder or even a break to
contend with. The students, who had gathered around at a
safe distance, were open-mouthed. They had seen Hacker in
action before and knew how dangerous he was at this game.

They waited for Mundy to topple, Hacker's cronies grinning in sour satisfaction.

Mundy swung round in a swift circle, using Hacker's power and his own momentum to complete the fall, but as his feet hit the ground, he was a sudden blur of movement, twisting in a counter move that ended seconds later with Hacker flat on his back. Mundy knelt down and locked an arm across his windpipe, though he exerted no pressure. The youth was helpless to resist, as though bound up in wire. He looked into Mundy's eyes and for a second shuddered at something, but then the teacher was grinning and swinging him to his feet.

"Very good, Darren."

"You beat me," said the youth, crestfallen.

"No. You beat yourself. You gave me the initiative. Your move, your throw, was really my throw. I'll show you how to do it."

Hacker had no time to feel sorry for himself, or, more importantly, to be jeered at by the students, who were totally absorbed. Mundy quickly pressed on, knowing exactly how Hacker felt, having been in the situation himself more than once at the military academy. Except that the instructors there were merciless and partial to a bit of student humiliation. There would be none of that here. Instead he showed Hacker exactly how to do what he had done and allowed the youth to counter-throw him a couple of times until the boy had perfected the move. Hacker was a natural.

Mundy got up from his last fall, brushing himself down. The students were waiting for him to thrash Hacker now, or at least to get him in some kind of nasty lock that would pay him back, but instead Mundy slapped Hacker on the back. "You learn fast, Darren. Very good. Okay, team, let's get into pairs. No, Davey Tolland, boys with boys for this one. You can do your cuddling up to the girls later on after lessons."

"Who would want to cuddle that git?" one of the girls said with real feeling.

"Now then, Marsha. If you use that kind of language, I *will* pair you up with Tolland."

There were hoots of laughter and even the seething Marsha managed a smile.

Mundy turned to Hacker. "Practice that counter-throw on Maele. Just don't break each other's arms."

Hacker nodded. "Okay, sir. Sir," he said, lowering his voice. "You're all right, sir."

Mundy smiled. "This is going to be a good team. The best."

· ✳ ·

Andrew Wilkinson leaned on the gates of the churchyard for a moment, puffing and catching his breath. It was almost midmorning and the sun was high and fierce, as it had been for days now. The young man had a habit of walking around at twice the speed of his contemporaries, a nervous trait that was costing him dear in this heat. He mopped at his face and neck with a kerchief, shoving it back into his pocket, drawing in another lungful of warm air and pushing open the gate.

Father Madding was bound to have some chores for him, or messages to take to someone. Wilkinson was proud of his role as helper. It was unique in the town, a role created for him by the priest since he was a boy. It was, Wilkinson knew, because he was good at it. Father Madding often told him how invaluable his services were and how he couldn't do without him. Mr. Trencher said the same thing.

The church door, unusually, was locked. Wilkinson was baffled for a moment, not quite panicking. Perhaps Father Madding was out on an errand. But, no, he had asked Wilkinson to come back here for about now. There were other doors into the church and its offices. Wilkinson would find one. He went around the side of the grey wall to the first of them. But it was also locked.

A little further round the building there was a gate. Beyond it was an area that Wilkinson rarely entered, a neat garden. Posh lawn and flowers, he thought. Father Madding's private domain. But perhaps if he slipped through quickly and found a way into the church, no one would know, or shout at him. Some of the Brethren would be about somewhere, the grey-garbed men who worked for the priest as a team of special helpers. Their tasks were all connected to the church, so they weren't *that* special, Wilkinson thought. Not like him.

He weighed up his situation quickly. Tentatively he pushed open the gate, careful to drop the latch as he shut it. Timidly he crept through the garden, turning towards the bulk of the church buildings. There were several clipped high shrubs, forming walls that boxed in the sides of the narrow path, and as he was about to emerge from it, he realized he had almost stumbled across a large yard. It was only now that he saw that it was occupied. Several of the Brethren were in the yard, most of them stripped to the waist, exercising. Slightly embarrassed, Wilkinson pulled back into the hedge's shadows.

His fascination for what was going on compelled him to watch avidly. The men were all solid-looking, bronzed muscles gleaming in the sunlight. Wilkinson thought they looked exactly like soldiers from the barracks, who all trained so hard their bodies were like granite. These men laughed as they wrestled and practiced throwing each other. One pair, shadow boxing, came close to where Wilkinson was partly hidden.

"Why don't you come out and get a proper look?" one of them said.

Wilkinson jumped as if he had been scalded, almost tripping over. But he shuffled out into full view. "I'm working for Father Emmanuel," he said hesitantly.

"It's the halfwit," another of the men called. They were all grinning.

"What you playing at, son? Being a spy?"

Wilkinson felt terrified.

"Want to do some training, do you? Get your shirt off and join in."

"Yes, come on, Andrew. Let's see those lily-white pectorals!"

The men laughed cruelly. Wilkinson could feel tears welling. He had no idea how to deal with the situation. He started to back beyond the sheltered hedge of the pathway. Maybe if he turned and ran for the gate, he could get away before they caught him.

As he did turn he realized that the way was cut off. But it was the priest who stood there.

"Andrew," he said. "What are you doing here, boy? You know this is out of bounds." But Madding's face showed no anger.

"Looking for you, Father. The church was locked." Wilkinson was shaking.

The priest put a fatherly arm around his shoulder. "Come along. Let's not disturb the Brethren. I know you'd like to enter their order one day, but it's far too soon, dear boy. Mustn't rush these things. Besides, I've work for you. You know I depend on you."

"Why do they have to be so, so *hard*."

Madding's eyes narrowed for a moment, but then tried to give a reassuring smile. "I'm afraid it's a hard old world, Andrew. We none of us know when we need protection."

"They're like soldiers."

"No, no. They just look after themselves. Nothing wrong with good health and fitness, Andrew. Soldiers! Good heavens, no. We've enough soldiers down in the barracks."

Wilkinson did his best to understand, but he was still shaking when they got inside the church annex.

· ✳ ·

Shortly after the school day ended, Goldsworthy said he'd introduce Mundy to Sebastian Wroxton. As they left the teaching area, Mundy quietly broached the subject of Drew Vasillius.

"I gather there was a detective investigating the case," Mundy said.

Goldsworthy looked a little sheepish. "Inspector Barrazelli. Little rat of a man. Appointed by the Authority. What about him?"

"I gather Drew's body was never recovered."

"Barrazelli didn't have much to go on. He interviewed a few of us and some of the kids. Made a few notes. Then went back to Londonborough. The Prime had a copy of his report. Short and to the point."

"Suicide?"

Goldsworthy nodded. He was about to say more, but someone among the crowd ahead caught his eye. "Sebastian! The very man! Meet our new recruit, Chad Mundy."

The Senior Magister joined them, a huge man, his jacket stretched to the limit, looking as though it had not been buttoned up over that vast torso in a long time. He had a broad head, a strong chin, and his hair was very thin. As Mundy shook hands with Wroxton, he felt an immediate sense of warmth emanating from the man, something in direct contrast to what Mundy had felt with Carl Trencher.

"So, what has enticed you to this last bastion of civilization?" said Wroxton.

"Frontier spirit, I suppose." Mundy smiled.

"Any local ties at all?"

"No. I don't have much of a family background. Both parents died when I was very young. I hardly knew them. Londonborough lost a lot of people over the years, since the

Plague Wars. I lived with an uncle until I went off to the military academy."

"Wellington, wasn't it? One of the better ones." Wroxton said wryly. "The Prime appreciates staff from the leading academies."

"You weren't at her latest address." Goldsworthy made a face.

"No, but I can imagine exactly what she told the staff."

"She has a very clear view as to how we should tackle things," said Mundy.

"Yes, very much an Authority person. Here, she *is* the Authority. Not one for compromise, not if she thinks there's any chance of it disrupting or undermining progress. Demands very high standards. You've just come from a very strict regime. So you'll know what that entails."

Mundy nodded.

"As for our students, I tell you now, they're a tough lot here, Chad. They need to be; they are going out into a tough world. But they come from a breed of survivors. As you said, frontier spirit. Families that go back to the Plague Years. I'm sure it was bad enough in Londonborough, but out here, it was chaotic."

Wroxton eventually made his apologies. "We must have a proper talk," he told Chad as he left them.

"He's a good man," said Goldsworthy. "He almost got the job as Prime. A lot of the staff would have been happier if he had. But the Authority appointed Vine. From her speech yesterday morning, you can see why. Sebastian would never have spoken to his colleagues like that. Not in a million years."

· ✳ ·

Mundy toweled himself down after a shower, and dressed slowly. He had a real appetite and the thought of Mrs. Bazeley's Canteen food had his taste buds dancing a jig. Military academy grub was filling, but basic. Here, Petra may be on the edge of the world, but the food was the best. He laughed to himself. *I'll be as fat as a bullock before long. All that pastry—*

There was a knock on the door. Mundy knew at once that it wasn't Goldsworthy: it was far too light. He finished dressing and opened the door. To his amazement he found Penn Ranzer standing there, an uncertain smile on her lips.

"Penn," he said, feeling more than a bit dumb.

"I was hoping I'd find you in."

"Sure, sure." He stepped aside. "Come in. I've just had a shower." *Idiot. Why should she care about that?*

She looked around the room casually and then turned her alluring blue eyes back to him. "Some of us are going across the river tonight, to Overwater. There's an old pub there that does good beer and cider. Makes a change from being inside the city walls. Different crowd. Bit more relaxed."

"Oh, yes?" He beamed at her.

"We wondered if you'd like to join us. Being new and all. I know that Brin is looking after you, but it'd be a change."

"Sounds great. I was just going to get some tea—"

"No need. They do good grub over there."

"Sounds good to me." *I'm gibbering.* "What time?"

"Join us in the Feathers at six. That okay?"

"Brilliant." Part of his mind was racing, wondering why on earth his ability to converse had suddenly deserted him. Penn must think he was a moron. She turned back to the door. "See you down there," she said with another smile.

The door closed behind her and it was a while before he realized he had been gaping at it for several long moments.

VII

PETRA: ACROSS THE WATER

AS USUAL THE Feathers was packed, the heat oppressive as flaming June continued to live up to its name: the air density had been building up during the day and by evening was like a soup in the bar. Mundy struggled through the crush, getting himself a pint of the heady local brew. He saw Penn and other staff members he had met, and he joined them, sitting beside her. She didn't appear to be attached to any of the men in the group and he wondered, for the hundredth time, if she had a partner.

"We'll be on the move in a minute," she said, finishing her own pint.

"So we're going over the bridge, to the outside?"

She nodded. "Sword and Anvil. Rough crowd, but much more interesting. This place is okay, but everyone talks shop."

Mundy wished he hadn't bought a pint, knowing that if he tossed it back too quickly it would have the effect of three strong pints of the stuff he was used to. In fact, he wasn't a great beer drinker. In Londonborough, Detroyd seemed more able to cope with his drink, as with anything vaguely debauched, Mundy recalled somewhat ruefully. Two of the young teachers, Dane Elland and Zak Miller, evidently good buddies, sat close to Mundy and Penn, and there were three others, two of them young women, who also appeared to be part of this regular group. They had happily let Mundy into their fold and looked to be at ease with him. Like him, they were from outside Dumnonia, although Penn had a strong trace of local dialect, which the beer seemed to lure out.

"I had a brief visit from our leader," Mundy told them. "Welcoming me aboard." He briefly recalled the Prime's un-expected dropping in on him before he had set out. Although she had welcomed him, she had seemed somehow offhand, as though performing a required task, something to be ticked off a schedule of chores. As with Trencher it was cold, unlike

Wroxton's far more credible geniality. "I don't know what to make of her. I think the idea was to make me feel like one of the family."

Zak, dressed in a scruffy jumper that must have been far too hot in the pub's stifling atmosphere, snorted. "And did you?"

Mundy shrugged. "To be honest, I felt a bit uneasy."

"Very diplomatic, Chad." Dane laughed again. "You mean you were shitting yourself!"

Mundy glanced at Penn, and could see by her amused expression that she was enjoying this.

"Tell you what," said Zak. "If you had a broken leg, she'd visit you, ask you how you were doing, were you okay and that, then she'd want to know if you were keeping up with your marking and how soon were you going to be back in class and out on the field. That's all that matters."

One of the girls, Daura Woollacott, who had been listening closely, leaned over and said in a subdued voice, "She didn't have much sympathy for Drew Vasillius. If she had been a genuinely sympathetic person, she'd have been nicer to him."

"She made him ill," said Zak. "Kept on at him."

"He *was* ill, then?" said Mundy, remembering what the student Maggie had told him in confidence.

"You wouldn't jump off a hundred-foot wall unless you were ill, would you?" said Zak, draining his glass.

"Come on, you lot," said Penn, steering the conversation away from the potentially morbid. "Let's get going."

Mundy left half of his pint, trying to slide it discreetly out of sight. But Penn's eyes betrayed that she had seen him do it. She was grinning, but deliberately avoided looking at him. He knew she was being diplomatic and savored it as a private thing between them.

Outside it was still very bright and cloudless. Mundy felt relief at the air on his face, but the evening was still unduly heavy.

"Is the weather always like this down here?" he asked.

"The last couple of summers have been pretty hot," said Penn. "It's okay until a storm builds up. Then you need to keep your head down. Last year we had a beauty and lightning knocked one of the old buildings in town over."

"Once the rain starts," said Dane beside them, "you need a boat. Last year Dunstan had to empty a couple of the roof tanks more than once."

They left through Petra's main gates and walked steadily across the narrow stone bridge that led to the houses known collectively as Overwater, which straddled the eastern banks of the river, whose grey waters flowed by swiftly, eddying and swirling in shifting patterns that hinted at treacherous currents. Mundy couldn't help but look back at Petra, draped in lengthening shadows behind them, overshadowed by the bulk of the Academy. The sun was dropping low in the west, half-erased by the long line of the sea wall. It dominated the scene, like a possessive mother enfolding its brood of buildings.

Once across the bridge, they turned to their left and followed the narrow road that dipped down and skirted the edge of the river, where several ancient hulks had been stranded on mud flats for what must have been decades. Their weed-smeared sides were breached and rotting, their cabins derelict, disintegrating slowly like corpses on a battlefield. Mundy shook himself. *No need to be so gloomy!* he told himself, turning instead to Penn, who was watching him with a curious expression.

"Looking a bit morose, Chad," she said. "Homesick?"

He managed a weak laugh. "No. I don't think I'd want to go back to Londonborough. There's no sunlight! Well, not like there is here. It's just that this side of the river is a bit strange. The landscape."

"Twilight zone." She grinned. "There's a cemetery up on the right. And a ship's graveyard along the riverside. There are a few houseboats, too, so it's not all doom."

"I was thinking," he said, nodding towards Petra and the distant silhouette of the Academy, "it's like something out of another world."

"That's how the locals view it." She laughed.

"Are they hostile?"

She laughed even more. "Not to us. But they don't care a lot for the military." She pointed across the river, which was well over a hundred metres wide here, to the naval base and its half dozen or more ships, motionless in their moorings downstream. "They don't mind the navy so much. It's a bit of a pirate town."

"Pirates? Really?"

"Pirates, smugglers, wreckers— the secret economy. This part of the world thrives on it and has for as long as people can remember. The navy is about as corrupt as you can get!

I doubt whether the Authority will ever come to grips with it. Does that shock you?"

Mundy grinned. "No. In a way it makes the place more human. I get the feeling that the whole area is very independent and survives quite happily without subscribing too much to the rules of the Authority."

"Didn't take you long to see that!"

"And is the Academy the same?"

"Ooh, leading question." She chuckled.

"What on earth do you mean?" He smiled, but he sensed that her apparent good humour was screening something.

"Well, Chad, you could be an Authority man. Sent here to keep an eye on the rebels. I could be sticking my neck out."

"You don't honestly think that, do you, Penn?"

She hooted with laughter and the others, who were a few paces ahead, turned to see what had so amused her. "Probably not," she said. "But you'd do well to assume that the locals will think so. Until you convince them otherwise."

"I'm Authority trained and suppose I generally subscribe to their aims. Grand Britannia needs to be organized if it's ever going to rise up out of the mire."

"The mire? Is that how you see Dumnonia?"

"No, no, I didn't mean it like that. I mean the mess across the whole country, the confusion, since the Plague Wars. It must have been very different once. Less primitive. Have you ever been to Londonborough and seen the endless miles of crumbling buildings, the rot that has set in everywhere? You need to be organized to have any chance of rebuilding it— never mind the world outside."

"Maybe Petra doesn't need the Authority's help."

"Surely it would benefit from its resources?"

"A compromise, then," she said. She had never stopped smiling since opening the conversation and he wondered if she was testing him or simply teasing him.

"I suppose I'm open-minded," he said.

"Good way to be. Here's the pub. Keep that mind open."

Inside it was not as crowded, the air less dense, than it had been in The Feathers. The group, including Mundy, swapped 'hellos,' but Mundy sensed that there were more watchful eyes on him, as if he were being weighed. He was an unknown quantity in a society that could ill afford to wear its colours on its arm. *Pirates, smugglers, and wreckers.* Penn's recent words drew an involuntary grin from him. *Why not? Catch as catch can in a broken world.* He knew that the undercurrent of crime in Londonborough was a fast-flowing body, a mirror of the great Temmswater River that bisected the heart of the metropolis.

Penn and her colleagues were evidently at home in the pub and soon found a table, frothing pints of local beer in hand. Mundy sipped at his cautiously. It was amazingly even better than the brew in Petra. And, he guessed, more potent. There were other Academy staff here at the Sword and Anvil. Those that Mundy had already met he acknowledged, and they nodded or waved in recognition. Three older men came in, saw Penn's group, and invited themselves to pull up chairs and join them.

"Chad Mundy, this is Rick Stanner, Jo Rudge, and Danton Connell. All former stalwarts of Petra Academy."

"Now escaped, released, or otherwise struck off the lists," said Connell, a tall, heavyset man with a shock of thick black hair streaked with grey. Mundy put him in his mid-fifties. His grip was fierce, but his smile was engaging. Stanner was much smaller, a few years older, shoulders hunched, eyes tired. Rudge was also in his mid-fifties, Mundy estimated, and had a grizzled beard.

"The ex-pats," said Penn. "Right bunch of rebels."

"According to the powers that be on the other side. And what brings a young man like you to the end of the world?" Rudge said bluntly but with a smile to Mundy.

"A sense of adventure."

"Are you a good team player?"

"Only way to play," said Mundy. "I guess you guys weren't."

Connell chuckled good-naturedly. "Too right. We're the awful rebels. What have you been saying, Penn?"

"Not a word. You're the one who said you were struck off."

"The Carnivore did not approve of our methods or our results," said Rudge. "We're too parochial in our views. According to your divine leader. And of course, the Authority wants no truck with local initiatives. It sees the state as all important. Communities are all very well, but their first duty is to the state."

"To which we say, quite openly," said Connell, raising his tankard, "kiss my arse."

Penn was sitting back, watching Mundy's expression with amusement. He, too, was trying to keep a straight face, but was failing. "But the military haven't taken you out and put you to the sword."

"No, we're harmless idiots," said Rudge, scratching his beard, as if to demonstrate the fact. "No one in their right mind would take us seriously."

"Apart from most of the *local* population," said Connell. "But they're all halfwits, too. Thus life goes merrily on."

"So if you were thinking of reporting us to any of those walking dead across the river," said Rudge, "be our guests."

Mundy chuckled. "Not me. I'm not a devout follower of all their doctrines." *Am I safe saying this? Shit, yes.* It wasn't just the beer loosening his tongue. He was convinced these guys were what they said they were. And sooner or later, someone like them was going to take him on one side and confess to being his contact from the Historical Society. So far he had no idea who that might be. Initially he'd thought it was going to be Goldsworthy. But as Brin had said nothing, it now seemed unlikely.

The food arrived, and turned out to be every bit as delicious as Penn had avowed. Mundy ate appreciatively but respectfully shunned the cider. He didn't want anyone to have to carry him back to the Academy. He wanted to focus his attention on Penn, but she was elusive. Not deliberately, he thought. She was just a popular woman, which was hardly surprising as she was so attractive. But Mundy found himself able to talk freely to not only the teachers, but also the three 'ex-pats' and many others in the pub. The conviviality and freethinking spirit of the place was refreshing. He instinctively felt at home.

At one point, standing slightly away from the group, drawn into a discussion about the river and some local yarns about its history, Mundy was standing shoulder to shoulder with a woman in her mid-sixties called Anna. The pub was packed by this time, and everyone was squeezed into a conversation, whether they wanted to be or not. Anna had good-naturedly asked Mundy who he was. He saw no reason not to tell her.

"What do you teach up there?"

"English is my academic subject."

"You like language do you, Chad?"

"Yes. It fascinates me."

"Are you originally from Dumnonia? You don't have an accent."

"No. I grew up in the city."

Her dark-ringed eyes studied him, as though she would look straight into him and assess what she found there. But he felt too relaxed by now to shy from her gaze.

"I thought so," she said. "How well do you know your English? Have you studied its history?"

A sudden flush of sobriety washed over him. *Is this my contact?*

"Its origins, its routes?" she went on.

He held her gaze, but she was clearly waiting for him to answer. As far as he could tell, no one else was aware of their conversation, or showed any interest in it.

"Yes, I've made a study of its origins. I probably would have majored in History, but to be honest, you have to wait to be chosen for that sort of thing. History is something of a sensitive area with the Authority."

She seemed to flinch at that but recovered herself. "I understand."

"I did my thesis on dialects."

She considered this with unfeigned interest. "Do you know the Old Tongue?" she asked.

Mundy again felt another flush. "Well, I wouldn't profess to be an expert."

"Few would," she said, this time smiling so that the skin at the corners of her eyes creased. She seemed now to be much older than he had first thought, that or much wearier. She leaned closer and whispered something.

Mundy hid his shock by sipping at his beer. The so-called Old Tongue! *She is speaking to me in a dead language from — how many centuries ago?*

"And I, Chad Mundy, greet you and give thanks for your kind welcome," he whispered back to her in as good a rendition as he could of the same ancient speech.

"We are being watched," she said, still in the Old Tongue, but in a casual way as if discussing the quality of the beer or the pleasantness of the summer. "I will leave you now, Chad."

"We must talk again," he said, also in the Old Tongue.

She bent forward to set down her tankard on a table and as she did so, she spoke slowly so that he could understand and, amazingly, it was as if his mind was free of obstruction, as though the ancient words pierced all mental barriers, resonating within an inner part of him that had been dormant all his life.

"You are in danger here in Petra," she said. "Guard your back at all times. Put on your warrior's face." The words shook him, somehow more frightening spoken in the Old Tongue. But she had one last comment to make and it really caught him unawares, as if she had punched him under the heart. It was only at that moment that he realized who she was.

And then she was gone, absorbed into the press of bodies, the swirling noise.

After that, the rest of the night in the pub sped by and somehow the beer had little effect on Mundy. The woman's parting comment rang and rang again in his head, more sobering than a douche of cold water. But he said nothing of it to his companions. He would need time alone to think about it and its disturbing implications.

I'm Drew Vasillius's widow, she had said. *And he did not commit suicide. He was murdered.*

VIII

PETRA: THE RIVER

MUCH LATER, HE and Penn and their original companions left the pub along with a spillage of others, all waving or shouting happily. Connell and the ex-pats made a point of wishing Mundy good night, urging him to visit them as often as he liked "for as much corruption and sedition" as he was up for. They each shook his hand and, with a few final ribald remarks, shambled off into the darkness, no doubt, Mundy thought, for a further, private drinking bout.

To his surprise, Penn took his arm. He tried to treat it nonchalantly, though his heart was thumping in his chest as if it would betray him. But she seemed to be totally relaxed. "So you met Anna Vasillius."

"Yes," he said, making no reference to what she had told him.

"Did you ask her about her husband?"

He frowned. "To be honest, I thought she'd be a bit loath to talk to me about it. Dead man's shoes."

"She wouldn't resent you. She's not that kind of person."

They followed Dane, Zak, and the others along the narrow street and back up the riverbank towards the stone bridge. They were within fifty yards when they saw a group of men, obscured in shadow, leaning on the parapets. Mundy felt a stirring of unease. Anna Vasillius's words about danger hovered about him like phantoms. The entire atmosphere of the night had changed since their arrival in Overwater.

"You okay?" said Penn, squeezing his arm. "You've gone very pensive."

He was about to answer when he heard the rustle of grass to his right where the bank slid down to the water, now as black as pitch.

"Sir. Sir," someone hoarsely, urgently whispered. Immediately Mundy was in a defensive mode, gently easing

Penn aside, putting himself between her and whoever had spoken in the darkness. A narrow track led down from the road, curving like a towpath along the muddy bank and under an arch of the bridge. Mundy could make out a shape now: someone seemed to be beckoning to him.

"Careful," breathed Penn. "Not everyone hereabouts is friendly. There are some odd characters around. They deeply resent anything vaguely related to the Authority, no matter what our views are."

"Okay, wait here while I check it out," he told her and went down the track cautiously.

"Sir!" He heard the voice again. With a start of surprise, Mundy recognized who it was. Darren was barely discernible in the moonlight.

"Darren?" Mundy stepped slowly towards him, watching the immediate shadows for any other signs of movement, but there were none. Almost as though something was focused on his presence. Across the water, Petra's winking lights were testament to its torpid slip into the inactivity of night. Downriver, between the town and the barracks, there were signs that the waterfront pubs were still very active.

"Don't go up on the bridge," said the youth, eyes fixed on the blurred shapes up there. The men at the parapet were looking in Mundy and Penn's direction.

"What's the problem?"

"I heard them. Me and Dean Wenner were up there, cadging smokes. I heard some of them saying you were coming. They've been watching you in the Anvil."

"Me? Why?" Mundy again replayed Anna Vasillius's warning in his mind.

"Dunno, sir. But they're gonna rough you up."

"What is it?" called Penn from further up the slope. "Is that Darren Hacker?"

"It's all right," Mundy replied, slightly raising his voice, one eye on the group of men on the bridge. He turned back to the youth. "Who are they, Darren?"

"They're dressed like soldiers from the military base. But I ain't seen them before. Could be new ones. Most of the ones that come over here, me and Dean know. They look like a hard lot, sir. More than usual. Sir, I can get you out of this."

"What do you mean?"

"I've a boat just down here, under the bridge. I can row us back over to Petra. Even if they followed by the bridge they'd not catch us. Tide's flowing out."

Glancing back, Mundy could see that Penn, who couldn't hear the conversation, was looking uncomfortable; the other staff were almost at the bridge.

"What about Miss Ranzer?"

The youth shook his head. "They won't touch her, or the others. Just you."

Mundy could see the others. They seemed to be in no danger. "Penn," he called. "Go on up to Dane. Be careful what you say to anyone on the bridge."

"What's happening?" she said, eyes widening. "What's going on?"

"Just go on up, please. If they ask about me, make some kind of excuse. Say I'm coming and will catch up in a few moments. Say I'm having a pee, or something. But don't hang about, not you, Dane, or any of them. Just get back across the bridge as quickly as you can. I'm sure you'll be okay."

"What about you? You can't stay here!"

"No. I don't intend to. Darren here has got a boat. I'm going over with him. I'll explain later— tomorrow. Just trust me."

She hesitated. "I don't like this, Chad—"

"Please."

She looked up at the bridge. The men were ignoring Dane's group, who were dawdling along, waiting for Penn and Mundy to catch up.

"Well, if you're sure you know what you're doing."

"Yes. Go on up before anyone realizes."

She nodded, still clearly in two minds about the situation, then started up the slope. The men on the bridge watched her like hawks, one of them moving to the top of the narrow road, as if waiting for her.

"Hurry, sir!" said Darren, turning back down the trackway. Mundy followed him, nearly slithering over on the slick bank, but in a few moments was on the level. Darren, a few steps ahead of him, pointed under the darkness of the first span of the bridge. A thin plank led across the mud flat to a rowing boat moored there, a pair of oars resting inside it.

As the youth made for it, another shadow detached itself from beside the stone arch, materializing out of thin air, having been completely obscured by the darkness. Arms reached out, preparing to make a grab for the youth. The man, who was dressed in military uniform, moved in quickly, intending to put some sort of arm-lock on Darren and swing him round to face Mundy, a hostage in whatever grim game was being played out here. But Mundy's horror turned to an involuntary wry smile as he watched Darren employ the very throw that he had taught him that morning, turning defense into attack. With a deep-voiced curse, the man could not prevent himself from being flipped up and over. He thumped down on the path, his head and shoulders meeting the ground with the full impact of a heavyweight's punch.

Mundy was beside the youth in a moment, steadying him gently. He could see that the soldier — if soldier he really was — was momentarily too stunned to move, the wind completely knocked out of him. And the men above on the bridge would not have seen the incident. From further down the pathway, upriver, there were several guttural curses. Others were coming to reinforce the assault.

Darren, slightly stunned by what he had done, recovered quickly. "I'll get in and do the rowing, sir," he said. "You untie us." He pointed to a thick pole thrust up from the mud. The mooring rope was secured around it.

Mundy nodded, watching the shapes that were now coalescing from the night no more than twenty yards away. Darren slipped into the boat, lithe as a cat, and took up the oars. In a moment, Mundy had untied the knot and was sitting in the stern of the rowing boat, facing the now breathless youth. With a few easy pulls, Darren had worked the craft out into the drag of the tide. Behind Mundy there were more curses as the pursuit was forced to a halt at the water's edge. Mundy could see over the side of the rowing boat that the river was flowing deceptively quickly. Darren, however, used the current with the consummate skill of a practiced oarsman, guiding the craft easily and steadily. In no time at all they were skimming along.

Mundy looked back to see the pursuers, together with the man Darren had thrown, glaring at them in impotent rage. They had no boat themselves. "Well done, Darren. I'd say you learned your lesson well. That guy will have a headache for a while after that landing."

Darren was watching the bridge as he rowed and could now see the soldiers up there, waving and gesticulating. Their voices carried on the still night air, the words muffled and incoherent, but the anger in them very evident.

"I owe you one," Mundy said to Darren.

Darren nodded uncomfortably, twisting round to see where the opposite bank was. His face was serious, with no hint of a smile. "I was shitting myself," he said. "When that bloke came at me. I told you they were after you, sir."

Mundy ignored the crude language. "And you've no idea why?"

Darren shook his head. "No, sir." He concentrated on working the boat into a position that would ease it across to a set of steps built into the nearing quayside, within the city wall. The tide was ebbing, having been full not long earlier and there were no more than a dozen dripping steps revealed. Darren's control of the boat had brought them across in a matter of minutes. As the youth prepared to maneuver to the steps, Mundy looked back at the receding bridge. He could see one group of figures crossing it— Penn and her fellows. Darren had been right: the soldiers were not following, remaining grouped at the eastern end of the bridge, knowing that they had been outwitted. Even if they had commandeered a rowing boat, the tide was far too swift for them to have caught up.

Mundy's attention was snared by a subdued groan from Darren. He had shipped oars and ducked down, pointing up at the quayside. Mundy struggled to see into the thick shadows there, but after a moment he detected the slightest of movements.

"More of them," murmured the youth, immediately using an oar to guide the rowing boat back away from the quay. "Can't land us there."

Mundy watched, certain now that there were a number of men moving parallel to them along the quay. It was an area that the night had completely claimed. No lights, no pubs, just obscure walls and buildings.

"I'll have to land us at the barracks, sir. But there may be more soldiers there, mates of the ones looking for you. I could go back across, but I don't reckon it would be safe in Overwater now."

"I don't want you to put yourself at risk, Darren. Can you outpace the men on the quay? Is there somewhere between here and the barracks? If I've got enough of a start, I could outrun them and slip back up to the Academy."

Darren nodded, clearly torn between keeping clear of trouble and helping Mundy. He sculled very quickly, propelling the craft along with the tide that, in the half-glow of night, seemed almost unreal. Anyone pursuing along the quayside would not have been able to keep up. Darren's face was a mask, etched by fear. His expression warned Mundy that the youth had seen something else behind Mundy's shoulder, as if the river was about to disgorge some hostile agent, intent on sabotaging their flight.

"What is it?" Mundy called. He looked back, but saw only the dark water.

"Blood on the water," said Darren. "It's a bad moon."

"What are you talking about? There's no blood."

"Trick of the light, sir. But it's a bad omen."

Mundy had forgotten how superstitious some of the local people were. There was no point arguing. The boy was clearly terrified by whatever he had seen, or imagined.

"Just drop me ashore, Darren. And you get yourself away as quickly as you can. Get back to safety. I'm sure they won't follow you."

Darren was too afraid to object. He turned and looked for the next set of steps, which were close. Already he had given them well over a sixty yards head start on the pursuers. It would have to be enough. Quickly he slid the boat to the base of the stone steps. As he did so, Mundy balanced himself and leapt. He almost slipped on the weed that coated the steps, but braced himself on the quay wall.

"Get going!" he called to Darren, not looking back as he clambered unsteadily up to the quayside. One glance up-river showed him that the pursuers were still not in sight. He only had a vague idea about where he was in relation to the Academy, but he ran across the quay into the first alley he came to. It was dark and wound tortuously between the squat houses, leading to a tiny maze of similar passages and tight little streets. *As long as I go upwards*, he thought, *I must be heading for the Academy.*

A hundred yards into the waterside buildings, he realised the street curved back towards the river. He would have to go back or risk going on before detouring up again. As he deliberated, he heard footsteps clearly ringing out on the street behind him. The pursuit was closing.

He made a bolt for it, down the street and back on to the harbour side. Fifty yards ahead, light spilled from a pub. On the quayside, bobbing slightly on the night tide, a large ship had been moored. To Mundy's untrained eye, it looked like a trawler. Certainly the sudden reek of fish and the sea suggested as much. There were men coming along the quayside and he knew there were others behind him. He raced on.

Shortly before he reached the pub, there was an alleyway. One look up it showed him that it led steeply upwards into darkness. It might just be what he needed, a way back up to the top of the town. Nothing else for it. He turned into it and ran.

Within moments he realized it was the wrong choice. The alley led a dozen yards on, ending in a wall, a dead end. There was a door set in it and for a second he drew back in surprise, confronted by a strange carving in the wood of the door, a wild face, wreathed in what looked like oak leaves. Recovering himself, he tried the wooden knob, but the door was immovable.

Behind him, by coming into the alley, the first of the pursuers had cornered him. He turned, partially obscured by the night, but knew he was trapped. His only advantage was that the alley was narrow. If they wanted to attack him, they could only do so two at a time at most. Normally that would have been something he would have been prepared to deal with. But there was nothing casual about this premeditated attack: the first two men coming slowly towards him both carried long knives. Their faces were obscured, their clothing rough and nondescript. He was immediately reminded of the incident with Barry Skellbow and the men who had so obviously been about to harass him. Were these the same ones?

Soon they were no more than feet away, regarding him coldly, noting his stance.

"You've got a long nose, son," said one of them in a voice that Mundy immediately recognised as not being Dumnonian. Like many of the military men here in Petra, he was from Londonborough.

"I don't know what you're talking about."

"Oh yes, you do, son. You've been sticking your nose in where it don't belong." He held up the knife, at least a foot of steel. "You're going to get it cut off if you don't watch yourself."

The other man also made sure that Mundy could see his blade. "You were in Overwater. Talking to the scum who frequent that piss-hole of a pub, the Anvil. One lady in particular."

Mundy felt a chill of unease. Anna Vasillius had warned him. She had said that her husband had been murdered. By these people?

"If I were you, I'd stay well away from that lady, Mr. Mundy. You just get on with your job. Stay away from Overwater. Stay away from all those pagan idiots. Very unhealthy lot. You understand me?"

Mundy kept completely still and said nothing. He was trying to decide which of the two would be his first target if he had to take the initiative. His main worry, apart from the knives, was the other group of men back down the alley.

"This is a small town. We see everything. We've got eyes and ears everywhere. You so much as fart and we'll hear you," sneered the first man.

His companion grunted with amusement. "This is just a friendly warning, son. You step out of line and—"

He was cut short by a strangled shout from the mouth of the alleyway. Mundy could not see, but something was going on down there. Voices were suddenly raised, snarls almost: a fight had broken out on the quayside.

The first of the two men that were menacing him turned around, trying to discern what was happening. The other, startled, took his eyes off Mundy for a few moments. Mundy acted with trained speed, aiming a hard kick up under the man's abdomen, his toe connecting between his legs. His victim squealed in agony, doubling up, dropping his knife. Mundy darted forward, gripped the man's arm, and wrenched it brutally to one side. The man's wrist snapped like a dried branch and he screamed.

Mundy swept up the knife from the floor in one continuous movement, jerking the man around and holding the blade to his throat. The man's eyes filled with tears of acute pain, his body unable to do anything to counter Mundy's grip on him. Down at the head of the alley, things had suddenly gone as silent as they had been before the abrupt scuffle.

Mundy's first assailant was going down the alley, oblivious to the fact that Mundy had his companion in a paralyzing grip no more than a few feet behind him. Mundy gently nudged his victim forward, the knife blade still touching his throat across his windpipe. It was impossible to see who was involved in the melee, but there were more men than earlier. And not all of them were part of the gang that had pursued Mundy.

There was a sudden flurry of movement and the first man with a knife gasped as if he had been thumped hard in the guts. He doubled over, his knife clattering to the stone floor of the alley. Whoever had attacked him grabbed him, hauled him to his feet, and hit him again, one blow landing on the side of his face with a sound like a hock of meat being smacked against concrete.

Mundy kept on easing forward. He was now very close to the mouth of the alley. There was light beyond and in its wan glow, he saw a different gang of men. They had the look — and the smell — of sailors. Maybe they were the fishermen from the large trawler he had noticed earlier. It was they who had piled into his pursuers, and Mundy could see now the resulting chaos. Several men were down, faces bloodied, at least three of them sprawled out, unconscious, or close to it.

The first of the men who had threatened Mundy with a knife was on his knees, retching into the alley. As Mundy stopped, still holding his second pursuer, two from the new group appeared on either side of him, gripping his arms so that he was powerless to move. They took the knife from him easily.

"People who play with knives ought to mind they don't go cutting themselves, boyo," said the first of them. Another of the men stepped forward and pulled the man away from Mundy and Mundy could not see but it sounded as if his former prisoner had been thumped in the stomach. The man let out a shuddering gasp of pain and sagged, and he was quickly dragged aside.

Mundy, still held in unbreakable arm-locks on either side, found himself face to face with a huge fellow with a mane of hair and a tangled beard that hung halfway down his chest. His eyes beamed at Mundy. "Fine mess you're in here, boyo. What have you done to upset this bunch of shite?"

"I don't know," Mundy said, shaking his head slowly. "I was in Overwater. They were waiting to jump me. I ran and got myself lost. They followed me here."

"Looks like they meant business." The man picked up one of the fallen knives. "You could gut a shark with one of these. I know, I've done it often enough!" He laughed. It was not a pleasant sound.

Mundy felt the grip on his arms weakening slightly.

The big man kicked out casually at one of his fallen victims. "I've told these bastards to keep away from our patch. The dock is out of bounds to the likes of them."

"Who are they?" said Mundy.

"Fucked if I know, boyo. And who are you?"

"Mundy. I'm new at the Academy."

"Teacher, is it?"

Mundy nodded.

"Well, you may be that, but you need to learn a few things. Like, you stay the fuck out of this part of Petra. You're lucky. Your god must be watching over you."

The men let Mundy go, but he was wary of making any sudden moves.

"You get off to your school, boyo. And keep away from the docks. Next time will be the last." He thrust the knife into a thick leather belt. "I mean, the last."

Mundy nodded. "I owe you for this."

The bearded giant grinned, but his expression was disturbing, slightly manic. "Stay away. That'll be reward enough for me." He said no more to Mundy, calling his men to him. Some of them glared at Mundy as if to say to their leader, *surely you're not going to leave this fellow alive, are you*? But Mundy was soon on his own: the seamen had walked away from their victims as though nothing had happened.

Quickly Mundy slipped back along the quay, checking each alleyway to see that none of his former pursuers were watching him. Then he found a street that did offer a climb up and away from the docks. He walked as quickly as he could, glancing back over his shoulder, but there were no further signs of pursuit.

He wondered if Darren had made it back safely. It seemed likely.

As he came to the upper part of the town and reached a junction where a torch set high up in a cresset burned what would be its last moments, he glanced down at his shirt and to his horror saw that one side of it was soaked in blood. He automatically reached inside it to touch his side, for one shocking moment thinking that he must have been cut in the skirmish. But it was not his blood. His unwitting rescuers must have used their own weapons on the men who had followed Mundy. Surely to God they wouldn't have killed any of them. Were they that ruthless?

Cautiously Mundy approached the gates of the Academy and slipped through. He knew that one of the caretakers, probably Jordan Creech, would be locking them for the night fairly soon. Careful not to be seen, Mundy went into the building and up the stairs to his room. As soon as he got in, he tore off the shirt together with all of his clothes, checking them all for bloodstains. Apart from the shirt, everything was all right, so he stuffed the shirt into the cloth sack that served as a litter bin and buried it under old papers he had discarded, tying the sack up tightly. Eventually one of the caretakers would remove it and incinerate it with all the other rubbish.

He ran a bath, mercifully still a hot one, and sank down into its blissful relief.

Who were his assailants? he kept asking himself. *Authority men? They had Londonborough voices. Warning me off Anna Vasillius. Don't want me talking to her. Because she knows her husband was murdered. By them, or others connected to them? Why? Why was he murdered? What could Vasillius possibly have done to warrant being killed? Whatever it was, it looks as if his killers don't want anyone poking their nose into it. Thank God for the seamen.*

And who were they? Mundy kept asking himself. The voice of the big man had had an unusual lilt to it. Not at all Dumnonian— he was no local. But if he was a fisherman, no doubt he and his crew plied their trade near and far along the coasts and out into the deep seas. He was used to killing sharks, he'd said.

God help the sharks. Mundy grinned to himself, drawing at least a modicum of comfort from the thought.

PART TWO
A STATE OF CONFUSION

IX

LONDONBOROUGH

IN THE OFFICE'S dim light, the detective pored over several documents, his mind anywhere but on the drudgery of the current job. Since he had returned from the sunlit fortress city of Petra, a million miles away from the gloom and grind of Londonborough, his enthusiasm for work, or anything else, had waned big time. So when the door opened and his secretary handed him the envelope, he prayed that it would be an omen.

"Some geezer left it for you just now," she said casually. "Said to tell you, one good turn deserves another." She left him staring at the creased envelope.

Slowly he opened it. Two keys fell out and a single sheet of creased paper. There was an address on it, a near derelict street not far from these offices. He knew what this was about.

Cursing, he got up, pulled on his coat, and was out of the offices in a matter of minutes. A brisk, four-hundred-yard walk brought him to the street named on the sheet of paper. No sign of life anywhere. He went down the street, checking out numbers on dilapidated doors.

He reached his destination. Rubbish was heaped in the tiny garden and rats scuttled off, vanishing under the heaps. He took a last look around before approaching the door. The larger of the two keys opened it. It swung in, scraping the worn floor tiles. There was enough daylight to be able to study the house. Dusty, cobwebbed, no indication of occupation for a long time, it was one of thousands in this part of the city. The two downstairs rooms and a kitchen were stripped bare, crumbling and damp. He climbed the rotting stairs carefully. At their head there was a landing, the first door shut. He tried the key, successfully.

Beyond was the only room in the house that had been decorated. It had a clean carpet, painted walls, was almost pleasant. There was a table, two chairs, and a bed. A safe

house, then. Light filtered in through the old window as if
the place was below water.

He looked down at the young man sitting on the bed, head
bent forward, hands over his ears. The detective had never
seen a more wretched spectacle.

"Mario," he said softly.

The youth, who was in his late teens, looked up, startled,
not realizing he had a visitor. Slowly his dark-rimmed eyes
widened. His mouth opened and momentarily it was as though
he could not form words. But he managed to force out one.
"Dad?"

The detective had to struggle to push down the anger that
was rising in him. "What sort of mess have you got me into
this time, son?"

They looked at each other, both warring with their emotions.

"How did you find me?" croaked the youth.

"I've always been a good cop, Mario. Always done things
by the book. Never compromised myself. Never taken bribes. I
prided myself that I told the truth. But now that has changed."
Because of you, he wanted to add. His son had been nothing
but trouble to him, lazy, mixing with bad company, living on
the dark edge of society. One scrape after another.

"I was sent to another city, to investigate a death. When I
came to write my report, I was told that it had been written
for me. All I had to do was sign it. If I did, you would be
returned to me."

"Who abducted me? Who locked me up here?" The youth
stood uncertainly. He looked as if he hadn't slept for days.

"It makes no difference. Better that we don't know. I signed
the report, Mario. Against my better judgement. I, Antonio
Barrazelli, am no longer beyond reproach. But you are free."
One good turn deserves another.

"You shouldn't have done it—"

"Don't tell me that!" Barrazelli snapped. "You're my son.
You think I would leave you to rot, in spite of all our differ-
ences?"

The youth winced. He knew well enough what his father's
fury could be like— he had invoked it enough times.

"I still have a choice, Mario. I can take you with me, forget
about the report I had to sign and we would be left in peace.
Or I could lock you up again and go back to my boss and
expose what has happened."

"No! They'll kill me—"

Barrazelli nodded. "So tell me, why should I take you with me? What do I gain by that, eh?"

The youth was shaking, tears springing from his eyes.

"Easy for you to cry, Mario. Listen, you come with me under conditions. No more stupidity. No more wasted life. And you go to an academy. You train and you *earn* your right to live."

Mario looked for a moment as though he would cry out in all his bitter frustration, but he could only nod, shivering, his cheeks streaming.

His father went to him then and did something he had not done since Mario was a child. He put his arms around him.

· ✳ ·

Deadspike's grey eyes fixed unwaveringly on the manuscript before him as though nothing else in the room existed. Each page was numbered and headed, *Chad Mundy.*

Behind him, through a tall window, one of Londonborough's incessant rainstorms lashed the glass, blurring the view. An occasional stab of lightning illuminated the endless procession of clouds. Deadspike ignored the muted din. He might have been a statue, his long, skeletal fingers lifting and turning the pages. His face was set like stone, in an expression his contemporaries often found unreadable.

His mind, however, was sifting information he had received earlier. News that intensely irritated him. Sunderman's goons were as ineffectual as their boss. Headless chickens. All they had to do was watch members of the Historical Society. How hard could it be to trace them to its base? But after a month of surveillance they had come up with nothing. Led up blind alleys and on wild goose chases. Sunderman, Deadspike cursed mentally, was embarrassingly inept.

Moreover he'd sent this man Mundy to Petra, not as an agent, trained and primed for Authority work at a time when it was so obviously needed, but as an independent operative. Ridiculous! Deadspike's thoughts returned to Mundy's dossier. What was it about his fascination for a *dead* language? The Old Tongue, it was called. Perfectly credible for it to be of interest to someone like Harrald Moddack, Mundy's main preceptor: the world of elderly academia was far too preoccupied, too self-contained to pose any real threat to the Authority.

But why should a virile, young man, exceptionally skilled in hand-to-hand combat, have any interest in something as stultifying as dialects and a dead language?

What am I missing? Mundy was praised for his self-discipline. It contributed much to his skill as a fighter. The file referred to the necessary disciplines at work in language, the complex use of metre, cadences, and so on. Deadspike was sharp enough to recognise that, although such things passed for the most part over his own head, they were nevertheless considered important. Discipline of the mind as well as the body. Natural forces, which Mundy possessed and exercised in his own peculiar way.

Deadspike closed the file. Perhaps he was being alarmist. *Perhaps.* From a drawer in the desk he removed another file and unclipped it. After a brief perusal, he sealed it in a large envelope and slid it into a briefcase.

Moments later, he left the building with the briefcase, pulling a hood over his head to keep off the driving rain. In the gusting deluge, no one would have known it was not late autumn. Midsummer may have been approaching, but it was constrained high over the city, beyond that barrier of murky cloud. The Enforcer was aware that he was being shadowed: it was easy enough to discern human movement against such an empty backdrop. But they would be his men, so much more effective than Sunderman's dummies. He went nowhere without protection and never took his safety for granted. In Londonborough, anything unidentified that moved was a potential enemy.

Deadspike's brisk walk took him along a labyrinthine route, down abandoned backstreets to a part of the central city that he rarely used. Its dangers were well known. The criminal element thrived in its morbid grip. But Deadspike had been capitalizing on its mystique for a long time. His needs and those of the underbelly of Londonborough often coincided.

His discreet walk brought him to an alleyway where a single inhabitant leaned up against a grimy wall, barely distinguishable from the sacks of rubbish and other detritus. From under a dripping, broad-rimmed hat, the man eyed Deadspike. Satisfied that he knew him, he stood aside. Deadspike entered the alley, reached a door that was peppered with woodworm, and pushed it open.

Another grubby character sat in an alcove inside, lit by a single candle. In here night was indistinguishable from day. But it suited Deadspike.

"Mr. Slake is expecting you, sir," said the man.

Deadspike nodded, walked on down a dusty corridor, and knocked on the brightly painted door at its end. It opened almost immediately.

"Mr. Slake is on his way," said another of the men who looked after this semi-derelict building. Like many others, its anonymity served its purpose well. Deadspike could feel reasonably certain of being undisturbed here. He removed his wet coat and tossed it onto a chair. Another door opened, admitting Deadspike's host.

Ottomas Slake was bent over, stocky, his grubby coat saturated. He was almost bald, a few wisps of hair plastered to his freckled head. In his gnarled hands he clasped a begrimed hat that had seen better days, crushed up in that grip. Slake's complexion was ruddy, his jowls evidently unshaven for a day or so. His rheumy eyes flicked about the room as if expecting to see something untoward. With a curt nod of dismissal to the other man, he shuffled forward as though partially lame, his mouth opening in a sidelong grin. "Foul morning, Mr. Deadspike. Very foul."

Deadspike grunted, non-committal. The private detective was a mess to look at, but Deadspike knew he possessed a sharp brain and had contacts in Londonborough's underworld that were second to none. Slake was aptly named the Londonborough Roach. Deadspike lifted one of the files. "Have you a report on Erroll Detroyd?"

Slake pulled a shabby notebook from an inner pocket and flipped it open. He made no attempt to sit down. "As you asked, Mr. Deadspike, I had him watched. I used some of my best boys. They don't miss nothing."

"That's what I pay you for, Slake. So what have you found out for me?"

"Like you said, Detroyd visits someone once or twice a month, down Belmondside. Big building. Mostly derelict. But I've had men on the place for days. It's a woman he visits. We've seen her coming out."

"Anyone else?"

"No one, Mr. Deadspike. There's a back entrance and a side one, but neither ever gets opened. Locked. We've tried them.

And of course, there's always one or two of Mr. Sunderman's staff watching. They don't see my boys, though." Slake managed a crooked smile. "We've followed the woman. Looks like she lives in the centre of town. She turns up, and then, an hour or so later, Detroyd turns up. Sometimes he comes out, later on. Then she comes out, later on again. Sometimes neither of them come out, as if they have another way out that we haven't found. But we will."

"What are they, lovers?"

Slake laughed, more of a snigger than anything. "Well, no accounting for taste, Mr. Deadspike, but I don't think so. Detroyd sees other women, more his age. He's a good-looking bloke, so he pulls good-looking birds. Can't see why he'd want the woman as a lover. She's old enough to be his mother."

"Or his aunt," said Deadspike, looking at something in the file.

"Like you say."

"Does she have a name, Slake?"

Slake referred to his tattered notebook. "Amelia Tannerton. Widower. An administrator."

"For the Authority?"

"Like you say. Based in Financial Records."

Deadspike scowled and Slake looked away. Deadspike's scowl had not been directed at him, but he knew it made Slake very uneasy. "Have your people been into the building?" Deadspike asked.

"Only so far. There's a lobby. Other than that it's all locked up, like some old warehouse that's never been used. Except that it *is* used. I smell them, Mr. Deadspike. Whoever has been in and out. You can tell that place isn't always deserted.

"More than just Detroyd and the woman meet there. Sometimes Detroyd has someone with him. Another young bloke, like him."

Deadspike leaned forward like a hound scenting blood.

"Neither of them came out, not by the front, any road. One time they went in together and came out together. And then, at other times, this other bloke goes in and out on his own."

"This other— *bloke*," said Deadspike, picking up the second manuscript and opening it to reveal a black-and-white drawing of a man's head and shoulders. "Would this be him?" He held out the drawing so that Slake could see it.

"Indeed it would, Mr. Deadspike! Him and Detroyd were, until pretty recently, living in the same house. Name of Chad Mundy."

Deadspike retrieved the picture and closed the file, setting it down slowly on the desk. "That's very helpful, Slake. Tell me, have you heard anything about a private group of individuals calling themselves the Historical Society? Do you know of anyone who might be connected with such a group? Think carefully, man. This is important."

Slake repeated the name to himself under his breath a few times, in case it would ring a bell in his extraordinary memory. But after a few moments he shook his head.

"The minute you do hear of it, let me know."

Slake was using a broken pencil to scribble in his little book. "I will, Mr. Deadspike. Rest assured I will."

"Keep the woman under surveillance. I want to know all the people she meets. Especially outside of her work. And if any of her working colleagues meet her privately, I want to know. The same goes for Detroyd. Just make damned sure none of them are aware that they're being watched."

Slake nodded his head, though his stooped frame made it more like a bow.

Deadspike opened another file. He handed it over to Slake, who took it gingerly as if it were in danger of falling apart in his clawed hand.

"His name is Moddack. Harrald Moddack. He's a lecturer at Wellington."

Slake studied the drawing of the man in the file. "It's a good likeness."

"What do you mean?"

"I've seen him. He's been to that same building."

Deadspike looked almost smug. "Has he, indeed? Well, I want the usual survey. Day and night. Who he meets, where he goes. Listen in on his conversations if you can get close enough. And above all, Slake, if he meets Amelia Tannerton or that young man Detroyd, you get straight back to me."

Slake nodded, pushing both the file and his notebook into some hidden pouch within his coat and buttoning it up again.

"Don't leave without this." Deadspike pulled another envelope from out of his inner pocket and handed it over to Slake, who took it with an almost reverential bow. He put his hand on the door handle, but turned slowly, as if he were in pain. "Mr. Deadspike, your interest in this Historical lot—"

"I expect your absolute discretion on that, Slake. The consequences of not exercising it would be, shall we say, very disturbing. Why do you ask?"

"If this bloke Moddack or the woman knows about the Society, we could easily take them on one side — discreetly — and ask them a few questions. Not too gently, mind."

Deadspike grimaced. "It may be necessary later, but not before I give the word. Your absolute discretion is vital, Slake. I wouldn't want anyone getting hurt."

"No heavy stuff. As you wish, Mr. Deadspike. Softly does it." He was about to go, but turned with a final lopsided smile. "That other business, with the boy."

"Barrazelli? Have you done as I asked?"

"My man left his father the keys. He took the bait. Father and son reunited."

Deadspike picked up his coat. "Keep an eye on them. Just for the time being."

X

PETRA

MUNDY WOKE WITH a shock of realization that he had overslept. Panic galvanized him. But something surfaced on the swirling pool of his thoughts. *Today's Saturday. Day off!* He slumped back among the sheets with a sigh of relief. He had had a dreadful night, invaded by bad dreams. Repeatedly he had relived the events across the river. And a strange, leering face, carved from wood and wreathed in oak leaves, mouthed at him in torment— the face he had seen carved on the door in the alley.

He got up and for once was content to splash cold water in his face and across his upper torso, wincing at its effect, but appreciating it. He must find Penn, and quickly, to reassure her that he was okay. The canteen? She might be there, or at least someone would be who knew her address.

There was no sign of her there, but as frustration gnawed at him, he caught site of a tall, blonde girl who he knew worked in her department. He approached her table with a forced grin and she looked up at him, puzzled. She knew who he was, but seemed surprised to see him here.

"Hi. It's Chad, isn't it?" she smiled. The man beside her, a muscular teacher who was busily chewing his way through a plateful of bacon and eggs, looked up quizzically at Mundy as though eyeing a rival.

"Sorry to bother you, Donna, but I need to speak to Penn Ranzer. It's important. Is she at home, do you know?"

"I'm pretty sure she is."

"What's her address?"

"She's on Argent Street. Number 16. But she'll be in the Feathers at midday. You're sure to see her then." Donna looked uncomfortable for some reason.

"Okay. Sorry to bother you." Mundy smiled at her and her burly companion, who nodded at him indifferently.

Outside, the air was already thickening, if anything more humid than the previous day. He knew that Argent Street was not far from the centre of Petra, down a very steep side street. The houses were tiny, squeezed together in long winding rows, with no pavements. Mundy was moving down the hill, reading off the numbers. He could see across the roofs of the town to the river, picking out Overwater's distant buildings on its far bank, which included the Anvil. It looked very different by brilliant daylight; the air of menace from the night before had dissipated.

Ahead and below him, movement caught his eye. There was a snatch of laughter— a girl's voice as she exited one of the houses. He recognized her at once. Penn! He was about to hail her, when another figure stepped from the house, closing its door. Penn's attention was fixed on the man, who Mundy guessed to be about his own age. The man put his arm around Penn's waist and she leaned across and kissed him gently on the lips. They stood for a moment, talking quietly to each other.

Mundy instinctively blended into the shadow of the nearest house, able to flatten himself against its wall, which curved slightly so that he was out of immediate sight of the couple. He inched his head forward. Penn and the man were moving off down the street, her arm around his waist, his arm around her shoulders. Their heads were very close together. Like lovers.

Mundy felt his cheeks burning. *Lovers*. He'd been an idiot. Why should he assume she wasn't spoken for? But last night, after they came out of the Anvil, she put her arm around him. As if encouraging him. *To what? It was late, it was dark. We were just returning to Petra. She must have just felt a bit more secure putting her arm around me. I was no more than a friend.*

Whatever, it was not the right time to speak to her. He could see now why her colleague, Donna, had been a bit uneasy. He waited until the couple were well out of sight and then turned back, more confused than ever by events. So why had she invited him out last night? Simply because he was new and she was playing the part of hostess. She was obviously a bit of an extrovert who enjoyed company. No reason to suppose that it was anything more than her outgoing nature.

Suddenly he felt hungry. With any luck he could still get some breakfast. Even if Mrs. Bazeley had finished serving, she might at least let him have something to take back to his room. Later, nearer midday, he would look for Penn in the Feathers.

· ✳ ·

Dunstan Fullacombe leaned on the balustrade at the top of the Academy watchtower and gazed down fifty feet at the length of northern wall that ran along the back of the Academy and fell away dramatically for a hundred feet to the rocks and curdling sea below. Endless white spume swirled down there, occasional waves flinging themselves upward in milky explosions. Fascinated, Fullacombe studied the patterns in the surf for long minutes. He could have stood there all day watching.

The wall ran slightly crookedly out to the east, right on down to the river. On its way, beyond the Academy boundary, it passed a long flight of incredibly steep steps that plunged to a tiny quay, where several small fishing boats bobbed on the one area of the shore where there were no rocks. Beyond that there were more steep cliffs and equally jagged rocks before the wall acted as the northern boundary of the military base. Below it, stretching northwards into a shimmering heat haze, ran a grey line of pebbles, a distinct ridge, dividing on its west a wide expanse of flat sand from an even wider expanse of low dunes in the east, as far as the eye could see.

Fullacombe sucked in the sea air as if it would pump energy into him. *Nothing like it anywhere.* He tried to let his thoughts about the seawall ease away. But it was his colleague, Barry Skellbow, who troubled him.

Stupid bugger. Late again this morning. Drinking far too much. I could smell it on him when he came in. Apologizing grumpily. He blames himself for the teacher's death. Why? No one is going to hold him to account for it. Not even the boss. She's said nothing to him. Nor me. It's like Vasillius never existed as far as she's concerned. She just wants to get on with running the Academy.

A sound behind him made him turn, reminding him why he was here. There was a pigeon loft near the top of the watchtower, its inhabitants cooing incessantly.

"I'm coming, my lovelies," he called, lifting up a small sack of grain he had brought with him. As he climbed a narrow set of steps, he looked out directly to the west's endless vista of ocean. Deep blue, flecked with spilling waves, it ended in that same heat haze, vastly empty, showing no sign of life. Above it the vault of azure sky was unbroken. The sun blazed. Looking across at the sea, Fullacombe's thoughts were inevitably drawn back to his youth and the days he had spent out on the water with his father.

· ✳ ·

He had been fifteen years old when he and his father, Roger Fullacombe, named by his mates the Bear for his huge size and apparently measureless strength, had put out across the wide bay that summer, seeking out the rich shoals of white fish that would by evening fill the hull of their little trawler. The Bear was all the crew this craft needed, he and his first son, Dunstan, who was already a strong, big-boned lad, eager to please and demonstrate just how well he would cope with a full day's fishing.

It had been a calm day, a few mares' tails of cloud over-head in an otherwise blue vault. By midmorning they had thrown out the first of the heavy trawling nets and started their work, the hard graft of drawing in the teeming nets. The Bear constantly cajoled his son, but his pride in the boy shone through and young Dunstan gritted his teeth and slaved away happily enough nevertheless, developing young muscles that would before many years bulge like his old man's.

Dunstan had been preparing another net for his father down in the already fish-deep belly of the craft when he heard a shout from above. On deck in a flash, he saw his father craning his neck, shielding his eyes from the sunlight, studying the bay.

"Shin up the mast, boy. Cast your eyes westward. Tell me what you see."

Dunstan was up the single mast, quick as a squirrel up a tree bole. Hanging off the cross piece, he studied the horizon and within moments had picked out what his father had seen. "Boat, dad. Not sure what sort. No sail. Don't look like she's out of Petra."

"How many on board? Can you tell?"

"Can't see no one. There are oars. But they're not rowing."

His father grunted. He didn't like his day interrupted, but this was a mystery that maybe needed looking into. Once Dunstan had dropped back to the deck, he set the sail, let her bell in the light breeze and tied the nets to anchored buoys that would hold them in place until they got back to them.

A short time later they could see the lone boat. It was a large rowing boat, unusual for these waters and certainly not from Petra or any of its small satellite ports. Dunstan's father steered them alongside, right hand gripping a steel hook that made a formidable weapon. Instinctively Dunstan picked up a long gutting knife. It looked as if his dad had interpreted the uncanny silence surrounding the boat as trouble.

He was right. No sooner had they secured the long rowing boat to their craft than they discovered chaos. There were sailors here, all right, but they had been in a fight and a right bloody affair it must have been.

"Mind your step, boy," said Dunstan's father. "There's death here and not a lot else." Ten of them, sailing men for sure. All cut to pieces.

"Who did this, dad?" said Dunstan, horrified, not least of all by the sickening stench of the blood and spilled vitals. He'd never seen the like in his life. If his old man had, he said nothing about it.

"Only one answer, boy. Fucking pirates. Must have been a whole shipload of the bastards. These here are a tough lot. Took some killing." His head spun round as he spoke. He had heard something.

There was life here, after all. The old man bent down over one of the fallen, lifting his head carefully. The man's eyes opened and he spoke through broken lips.

"Get fresh water from our keg, boy," growled the old man. "And a bowl. I'll clean him up. Keep your eyes peeled. If they come back, we're fish food."

Dunstan obeyed at once, and in a while his father was bathing the face and neck of the wounded man. His eyes were open, but he looked in a bad way.

"He's Erish," said the old man. "From way across the sea. High Burnam. And I was right. Pirates jumped 'em. Killed 'em just for the hell of it. I wouldn't want to be in their boots when the Erish find 'em. They'll die slowly, every last one of 'em."

Dunstan felt his flesh crawl. This was an unfamiliar world. He tried not to look around him at the carnage, which made his guts churn. But he was determined not to heave. As he watched the sea, while his father continued to help the one living sailor toward some kind of recovery, Dunstan saw a sail out in the bay. It was a much bigger craft, this, a high, deep sea-going vessel for sure, far larger than anything he had ever seen docked at Petra. It had come upon them with unbelievable speed.

His father confirmed his fears. "Erish raider. Nothing for it, boy, but to wait on her. Just pray this one here survives long enough to greet 'em."

By the time the big sailing ship hove to, the fallen survivor had managed to sit up, propped on the rowing boat's gunnel. He eyed the newcomer with an ugly grin.

Dunstan could see several dozen sailors glaring across the water, now no more than a few yards away. These were no fishermen: terrifyingly, they all looked to be armed for war. One of them, swinging from the rigging, hailed his father.

"I'm thinking that's our longboat you've got there, matey," he called in a voice that almost obscured the words.

"Your men have been attacked," the old man called back. "Pirates' work. There's one left alive. My boy and me just found 'em." He tossed aside his steel hook and Dunstan let the knife he was holding fall to the deck.

The warriors boarded the longboat then, six of them and the one who was evidently their chief. He had a shock of bright ginger hair and wore a necklace of small bones. In his belt were three vicious-looking knives that made Dunstan's flesh crawl with terror. This man leaned down and spoke to the survivor while his men watched Dunstan and his father like hawks. Neither of them moved a muscle.

"Kruach says you saved him," said the ginger man, although to Dunstan his face seemed like thunder. "That was a kindness that has saved you, fisherman. Did you see the pirates? Where they were headed?"

Dunstan's father shook his head. "They normally keep their distance from Petran waters."

"Petra? That your port?"

"Yes."

"Maybe we won't come calling then," said the ginger man and spat noisily over the side. "Murtagh! Finnian! Carry this useless sack of turds back on board and clean him up."

The fallen man beamed, regardless of the insult. "Sure, you're all heart, uncle," he grinned, wincing with pain at the effort.

"You'd better cast off and get back to your pretty little port," the ginger man said to Dunstan's father. "I'll be remembering this."

Later, safely distanced from the Erish raider, Dunstan's father had breathed a deep sigh of relief. "You heard 'em, boy. They owe us for that man's life. Lucky he didn't die on us. Petra won't be molested. And it's likely that these waters will be free of at least one pirate rabble for a while."

It had been a long time ago, but Dunstan Fullacombe had never forgotten it. The Erish had never since raided Petra or its environs. He heard that Petra's navy sometimes clashed out on the seas with them, but otherwise those seas were quiet.

· ✳ ·

Fullacombe fed the pigeons, checking the returning loft. Sure enough there was a bird in there, half-asleep. He could see the tiny scroll strapped to its right leg. Message from afar. The bird must have come in last night. Londonborough. Gently he caught the bird, spoke softly to her, and unwrapped the message with surprising delicacy for such a big man. He lightly kissed the bird, set her down, and gave her some grain, which she started pecking at instantly.

As he went back down into the Academy, knowing that Trencher would be working, even though it was Saturday, he spared a final thought for Skellbow. *I'm going to have to talk to him again, before he makes himself ill. The last thing we want now is him fucking up when we've got another Inspection coming after the summer.*

· ✳ ·

The tall room was mercifully cool, away from the glare of the morning sun, its high, anachronistic windows facing the west. One wall of the room was lined with books, some of which appeared to be very old, though there was no hint of dust on or around any of them. Someone evidently took pains to see that everything in this room was kept in very clean condition. The carpet, richer in pile and texture than most others in the Academy, was bright, well manicured. The wooden furniture was polished, gleaming. The huge desk was uncluttered, everything in neat little piles, the quill pens in their jar, the pencils in a wooden box.

Carl Trencher, the Senior Magister, and Father Emmanuel
Madding, the Academy's priest, sipped ice-cold well water
together. The two men could not have been more opposite
in form. Trencher's stockiness contrasted with Madding's ro-
tundity, the priest's pudgy hands protruding from the sleeves
of his black, voluminous cassock. Trencher's pale face and
white forehead gleamed in the light, while Madding had a
ruddy, florid complexion, his eyes set deeply, squinting as if
against the glare of day. Trencher's eyes were cold, his lips a
thin, bloodless gash, while Madding's were thick and moist.

The priest was evidently highly agitated. Around his neck
he wore a somewhat ostentatious chain, from which hung an
elaborate crucifix. As he spoke, his fingers fiddled with it.
"That damned summer festival will be upon us in no time.
And you know what it will mean. The atmosphere in the
town is unsavoury, to say the least. Since Vasillius's death,
the locals have been stirred up like hornets."

"Why should they be?"

"He was a popular man. He was not one of my fold and
was quite blatant in his rejection of our religious tenets. I
am not saying he died a martyr, Carl, but far too many of
the pagan element are ready to capitalize on his death. The
festival will give them a perfect opportunity to strengthen
their grip on Petra."

"You're panicking needlessly, Emmanuel. With more and
more troops being sent in, the Authority's position here is
very strong. It's last night I want to know about."

Madding's face soured. "It's not good news. The Brethren
were watching this new man, Mundy. He was in Overwater,
talking to, of all people, Anna Vasillius."

"What?" Trencher's features clouded.

"It may just have been chance, not necessarily planned.
As a precaution, I arranged for the Brethren to watch Mundy
and, if need be, warn him off. Usually they are very efficient
at that sort of thing."

Trencher scowled. "You say it as if something went wrong."

"Mundy slipped their grasp by the Overwater end of the
bridge, but others on this side cornered him and warned him
off getting mixed up with the dissidents and specifically Anna
Vasillius. They were discrete— there was absolutely nothing
to connect them with the church."

"So what happened?"

"You know what the wharf is like. There are unwritten rules about who controls it. Those accursed trawlermen were in port. They like nothing more than a bit of thuggery. If they're not braining each other, they'll attack anyone who steps into their territory. I don't know why our navy doesn't put a stop to it."

"Tithecombe probably thinks it's easier to let the trawlermen have their head than try to expunge them altogether. Otherwise it could end up in a nasty conflict."

"Have their head! God, Carl, they had that, all right!"

"Are you saying they attacked the Brethren?"

"Yes! Two of my men were *knifed*. Oh, they'll recover. But they won't be on duty for a few weeks."

"What about Mundy? He wasn't injured was he?" There was no disguising his concern.

"In the chaos, he got away. We can only hope that he'll have the sense to take note of the warning and keep his distance from Overwater. The whole business will have shaken him, I'm sure. But we must watch him—"

They were interrupted by a knock on the door and both froze for a moment. But Trencher recovered his wits promptly and called out a curt instruction to enter.

It was Dunstan Fullacombe. His eyes took in the scene at once. "Begging your pardon, Carl, but I didn't realize you had company. Father Emmanuel, I'm sorry to interrupt."

"That's perfectly all right, Dunstan," said the priest, rising. "We've concluded our morning's business. I was just about to leave. How are you keeping?"

"Very well, Father. But I need to speak to you about a colleague. Would there be any possibility of your talking to me in a moment?"

"Of course," nodded the priest affably. "Who is it?"

"It's Barry Skellbow, Father. I don't think he's too well. I think a few words from you would ease matters."

Madding and Trencher exchanged the briefest of looks, and the priest's ruddy features creased in a condescending smile. "Certainly. I have a little time before I'm needed at the church."

Fullacombe nodded in evident relief. "Very grateful, Father."

"What did you want to see me about, Dunstan?" said Trencher.

Fullacombe reached into an inner pocket and pulled out an envelope. "I've come from the watchtower. We had a bird in this morning. You did say to bring any messages to you as a matter of urgency."

Trencher took the envelope, brows slightly raised. "That's good of you, Dunstan."

Madding excused himself and in a moment had quit the room with Fullacombe, who closed the door quietly behind him.

Trencher cursed under his breath. *Skellbow. Why the hell does Dunstan want Skellbow to speak to the priest? Christ! But then again, maybe the tactic of frightening the crap out of him is working. Maybe Skellbow just wants a little spiritual guidance, rather than to blurt out some kind of confession. Maybe he needs something to keep the darkness at bay.*

XI

PETRA

PUTTING THE CARETAKER from his mind, Trencher pulled from the envelope a single sheet, holding it up to the light. One glance told him it was from Londonborough. It was headed STRICTLY CONFIDENTIAL. As he read it, Trencher gasped. Madding's summary of the night's botched events suddenly took on a new importance.

> RE: YR NEW TEACHER CHAD MUNDY.
> STRONGLY SUSPECTED OF COLLUSION WITH
>   EXTERNAL AGENCY
> VITAL HE IS UNAWARE OF OUR KNOWING
> HE MAY HAVE LINKS IN PETRA
> KEEP HIM UNDER SURVEILLANCE BUT NO OTHER
>   ACTION
> REPEAT: NO OTHER ACTION.

The note was signed "Nightingale" which meant that it was from the Enforcers who had been here for the Inspection and with whom Trencher, recruited by them, had formed a specific relationship. He guessed that Nightingale was either Luther Sunderman, the bureaucrat who had led the Inspection, or one of his right-hand men.

He read through the note again, and then took it to the large fireplace behind him, which was empty; there were several paper spills in a brass container beside it. Using a flint, he ignited one of the spills and carefully set the message alight, putting it down into the grate and watching it incinerate until there was nothing left of it but a tiny trace of grey ash.

Chad Mundy again. The replacement for Vasillius. So is the Academy rid of one agitator only to have another spring up?

He smoothed back his black hair and sat in thought for several moments. He had met the new teacher at interview. Bright youth, with an impressive record at Wellington. It was time he looked him up and had a deeper discussion with him. Monday morning would do.

· ✳ ·

The priest sat in Fullacombe's sombre office, hands squeezed together as he waited impatiently for the big man to return with Skellbow, who he had gone to fetch. His mind was more on the message that Trencher had received than on this duty Fullacombe had asked him to perform. The pigeon must have been from Londonborough. Madding knew that Trencher would share its contents with him at the earliest opportunity. The Senior Magister relied too much on his support now to keep him in the dark about any developments.

Madding pursed his lips in a wry smile. *Yes, Carl, you are such an ambitious man. An Authority puppet through and through. No one will stand in your way— not even me, if push comes to shove. But we do need each other. With the church behind you, well, Petra is only the first step. Success here will bring you an academy of your own. Londonborough recognizes its generals.*

His reverie was interrupted by a hesitant knock at the door. He looked round to see a disheveled figure standing there. Unshaven, eyes bloodshot with lack of proper sleep, it was Barry Skellbow.

Madding stood up and opened his arms. "Barry, dear man. Do come in. Come in. Close the door."

The caretaker looked startled, as if about to bolt, but he made a huge effort to pull himself together, closed the door and shuffled in.

Madding enfolded him in a hug. "I know you are a troubled man, Barry. But you've done the right thing in coming to me. Sit down, sit down."

Skellbow did so, unable to meet the priest's gaze. The caretaker looked visibly intimidated by Madding, crowded by him as if he were about to envelop him again.

"What is it you want to tell me?" Madding could see the signs of deep stress in the man, his shaking hands and nervous shifting of the head.

"I'm scared, Father," he murmured, almost so quietly that the priest didn't hear. But Madding leaned forward in his seat so that he was almost on top of him.

The priest reached out and took both Skellbow's hands in his own. "Listen to me, Barry. Here, there is only you, me, and God. Through me, God is listening to you. There is no need to fear Him. You are not here to be judged. You will receive His patience and understanding. His love, Barry. Do you understand that?"

"Yes," said the caretaker, but his manner belied his answer.

"We are all sinners, Barry. Every day we sin. It is human nature. Just as it is God's nature to forgive. He created us, with all our flaws. So He listens to us. He is listening now. Through me. Do not be afraid."

Skellbow drew in a deep breath, as if about to plunge underwater. His words came out, halting and broken, tears forming in his eyes. "They're going to kill me. Like they killed Mr. Vasillius."

Manning's face, inches away from the caretaker's, remained impassive only through an immense effort of will. There was a moment of silence, as though everything had stopped, stunned by the caretaker's claim.

"No one is going to kill you, Barry," said the priest, squeezing the caretaker's hands. They were dry and coarse, while Manning's were sweating and soft.

Skellbow looked down at the floor, trying to compose himself. "I saw things."

Madding felt a wave of unease. "You had better tell me everything, Barry."

Skellbow seemed to make a huge effort, but finally won some internal battle with himself and began to talk. He spoke of the night the men had come to the Academy and what had really happened to Drew Vasillius. Madding listened patiently, coaxing as much from him as he could, pouring out reassurances with every breath, though his own mind was in turmoil.

"If this was murder, something has to be done about it," said the priest convincingly.

Skellbow gripped the priest's forearm. His fingers were like steel. "But if they find out I've blabbed, they'll go for my *wife*! They've already tried to warn me off."

Madding gently eased himself free of the grip. "I don't understand—"

Again Skellbow talked, explaining in halting, frightened tones how he had almost been trapped outside the pub. He said nothing about Chad Mundy, though.

"Do you think they've threatened Mr. Trencher, too?" he added.

Manning again put a comforting arm around him. "Possibly. I will find out. For the moment, I would ask you to do and say nothing. Not a single word to anyone. You've not told your wife about this, have you?"

"She's not very strong. It would worry her to death."

"No, you mustn't say anything. But you did well to talk to me, Barry."

"I'm glad someone else knows."

"Well, it's my burden, now. You must let me deal with this. Will you?"

"What are you going to do, Father?"

"I know Mr. Trencher very well. We've worked closely together for a long time. If he has kept silent on this matter, there is a reason for it. But he will know, like you, that if he speaks to me, his words will be private. They will go no further. This is a matter for God and for us alone. You, me, and Mr. Trencher. We are the ones who have to resolve this matter. Where are these men now?"

"They said that they would be well on their way back to Londonborough the next day. There was something else, too, Father."

Madding steeled himself. This damned mess was just getting worse by the minute. First the previous night's debacle with Mundy and now this. "Tell me."

"They said the place was *marked*. And they'd be watching, Father. The birds, even the wind. They were agents of the Devil, father, I swear it." His voice had dropped to a whisper and Madding knew that this was the real nub of his fear. The old, old supernatural fear, bedded deep down in these people, immovable and indestructible.

Madding held up the crucifix. "They are impotent against the power of God, Barry. You must put your faith in Him. There are other things that I must tell you." The priest took off the crucifix and slipped it over Skellbow's neck. The caretaker gripped it with both hands like a man in a turbulent sea gripping a lifesaving piece of flotsam. "You are right about the Devil being at work, Barry. He has marked Petra and only the strongest of us will be able to withstand him."

Skellbow's terror rose up as if he could see something satanic coalescing in the very air around them. His mouth had gone dry.

"There are those in this town, Barry, who have begun very evil work, conjuring up blasphemous powers. These beings you saw, for I am not convinced that they were men as we know men, were part of these terrible rituals. They are coming to a head. Through the pagans."

"They'll send someone or something for me—"

"They won't know you've told me, Barry. My church is sacred ground. They cannot penetrate its defences. And you must keep absolutely silent. This is God's work now. Do you hear me?"

Skellbow nodded, close to tears again.

"I will speak to Mr. Trencher in strict confidence. He and I will deal with this in our own time. In the meantime, I will conduct a private ritual for you. If you are being troubled by outside forces, I will exorcise them. But if you share any of this, *any of this at all*, with anyone, Barry, you will disturb the protective spell."

"I won't. Keep them away from me, Father."

"Very well. Keep that crucifix about you. It is a very old relic and very powerful. It will serve you well. I have others to protect me. Have you finished work for the day?"

Skellbow nodded.

"Now, you're sure that no one else knows anything at all about what you've told me?"

Skellbow shook his head.

"Good. Come on, up you get. Go home and sleep. God is watching over us, Barry. He will not be angry with you. And He will guide me. He always does."

· ✳ ·

"You got back all right, then," Penn said softly to Mundy as he joined her in the stifling atmosphere of the Feathers. "I was worried stiff."

Mundy smiled thinly. *You didn't seem that worried earlier on today.* But he pushed the image of her with the other man from his mind.

She was glancing round nervously as she spoke, her eyes not meeting Mundy's.

He told her what had happened, carefully editing the story.

She looked even more horrified. "But why?"

He leaned closer so the general noise level of conversation muted his words. Even so, he felt uncomfortable. "How well do you know Anna Vasillius?"

She looked puzzled. "Not that well. Brin Goldsworthy was a big mate of Drew's. He knows Anna well. Why?"

"Something she said to me in the Anvil. Two things actually. She said we were being watched. Obviously she was right about that."

"Why would anyone watch you?"

"My guess is that it was because of what she told me. I'd rather not say what it was, Penn. I think I ought to talk to Brin about it first. If you don't mind."

"No, no, that's fine," she said. If she was hurt, she didn't show it, though she seemed a little edgy. Given what he had told her, it seemed only natural.

"The men who accosted me weren't soldiers."

"Maybe it was a warning for you to stay on this side and keep to accepted places. Avoid the dens of iniquity."

He shook his head. "I'm sure it's related to what Anna told me."

"I know you don't want to say what it was, but is it something that the Authority wouldn't want you to know?"

He nodded slowly. *It means the Authority was involved in the death — the murder — of Drew Vasillius. And they want me to keep my nose out.*

Penn was watching him as though trying to read his mind.

Who else knows about this? he wondered. *Who the hell can I talk to about it? Ideally, I need to see Anna again and find out more. Other than that, the only one I dare trust is Brin, as he's a good friend of the Vasilliuses.*

"We'd better take some extra muscle with us when we go to the Anvil again," she said, smiling in spite of her concern.

"I'm certainly not going to avoid the place."

"Here's Brin." Penn waved to him and shifted aside to make room for him on the bench, as there were no other seats available in the packed pub.

"Morning, young people!" Goldsworthy beamed at them. "Thanks," he added, squeezing in between Mundy and Penn. "How are we all this bright and sizzling day? Are they looking after you, Chad? I didn't want to dog your every move."

"It's been fine. We had a bit of an adventure last night. Across the river."

"Not the Anvil?" Goldsworthy laughed. "Gets quite lively over there sometimes. So, tell all. Who've you been mixing with?"

Mundy leaned as close to him as he could and said, very softly, "I met Drew Vasillius's wife. I need to talk to you about it." He was watching Penn as he spoke, but she seemed to have suddenly become embroiled in a conversation with one of the other female teachers at an adjoining table, leaning back to speak to her.

Goldsworthy was watching the faces of everyone around him. Satisfied that he could speak freely, he nodded. "He was a good man. And Anna."

"Last night Anna told me about his death. I assume you know the truth."

Goldsworthy nodded, face half-hidden as he took a swig of his drink.

"Do you know who was responsible?" Mundy went on. "Can you tell me?"

After a long, thoughtful pause, Goldsworthy said, "Yes. But not here."

"Do you know why it happened?"

"We think so."

"She told me that she and I were being watched. When we all left the pub, there were a group of men lounging about on the bridge. Waiting for me. I think the idea was that they gave me a fright. Warned me off." He told Goldsworthy the same version of the story that he had told Penn.

Goldsworthy remained impassive, as though they were discussing the teaching schedules for the coming week. "Whoever they were, they may still be watching you."

"Do you know why?"

"I could guess. You need to go and see Sebastian Wroxton. Tell him what you've told me. You've trusted me. I'm telling you, I trust Sebastian."

· ✳ ·

A short time later Mundy sat alone with Sebastian Wroxton in his office.

"Before we talk, Chad, you need to know that you're among friends." Wroxton pulled from inside his jacket an envelope, handing it to Mundy. "Read that. Satisfy yourself that it's genuine."

Mundy unsealed the envelope and unfolded the letter it contained. It was addressed to him. With a start, he recognized

the handwriting and then saw the signature: he knew it was
genuine. Hewitt Marlmaster.

He read the elegant script:

> *Dear Chad,*
>
> *When you read this, you should be sitting with one of
> the Society's most valued and trusted servants, Sebastian
> Wroxton. He has been a member for even longer than I
> have. In his hands, you will be as safe as it is possible for
> one of our beliefs and commitments to be.*
>
> *I did say to you on the occasion of our last meeting that
> you would be contacted in Petra. Ask for the password
> we spoke of.*
>
> *Good luck in everything you do.*
>
> *Hewitt Marlmaster.*

Mundy read the letter through twice, nodding slowly and
then looking up into the level gaze of the Senior Magister.

"Sorry to be circumspect," said the big man. "But you
know how the Society works. Secrecy is key to our survival.
In fact, no one here but you knows that I am in the Society.
I'd like to keep it that way."

Mundy nodded. "Fine. But you need to give me a password."

Wroxton smiled. "Hand me the letter."

Slowly Mundy did, and Wroxton took it, turning. There was
a small fire grate behind him and in a moment Mundy saw
smoke curling upwards as Wroxton incinerated the note before
turning back and saying quietly, "The password Marlmaster
gave you was 'Daybreak.'"

Mundy sat back with a great sigh of relief. "Thank God
for that."

"God?" said Wroxton, chuckling, his huge girth shaking
gently. "Are you a religious man, Chad?"

"I'm a bit unresolved on that. We had religion more or
less beaten into us at Wellington. It's the Authority's way."

"Have you met our local religious representative yet? Father
Madding? He's something of a fanatic. And a very frustrated
man." Wroxton grinned hugely. "Madding is bitterly opposed
to anything that smacks remotely of the *pagan*. Just as the
locals in Petra and Dumnonia generally have a tendency to

buck the Authority, as our venerable Enforcers have been quick to point out in their less than glowing report, so the pagans have their own beliefs.

"Religion since the Plague Wars, as you may know from your own secret studies, is a strange brew these days. A fusion, a melting pot."

"There were once a whole lot of religions, here in Grand Britannia as well as in the outside world, if what I've read is true."

Wroxton nodded, obviously enjoying the freedom to talk of such things. "The Authority was behind the coordination of them all. What we have now, as far as the *official* church is concerned, is a universal religion, based on predominantly Christian tenets. Madding subscribes wholeheartedly to this faith. Not only does it bring all his flock together, in theory at least, but it gives him *power* over it."

"Endorsed by the Authority."

"Absolutely. Madding is its pawn, but he revels in that. If he ever desired to initiate an inquisition, he would probably have the backing of the Authority."

"You're not one of the Father's disciples, I guess."

Wroxton laughed. "I have to appear to be, as with any number of things. I'd say I'm considered to be the right hand of our Prime (being the designated deputy) but in reality that's Carl Trencher. As much a willing tool of the Authority as Madding. He's even more ambitious than Madding. While Madding would be content to sit astride Dumnonia as the head of its church, Carl takes the wider view. His future lies elsewhere. One of Londonborough's military academies, I should think. He's insidious, Chad."

After a while, Wroxton turned to the previous night's incident, which he obviously knew about. Mundy spoke as reservedly to him about it as he had to Penn and Brin. Wroxton was intrigued by his meeting with Anna Vasillius.

"She's well versed in the Old Tongue, so I was happy to talk to her."

"I gather your grasp of the Old Tongue is very good. Well enough to understand what Anna told you." Wroxton's eyes were fixed firmly on him, evaluating him. "I know what she would have said, about Drew. You understand the implications?"

Mundy nodded uneasily. "Do you know who killed him?"

"The Authority, of that I have no doubt whatsoever."

"But why? I understand he was a bit of a rebel. But then, so are half the people across the water. Have others been killed?"

"No. Just Drew. Yes, he was openly opposed to many of the Prime's strict policies and procedures. He pressed for more open debate, more understanding of the local will. And he was pretty contemptuous of the church. He was far more interested in the pagan elements of society. Never mind all that— he was killed because he *knew* something, something of significant importance. The problem is, no one else knew, not even Anna. Drew shared it with no one."

"But his killers knew."

"Undoubtedly. Petra is a volatile place, a focal point for various forces. But this is not just some parochial squabble. It's a major conflict. Those of us involved face some very daunting challenges. I'm determined to find out what Drew Vasillius knew and why he was silenced so brutally. Are you prepared to help? Your command of the Old Tongue would be invaluable."

"Of course. So, what do I do?"

"My guess is that the Authority, through Trencher, is behind the threats to you. It doesn't want anyone snooping around Drew's death. There was a detective here, sent in by the Authority."

"Was that Barrazelli?"

"Yes. I thought at first he would simply go through the motions of investigating Drew's death and just pronounce it suicide. All neat and tidy for the Authority. But initially Barrazelli showed real signs of being impartial. I'm sure he smelled a rat. But somewhere along the line, he drew back from whatever suspicions he may have had. Abruptly the investigation ended and his report dismissed the matter. The key factor was that Drew's body has never been found."

"Convenient for the Authority."

"It leaned on Barrazelli. God knows what threats it used. Same as were used on you last night, I would guess. But the Authority knows nothing about your involvement with the Society. You have to convince its people, especially Trencher, that you're actually an Authority man. The route to him is Madding."

"So what do I say to him?"

"Express your horror at having been threatened and almost attacked by what you assumed were the pagan elements.

Nothing is more guaranteed to fire Madding up than hostile action by the hated pagans. If you convince him you're no dissident — you came to Petra as a devoted Authority man — he'll do his damndest to win you over. He'll sway Trencher to believing you're ripe for recruiting. Persuade Madding that you've no interest in Anna Vasillius— that meeting was pure chance."

"Then I go to church tomorrow?"

"Exactly. You're a new boy. Madding will not be able to resist taking you aside at some point. For a little chat. But do tread carefully."

XII

PETRA

CARL TRENCHER EYED the priest uneasily. The Father was undoubtedly troubled by something, rivulets of sweat running down either side of his plump features.

Madding mopped his brow with a handkerchief. "It's that damned caretaker! I've not long ago interviewed him."

"I hope you're not going to tell me that he's losing his nerve?"

"That's precisely the problem, Carl! He was practically blubbering. Panic, pure and simple. He saw what happened—"

"What do you mean, *saw*? He didn't actually *see* Vasillius thrown off the wall? I thought he was on the stairs?"

"Yes, yes. But he *knows*, Carl."

"Has he spoken to anyone?"

"No, he's too terrified. He said threats had been made against him and his wife. And he sees and hears demons all around him."

"Isn't that enough?" said Trencher, stiffening with suppressed annoyance.

"It should be! I told him that absolute silence was the best policy. He thinks one word out of place and the men will send something to harass him and his family." Madding squeezed his hands together as if he could wring some kind of answer out of the air. "He's drinking too much. I just think he might do something stupid. I don't know, Carl. Perhaps I'm overreacting."

Trencher sat back, lips pursed. "Given that he's seen you and that he's showing signs of stress, I think you'd better keep an eye on him. It would seem perfectly natural for you to want to help one of your flock in times of trouble. No one would think it odd."

"I could use the Brethren again."

"I leave that to you. What about Skellbow's son? He's finishing his last year with us. He may not go on to the military academy. Apprenticeship lined up, I believe." Trencher steepled his fingers. Then his thoughts seemed to swerve elsewhere. "Oh, by the way, that note earlier today that Dunstan brought in. It was from Londonborough."

Madding's face looked slightly pained, as though he had anticipated bad news.

"It was about the new recruit. Chad Mundy. They suspect him of collusion with what they call 'an outside agency.' We're to watch him."

"Dear God," sighed Madding. "Does this mean that we've inherited the same problems that we had with Vasillius?"

"I don't know. I haven't met with Mundy since he started. You'll probably see him before me, assuming he attends church tomorrow. I met him at interview and he seemed a little ambivalent about religion when I spoke to him privately afterwards. When Cora quizzed him formally, he was fairly cautious with his answers. Obviously didn't want to blow the interview. But I'd be very surprised if, during his first couple of weeks, he doesn't try to toe the line to some extent. If he's in church, talk to him. If not, go and find him In the meantime, attend to that wretched caretaker."

· ✳ ·

Skellbow left the Feathers just before the landlord called closing time. He'd had a skinful by the time he'd shuffled out into the stillness of the night, waved to a few familiar faces, and moved off down a side street, headed for home.

His head was full of conflicting thoughts. His meeting with the priest that morning was something he kept revisiting. Father Madding was quite right: he should say nothing to nobody. No point in doing otherwise. Look after number one. Those three bastards who'd done for Mr. Vasillius were not to be messed with. But was Trencher involved in this? Why? Why was Vasillius killed? It didn't make sense. Just because he hadn't liked the Authority?

"People should make up their own minds about what they want, Barry," Vasillius had once said to Skellbow. "Not be herded like cattle."

Skellbow didn't mind being part of a strict system. He liked to know where he was. Go to work, do your job, regular. Everything in its place. Make things work properly. The Academy had to run smoothly— bit like a machine. It suited him.

*But just because Mr. Vasillius was a bit of a rebel was no reason
to kill him.*

Skellbow stopped along another side street. Although he
had sunk several pints, he didn't feel particularly drunk. It
took a lot at the moment to get him really pissed, but his
bladder was getting weaker and he did need a leak. He cursed
softly and went down a sloping alleyway leading to the river,
finding an old doorway. While he was relieving himself, he
caught a brief glimpse of movement back up at the mouth
of the alley. Someone else on the way home.

But as went back up, he sensed that he was being watched.
He swung round. There was minimal light here and a dozen
places for anyone to hide out of sight. Up on the roofs he
heard the flutter of wings. Pigeons settling down for the night.
Must be. Either that or— but he switched the thought off,
telling himself that Father Madding had promised to exorcise
anything evil sent to watch him. Gripping the crucifix the
priest had given him, hidden inside his shirt, he moved on,
listening out for any suggestion of footsteps. But he heard
nothing. The night was breathless, any sounds in the town
muffled by the packed buildings and warehouses here along
the riverside.

When he reached his house, a modest cottage set back
from the side street with a minute courtyard garden at its
front, he turned at the gate, looking for signs of movement.
Night shrouded everything. Moonlight gave the faintest of
glows to gables and doorsteps. But that was all.

He let himself in, surprised to see a candle burning in the
front room. By its steady glow he saw a face, hovering like a
ghost's. He suddenly drew back in a flush of alarm.

"It's only me, Barry. Who else were you expecting?" It was
his wife, sitting at the table. Her long grey hair, which usually framed her face, had been scraped back, for a moment
unnerving him.

"Hell, Myra, you scared the crap out of me."

"Edgy, aren't you, Barry?"

"What do you expect? Come leering out at me in the middle
of the night!"

"Sit down," she said in a tone that he recognized. There
was no point in arguing when she was in this kind of mood.
She was not a healthy woman, but her will was strong enough
for two.

He did as she said, pulling up a stool. "What's this about? I've been out for a few drinks, that's all. It's not that late."

"You know I don't mind that." It was true. She never usually complained. She leaned forward, her face again highlighted by the candle's glow. "Just lately you've been as nervous as a cat. I know when something's bothering you."

"Nothing's bothering me!"

"Doesn't sound like it! And you don't normally drink every night."

"It's nothing, maid. It's been a hard term."

"Is Dunstan riding you too hard? Trencher? Or is it the Prime?"

"They're fine! She's driving everyone hard at the moment." He seized on the opportunity to ease himself out of this. "The Enforcers have got to be satisfied. We all have to knuckle down."

"You've nothing to worry about. You work damned hard. There's no reason for them to lean on you. Seems to me the trouble started when Mr. Vasillius died."

He clenched his fists under the table. "They can't blame me for that!"

"I should hope not! Do you? Is that it, Barry?" Her eyes searched his face for an answer, some clue to his misery.

He shook his head. "No, no. I don't normally do security, but they can't blame me. He just— just took everyone by surprise, that's all. No one could have known he'd do what he did."

"Have you see Father Madding?"

Her words hit him like a slap across the face. "Why do you say that?"

"Have you?"

"I saw him this morning, just for a few minutes. I... I met him by chance in the Academy. He wanted a few words."

"Did it help to talk to him?" she said, trying to encourage him. "Sometimes it does. We go to church, but neither of us have had much to do with the Father for a long time. Maybe we should."

"No! No, there's no need."

"So what did you say? Did you talk about Mr. Vasillius?"

"No. I can't remember. Why?"

"Someone was here earlier. One of the Brethren."

Skellbow felt a wash of cold air. "What did they want?"

"A message for you."

Skellbow was as sober as a stone now, his mouth dry. He struggled to get his words out. "What message?"

"He just said Father Madding had asked him to see if you were in. Just to say, don't forget your little conversation this morning and that he would always be available. You could always talk to him. He made a point of saying that. Always talk to him. And that the Father had cleared the air. What did he mean by that?"

"Just a manner of speech. He's just doing his job. Looking after his flock."

"Well, there's nothing wrong with sharing your problems with the priest, Barry. But if you're that troubled, you could talk to me more. You don't have much to say at home these days."

"It's not that," he said. "I'm all right. Really. Just tired. You work hard, too, Myra. You don't want to be bothered with my moans and groans about work."

"I don't want you making yourself ill. Speak to the Father tomorrow, if you need to."

He looked across at her, holding down his panic with difficulty. "Okay, maid. We'll go to church. Sure."

She stood up. "I'm going to bed."

"I won't be long. Just need some fresh air."

She nodded, studied him for a moment as if she would say more, but appeared to change her mind and went out to the stairs.

Skellbow rubbed his face. Bloody headache coming on. Back outside in the garden, he leaned on the wall. *So the Father sent someone to remind me about this morning. Always talk to him. No one else.* The real message was clear, reinforced. *Forget what I saw. Wipe it away. The church will protect me.*

He was about to go back inside when he was sure that there was a movement on the edge of vision. He peered down the street. It was only instinct, but he was *sure* something was there. With a quick look back at the house to satisfy himself that Myra hadn't joined him, he went into the side street.

"Don't bugger about with me!" he hissed, barely controlling his fury, but he was not afraid to defend himself if he had to. His fists hung at his sides like hams. He would use them.

"Help me, Barry," came a soft voice from a doorway a dozen yards away. Then a figure slipped into the dim light, hunched over, watching him, its face not quite in focus.

Skellbow halted in his tracks, a shudder traveling the length of his spine. "Who are you?" he whispered, but the still air amplified his voice.

The figure edged away from him down the alley, looking back over its shoulder. "You know me, Barry," it said. With a stab of horror, he realized what he was seeing. That hair, that coat. He *knew* that coat! But it was impossible!

"Mr. Vasillius?" He shook his head, again gripping the crucifix.

"Don't come near me, Barry. Not safe. I can't stay. Don't belong here any more. I'm in a terrible place." The figure edged further away.

"What do you want?"

"To warn you. Keep quiet about me. I jumped. Say I jumped. There are things here in this place that would hurt you if you don't say it."

This place? Skellbow's mind echoed. *God in Heaven, what does he mean?*

"I must go. I can't escape them, but you can." The figure moved up the alley, seeming to glide. Skellbow was rooted, his mouth dry, his whole body iced by fear.

For a long time after the figure had gone, Skellbow stood as if carved from stone. Slowly the sounds of the night filtered back into his conscious mind. And again he heard something scratching up on the roofs above him.

I imagined it, he told himself. *I did not see Drew Vasillius. He's dead. Dead and gone. I did not see him.* As if to convince himself, he edged down the alley to where he had last seen — imagined he'd seen — the figure. He came to where another alley crossed over and looked up and down. But there was nothing, darkness closing in. He looked down at his hands. They were shaking badly.

Satisfied that there was nothing to be found, he made his way home. He was part way there when more shadows detached themselves from the darkness, blocking his way back.

"Well, then, Barry. We meet again. And you don't seem to have your guardian angel with you this time."

Skellbow almost cried aloud with terror. He recognized the leader of the pack who had threatened him the other night outside the Feathers. Had they seen that... thing? God, had they somehow *summoned* it?

"Why are you bothering me?" he said, finally mastering his dread.

"Just keeping an eye on you, Barry. You and your missus. And your son."

Skellbow swore crudely. "Why don't you just leave us alone?"

"We will, Barry. You keep your part of the bargain and we'll keep ours. That's simple enough, isn't it?"

"I told your mates up on the seawall that I'd say nothing."

"Careful, Barry. I don't know about any mates. And the only seawall I know about is the one Mr. Vasillius threw himself from. I am right, aren't I?"

"I fucking said so, didn't I? How many more fucking times do you want me to say it!" Skellbow's voice was lifting, his face reddening.

"So you haven't said a word, eh? To anyone? Like the *priest*?"

Skellbow shook his head. Part of him wanted to stride forward, take hold of this bastard and rip him apart. But he knew it would go badly if he did— the others, probably the same five he had seen before, must all be there in the shadows. And God knew what else. Vasillius had said— but no, he must not think about that.

"I've told you I've said nothing."

Before Skellbow could do anything to defend himself, the man lashed out and smacked him hard across the face. "Don't lie to me, you bastard!" he snarled. He kicked out viciously and Skellbow felt a jarring pain under his knee. He dropped down and another powerful kick landed in his midriff. The cross was no protection against this.

"I've said nothing!" he gasped, tears of pain streaming from his eyes.

"I told you we have ears and eyes everywhere. This place is marked, Barry. *Marked*! You don't breathe without us knowing. You spoke to the priest. Father fucking Emmanuel. Didn't you?" Another kick landed.

"Not about Vasillius," Skellbow gasped, too shaken up now to rise.

The man was about to administer another kick when he heard one of his cronies call to him. He swung round to see what had interrupted him. There was more movement among the shadows. Other voices were raised and it sounded as though an argument had broken out.

A group of men who had been in another pub was coming up the narrow street and had happened upon the assault. The foremost of them, Danton Connell, had shouted angrily when he saw the caretaker on his knees, about to be kicked.

Warily the six men who had cornered Skellbow stood aside. Their leader spat pointedly. "You guys would do better to mind your own business and move on."

Connell stood over Skellbow. "I think this *is* our business, pal." He gripped Skellbow's elbow and got him to his feet. The caretaker winced with pain.

"What's this about, Barry?"

Skellbow shook his head, holding his ribs as if trying to stop himself from physically falling apart. "I'm okay. Too much to drink. Let it go."

Connell kept an eye on the ring of assailants. He could see they were spoiling for a fight. And they had the look of hard men, men who could look after themselves.

"Another guardian angel, Barry," said their spokesman. "Someone is looking after you. And you," he growled at Connell. "You don't want to get mixed up in his troubles. Bad for your health."

"What troubles?" said Connell, as Skellbow remained still beside him.

"They've got hold of the wrong end of the stick," said the caretaker. "Just a misunderstanding. Forget it."

"That's fine by me, Barry," said his assailant. "You get yourself home to that lovely wife of yours and young Davie."

Connell edged forward, now no more than a foot from Skellbow's tormentor. They were a breath away from violence. "That wouldn't be a threat, would it?"

Skellbow tugged Connell back. "It's okay, Mr. Connell. Just let me get off home."

Connell nodded, easing him back further along the street. Two of the assailants suddenly pressed forward as if they were going to block Skellbow's passage to freedom, but Connell's companions immediately stepped in, shoving the men back. It was the trigger for the first punch to be thrown and in a moment several of the men were scuffling, swearing in the half-light.

"Come on, away," said Connell, shepherding Skellbow towards his home. "You're mixing with the wrong lot, Barry."

"I'm okay," said Skellbow, but he still groaned every time he moved. He'd be lucky if nothing was broken. "It was a mistake. But thanks, Mr. Connell."

Connell had got him to his gate. "Buy me a pint or two sometime, eh?"

"I will."

Connell watched him struggle into his house and shut the door.

· ✳ ·

By the time Connell had rejoined his companions, the brawl was over. A couple of them were nursing split lips and one man had a rapidly closing eye.

"Hell, Joss, you'll need a beef steak on that bugger," someone said and there were muted hoots of laughter.

"The other fucker will need more than a steak, sunshine. They'll be carrying him home."

Connell chuckled, but his face was etched with anxiety. He knew who the bastards were, but why were they leaning so hard on Barry Skellbow? Barry was a tiny fish, a bit player in Petra's intrigues.

· ✳ ·

Andrew Wilkinson was feeling well pleased with himself. He'd been able to help Mr. Lurrell, the PE teacher, with a football match this afternoon and then Mr. Miler with more football training with the boys. They were always much more friendly on Saturdays. Wilkinson wasn't much good at football and the kids took it out of him, but they never did him any real harm. He didn't like some of the names they called him, but he put up with it because he loved the company. And afterwards! Today had been great, because in the pub Mr. Miler had bought him *two* drinks! He wasn't allowed alcohol, so he had had lemonade with ice. It was just brilliant to be able to sit with some of the staff and just talk. He hadn't seen Mr. Mundy, whom he liked. But Mr. Goldsworthy had turned up later and made him feel even more at home.

Now, closing time had been called — he had stayed *that* late! — and he said his good-byes, still flushed with excitement.

Goldsworthy watched him striding up the hill towards the church. "Just hope Father Emmanuel doesn't give him a thick ear for getting in late."

Wilkinson had reached the church gates, which would be locked up soon, when he heard several men coming from another street towards him. Before he could duck back into the shadows, they were abreast of him. He didn't recognize them at first, but when the leading man called out, he knew the hated voice at once.

"Andrew, you little turd! What are you gawking at? You should have been in bed hours ago."

Wilkinson merely stood, shivering with fear, watching as the group came into the light. There were six of them, and two were helping one to walk. His face, briefly illuminated, was a bloody mess. *The Brethren. They've been fighting!* Wilkinson realized with another jolt of fear.

The men went in through the gates and their leader turned to him, spitting noisily. "Don't stand there like a dick, boy. Get inside!"

Wilkinson obeyed automatically. As Wilkinson passed the man, he smacked the side of his head. "Hurry up, or I'll tell the Father that you've been pestering the girls."

Wilkinson wanted to shout his outrage at that, but he was too afraid. These men, they *were* like soldiers, no matter what Father Emmanuel said.

XIII

PETRA

SUNDAY MORNING OPENED another stifling day, cloudless and airless. Petra bathed in the intense heat, its streets empty but for the occasional members of the church congregations making their way to either one of four town churches or the one at the Academy's western end, against the sea wall. Within the church there was a gathering of two score or more people, all from the Academy, although people from outside were always welcome to join. Few ever did. In the city churches, Father Madding knew, numbers were dwindling.

Chad Mundy sat alone to one side, paying lip service to the morning's session. Not one for religion, his mind was fixed on his real mission and the various recent conversations he had had. Up in the pulpit, Father Madding conducted ceremonies with gusto, his voice loud during the singing and urgent when giving his sermon, which focused on the true path of belief and the perils of straying from it. The priest's frustration at the local interest in paganism could be heard clearly in his tone and seen equally clearly in his face.

After an hour, the service ended and people began to leave. Mundy remained, head bowed as if in prayer, something he had not done since he was a youth and then under duress. He was mentally preparing what he would say to the priest, when eventually he heard someone beside him.

"Good morning!" boomed the priest, looming over him "You'll be a new member of our little flock?"

"I'm Chad Mundy, Father. Recently arrived."

"Excellent!" Madding shot out a hand and gripped Mundy's enthusiastically, pumping it up and down. "Good to see you in here, Chad."

"I was hoping to have a quiet word with you, Father."

"Well, come along to my rooms. I've got some fresh water from the well. Need it after all my tub-thumping, eh?"

Mundy smiled politely and let the priest shepherd him to the far end of the nave. A room beyond served Madding as an office and Mundy took a proffered seat and a glass of the ice-cold water. It was delicious.

Madding sat opposite him, his face gleaming with perspiration. The heat seemed to be making him a little breathless. "How do you like Petra? Bit of a law unto itself. You probably picked up from my sermon that I'm more than a little concerned about some of my lost sheep."

"That's what I wanted to talk to you about, Father. When I was in Londonborough — I was educated at Wellington — I was used to the strict regime. I've always tried to be a good citizen. I respect the Authority and once I'd decided to make teaching my profession, I found it easy to comply with its codes and standards. I've come here prepared to carry out my work as a part of that system."

Madding nodded encouragingly.

"At Wellington, we all had occasion to, well, spread our wings a bit. Being young people, we needed to try a few things out."

"Forbidden fruit?"

"Sort of."

"Always the most tempting. I know exactly what you mean. It's refreshing to hear such honesty, Chad. But do go on."

"I didn't do anything dishonest, or radically against the Authority's rules. You don't need to know some of the pranks we got up to. Let's put it down to the process of education. Life experience. But I was aware that there were some people in the city, groups, perhaps, who *were* straying from the right path."

"Did you discuss this with anyone in the Authority?"

"No, I just made sure I didn't get involved myself. I think people have a right to choose for themselves what they do and how they pursue life."

"I see. More water?"

"Thanks." Mundy held out his glass and let the priest fill it. "I wouldn't have brought it up now, Father, but something happened the other night, here in Petra."

"Now I am intrigued."

"Your sermon hinted at there being a fairly active pagan element in the local society. My colleagues at the Academy have been very good to me. Considerate and very welcoming.

As part of that, they've taken me out and shown me around. On Friday evening some of them took me to Overwater. I have no reason, even now, to suppose it was anything but an innocent trip to see another part of the town. After all, a lot of our youngsters come from that way."

"Yes, they do."

"It was fun. I met new people — some ex-members of staff, who were a bit radical, if I'm honest — and heard various views. The sort of things you always hear in a pub. Some people want to change the world." He smiled.

"I do know what you mean, Chad," Madding said patiently, but Mundy could see that he'd hooked him. The priest was eager for revelations.

"I heard nothing that revolutionary that I needed to go back to my senior colleagues and report it. It was all pretty harmless. But later, as I was leaving the pub — the Sword and Anvil — I was warned that some men were waiting to see me. They turned out to be a right bunch of ruffians." Mundy then gave the priest a careful summary of the events by the bridge and back on Petra's quayside.

"Heavens, you say they were armed?"

"With knives. It was meant to be unnerving and I tell you, Father, it was."

Madding looked horrified. If it was an act, as Mundy suspected, it was a very convincing one. "Things are far worse than I had realized."

"I was lucky, Father. The trawlermen saved my bacon, but if they hadn't been passing, or been so territorial, I would probably have come off a lot worse."

The priest also sat back, mouth slightly open. "This is dreadful news, Chad. I am very sorry that you've been put through this, of course, but the implications —"

"Who do you think they were, Father?"

For a moment the priest's eyes narrowed. "I can't imagine why anyone would want to threaten you. Although, if you were perceived as a dedicated Authority man, the dissidents would be the most likely ones to harass you. They are becoming more and more aggressive in their criticisms of the Authority and the church with it."

"I've been fairly open about my support for the Authority's ideals. Not only in the Academy, through my interview and with new colleagues, but I suppose I was pretty outspoken in the Anvil. I just didn't think that the dissidents — the pagans — would be so incensed by my views. Perhaps I was being a bit naïve."

"Have you said anything to anybody about this?"

"Well, I was with Penn Ranzer—"

"Yes, I know the young lady. PE teacher."

"She didn't see the attempted attack by the bridge, but obviously she was surprised that I made my own way home, across the river. I saw her the next day and made light of the whole affair. I just said that some of the locals had made obnoxious remarks about the Authority. She said some are far more outspoken than others. They don't like newcomers, especially from Londonborough. And they don't like them visiting their side of the river. I didn't tell her about the attack over here. So as far as my colleagues are concerned, that's the end of it."

Madding nodded slowly. "I'm glad you've told me, Chad. This is very disturbing. Can I ask you to do something for me?"

"Of course, Father."

"Keep me informed. Anything like this, I need to know about. We are concerned about so-called pagan activity. It's not healthy. Some good people are trying to rebuild things in our world. Working together, even if our controlling rules are very strict, is essential. If we have groups splintering off, it will weaken us all."

"As I said to you, Father, I saw something like this in Londonborough. But it was never my path."

Madding looked at him intently. "You're wise, Chad."

Mundy rose and set down his empty glass. "Well, I'd better go and prepare some work for next week."

"We could always do with an extra pair of ears and eyes," said the priest, again shaking Mundy's hand.

"If I can help, Father, I will do. It sounds to me as if you've a nest of vipers here and it needs dealing with."

· ✳ ·

Carl Trencher studied Andrew Wilkinson, the young man who stood before him almost at attention. He seemed hardly older than the students he helped with, a thin, wiry specimen who sported the beginnings of a moustache. At this

stage of its growth it did more to accentuate his youth than
enhance his age.

"Andrew," said the Senior Magister warmly. "Everything
okay?"

"Yes, Mr. Trencher, sir." Wilkinson had done his best to
blot from his mind last night's clash with the Brethren.

"Good. Didn't I see you helping Mr. Lurrell yesterday?
At the football?"

"Yes, sir. I'm not very good, but he let me help."

"I'm glad to hear it, Andrew. Everyone has a job to do
and we are all important in the scheme of things. Even you.
Remember that."

Wilkinson beamed. Father Emmanuel always said that, too.

"I meant to ask you, Andrew. How is our new teacher
Chad Mundy getting on? Settling in okay?"

"Yes, I think so, sir. He's a kind man. Like Mr. Goldsworthy.
Father Emmanuel says it's one of my duties to help new staff."

"Andrew, you do know, don't you, that there are some
people in Petra and in Overwater who don't behave as well
as they should do?"

"You mean the pagans, Mr. Trencher?"

"I do, Andrew. We must all be careful. Now, Mr. Mundy
won't know much about them. We need to protect him. But I
don't want him worrying. So we need to keep an eye on him,
sort of secretly. You would be very good at that, Andrew."

"No one notices me, sir. I could do it."

"I don't want you to *spy* on Mr. Mundy. Just let me know
whom he speaks to and sees in the pubs and around the town.
If necessary, I can talk to him and, well, guide him. Do you
think that sounds like a good arrangement?"

"It is, Mr. Trencher." Wilkinson thought again of the Brethren
and their crude comments to him. They were the sort of people
Mr. Trencher was talking about.

· ✳ ·

Father Madding finished seeing out his small congregation
from the Sunday evening service and closed one of the front
doors to the church. Outside it was still very bright, the air
mercifully cooling down. If this weather went on much longer,
he knew there would be a storm, probably quite a fierce one.
He watched the last of his flock winding away through the
tightly packed streets, and he turned back inside the building.

He made his way through the musty cloisters that led to the private sector, out to where his Brethren were based. Quietly he entered one of the side rooms containing a number of beds that suggested a dormitory. Two were occupied. The men propped up on pillows acknowledged the priest's entry with curt nods.

"How is it?" Madding asked them.

"Doc said we'd be fine in a day or so. The bastards who cut us — sorry, Father — they knew what they were doing. They weren't aiming for any vital organs. They knew how to use a knife. Reckon if they had done for us, they knew they would have had to face the navy and probably the noose for it."

Madding winced squeamishly. "Let's be thankful for a small mercy."

Behind him another man entered, the sour-faced leader of these men.

"Jarrold," said the priest. "Your companions seem to be on the mend."

"We were unlucky, Father. We had Mundy cornered like a rat in a trap. A few more minutes and we would have scared the— well, we would have made sure he got the message, all right. We should have had someone watching out for the trawlermen. It's their patch, not ours."

Madding's eyes narrowed. "Was it just chance that they came along, do you think? They weren't *protecting* Mundy, were they?"

Jarrold shook his head. "Nah. They're a law to themselves, Father. They'd carve up their own mothers if they annoyed them. Mad bastards, the lot of them, if you'll pardon me."

Madding wished the men a speedy recovery, and went outside with Jarrold. "What about last night? The business with the caretaker?" said the priest.

"Worked a treat. His face was a picture when he saw what he thought was the ghost of Vasillius. Hah!"

"But you ran into some trouble?"

"Nothing to it, Father. Bunch of drunks from a pub. Danton Connell, who used to work at the Academy. He knew Skellbow from there. By the time he saw us, we'd done the necessary. A few punches got thrown. Zennet's a bit bloody, but he'll clean up. Worsley and Batch in there will soon be on their feet. Itching for a fight, too."

"Well, there may be more work before the week's out. You keep an eye on Mundy. He may be okay, after all. But I'd like to know who he mixes with."

· ✳ ·

Madding returned to the nave and found Trencher waiting for him.

"Did you get to see Mundy?" said Trencher.

Madding nodded. "He was here this morning. We had a very enlightening conversation." Madding quickly related what he had been told after the morning service. Trencher listened attentively, nodding occasionally. "It seemed to me," finished Madding, "that Mundy wasn't speaking like a dissident at all. He talked about his time at the military academy, his antics with friends. He quite openly admitted that they had been rebellious to a degree, but he claims that he knuckled down to work and committed to the right kind of future."

Trencher was looking into the middle distance, trying to picture the events of Friday evening. "So when he spoke to Anna Vasillius, it may just have been part of the evening's general chat, is that what you think? A case of a new recruit meeting people and circulating. Did we overreact in sending the Brethren after him?"

"Is it possible that Londonborough's got this wrong, Carl?"

"The note said 'strongly suspected of external collusion'. So they don't sound certain. You said Mundy admitted he'd been a little wayward. Maybe that's what has alerted Londonborough. They said to have him watched. No action. But our talking to him will do no harm at all. If he is Authority material, we must cultivate him."

"He expressed a willingness to keep me informed."

"If this works out as we would want, it would be a real string to our bow, Emmanuel. I rather like the idea of Londonborough having to rely even more on us."

The priest smiled, indulging in a little smugness. "Indeed."

"I'll send a note to Nightingale, confirming that Mundy is under surveillance. No more than that. Let's keep our options open."

"And if Mundy shows any sign of collaborating with the dissidents?"

"Well, if the Brethren have to deal with him again, he won't be lucky enough to have a bunch of dockside thugs blundering in to his rescue."

· ✱ ·

That evening, Mundy entered the Feathers, collected a pint, and joined Penn and her companions. It was already becoming something of a routine. He had automatically checked if there was any sign of the young man he had seen Penn with, but there wasn't, as though for some reason the man kept away from the Feathers. *That reason being me*, Mundy assumed. Sooner or later he thought he'd have to introduce the man's existence into the conversation. *But why?* Mundy asked himself. *What business is it of yours who Penn sees?*

Penn pushed out a seat for him beside her and he dropped down. "Another blisteringly hot day," he said.

"Not for much longer," she said. "There'll be a storm soon. This air will pile up and thicken and then all hell will break loose. Happens every year at this time."

Once the small talk was over and the group's attention focused elsewhere, Mundy moved closer to Penn. "Has Brin told you what I'm up to?" he said softly.

She put her hand on his arm and he felt himself tensing. *Relax, for God's sake relax*, he told himself.

"You will be careful, won't you?"

"There's something very creepy about the priest."

"Do you mean apart from the fact that he's a lascivious, wet-mouthed toad who looks at women as if they weren't wearing anything?"

He laughed softly. "Is that how he comes across?"

"To any self-respecting woman, I'd say, yes."

"I'd trust him as far as I could throw him. Even if I hadn't known he and Trencher are as thick as thieves."

"Petra is a place full of people wearing masks. I'm a bit more volatile, I suppose. I like people to be up front with me."

So who is the other man? The question persisted, but he just couldn't bring himself to frame it. *Be up front with me and tell me about him.* "Is there anything else I should know?" The words were out before he could stop himself.

"About who? The group?"

He nodded, masking his embarrassment. "The group. Or you."

"Me? Not much to tell. I'd only bore you."

"I doubt that," he said.

But she looked away, her own smile forced. He could see that he had touched a nerve.

"A bit later, Anna will be here," she said, almost as an afterthought. "There's a private room in the back. She wants to talk to you."

XIV

LONDONBOROUGH

DEADSPIKE SAT IN the elegant old chair, seemingly oblivious to the decor and art of the large hall where he waited. Here, in the heart of Wellington Military Academy, there was an air of distinct tradition and old glory, something which the armed forces of the city relished, regardless of the caveats invested in historical knowledge. But Deadspike was far from indifferent to the varnished cabinets, display stands, and shelves and the array of weapons and artefacts they displayed. To any of the many young men and women who constantly passed through this atrium to the inner academy he would have seemed no more than an Authority official, patiently waiting to be called, but he was in reality highly attentive, those cold grey eyes missing nothing. While discreetly studying the spears and swords, he was also reading a report, given to him by Ottomas Slake. As usual the private detective had left no stone unturned in his efforts to uncover information for his employer. The Londonborough Roach at work— Deadspike grinned mirthlessly to himself as he thought of that drab figure burrowing through the mangled landscape, digging out, laboriously poring over and passing on nuggets of one kind or another.

With an almost imperceptible start, the Enforcer saw what he was looking for. Casually he went across to an open display case in which five long-bladed knives were on show, each of them labelled. The style of their handles and slight curve of their blades proclaimed them to be early examples of military weapons associated with an academy. As Deadspike stood beside the case, still looking at his report, a group of students passed through, wrapped up in animated discussion. Then for a while it was silent in the atrium.

Deadspike had chosen one of the knives and now, with a deft movement, reached into the case, lifted it, and transferred it to the inside of his jacket. Another student passed through, but his attention was on something distant and he did not notice Deadspike. Once he had gone, the Enforcer gently spread the remaining four knives in the case apart at equal distances. Only a curator or someone reading through the small labels would have realized that one blade was missing.

Deadspike sat down again, just as more students appeared. One of them came across to him. "Mr. Deadspike? Would you please come with me, sir?"

After a short walk through into the inner workings of the military academy, Deadspike climbed to an upper level, ushered into a large office, itself lavishly decorated with old paintings, uniforms, works of art and other reminders of times past. The figure awaiting him looked prematurely aged, a man whose eyes were lined with anxiety.

Another of the Historical Society's irritating adherents, Deadspike thought as Moddack introduced himself. *But not for much longer.*

"From what I have seen of your students and from what I've read, they are more than ready to go out into the world and contribute to its rebirth," said Deadspike bluntly. "Which is the reason I'm here. In a word, recruitment."

Moddack looked a little bemused.

"The Authority likes to choose its new recruits," Deadspike said with an unnerving grin. "It likes to have first choice. The cream."

"Ah, you're looking to take some of our students into your own organization?"

"Just one, Mr. Moddack. I've taken the liberty of asking him to join us. He should be here soon."

Moddack felt a coldness within him, spreading to every limb, but he forced himself to maintain a cool exterior. *This business is somehow off kilter,* he thought. *Maybe I'm just too old for these cat and mouse games. Maybe I'm jumping at shadows.*

Deadspike said, "A young man by the name of Erroll Detroyd."

Moddack felt his heart shiver. *No, this is no shadow. I was right all along.*

Like a venomous snake about to strike, Deadspike studied Moddack.

"Erroll, yes," said Moddack, forcing himself to enthuse. "A fine student. Sure to graduate with top honours."

"I certainly hope so, Mr. Moddack."

Moddack grimaced. *Hope so? What does he imply by that?*

"Language and Archery. Odd combination," said Deadspike. "But from what I gather, he's a top archer. One of the best in your academy." Deadspike was leafing through the folder, but Moddack was unable to read any of it from where he was sitting.

No doubt it's comprehensive, he thought.

Deadspike went on, "Doesn't seem to be any reference to the Old Tongue?"

"No," said Moddack. "No, Erroll is far more interested in modern trends."

There was a knock on the door and a moment later Erroll Detroyd entered. Deadspike introduced himself and then waved the youth to the remaining seat. Detroyd was tall, good-looking, and dressed smartly. He sat down quietly with an air of self-confidence that suited him. Deadspike studied him openly for a few moments and then turned his cold gaze back to Moddack.

"Well, Mr. Moddack, what would you like to tell me about this young fellow?"

Moddack glanced across at Detroyd, who smiled but remained impassive. "I wouldn't want to embarrass him, Mr. Deadspike, but it is fair to say that he is one of our finer students. He is predicted to get the very best grades."

Deadspike nodded slowly. "Yes, I can see a bright future ahead. What are you thinking of doing, Mr. Detroyd?"

"I'd like to go into the army and train to be an instructor."

"You'd like an active life. Not a desk job." Deadspike looked directly at him. "Of course, life doesn't always turn out the way we'd like it to."

Moddack felt himself tensing. Whatever game Deadspike was playing, he was about to show something of his hand.

"I appreciate that I'll need to graduate. I wouldn't want to take that for granted. I hope I'm not overconfident."

Deadspike smiled. "According to what I've been reading about you, I would say that's good. How disappointed would you be if you had to work in an administrative role, rather than the sort of role you've described?"

Moddack avoided looking at the youth. He'd had no opportunity to prepare him for this interview. Deadspike had sprung it on them both at the last minute. But, of course, that was part of his *modus operandi*.

Detroyd's face was creditably calm. "Naturally I would be a little disappointed, sir. I've rather set my heart on the military life. I think it would be the best place for someone of my skills."

"You have many skills. Many interests, I expect? What sort of things interest you— apart from your work?"

"I play a bit of sport. Cricket, football, tennis."

"I imagine you have a lively social life."

Again Detroyd smiled, but the first sign of uneasiness had crept into his voice. "Yes, I suppose I do. Work hard, play hard."

"A wide circle of friends?"

"Well, acquaintances. Only a few are what I would call close friends."

"Oh yes, I read somewhere that you shared rooms with Chad Mundy. We've recently sent him off to his first job. Presumably you had a lot in common?"

"We got on very well."

"You share his interest in language?"

"My field is literature, less so language. Obviously, as an English teacher, I studied language, but Chad was particularly passionate about it. I wouldn't say I was."

"I gather he was very well versed in something called the Old Tongue." Deadspike turned to Moddack as if for confirmation. The latter nodded, though Deadspike could see from his face that he was deeply uncomfortable at this turn of the conversation.

"Yes." Detroyd smiled again, affecting indifference. "I teased him about it. We were good friends, but that was way beyond my interests. It was intriguing, up to a point. But enough was enough."

"I imagine Mundy felt the same way about cricket."

In spite of himself, Detroyd laughed. "That's true, sir. Chad was not a fan of cricket. He could play football and quite well. But physically he was very disciplined. Unarmed combat. Drill, drill, drill. I admired his commitment."

"I'm sure you are no less committed to your speciality. Well, I'll come to the point, Erroll. Part of my job is to find new recruits for my own organization, which, I'm sure you are aware, is a branch of the Central Authority. We are called, rather dramatically, I think, Enforcers. The name does have a draconian ring to it, but on the other hand, our task is to ensure that certain things happen. In my case, in education."

Moddack felt his guts tightening. *There's something more to this*, he thought. *Erroll wouldn't be at all suited to working for the Enforcers, nor in an administrative role.*

"I have a vacancy coming up very soon," Deadspike went on. "I'll be blunt. I want you to fill it."

Moddack knew that Detroyd must feel horrified.

"Clerical to begin with," said Deadspike.

Detroyd almost said something, but somehow remained outwardly calm.

Moddack's mind was racing. *Clerical? A basic role? This is absurd. With Erroll's qualifications and skills, why on earth should they want to put him in a clerical role?* He cleared his throat. "Pardon me, Mr. Deadspike, but surely that's a very *modest* role for a man of Erroll's talents?"

"Oh yes, indeed it is. Chosen with that in mind."

"May I ask why, sir?" said Detroyd. His tone suggested that he was offended in spite of his demeanour.

"I would like to put you somewhere where I can keep an eye on you. Somewhere where the temptations of the outside world will be minimized."

"I'm sorry, sir, but I'm afraid I will just have to refuse your offer."

Deadspike sat back, interlinking his fingers. He appeared to be completely relaxed, not in the least annoyed by Detroyd's comment. "Refuse? I don't see that as an option, Mr. Detroyd."

"What are the options?"

"Options. Let me see. If you refuse to take up the post I am offering you, you will not graduate."

Detroyd said, indignantly, "*Not* graduate? That makes no sense."

"No, I agree. It would be a shame to throw away all that work. It would have a disastrous effect on your future. No qualifications, not a great deal of respect in the work market, poor prospects. Well, you can imagine the rest."

Moddack could not contain himself. "But why would you engineer this?"

"Engineer? Yes. Precisely. I have absolute discretion in such matters. For the good of the Authority. So, you will join us?"

"That's it? My only option. Join or be damned?"

"Aptly put, Mr. Detroyd. Join or be damned."

"And what exactly, does this post entail?"

"I haven't decided yet. But it will probably be very mundane. I'd go as far as to say soul-destroying." Deadspike made no attempt now to disguise his animosity.

Moddack looked pale. He sensed that Deadspike had not yet put all his cards on the table.

Detroyd looked across at Deadspike again, as though on the point of giving voice to his outrage.

There have to be other channels, Moddack thought.

"There *is* one other option," Deadspike added, as if something had just occurred to him. "Mr. Moddack, I wonder if you could leave us for a moment."

Moddack stood up slowly. Still he said nothing. He wanted to reassure Detroyd, but there was nothing he could say. Deadspike had absolute power over both of them and he well knew it. Moddack's superiors would have no leeway with Deadspike and certainly not those he served. Moddack would have to wait until he got a chance to see Detroyd alone.

Deadspike stood up and paced the room very slowly, thoughtfully.

Detroyd watched him, furious but determined not to show it. *How much does this bastard know?* he thought. *It's no coincidence he brought Harrald in with me. The little shit is showing off. He knows something about the Society. That's what this is really about.*

"Let's be blunt, Detroyd. You have something I want. I'm prepared to be reasonable."

"It didn't sound like it just now."

"No, that was a threat, wasn't it? I can soften that. You really don't want to be shunted to some godforsaken hole for the rest of your days, with no hope of promotion or release. Not an active chap like you. As I see it, it's just a case of how much you are prepared to compromise."

"What exactly do you want?"

"Simply information. There's no need for you to work for my department at all. I can arrange for you to pass everything with flying colours, although I'm sure you would do anyway. You are an excellent student, no doubt about it. I can also arrange for you to have a career in the best military academy available— probably here at Wellington, as it seems to be progressing so well. You can have the best training staff looking after you. In no time at all, you could be at the peak of your profession. Is that not a tempting scenario?"

Deadspike was standing behind Detroyd's chair now and he patted the back of it.

Then he walked over to one of the tall windows. He could see out over part of the city, its bleak, jumbled terrain, a mixture of revived buildings and squalid old ones, ripe for reclamation or destruction. The perpetual clouds scudded overhead, driven by endless winds.

"I want everything you know about the Historical Society. Names, contacts, and whatever it has learnt about our past."

"I don't know what you're talking about."

Deadspike sighed, his eyes fixed on the outside world. "Do we really have to go through all the motions? The conclusion will be the same. I *know* that you're a member of the Society. I've had you watched. You, Moddack, a dozen others."

Detroyd clenched his fists. He couldn't bring himself to speak, knowing he'd only goad Deadspike to even more unpleasantness. *Yes, you bastard,* he wanted to say. *I'm sure you have. And you're scared of us. You and your fucking Authority. You know that you can't nail us. That we're growing. And that one day, we'll bring you and your sick empire down.*

"And of course," Deadspike went on, turning theatrically and approaching him. "Chad Mundy told us all about you."

But Detroyd was not taking the bait. *No, I don't buy that. Chad would never have succumbed, even to torture,* he thought.

"He couldn't pass up a good offer," said Deadspike. "A chance to study the Old Tongue firsthand. In Dumnonia? Imagine his delight at that. A good post, excellent prospects. He took the sensible route. You should do the same."

Detroyd shrugged. "I'm sure I will," he said, again clamping down on his thoughts. *Bullshit. I don't believe a word of it. If Chad had betrayed us, you wouldn't be here now, trying to get me to cooperate. You'd just have us all put away. If there's one person we can rely on to keep his mouth shut, it's Chad.*

"So how does this play?" he said as casually as he could.

Deadspike returned to the window. "Come here a moment."

Detroyd did as bidden. Even if what he really wanted to do was shove him through the glass and watch him tumble out into the murk.

"What do you see out there, Erroll?"

Detroyd shrugged. "A wasteland. Mile upon mile of an old city that barely survived the Plague Wars."

"Yes, but it's not a terminal illness. Day by day, inch by inch, Londonborough is rising up from its own ashes. People like you, Erroll, and I'm not being in the least patronizing when I say it, people like you are making the rebirth possible. And, like it or not, people like me. Someone has to take a hard line."

Detroyd said nothing.

"That's all we're really interested in, isn't it? Rebirth. A strong community. Strong enough to survive and especially strong enough to withstand any invasion."

"If one ever comes."

"Yes, if one ever comes. Many doubt that it will. But complacency is a serious weakness. If we rebuild Londonborough and the Invasion does happen, think what it would mean if we simply capitulated to our enemies. If Evropa just walked in and took control. You don't think that's worth guarding against?"

Deadspike's words were seductive, oh yes.

"It would be replacing one form of control with another," said Detroyd.

"The Authority? So you see it as evil?"

"I believe in free will. I see very little of that in our world."

"I do understand, you know," said Deadspike, turning away from the window. "I'm not totally without sensitivity. Perhaps I have less faith in too much free will than I do in order."

"If the Authority was a genuine servant of its people, I'd have more respect for it. But it is corrupt, self-seeking."

Deadspike did not react. His eyes remained cold, but were devoid of anger or bitterness. "Without the Authority, humanity would collapse. Grand Britannia as it is today would simply retrogress. A new Dark Age would swallow us all. Corruption among the powerful is something that cannot be avoided, at least to some extent. We have to police ourselves. Men like you, Erroll, are probably the ones to do it."

"And men like you?" Detroyd turned and faced Deadspike, watching that cool expression, those unblinking, grey eyes.

"I *am* ambitious, I do not deny it for a moment. I am ruthless, Erroll. My methods are necessarily blunt and direct. I believe some things have to be taken by force. But the weak have to be protected by the strong."

Detroyd would no more trust this man than he would a mad dog. But he remained calm, as though swayed by the glib words.

"I will give you one day to think about my offer," Deadspike ended. "We'll meet here tomorrow at the same time." He picked up his folder and left without a backward glance.

· ❋ ·

Later, Detroyd told Moddack what Deadspike had said.

"Well, we always knew this could happen," said Moddack uncomfortably. "We do have an exit plan. The Society will have to go even further underground. Amelia, Hewitt, and I will just have to disappear. We can no longer operate as 'normal' citizens. Deadspike will already be watching all of us. God knows what he's contemplating. I daresay even *torture* would not be beyond him."

Detroyd looked disgusted. "That stuff about Chad— that was bullshit, wasn't it?"

"I'm sure it was. Chad would never turn his coat for these monsters. By now he'll be under the wing of our man in Petra." Moddack frowned deeply. "Your situation is very difficult, Erroll. If you refuse to cooperate with Deadspike, he'll do everything he threatened. He has that power. They will reduce you to nothing."

"I'm damned if I'll cooperate."

"You could appear to. Listen, my cover is blown, and other key people are also in my situation. We know that. You can confirm for Deadspike what he already knows. It won't matter to us. By tonight we will be gone. Be selective about what you tell him. Pretend to sell him your soul and work for him. Say you can find us. And everything we know. He might just fall for that. He's flying blind, to some extent. This is a game of bluff and double bluff."

"It sticks in my craw, Harrald. Even pretending to work for that little shit."

"Handle it carefully and you could be working against him. Eventually we'd get you out. Maybe to Petra, where Chad is. Or somewhere like it."

"There is another path I could take. I could just disappear, right now, today. It's the one thing they wouldn't be expecting."

"But you'd be no better off than if Deadspike shackled you. Worse, you'd be a renegade. Hunted. Possibly even killed on sight."

"I'd be my own man. There must be others like me out there. You could help me get away."

"We could, but it would be such a waste!"

"We dare not afford to delay. He expects me back tomorrow."

Moddack was thinking furiously. "Very well. Meet me in the main library at lunchtime. Selwinn will find us somewhere where we won't be disturbed, or watched. We'll take it from there. As soon as you go through that door, assume you're a marked man."

XV

PETRA/LONDONBOROUGH

MUNDY MET ANNA Vasillius at the rear of the pub in a room discreetly set aside for them. She sat at a table, a cup of water and a few slices of fresh bread beside her. Her face looked tired, her eyes slightly pained.

"How did your meeting with Father Emmanuel go?"

He went over it with her, laughing at the priest's attitude towards the dissidents.

She smiled and for a moment a dozen years fell away from her. "Manning hates us, Chad. Servants of Satan that we are. He's desperate for power. It's like a cancer. Gnawing away at him. His followers are dwindling."

"And he would kill to change things?"

She nodded slowly. "He's far too spineless to get his own hands dirty. But when it suits his cause, oh yes, he'd kill."

"Was he implicated in your husband's death?"

"You need to know about Drew. The official story centers on his disaffection with the Academy. He loathed the strict rules, the unreasonable demands put on staff to meet targets, to attain something that the Prime referred to as capacity. Her thinly veiled threats of dismissal. Whatever dictates come down from the Authority she uses as watchwords for progress. But it's a stick to beat the staff with. People like Drew feel very stressed. Some cope better than others.

"The Prime has a set method of dealing with any kind of resistance to her measures. A slow, grinding series of 'interviews' designed to drive the offenders into submission. Psychological bullying, threats. Improve or, sadly, you will be axed. You met some of the 'rebels' who suffered this. Good teachers who know more about controlling kids and relating to them than the Prime ever will.

"The official reports say Drew cracked. He was working too hard and the Inspection was the last straw. It all became too much and he committed suicide. It is possible that the

Prime actually believes this herself. She may not have known what really happened. I could believe it. But her regret of Drew's death was short-lived. Once the inconvenience was over, she moved on as if it had never happened. I doubt if she ever gives him a thought now."

"But it was a front?" said Mundy. "A lie to cover up what really happened?"

"Yes. The blame culture that is the Academy lives on and others feel the slow grind of its stress. But the reason for all this subterfuge is that Drew was the keeper of certain knowledge. Secrets, Chad. How melodramatic is that?"

He watched her face, the undisguised wretchedness.

"Secrets that no one else was allowed to share. Not even me. Drew told me long ago that he carried them with him but would never share them with me because if he did, my life would be in danger: there were ruthless people who would have no hesitation in torturing, even killing for them. So we agreed I would never know. He was safe as long as no one knew he was in possession of the secrets. And that was the case until only recently."

"Do you know anything at all about these secrets?"

"Yes. They were a family inheritance. Drew's family were the keepers. These secrets go back a long way. As far as I was able to find out, Drew's grandfather was in possession of them. Before him, I don't know. He was called Matthias. His son, David — Drew's father — inherited the secrets when Matthias died. And when David died, he passed them on to Drew. Down the family bloodline. It's something to do with genetics. The information is inherited like a family trait." She paused, looking into the half-darkness, but she slowly recoiled from whatever disturbing visions she had seen there.

"Were they all Dumnonians?" said Mundy quietly, almost afraid to stir the air.

She shook her head. "Matthias lived in Londonborough. David came here to Petra as a teacher. Drew was born and bred here. Trained, like you, as a teacher. Attended military academy in Londonborough. Came back here and worked alongside Sebastian and other colleagues."

"So his grandfather, the original keeper, was a city man."

"Yes. A scientist. He did some teaching, passing on his own knowledge to others. In his day, Londonborough was an even darker place than it is now. Isolated, forlorn, weak.

Men like Matthias labored long and hard to drag it out of the darkness following the Plague Wars. Drew was reticent on the matter. Because Matthias had been the keeper, he was almost totally off-limits as far as conversation went. It was part of Drew's vow of silence, Chad."

"And the same with his son, David?"

"Yes. Perhaps Matthias decided that Londonborough was not a safe place for his son, so he sent him here, out of harm's way. And, I suspect, because he must have known that in Petra the secrets would be far from the eyes and ears of anyone who might have been seeking them. Whether the original secret is something that Matthias discovered, or whether it was passed to him from his own bloodline, we don't know. My suspicion, and it is only that, is that, as a scientist, Matthias stumbled on to something."

"So if Drew had lived, who would have inherited the knowledge from him?"

Anna drew in her breath slowly and Mundy could see that she was holding her emotions in check, her body suddenly tensing, the years never more apparent than now. "We had no children of our own," she breathed.

He could see what it had cost her to speak of this; he felt immediate regret at having posed the question.

She held her hand up to save him from commenting. "It's all right, Chad. You couldn't have known. We tried. We wanted a family. Drew would have been a good father. He loved children. But for some reason we were denied them. So there was no one to inherit Drew's knowledge."

"It died with him?"

She looked doubly uncomfortable, nodding slowly. "Perhaps it would have been better if he had confided in me."

"Could he have confided in anyone else?"

"He could have. The one person who would have been an obvious confidante would have been Sebastian. Drew looked up to him more than anyone. Brin Goldsworthy was Drew's closest friend, but he would never have compromised his safety. It's a paradoxical situation. On the one hand, you need someone you can trust absolutely. But on the other, you don't want to put your friends, or your wife, at risk."

"Maybe the knowledge is so terrible that we're better off not knowing?"

"Sebastian thinks it's vital that we recover it."

"Does he have any idea what it is?"

"No. But I think he understands the implications. If — *if* —, Drew shared the knowledge with anyone, it would have been someone steeped in the old ways. A true pagan sympathizer. Well, our faith is vested in something far older than Father Madding's. Drew had contacts beyond Petra. He attended pagan ceremonies, more so than me. It is possible that he passed the secrets on to someone in that faith. You've seen the edge of the forest lands, Chad. Have you any idea how far they stretch? Across Dumnonia alone they encompass thousands of square miles. There are groups out there, in the deep lands.

"The festivals begin soon. Talk to Penn and the others. Get involved. There will be ceremonies across the river and beyond. It's an opportunity for you to meet the true pagans."

In spite of a deep feeling of unease, Mundy also felt a stirring of something else within him. Some atavistic force, perhaps. *True pagans.*

Anna picked up her bread and broke off a small piece. "You need to meet someone called the Green Man. If anyone can unlock this mystery, he can."

He was about to ask her more, but he had become ever more conscious of her unhappiness, her loneliness, wrapped around her like a mantle. She chewed slowly, looking away now as though he was no longer in the room.

Back in the main part of the pub, Mundy was plunged into a rowdy wall of gaiety and boozy excitement. Penn and the others, more flushed now than earlier, welcomed him back with gleeful hoots and exaggerated bonhomie. He pretended to take it in his stride, sitting once more with Penn.

"Is she all right?" she asked him with genuine concern.

"She misses him. Acutely."

Penn put her hand on his arm as she had before, as though they shared a personal tragedy. "Yes, she does."

"Whoever did this, they must be found," he said. "Whatever else we get out of this business, we have to bring those bastards to justice."

"That's what I like to hear," she said.

"So," he said, taking another long pull at his beer. "Tell me about the festivals. I keep hearing about them. Term ends soon and Petra goes festival mad, I gather."

"Right! Where shall I start?"

"Tell me about the Green Man."

· ✳ ·

Fog thickened, curdling like milk. The streets of Londonborough filled as though the waters of a lake had risen up and churned through them, swallowing everything, blotting out what weakened daylight could get through. Where figures did stir, they moved like ghosts, ethereal and vague, silent and self-contained. It was an even more alien landscape than usual, with few of the city's inhabitants prepared to trudge through it. Perfect conditions, however, for certain darker pursuits.

Two men, both dressed in nondescript clothing, indistinguishable from any other citizens, slid into the shadows of an alleyway, pulling up the thick lapels of their jackets against the drop in temperature that came with the coiling fog. Hands thrust deep in their pockets, they listened to the all-enveloping silence. Somewhere they could hear the *dripdrip* of water from a conduit, condensed fog running off a tiled roof.

"You ready, Spragg?" one of the men grunted.

The other nodded. "You?"

"The way I see it, we got no choice."

"Bit late to think about choice, Munk. Either we get on with this, or we make a run for it. Don't fancy our chances if we do that. We'd be picked off like fish in a barrel. You got cold feet?"

"Nah. Deadspike is the right man to be working for, mate. His star's rising. We do our job and we'll rise with him. After this, he said we'll be shipped out of here for a year or so. No one'll know we exist."

"Yeah. You know anything about this Petra place we're going to?"

Munk nodded, watching the shifting murk around them. "I spoke to Marsley. Him and some of the others have not long got back from a tour down there. Said it was okay. They had to take care of some business for Deadspike. Otherwise they said it was pretty cushy."

"They're well in now."

Munk nodded again. "Promoted. We'll be the same. Deadspike will always need men like us, Spragg, my son."

Spragg grinned, then turned stiffly around like a hound, attention fixed on the mouth of the alley and the street beyond. "He's coming."

"Softly does it."

They became even more like wraiths, invisible in their hiding place. The man they were waiting for passed this way each evening at the same time, his tour of duty over for the day. He was based not far from here and in conditions like these would be in a hurry to get home.

Sure enough, a spectral figure in a long coat appeared in the mouth of the alley. It paused, sizing up the terrain ahead, but with a brief glance to either side, it entered the narrow confines. A dozen quick strides in and the man found himself confronted by someone who had clearly been waiting for him.

"You on Mr. Sunderman's team?" Munk said, his voice grating in the semi-darkness.

The man was about to pull his hand out from one of the coat's pockets, but he felt an arm grip him from behind before he could complete the movement. There were two of these men.

"What's it to you?"

"It's okay, pal. We're all on the same side."

"I don't know you."

Munk shook his head. "You know how the Authority works. You been following Marlmaster?"

The man was very still. "I report to Sunderman. I wasn't told to report to anyone else."

"That's okay. We've been drafted in. The Authority is hotting up the hunt. Marlmaster, Tannerton, Moddack. Surveillance every minute of the day and night."

The man seemed to relax at that, but the grip on his arm did not.

"The Historical Society," said a voice at his ear, as guttural as that of the man in front of him.

"Yes, I've been following Marlmaster. He's gone to the address where he stays. He'll likely stay put for the night. But my relief is watching him."

Munk smiled, but it was not a cheering expression. "Your job's done, then," he said.

These particular words were a signal to Spragg, who reacted with lightning speed. His hand moved up to the neck of the man he held, gripping it with fierce intensity, and his other hand was a blur in the darkness. The knife he held drove home through his victim's clothing, and up under the rib cage, tearing into the heart in one powerful motion. Spragg closed his free hand over the man's mouth to stifle what would have been a scream of pain. The man thrashed, but Spragg was unusually strong. He had been carefully selected for this killing.

Several minutes passed before the victim's helpless struggles ceased. Munk went to the mouth of the alley, leaning on one of its walls casually and watching, listening. But beyond him there was only the writhing silence of the fog. Satisfied that the bloody act would not be discovered, Munk went back to Spragg and between them they lifted their victim like a sack and took him down the alley.

It debouched into a small square where a horse and small cart had been tethered to a rail. The horse turned to look at them in a disinterested way, waiting for them to untie it and move it on. They loaded the dead man in to the back of the cart.

Munk clambered across to the driving seat and waited.

Spragg checked the corpse a last time and then pulled a sheet over it. He jumped down again, undid the reins, and got up beside Munk. Both men listened to the night, but the silence was complete. Munk spoke to the horse, flicking the reins, and it obediently moved out of the square.

"Is that knife secure?" Munk asked his companion.

"Sure. It'll take a bloody good yank to pull it free of his chest."

"That's good," Munk nodded. "Mr. Deadspike was very specific about that. What is it, that knife?"

"Dunno, mate. There are far better weapons around these days. Looked like an antique to me. Something out of a bloody museum."

· ✳ ·

Lionel Canderville walked stiffly down the corridor, Deadspike beside him, two guards armed with handguns behind him. They were deep under the Enforcers' base in the heart of the city. Canderville had a face that made it all too clear that he was in the foulest of moods.

"I say again, Deadspike, you'd better have a bloody good reason for dragging me down here at this time of night."

Deadspike, unmoved, led him to a steel door, pausing only to unlock it. A single guard waited within, saluting the men as they entered. The room was empty save for a long steel table. Stretched along this was the body of the man lately murdered by Deadspike's staff.

"What the hell is the meaning of this?" Canderville fumed. He looked down at the body, which was still fully clothed. The hilt of a long knife protruded from its chest, the coat soaked in blood.

"Who is this man?" Canderville demanded, staring at the hilt of the weapon.

"His name is Pollander, sir," said Deadspike. "He works for Mr. Sunderman. Part of his surveillance team."

"Why have you brought *me* here to see him? I can see he's been butchered. But why haven't you taken him to Sunderman? Does he know about this?"

Deadspike remained completely calm. "No, sir. I think this is a rather delicate matter." He indicated the guards.

Canderville dismissed them all with a wave of his hand.

Once he was alone with Canderville, Deadspike pointed to the knife. "Mr. Sunderman had members of a certain Society watched. The Historical Society."

Canderville nodded, his interest beginning to focus.

"I strongly advised Mr. Sunderman to take firmer action against this Society, sir. In my view, it is an extremely treacherous organization. Mr. Sunderman felt that it was sufficient to keep it under surveillance. This man, Pollander, was one of a team observing its movements. In particular, Hewitt Marlmaster."

"I know him, yes."

"Earlier tonight, Pollander was killed, as you can see."

"Knifed," Canderville grunted.

"It's no ordinary knife, sir. It's from Wellington Academy. I think an inspection of its militaria will confirm that this particular knife is missing."

"You're saying that Marlmaster killed this man? But he's an old man. He'd not be capable of this."

"The Society, sir. That knife was taken from an old collection in Wellington Academy. Either by Marlmaster, who would have had access, or, I suspect, Harrald Moddack. Both highly involved with the Historical Society. And the killing was clearly the work of a man or men working to Marlmaster's instructions. At least, that's my view."

"And you did not think to share this with Sunderman?"

"To be perfectly candid, sir, no. I am afraid that Mr. Sunderman is far too gentle in his approach to these matters. I believe, sir, it is time for much more stringent measures. I think we should deal with this Society once and for all. Before there are any more— embarrassments."

Canderville studied the corpse in silence. Deadspike and his methods were not something he embraced with any pleasure. But neither was murder. This accursed Society had gone too far. And it was true, Sunderman was much too soft. Perhaps he was becoming a liability. It was the last thing Canderville wanted with his own potential promotion in the offing.

"Very well, Deadspike. Do what you think is necessary to bring them to book. Keep me well out of it, mind. My name must not be associated with the sort of measures that you may need to take. Just keep me informed."

"And Mr. Sunderman?"

"I'll tell him the matter has been taken out of his hands. That's all he needs to know for the time being."

XVI

LONDONBOROUGH

ONCE ERROLL DETROYD had left, Harrald Moddack began writing brief, coded letters to both Hewitt Marlmaster and Amelia Tannerton, his two immediate contacts in the Society. They would all have to go into hiding immediately. Even now he could feel Deadspike's cold eyes upon him, with the promise of dire consequences if he didn't act expediently. He slipped the letters into envelopes and sealed them, stamping them with his own private crest so that the recipients could be sure they were genuine.

He hurried down into the Academy's wide Reception Area. Behind the main desk, Mrs. Verriton, the head receptionist, gave him a slightly nervous look.

Moddack handed her the two envelopes. "Good morning, Mrs. Verriton. I need these letters delivered as a matter of some urgency—" he began, but although she took them from him, she was shaking her head.

"I'm very sorry, Mr. Moddack, but I'm afraid they can't go out just yet. There's been an incident." She sounded like a conspirator. "The Deputy Commander has asked that no one leave the building while he carries out an investigation."

"An *incident*?" said Moddack, puzzled.

Mrs. Verriton leaned forward. She had been here a long time and had known Moddack for most of it. "Something has been taken from the militaria collection in the main waiting room."

"Stolen?"

Mrs. Verriton had clearly said all she was going to say, but the look in her eyes implied that Moddack was correct in his assumption.

Moddack turned to see Philbertsmith, the Deputy Commander of the Military Academy, approaching him in a highly agitated state. He was a short man in his late sixties, with a thick moustache and thin, yellowish hair.

"Osbert, what the devil's going on?" Moddack asked him.

"All very embarrassing," Philbertsmith snorted. "A knife is missing from the old collection. Whoever took it reshuffled the others to try and cover up the theft."

"When did this happen?"

"Don't know yet. Had a note about it from one of our visitors— an Enforcer, of all people. He was waiting to see you and he happened to be studying the collection."

Moddack felt his blood running cold.

"You know what these damn people are like. Miss nothing. He saw that a set of knives had been disturbed. Only four instead of five. As he was leaving, he left a note. Smug bastard. But he was right. A knife has indeed gone."

Moddack's mind was swirling. *It was Deadspike. He had reported the knife missing as he left. Not immediately. Which meant he must have taken it himself.* "It's probably a stupid student prank, Osbert. With the end of year coming."

"I hope so. Look, it's shutting the stable door after the horse has bolted, but I've put a brief lockup on the building. No one goes out for the next hour or so while I have this checked out. I hope you don't mind helping out."

Moddack could hardly think straight. Why should Deadspike take the weapon? It could only mean trouble. Part of his scheme to discredit the Society? He had threatened as much.

"Once the lockup is lifted, Mrs. Verriton, could you arrange for those letters to be sent as quickly as possible?"

"Of course, Mr. Moddack."

He had no choice now but to get out. Every minute counted. He returned to his rooms and thrust a few papers into a slim case, preparing to leave. *Detroyd! Did he get out before the lockup? Damn, I should have asked Mrs. Verriton. She sees everyone in and out.*

But he dare not go back to the main reception now. Instead he slipped quietly along corridors and down narrow stairways: he must leave by any of the side doors. In a lockup, they would be secured, but he had a master key. To his relief, no one was about. Everyone would have been called to the three central assembly halls to face the wrath of the Deputy Commander and his chief staff.

On the ground floor, Moddack marched cautiously towards the outer area. Anyone he saw on the way he chivvied along to the halls. No one questioned him. His body was soaked in sweat, his breath laboured as he reached the corridor to a small set of steps down to an exit. Satisfying himself that he was alone, he descended to the thick, wooden door. It was locked. He slid his master key into the lock.

"Mr. Moddack?" said a voice behind him at the top of the steps, and he felt his heart give a lurch of dread. He swung round, trying to look composed.

"David," he said. "You gave me quite a start."

It was one of the security guards, smiling uncomfortably. "Did you know about the lockup, sir?"

"Yes, I'm assisting Mr. Philbertsmith in an investigation. I need to slip out for a moment. Can you wait here until I get back?"

The guard came down the steps slowly, uncertainly. "Of course, Mr. Moddack. But if you don't mind, sir, I have to search you."

"Of course, David, that's absolutely fine." Moddack lifted his arms. The guard, clearly embarrassed, carried out a perfunctory search, stepping back.

"Sorry about that, sir."

"No problem. I won't be long. Lock me out and wait for me here. I'll let myself in. Ten minutes, no more." Moddack fumbled with his key, but got the door open. For once the enveloping fog of Londonborough's streets was a welcome relief. He heard the turn of the lock as the guard secured the door again. For a moment he closed his eyes, concentrating on the route to the safe house that he had committed to memory, then he moved off through the narrow streets.

· ✳ ·

The first of Moddack's letters, addressed to Amelia Tannerton, was delivered to the administrative centre where she worked almost two hours after Moddack had given it to Mrs. Verriton. She in turn had arranged for one of the Academy's couriers to take it by hand to the centre where one of Amelia Tannerton's colleagues received the envelope. It was marked as confidential, so he did not attempt to open it. Several office workers were near at hand, heads bowed over their piled desks, endlessly sifting through papers and documents.

"Has anyone seen Amelia?"

Heads looked up in unison, but there was initially no response. Finally someone entered the long room and said that he thought he had seen her downstairs about half an hour previously. Consequently the letter was placed on her desk in a prominent position, so that when she did return, it would be the first thing she saw.

She did not, however, return.

· ✳ ·

Hewitt Marlmaster read and reread the contents of his own envelope, which had arrived late in the afternoon. It was a brief note, referring to some very minor paperwork. But the wording was a coded message. No matter how many times Marlmaster studied it, he knew what it meant. The Authority was intent on moving against the Society. He had to act and quickly. The words implied urgency.

He paused only to collect a few things, put them in an old case, and change his clothes. He had eschewed buying any new ones for many years; what he possessed were seedy and dilapidated. He donned a very tattered overcoat and left his home with a brief glance back, knowing that he would probably never see it again. The fog that had begun to congeal earlier had set in for the night. He just hoped that he could remember the way to the safe house. It was over two miles away and in this soup-like atmosphere he could easily lose his bearings.

I'm too old for this nonsense. Maybe I should just let the Authority pull me in and have done with it, he thought, feeling the weight of years. But he knew too much. If they did get hold of him, they would extract things from him by whatever brutal means they chose. He would resist, of course, but he was not strong any more. Nevertheless, he owed it to the safety of others to defy the Authority. He must run.

He was a mile or more into his flight when he knew he was being followed. Whoever was dogging him was very good. Each time he paused and hid himself well out of sight, silence descended. It was only when he moved on that he thought he could hear something. Perhaps Moddack's warning had come too late and the Authority was already on to him.

But he pushed the thought aside. It could just as easily be footpads. If they jumped him, they would soon realize he had nothing of use to them. It had happened to him before and he had never been considered worthy of a beating or even of being robbed.

He was within a short walk of his destination when two men stepped out of the fog, blocking his path. He realized the way back would also be blocked.

"Mr. Marlmaster?" said a rough voice. The two men were not dressed as he would have expected Authority officials to be. But footpads would not have known his name.

"No need for concern, sir. We're here for your protection. Mr. Moddack asked us to meet you."

Marlmaster was uneasy. This wasn't part of the agreed plan. But Harrald had obviously been very concerned when he had written that letter.

"We're to take you to the safe house. There are people about, sir. Not all of them likely to be friendly."

Marlmaster knew he had little choice: the two of them would have overpowered him easily if he had resisted. He nodded and they indicated that he should follow them. Others were backing up and in a moment the group slipped away in silence. It was obvious to Marlmaster that their destination was not the safe house he had been heading for, as directed in the coded letter. His spirits were rapidly waning.

"Where are we going?" he called to one of the men in front.

Something jammed into his back and a hand gripped his right arm. He felt his tendons protest. "Keep walking, mate. Soon be there. No noise, okay? There's no one around to hear you."

The leader abruptly ducked up an alleyway and the small party followed. The man opened a door, a pale wash of light emerging, and Marlmaster was pushed roughly inside into a bare corridor. He heard the door close and the lock turn. With it went any hope of completing his getaway. These men were professionals, hard and uncompromising.

One of them opened a door off the corridor and Marlmaster was thrust into the room beyond. A solitary candle burned low. But by its light he recognized the two gaunt faces that stared up at him. At that moment he knew real despair.

"Hewitt," said Amelia Tannerton, voice full of anguish. "We prayed you'd slip away in time." Beside her Harrald Moddack looked equally as drawn.

"Who are they?" said Marlmaster. "Authority goons?"

"I'm sorry, Hewitt," said Moddack. "But my guess is, this is Deadspike's work." He lowered his voice: they appeared to be alone and their captors had left but Moddack was clearly being very cautious. Moddack recounted for Tannerton and Marlmaster the conversation he'd had earlier with Erroll Detroyd.

"Did Erroll get away?" said Marlmaster anxiously.

Moddack merely shrugged.

"Let's take heart from the fact that he's not here now," said Amelia.

"I pray he gives Deadspike the slip," said Moddack. "Because someone must find a way to warn Chad Mundy. Deadspike mentioned him, quite casually, so may not have any further interest in him. But Deadspike is going to want information about the Society. And he'll want the names of all its members that we know of."

· ❋ ·

Erroll Detroyd had left the Academy before the lockup had been actioned. He had wasted no time in considering Deadspike's ultimatum. As he had told Moddack, there was only one choice open to him and he focused on that now with single-minded determination. Going out through the main entrance of the Military Academy, he noticed at the reception desk several people involved in a heated discussion. But he was gone before anyone noticed him and was away before the Deputy Commander sealed the building.

Detroyd made his way home as quickly as he could. He changed into the soiled and torn clothes he had set aside for just such an eventuality as flight, including an old jacket with a hood. He was least likely to attract attention in them. He took also a long case, in which he kept his bow and two dozen arrows. It was an awkward thing to carry, but it was the last thing he would have wanted to part with, especially given the coming journey.

He exited by an upstairs window, climbed onto an annex roof, crossed it and three others, and slipped down into the fog and darkness some distance from the house. He did not know it, but by doing this he gave his watchers the slip for a vital period of time. *Always assume you are being watched*, he had been told— advice that he clung to at all times.

The time he had won himself enabled him to get far enough through the maze of streets to a safe house where he was given a horse. No one at the house, three miles from the administrative center, questioned him. He was a known member of the Society and the men looking after the safe house were dedicated and used to swift action. Detroyd rode northwards through the clouds of fog to an area where it began thinning at last, enabling him to speed up. Unknown to him, by that time his pursuers were back on the trail, an eager pack of hounds. They knew the layout of Londonborough better than anyone, every last rat run. Inexorably they closed up the gap.

He rode for several hours through that graveyard landscape, skirting at least two huge Plague Pits, the massive, domed constructions that were like gigantic mausoleums, whatever horrors they concealed walled up inside them. He saw no one for miles, occasionally passing a small group, though no one attempted to stop or even hail him. People in these places kept to themselves, fugitives from their own shadows. It was evening when Detroyd reached his destination, another safe house in Greywalls, a drab area at the very borders of the city. He slowed his mount, speaking to it softly, and entered the courtyard of the big ugly building he had been told about. It was as dark and forbidding as most of its surroundings and there were no lights.

He dismounted, tethering the horse to a rail. He stood at the gates, listening. He heard nothing, no distant clatter of hoof beats. The fog had not reached here, but a thin sheet of drizzle blurred the view as night closed in, the dead sky losing the last of its dirty rusted sunlight. He studied the terrain outside, but it was lifeless, low buildings like tombstones.

Satisfied that he had arrived without detection, he found a door and rapped several times. Eventually it opened and Detroyd found himself staring into the 'o' of a handgun.

"You're in the wrong part of town, sonny," said the hugely overweight man pointing the gun in his face. "Just remount your horsey and ride back the way you came."

"I'm here to see Norrisall. I'm from Mr. Marlmaster. I'm *paid* for."

This last seemed to do the trick. The gunman waved Detroyd inside, where he instructed one of his cronies to see to Detroyd's horse. Only when they were walking down a long corridor, deep within the building, did the big man slide his gun back into his belt.

· ✳ ·

In the dreary seclusion of an ancient pub, its stale air barely more breathable than the fog outside, Deadspike watched his companion, Ottomas Slake, recount the events leading to the rounding up of certain members of the Historical Society. The private detective and his network had again proved to be the most effective method of dealing with the situation. Marlmaster and his companions had bolted, just as Deadspike had guessed they would. It would be seen by Canderville as tantamount to a confession of the murder of Sunderman's lackey and thus a vindication of Deadspike's methods, rather than those of the plodding Sunderman.

"Nearly all accounted for, Mr. Deadspike, as you required. One short of a set, for the moment." Slake tried to look comfortable, but his hands, as usual fiddling with his battered hat, betrayed his uneasiness. Mr. Deadspike liked things *right*.

"Erroll Detroyd," the Enforcer said through gritted teeth.

"Like you say, Mr. Deadspike. Mr. Detroyd took off at a right lick, straight towards the outer areas. We nearly got thrown off the scent when he got himself a horse. Someone had it ready for him. But we're used to people trying to wriggle off our hooks, sir. Always got backup when we need it. No, Detroyd took off on horseback, and we did the same. It was a long ride. Out to the Greywalls district. Do you know it, Mr. Deadspike?"

"I know of it, Slake."

"You don't go out there, sir, unless you have friends or contacts. And even then it's not somewhere as you'd want to spend much time. Some very tough boys out there. Can get a bit nasty, that Greywalls turf."

"And Detroyd?"

"Turns out he was looking for help."

"Are you saying that the Society has contacts out there?" Deadspike's humour was not improving.

"From what I can gather, seems like it. It's all about resources, Mr. Deadspike. I know the Greywalls boys. Very independent. Easy enough to do business with, on their terms. Always up for a bit of barter, a bit of dealing. Anything that pays. It's your black market centre. I got to be careful what I say, Mr. Deadspike. Don't want to compromise no one."

Deadspike knew well enough when not to poke the goose that provided so many golden eggs.

"Suffice it to say that Mr. Detroyd got himself a bed for a few nights. No questions asked. Someone would have paid off the Greywalls boys. It's not for my crew to ask them, but, like you say, very likely the Society."

Deadspike nodded. *The Society has rooted even further afield than we realized.*

"What Mr. Detroyd really wanted was a way out," said Slake.

Deadspike's expression hardened. "Out? Out of where? Londonborough?"

"Like you say, sir. To the outside. The wild lands. There are ways out, sir. I expect you know that."

Deadspike was looking at the hunched figure before him, but his eyes saw far beyond him, out to the wild forestlands beyond the furthest walls of the city. The last retreat of the desperate. So Detroyd had chosen that path, rather than betray his colleagues? *How noble,* he thought cynically.

"He's just waiting for a guide. That's how it works. The Greywalls boys fix it up and arrange for someone to take you outside. Once you're out there, you're on your own. You'd have to be bloody desperate if you ask me. Excuse my saying. Chances are the dogs'll get you in no time. Packs of them, sir. Forest is full of them. Word is, there are worse things than that. So going out is for mugs, sir. If Mr. Detroyd's going out, you can write him off your list."

The hint of a smile crossed Deadspike's pale features. "It's not in my interests for him to leave Londonborough."

Slake nodded. "Doesn't have to happen, sir. Like I say, I have my own contacts with the Greywalls boys. Be easy enough for me to arrange it so that Mr. Detroyd's guide is one of my people. Mr. Detroyd wouldn't rumble the deception, not until it was too late. We could have him back here, or wherever else you want him, in no time."

Deadspike sat back again. "Yes, that would be very appropriate, Slake. I'll have a think about where we detain Mr. Detroyd. But you go ahead. Let him think he's being escorted out of the city. For the time being, secrete him somewhere remote, far from prying eyes. Away from the others you've got penned up for me. When I'm ready for him, I'll let you know. And, of course, Slake, there will be a suitable reward for your efforts."

Slake inclined his head in a kind of bow. "I'm sure it will be appreciated, sir."

PART THREE
A CONFLICT
OF INTERESTS

XVII

PETRA / LONDONBOROUGH

DUNSTAN FULLACOMBE STRUGGLED with the piping, reaching behind the wall from which it emerged and bending it around the edge of the crude tool he was using. On his hands and knees in semi-darkness, he cursed richly.

"Don't know why you fucking bother," growled Skellbow nearby. "Why don't we leave this and get on with other things?"

"I'll get it working," said Fullacombe. "Got that spare length?"

Skellbow lifted another piece of piping and eased it towards his companion. Fullacombe took the end of the pipe and pulled it towards him. "No, the other one. This one's too thick. I showed you! There. Pass it up. Come on, my hand's dropping off."

"I can't see it."

Fullacombe cursed, patience fraying, released the pipe emerging from the wall and got to his feet. He was covered in grime and dust, hair tangled, sweat streaking his face. "For God's sake, Barry! What's the matter with you?"

"Nothing! Just didn't see it, that's all. This one?"

"You're no help at all. Look, I know you don't give a toss about the old boiler, but I say it will work and it *will* work. Nothing's ever gained without a bit of bloody hard work. You're too fond of an easy life."

"What the fuck do you mean by that?"

"We can't afford to take things easy. The Prime is leaning on all of us. If we don't pull our weight, we'll be in the shit. Now, *wake up*."

Skellbow flung down the pipe and swore again. "I'm not having it, you hear me? You calling me a slacker. That's a fucking laugh. I work as hard as anyone here. I do my job and I cover when I have to. I don't have time off. I get here on time." His voice was rising and rising and only the poor lighting hid the redness of his face.

"I'm not calling you a slacker. Don't be so stupid!"

"I'm not fucking stupid!"

Fullacombe's anger was about to shout him down with a verbal mauling of his own, but an inner voice warned him to ease off. There was something not right about Barry this morning, probably the result of another drinking session. Barry had some kind of bruise down one side of his face and every now and then shook his head slightly, as if to clear it. And he was moving slightly stiffly as if protecting more bruises. Maybe he'd been in a fight.

Fullacombe took a deep breath. "Look, Barry, I know you don't want to bother with the old boiler. But all I want you to do is—"

"Do this, do that, fucking stand on your head! Check the doors, fix the windows. Keep the Prime happy." Skellbow was ranting, ignoring Fullacombe now, locked into his mounting fury. He paced about as he swore.

"All right, Barry, calm down."

"Calm down? How can anyone stay calm in this place? Whatever you do, it's wrong! Or it's not enough. Or it's too fucking late. I'm sick of it. You can stick your fucking job!" He stood rigidly, fists clenched in impotent fury.

Fullacombe, surprised by the extremity of his reaction, took a step or two towards him. "Hey. Barry. Will you just stop a minute," he said quietly.

Skellbow glared at him, and even in the poor lighting his eyes were wide, alive with emotion. He shook his head again, sweat flicking from it.

"I'm just asking for a bit of help, that's all. Come on, let's take a break."

"I don't want a break." He picked up the pipe that Fullacombe had wanted. "This it?"

Fullacombe nodded. "Yes." He went back to the wall, knelt down, and reached for the pipe he had bent. Leaning back, he called for Skellbow to ease in the new length. It came, but Skellbow pushed too hard and it caught Fullacombe's fingers and jammed them up against the wall. The big man yelled with pain.

"Now what the fuck's the matter?" snarled Skellbow, again dropping the pipe.

Fullacombe was on his feet again, nursing his fingers. "Shit, that hurts!"

"I told you this was a stupid idea."

"Fuck off, you bloody idiot! Go on, find something else to do. I'll finish this myself. Go on, get the fuck out of it!" Fullacombe's anger broke like a bursting boil, his patience drained. Skellbow mouthed an obscenity, turned on his heel, and stormed off.

Later in the day, when Jordan Creech came on duty he sat with Fullacombe, swigging from a water bottle as he listened to Fullacombe's comments about Skellbow's behaviour.

"Seems like Barry's getting worse," said Creech. "Like a fucking cat on a hot tin roof. Can't say anything to him. I swear he's got a crucifix under his shirt! Keeps muttering about being watched. He don't mean the Prime, he means ghosts. Bloody too much beer, more like."

"Well, I'm getting pissed off with it, Jordan. Look at that." Fullacombe held out his hand and the two fingers that were badly swollen. "I almost thought the twat did it deliberately."

Creech shook his head. "I'd say he needs a break."

"Worst possible time. With the holiday coming, Trencher will have a full program of works lined up."

"Bloody world revolves around the Enforcers. So what are we going to do about Barry? You can't report him to Trencher," Creech said. It wasn't their way to shop their companions. They preferred to deal with these things themselves.

"You talk to him, Jordan. You know him best. It comes better from you. Just keep the bugger away from me for a bit."

· ✳ ·

Detroyd sat quietly on the single bed in the bare room provided for him. The only other furniture was a table. On it there was a bowl of clean, cold water. Above the bed a solitary window, barely three feet square, framed a patch of early morning sky, no less drab than it would have been in the center of Londonborough. He had slept unevenly, surrounded by silence.

They had told him they would need a little time to find him a guide to take him outside. He was dealing with a very dubious bunch, the notorious Greywalls boys, but the Society survived because it was flexible enough to recognize the need to utilize whatever resources came to hand. Dougal, his host, that huge bear of a man, grizzled and scarred by physical combat, had fed Detroyd frugally last night. Dougal had promised him anonymity until the guide showed.

Detroyd went over the events at the Academy for the dozenth time. *What of Moddack, Marlmaster, Amelia? Their cover is blown. That ghoul, Deadspike, is on to all of them. They'll have a contingency plan. An escape route. Harrald seemed almost relieved. Must have known that the Authority would stamp down eventually.*

He got up and went to the door, listening. There was no sound from the outside corridor. They appeared to have left him alone. No one had questioned him about the long bag or asked what was in it. Here in the outer city everyone kept very much to themselves.

Time plodded on to midday and beyond. Still no sign of anyone. *How long is this going to take?* He went back to the door, this time gripping its handle and giving it a slow twist. He pulled but the door resisted. Several times he tried, but only then did he understand. They had *locked* him in. Why?

Precaution? Make sure no one who might be snooping around sees me? Maybe. But this building is one of many that the Greywalls boys control. The only ones snooping around here will be their lot.

Another hour seeped away. He didn't like the silence. He began to have visions of the door opening and someone from the Authority standing there. Deadspike even.

By the time the evening was well advanced, still no one had come. Detroyd had become more and more uneasy. *Just nerves,* he told himself. But he could no longer afford to take any chances. The outside could not be far and he must get to it, guide or no guide.

He twisted the bed around so that it was upside down, its small legs pointing at the ceiling. It was only a light-framed affair and easily propped against the wall under the window. Carefully he hauled himself up and came level with the window. The light outside was failing fast, but he could see an enclosed courtyard beyond, a drop of about twelve feet. Other windows looked out onto the yard and at least one door, but there were no lights on.

He felt around the window frame for a latch. Along its bottom edge, caked in old paint, there was some kind of rusting lever. He pulled at it, almost dislodging himself from his perch, but he clung on to the narrow ledge and worked at the lever. With a splitting of old wood, it came away, and he lowered it gently down onto the sloping bed. He pushed at the window frame until it opened outwards.

Dropping to the floor, he lifted the bag onto his shoulder and heaved himself back up to the window, which was just about large enough for him to squeeze through. He felt committed now. No turning back. If they caught him and his fears were unsubstantiated, he would just laugh and say that he panicked.

Carefully he pushed his long bag through the window and lowered it by its straps as far as he could before letting it go. It dropped softly to the stone courtyard, its contents cushioned from the fall by the clothes inside it. Detroyd gripped the window frame and swung a leg up, getting it over the sill with his second attempt. He wormed his way around until he could get both legs out, resting on his stomach. He paused, listening to the interior of the building beyond his locked door. Still no sound.

Gripping the sill, he lowered himself to his full length, drew in his breath, and dropped. He hit the stone floor seconds later, bent his knees, and rolled sideways. By now it was dark and he was cloaked in shadow. Again he waited, but the night remained motionless, the starless sky above him like a ceiling.

He took up his bag, swinging it over his shoulder. From a side pocket he pulled a short knife, wide-bladed, six inches long. He had never used it on another human being, but he knew how to.

In the courtyard he could see two doors. One was opposite the window from which he had emerged. He tried its old handle and it opened with a faint creak. Silent as a ghost, he slid into the darkness within. It was a long corridor: he had no idea which way he should go. There were no lights to guide him, no distant voices or sounds of any kind. He took a chance on a right turn and started forward. He had got so far when he sensed a cross corridor ahead. He heard voices coming from it. At least two men were talking: in a moment they would come into view. And no doubt see him.

· ✳ ·

"Barry, come in, mate. Sit down." Trencher smiled, pushing a chair forward.

Slowly the caretaker lowered himself into it. His expression was clouded, his anxiety ill-disguised. Part of his face, Trencher now noted, was bruised. It bore out the concerns

that Dunstan Fullacombe had been expressing to him earlier
when he'd urged Trencher to recognize the strain Skellbow
was so obviously undergoing. "Since the incident on the wall,"
Fullacombe had said, with some reluctance.

Skellbow certainly bore all the signs of stress: apart from
his scruffiness, his eyes were bloodshot, his hands slightly
shaking. He avoided Trencher's eyes.

"Nothing bothering you?" Trencher said, trying to sound
concerned. The Brethren must have shaken him up pretty
badly. *As long as it shuts him up.* "Mrs. Skellbow all right?"

The caretaker shuddered inwardly, recalling the last time
someone had brought her name into this. The threats. He
could only nod, unable to speak.

"Your lad, Davie, I gather he's doing pretty well here.
Looking forward to finishing this term and then what? Military
academy? Oh no, he's hoping for an apprenticeship, isn't he?"

Hoping? It's all been arranged. What's he trying to say? "Davie
wants to be a blacksmith. He's going to Kelvin Rudge."

"Well, I'm sure that if he does as he should do for the rest
of his time here, that'll work out fine."

"He means to work hard."

"We all have our roles, Barry. We all need to carry out
instructions of one kind or another. We know what to say and
what not to say, don't we? In order to make things happen for
the best. None of us want anything to go wrong." Trencher
was leaning forward, fixing Skellbow with a deliberate stare.

Skellbow could not meet that gaze. He knew only too well
what the Senior Magister was implying. They were all the
same. More threats.

He nodded.

"Good. If we can all do that, everything will be okay.
Young Davie will do just fine."

Skellbow could feel the sweat trickling down his spine,
soaking through his shirt.

"Okay. Let's talk about security."

· ✳ ·

Detroyd forced himself to remain calm, to follow the prompts of
his meticulous training. No good if it couldn't be put to practi-
cal use. He glanced back the way he had come. A doorway. He
edged over to it, tried the handle. Open. In. Shadows. Large
storeroom. Wait here. Hold the door almost closed. Listen.

The two men who had been speaking up ahead must have turned the corridor into the one he had just vacated. He heard them stop walking. And their voices.

"Change of plan." It was Dougal. "Norrisall says. You okay with that?"

"Is this guy going out or not?"

"No. But he thinks he is."

Me. They're talking about me, Detroyd's mind hammered.

"Slake's been here."

"Slake? Shit, the old Roach himself?"

"Yeah. He's seen Norrisall and done some kind of deal. Now Norrisall don't want this guy taken outside. But you got to make him think that's where he's going. His lot have paid for it."

"So it's a double-cross. Shit, I don't like that."

"Fuck you, Graddis. You do what you're paid to do."

"Thought I was paid to guide people out. This guy's been paid for."

"Look, you just fucking do what Norrisall wants. If there's any shit to come, that's Norrisall's problem, not yours. You want to get prim and fucking proper, you can take it up with Norrisall. You lead this guy out now, boy, and Norrisall'll string you up."

"All right, keep your fucking hair on, Dougal. So where do I take him?"

"Block Seven. Tell him that he'll be met by someone from outside and they'll take him on to the next stage. That's all you got to do. As long as he thinks he's getting out, he won't give us any trouble."

"So what's going to happen to him?"

"Fuck knows! It's none of our fucking business! You'll get paid. Fuck me, Graddis, it's a piece of piss. Just get on with it. Here's the key. Lock him in one of the old patient rooms. This key serves all of them. Slake will take care of the rest. When you've done it, get out of it quick."

"So where's this guy?"

"Here's another key. He's in wardroom 2B. Give me a few minutes to leave and then go and fetch him out. Get him over to Block Seven quickly, then you can bugger off."

The voices stopped and Detroyd heard one of the men moving off, presumably Dougal, who had gone back into what must be the main body of the building.

Detroyd held the door almost closed, his eye to the slit of opening, waiting to see if the man called Graddis would come past. After a prolonged silence, he heard the soft shuffle of feet. Graddis, who was a thin, short man dressed in very drab, creased garments, slipped past the door. Detroyd knew that he had only seconds to seize the initiative.

He opened the door silently, slipped out into the corridor, and was behind Graddis before the man realized it. Detroyd's left arm came up and locked Graddis in a paralyzing grip, his right hand holding the knife to his neck.

"Not a word," he breathed. "I'll open you from ear to ear. I mean it."

Graddis nodded, though his head could barely move. He knew from the hold he was in that he was dealing with someone who knew about this kind of combat.

"You will take me to the outside, is that clear? So— which way? Voice down, nice and low."

Detroyd eased his grip just a fraction, so that the man could speak. "Back the way we came."

"So that Dougal can pick me off?"

"No. He's gone the other way."

"Okay. Swing round slowly. Nice and easy. Very good, Graddis. You'll come out of this in one piece if you just co-operate."

"Who are you? The guy they want to—"

"Double-cross, yes."

"I don't like it. I like to play straight."

"So do I, Graddis. So here's the deal. You get me out, just like the plan. And you get to live. Any tricks and I finish this."

"Slake'll have me filleted anyway."

"You'll find something out there. You don't have a choice." Detroyd twisted his grip a little harder.

"Okay, okay. We have to get to the corridor ahead and then go left."

· ✳ ·

The Prime strode along the corridor, her thoughts organized, her mind grappling with one of a dozen problems that required her specific attention, when a figure almost collided into her, backing out of a room carelessly. It was Barry Skel-lbow, who turned and stared in horror as he realized he had almost thumped into the Prime.

"Sorry," he gasped, leaning back.

"Are you all right, Barry? You don't look too well." There was an empty classroom beside her and she opened its door. "Come in here. I want a quick word."

He seemed to draw himself together with a huge effort and then went into the room. She followed him and shut the door.

"I realize that life's been a bit of an ordeal lately. Things aren't easy. None of us have been able to relax very much. It's difficult for me, having to ask everyone to pull that little bit harder. We can't afford to let things slip now. I'd suggest you take a few days off, but there's so much work to do right now. Do you feel up to the job?"

He looked at her as if he had been slapped. "Yes. I work hard."

"I know that, Barry. But I've noticed that a few things aren't as they should be. Windows upstairs still need repairing. And at least two classroom doors don't lock. They've been like it for a month, Barry. Now, I simply cannot afford to have the Enforcers in here with this place not ready. Everyone has *got* to pull their weight. If it's getting to be too much, or if you think there could be a slip up—"

He shook his head violently. "No. I won't slip up. I won't." He stared at the floor, fists bunching.

"That's all right," she said, then added, as if in an attempt to cushion the admonition, "I just wanted you to know that you don't have to feel no one is interested in you and what you're doing, or how you feel. Okay?"

He nodded. But inside, his heart thumped against his ribs. In the buildings or out on the streets, he was being watched. *This place is marked.*

XVIII

PETRA / LONDONBOROUGH

"**THE GREEN MAN** is a symbol of unity with the earth powers," Mundy said to Penn. "The embodiment of regeneration and harmony of all things living? Very pagan. Complete anathema to Father Emmanuel. So are the festivals related?"

"Yes. We have our own Green Man ceremony here in the town. Quite a gentle, fun affair. Harmless and peaceful. The priest tolerates it, but his teeth are gritted all the way through the ceremonies."

Mundy laughed. "I think I'd enjoy that. Anna told me I should talk to the Green Man. Who is she talking about?" In his mind he pictured the carved oaken face, wreathed in leaves, which he had seen in various places around town.

"Out in the forests there is a large community. Sort of a clan. Every year one of the leaders takes the role of the Green Man in the ceremonies. As far as the Authority is concerned, they don't exist, but in truth they're considered to be outlaws. If the Authority had more control here, it would hunt them down. In time, it will happen."

"Through the military?"

"Their Commander here is Storm Gunnerson. He's discounted the outlaw problem. Says it's not worth pursuing. A waste of time— the wilds are pretty vast."

"So what does Sebastian make of this Gunnerson? He's linked to him."

"He gets on with him. He suspects that Gunnerson is a closet sympathizer. The Commander isn't one for action. He likes a quiet life. He makes sure his base is well run and that his soldiers train hard and are ready for the so-called Invasion. But he won't commit them to any serious efforts out in the wilds. And he certainly wouldn't want to get involved in any repression of the pagan festivities. Not unless they presented a very real threat."

"So when Anna suggested that I talk to the Green Man, she meant whoever will take the role this year. Anna thinks that Drew may have shared some information with him. Something that may have a bearing on Drew's death. Penn, I'm sure it was more important than anyone realizes. Not just because it was murder. Sebastian is right. We really have to find out why he was killed. What it was he knew."

"You think he told this year's Green Man? Drew mixed with the forest people more than anyone. And some of the guys you met in the Anvil, you know, the ex-pats, Connell and his gang, they were as much at home in the forest as in Petra. All good mates of Drew's. You mentioned earth powers— well, Drew was a firm believer in that. The Green Man of antiquity and Gaia. Do you know about her?"

"The Earth Mother."

"Your knowledge surprises me."

"There's a lot about me you don't know." He grinned, but felt himself flush with embarrassment, though she was laughing, squeezed up very close beside him.

"Drew's paganism was another reason why the Prime didn't like him. She saw him as a corrupting influence. He was very popular and got on with the kids. It galled her to think that he could control them and bring them on while others more loyal to the Authority couldn't. Brin's the same. The kids respect him. They see him as fair and understanding. He kicks ass when he has to, mind. But the kids know when they deserve it."

Mundy nodded. "It's a natural gift. Brin has it in spades. Does he have contact with this year's Green Man?"

She looked around, but if anyone was trying to listen in, they would have found it impossible to eavesdrop in the general hubbub. "Yes."

"Can he arrange for me to meet him?"

"There will be an ideal opportunity during the festivities, soon. In a week's time, there'll be a ceremony across the river, about five miles inland. In an area that's officially out of bounds. Quarantined."

Mundy frowned. "Something to do with the Plague Wars?"

"Yes, an old quarry. The Authority has declared it taboo— it's supposed to be a plague pit. The main one for the area, where literally thousands were dumped after the Wars. Officially it's a disaster area. Far too dangerous to visit."

"But obviously, if you use it, it isn't."

She grinned. "It's where they mined all the stone to build the walls of Petra. And they did that years *after* the Wars. So it can't be a plague pit. We use it for some of our ceremonies. We've managed to keep the Authority's nose out of it. As far as we know, they think the place is shunned."

He would have said more but noticed someone pushing through the crowd towards them. It was the young man he had seen Penn with when he had gone looking for her. He had thick, blondish hair, and although he was wiry, he looked as though he had trained to the point where his muscles were like iron. He wore a vaguely angry expression and when he saw Penn he glowered as he came forward.

To Mundy's amazement, the youth grabbed her arm and yanked her to her feet. "I want a word with you," he snapped.

"Guy, for God's sake, what's wrong!" she protested as he pulled her away.

"Not in here," he growled.

Penn turned to the bewildered Mundy. She shrugged. "Sorry about this."

· ✳ ·

The young man pulled her with him through the crowd, elbowing people aside. Some tried to remonstrate with him but he ignored them, making for the door. He drew Penn outside, which was barely lit by an overhead cresset. He seemed glad of the poor lighting, not eager to share their conversation with anyone coming in or out of the pub.

"What on earth's the matter with you!" she snapped, tugging free.

"I thought I'd find you in there."

"So what? Since when do you monitor all my movements?"

"Since you started playing up to that new guy. Mundy, or whatever he's called."

"Don't be so stupid."

"I'm not stupid. Or blind. You're in there making a bloody fool of me. The whole fucking Academy is in there watching."

"Guy, I was just talking to Chad and the others."

"You were practically sitting in his lap."

"You're an idiot."

"Don't call me an idiot," he said bitterly, his hands clenching so that she thought he might be on the point of striking her.

"Okay, okay, calm down," she said, putting a hand on his arm, though he shrugged it off irritably. "Look, Guy, I need to talk to him. It's part of what Brin and Anna and I are trying to do."

"Not this bloody Drew Vasillius business again, Penn? What's the point? We've been over this."

She began to look more annoyed herself. "I know you don't think anything of it, but I told you, there's something behind it."

"Why can't we just get on with our lives? As if we haven't got enough to do. We should be focused on the kids, this inspection."

"I *am* focused on it."

"And why do you keep on with these bloody— pagans?"

"How come you've got religion all of a sudden? You never used to give a damn. There was a time, Guy, when you wouldn't go near a church."

"Here we go. Same old bloody thing. I told you, if I've got to be involved, I'd rather be involved with the church than that bloody crowd. They're asking for trouble. Sooner or later there'll be hell to pay. And I don't want you mixed up with them when the shit starts flying. I won't protect you."

"I don't need your *protection*." Her voice had become icy. They had retreated a little further into the shadows, their heads close, their mutual anger passing between them like a current.

"What's that supposed to mean?"

"It means, *I don't need protecting*, Guy. I have a mind of my own."

"So my feelings don't matter?"

"Your feelings? Your entire universe is built around your fucking feelings! Since when did you ever consider *my feelings* and what I want?"

"Now you're just being stupid."

"Don't call *me* stupid," she snapped.

This time he really did seem to be on the point of launching himself at her, but a small group of people were coming out of the pub. They nodded at Guy briefly and disappeared into the night.

"So are you coming home or not?" he growled.

"I'll come when it suits me."

His mouth curled in an unpleasant smirk. "Okay. Just don't expect me to be there when you get in."

"Now you're just being childish."

"Fuck it," he muttered, then gave her a dismissive wave, turning on his heel and leaving.

"Idiot," she said under her breath and went back inside.

At the table, Mundy was talking to one of the others, relieved to see Penn returning. Evidently distraught, she sat down and took a long swig of her drink.

"I know it's none of my business," said Mundy. "But are you okay?"

She snorted. "That was Guy. You had to meet him at some point. He's my... I don't quite know how to put it. Lover, I suppose. The way things are going, he'll be my ex-lover. Bastard."

Mundy wasn't sure how to respond, so he said nothing.

"Sorry, Chad. It's Guy. I'm fed up with making excuses for him. He's highly strung. Not to mention selfish, inconsiderate, and unfeeling. God knows why I put up with him." He could see that she was close to tears.

"Why do you?"

"I don't know. He's not always like that. Believe it or not, he does have a more caring side. It's just that lately he seems to be getting more and more wound up."

"Is it work?"

"No. He's fine. He gets good results. If it wasn't obvious, he teaches PE. He resents my being involved with Brin and the others. When we were first together, he didn't care one way or the other about religion or the church. But it's as if he sees my faith as a threat. As if we were in competition. I don't like sharing some of what we do as a group with him, and, naturally enough, he hates that. But I can't trust him— his temper I mean. I haven't said very much to him about next week's ceremony. I really don't want him to come, though I don't think he would anyway."

"Is he a strong Authority man?"

"He never used to be. But now I'm not sure. Maybe someone has spoken to him. The priest is always trying to inveigle people into his congregation. Guy wants to get on in life and thinks that being a good servant to the Academy is the way to do it."

"Strikes me he's the jealous type."

She looked directly at him and then away. "Yes."

"I hope I haven't caused any problems."

She shook her head. "I talk to who I like."

"Does this mean I'm to be excommunicated?"

She turned back to him and couldn't help smiling. "Don't be stupid."

"That's a relief. I don't want to miss out on this trip across the river."

She looked serious again. "Don't joke about it, Chad."

"You think it will be risky?"

She took a deep breath. "I don't know. It's like this weather. Everything is brewing up. I get the feeling that this year things are coming to a head. I don't think Guy is the only one spoiling for a fight."

"Hadn't you better go and see to him?"

She shrugged, clearly exasperated. She stared into the distance for a moment.

"I think you should," he said, breaking the awkward silence.

"You're very understanding."

"I'm the nice guy."

She squeezed his arm, rising, and left him to his thoughts.

· ✴ ·

Norrisall sat back comfortably in his elegant chair, drawing on the dark cigar. He was running to fat, the classic sign of good living, his hair slicked back and thinning. His clothes still fit him well and were the best that could be found anywhere in Londonborough. His office, which was more like a private penthouse, displayed numerous *objets d'art* ransacked from the city and was lavishly carpeted. Appearances were important to Norrisall, as the head of the Greywalls boys, reputedly the toughest, most successful black market enterprise out on the city edge.

The Londonborough Roach sat opposite him, a direct contrast. Slake hunched forward on the edge of his seat, hat across his knees. His own coat was grubby and the man looked dishevelled, little better than a street wanderer. But Slake was anything but a vagrant. He ignored the fumes drifting up from the cigar, which had so obviously been brought out for show.

"I hope you are pleased with your latest acquisition, Norry," said Slake.

Norrisall gazed over the Roach's shoulder to an opened crate. Its lid was propped up alongside it, a curiously inappropriate item for such opulent surroundings. "Indeed I am, Mr. Slake. Delighted. Only too glad to do business with you."

"Ah, yes. And you've got this geezer ready for me?"

"Ready for collection, as promised."

As if to punctuate his words, the door opened quietly and a tall, severe looking man in a very smart suit entered. The man went directly to Norrisall and leaned over, whispering something to him. Whatever he said did not go down well with the gang leader.

"You better send him in," said the latter, irritably stubbing out his cigar in a cut-glass ashtray that was the centrepiece of a very stylish coffee table.

"Is there a problem, Norry?" said Slake calmly. "Want me to leave you for a moment or two?"

"No. You may need to hear this."

Slake nodded and watched as the suited man led in yet another. But the huge, sweating man who now joined them was in direct contrast. He wore a cotton shirt that his large frame stretched to the limit, with at least two missing buttons. A worn belt held up his stained trousers and his shoes were faded, their leather cracking.

"So, Dougal, what's all this about?" said Norrisall.

The big man had seen Slake: he knew who he was. He wasn't fooled by the grubbiness of his boss's guest. The Londonborough Roach was, if anything, even more powerful in his way than Norrisall. People who messed with him and his sprawling network tended to disappear.

Sweat poured down Dougal's face. "I came as soon as I found out, Mr. Norrisall."

"Found out what?"

"It's the bloke from the military academy."

Norrisall glanced at Slake. "Detroyd? What about him?"

"He's gone, Mr. Norrisall. Disappeared."

"What the fuck are you talking about?" Norrisall snapped. He sat up straight, now ignoring Slake.

"I told the guide, Graddis, to take Detroyd out of room 2B over to Block Seven. Gave him the keys."

"He knew about the change of plan?"

"Yeah. I told him straight. Said if he fu-, if he messed up, he'd be for it."

"So what happened?"

"A bit later, I went to room 2B to see that it'd all gone off okay. Expected to see the key left in the door of 2B. But when I got there, the door was locked. I would have left it. I thought maybe Graddis had just forgotten to leave the key in it for me. But I thought I'd check. Inside."

"And?"

"Room was empty, but something was wrong. The bed was propped up against the wall. The light was poor— I only had a small oil lamp with me. But I could see that the window had been tampered with. Found this on the floor." He held up a rusting latch, fragments of worm-eaten wood still clinging to it.

"You mean," said Norrisall, his voice dropping in barely controlled fury, "that Detroyd went out the fucking window?"

"I thought he must have. So I went over to Block Seven and looked around. The room I'd set aside for him was locked. Freddie was about, but he hadn't seen anyone. Not Graddis nor Detroyd."

"So where the fuck are they?" snarled Norrisall, getting up now as if he meant to take it out on Dougal's vast bulk.

"The boys are looking. So far we ain't found them."

"Excuse me butting in," said Slake, himself rising slowly, almost lazily, from his seat. "But does this mean that Mr. Detroyd has gone— outside?"

"No way," said Norrisall coolly. "He'd never find his way out without help. Not without Graddis or one of the other guides."

"But Mr. Graddis is missing?" Slake persisted.

Dougal was nodding, his whole body quivering as Slake turned his bland gaze upon him.

"Shit!" growled Norrisall. "Okay, Dougal, get your fat arse out there and round up everyone you can find. Turn this whole fucking place upside down until you find them."

"Yes, Mr. Norrisall," said the big man, glad to lumber out of the room.

Norrisall turned to Slake, himself very uneasy. "There's no way that bastard will get away from us, Mr. Slake."

Slake seemed surprisingly unconcerned. Either that or he was a master at concealing his own emotions. "Mr. Detroyd is a slippery young man, Norry. It doesn't surprise me that he wriggled out of his room. Maybe he suspected something."

"He won't get far at night."

"No, I'm sure. But if he gets out, then what? My employer would be pretty pissed off if he evaded recapture and was lost to the wilds."

Norrisall was sweating now. This was not good.

"Let me make a suggestion," said Slake. He moved across to the crate and looked down into it, a hint of a frown creasing his features as if what he saw within was unpalatable. "Your new toys, Norry." *Far more valuable than anything the Historical Society would have paid you.*

Norrisall came over. He also looked into the crate, but his face displayed only pleasure. "Oh, yes." He leaned over. "Very nice, Mr. Slake. Top quality, if I'm not mistaken."

"Certainly. Don't get many being made these days. But the skill isn't entirely lost. I reckon there'll be more and more of these showing up."

"These from the Academy?"

Slake grinned. "Best not to ask, Norry. But, yes. They are. Can your mob handle them?"

"Be the same principle as the guns they're used to. Slicker, obviously. Less likely to blow up in their faces."

Slake nodded, reaching down and picking up one of the weapons. He lifted it and swung it easily as if used to its balance. The mouth of the rifle casually lined up on Norrisall's chest.

"I hope this isn't a double-cross, Norry. I hate double-crosses. They get so messy, don't you think?"

Norrisall stared in dread at the gun. "Come on, Mr. Slake! I'm your client. We'll find that bastard. No question."

"If Mr. Detroyd has gone outside, you still need to find him. Bring him back, if you can. Preferably alive."

"But if not?" said Norrisall, cringing.

Slake sighted down the barrel and pulled the trigger. It clicked on an empty chamber. "If you have to shoot him, do it," said Slake, with an evil grin. "Don't hesitate. I wouldn't."

XIX

LONDONBOROUGH

DETROYD EASED GRADDIS along the corridor until the guide gasped instructions. "Down those stairs. Door at the bottom. I've got the key." It was an effort for him to speak: Detroyd's grip around his neck showed no sign of weakening and the blade felt cold at his neck.

The stairwell was unlit, running down into darkness. "Keep going," prompted Detroyd. The long bag strapped to his back was becoming a burden, his shoulder muscles aching.

"Let me go for a moment. I'm not going anywhere."

"Just take it slow and easy." Detroyd nudged him forward and Graddis very gently moved to the stair head. Step by step he went down into the well. Detroyd glanced up and down the corridor, but there was no one else visible. At the small landing, Graddis swore as he stumbled slightly, but Detroyd righted him with a jerk. Then they were climbing down into deeper darkness. They had to turn another three times at landings but eventually Graddis halted. The silence closed in on them like a fist. Detroyd could feel the man's heart thudding as he fought panic.

"This is it. There's a door. I need the key. It's in my left breast pocket."

"Okay, slip it out."

Graddis struggled to get his right hand up to his chest, but after a brief fumble pulled out a key. "Door's in front of us. Move me closer. Can't see a fucking thing."

Detroyd moved them together, crab-like. Graddis used his right hand to feel for the door outline, grunting when he got it. He fingered the darkness, locating the keyhole and twisting the key in place. A dull click sounded.

"Open it," said Detroyd.

Graddis did and there was a brief squeak of hinges. A waft of cold, musty air spilled over them, the reek of rotting vegetation.

"Stinks, don't it?" said Graddis. "Bat droppings. But they'll not be back until dawn. There's a platform inside. And some makeshift torches. Always got a few ready to use."

They edged inward. "Close the door and lock it," said Detroyd.

Graddis did so.

"Who else has a key?" said Detroyd, knowing that Graddis could easily lie.

"Only one of the others upstairs. And a couple more guides, but they're outside, until they're called in. Shit, you going to ease off now?"

"Get us some light and we'll see."

Graddis worked them over to a wall, groped about in the pitch darkness and pulled from a hidden niche a torch. "I need to get my flint from my trouser pocket."

"Okay. Slowly."

Graddis obeyed and a moment later was holding the flint. "Can't light the torch with one hand."

Detroyd paused, thinking it over. He released his grip, but kept his left hand on Graddis's shoulder, the knife blade in his right hand still touching the man's neck.

Graddis gripped the torch and stroked his flint down the roughness of wall. Sparks zipped and surprisingly quickly he had ignited the torch, a length of wood, rounded like a thin branch, with what looked like rags bound around the top section. These had been soaked, probably in oil, and now burned with a vivid orange and yellow flame. The shadows retreated from the glow like a great flock of birds and the sight revealed made Detroyd grunt in amazement.

For a moment his attention was off Graddis, but the guide just held up the torch so its light could reveal as much of the immense chamber as possible. Detroyd was torn between gaping at the view and watching Graddis.

"Enjoy the scenery," said the guide, stepping forward to the edge of what was a steel platform, high up above the chamber's floor. "I ain't going anywhere. I told you, I can't go back on my own. If they know you've got away, they'll do for me. Mr. Slake doesn't like mistakes."

Detroyd nodded, but made sure he was between the guide and the locked door. There were twisted metal stairs leading from the platform down towards a series of several more, a drop to the semi-visible floor of about sixty feet. The chamber was the size of a cathedral, its ceiling another sixty feet or more overhead, almost completely obscured in shadow. It contained a mass of the most bizarre, contorted shapes that Detroyd could have imagined. Huge, fat pipes and long runs of steel wire ran in all directions, some emerging from the high wall behind the platform, others dropping down into the floor, while yet more curved across to the obscurity of the far wall.

"What the hell is it?" said Detroyd, unable to mask his surprise.

"Dunno exactly. Engines and pumps. That's what people call this lot. Something from before the Plague Wars. Mostly it's all dead, but then again you get weird noises sometimes, like the pipes are full. Maybe they take the rain away when we get a storm. See how thick they get?"

Detroyd nodded, but he was more fascinated by the state of the place, which looked as though someone had sculpted a grotesque landscape out of candle wax or something equally glutinous and white. Everything was either coated or smeared in the stuff and in places it hung down like frozen waterfalls, thick globules of muck suspended in mid-movement. "What *is* that stuff?"

Graddis chuckled. "Bat shit, mate. A million tons of bat shit. You wait till you see the buggers! The ceiling heaves with them when they come back in."

Detroyd suddenly appreciated what he was seeing. The bats must have been nesting in here for countless years and the accumulation of their droppings had built up this unique residue. And it accounted for the pungent smell.

"So how do we get out?"

Graddis pointed to somewhere across the vault, way down below them. "There's a couple of places where the ivy and stuff outside has breached the outer wall. Just enough for us to squeeze through. Luckily the bats don't use the same passages." He held up the torch again, throwing as much light across the yawning chasm as he could. However, the upper wall was too far across to be seen in much detail. "They use some opening up there to come and go. Just as well. You wouldn't want to get caught up in that lot. They're harmless and they can't hit you when they're flying. But they scare the crap out of you, believe me."

Detroyd was almost amused by Graddis's enthusiasm for the place. But it was the guide's domain and he was evidently proud of it.

"Soon as daylight appears, in they come."

"Then we need to get moving."

Graddis glanced across at him, his face abruptly wrinkled in concern. "Moving? Where to?"

"Outside," said Detroyd. "What did you think?" He lifted the knife slightly.

"It's *night* out there. You don't want to go out there now. You need to wait."

"For what?"

"Daylight. I told you, the bats won't bother us. They'll be above us. But if we try to go outside now, the dogs will be on us. The woods are outside, pressed right up to the wall. The trackways are narrow and there aren't many of them. So the dogs use them, just like us. And they hunt in packs. Big packs, some of them. Nasty bastards. Rip you to pieces. It's bad enough in daylight. But at night, forget it. We wouldn't get a hundred yards."

"You said if you went back, Slake would get you," he said. "Who's he?"

"I work for different people along the outer walls. This north-western section is run by the Greywalls boys. Their boss is Norrisall. Now, he's a tough character is Norry. No one messes with him. Not even the nobs from the city. But Mr. Slake runs an even bigger network. Everyone knows him. They call him the Londonborough Roach. There's nowhere that he doesn't know: he's got contacts everywhere."

"What's he got to do with me?"

Graddis glared at him for a moment and then must have decided that there was no point trying to be deceptive. "I was told by Norrisall's lot there was someone to take outside— you. Detroyd, is it? I was all fixed up to get you out in the usual way—"

"You do this a lot?"

"There's always someone wants to get outside. Usually with a price on their head. Slake told Norrisall that you weren't to go outside. His boys told me to take you to somewhere else but pretend to you I was taking you out."

"Where were they going to take me?"

"To Slake, for sure."

"I've never had anything to do with him. What could he possibly want with me?"

"You must have upset somebody, pal. Somebody wants you."

In the guttering light, Detroyd realized who it must be. "Does Slake have contacts with the Central Authority?"

Graddis screwed up his face as though Detroyd had uttered a profanity. "Those bastards? Come to think of it, the Roach would swap his own mother for a bundle of contraband. Yeah, you're probably right. You upset the Authority?"

Detroyd didn't answer.

"So what do you want to do? Hide? Until dawn? If we go out now, you might as well slit both our throats. I tell you, we'd be fucked out there."

"If this man Slake catches up with us, you'll be a dead man. And I might as well be. I think I'd rather take my chances with the dogs."

"For fuck's sake!" gasped Graddis. "I'm serious, pal, we're dead meat out there. Look, I can keep us out of sight until dawn. They won't find us. They don't know this place like I do." His terror was genuine enough.

Detroyd paused to let him sweat for a bit longer. "Okay. Take us to somewhere safe. But, I've warned you, if anything goes wrong, I'll use this knife. If you can be sure of one thing in life, I will finish you."

"You've made your point! Fuck it, I hear you." Graddis studied the eerie landscape and gestured with the torch. "There's a way further along the wall. It's pretty shitty, but we'd soon be out of this area. They'll spend days looking for us. Even dogs would never sniff us out in that stuff. You wait till you get below. Where we're going, you'll need to cover your face. It stinks like you wouldn't believe."

Detroyd hefted his bag and motioned with the knife for Graddis to descend. The guide did so, laboriously working his way down the steep metal steps, careful to avoid the worst of the bat droppings that made it slick and dangerous. Detroyd followed, periodically looking back up at the door they had locked behind them. But no one appeared. It was a long drop downward and as they reached the final rungs, the canyon of pipes into which they had debouched rose up intimidatingly on either side.

In a perverse way Graddis seemed to be enjoying the flight. The stench of the bat droppings had become almost overpowering and Detroyd almost gagged more than once, but the threat of capture spurred him on through the deepening muck underfoot. It was a long trudge through more rows of pipes and metal spars, across to the far wall of the chamber and then along it, avoiding broken edges of metal and snarled chunks of detritus.

After what seemed like half the night, Graddis pronounced their surroundings safe enough. "I can't see anyone digging us out of here," he said. "But it's not a good idea to keep the light going." He waved the torch, which was burning lower, almost out anyway. He had brought two spares with him from above. The prospect of being plunged into darkness was not something Detroyd relished. What he really needed now was a decent sleep for a few hours. He was getting very tired, his shoulder aching like hell with the weight of the bag, but he dared not risk falling asleep with Graddis here. It would be easy enough for the guide to slip back above and bring the thugs to recapture him. And save his own arse.

Detroyd sat on a pipe section that had somehow avoided being coated in muck. He undid his bag and reached in for something. Graddis watched him from across the narrow gap, like a dog awaiting a command to make a break. Detroyd pulled out a roll of twine, used mainly for stringing his bow. Slowly and deliberately he cut a length and put the roll back in the bag.

"If I take a nap, I want you here when I wake up." He eased over to Graddis, who looked appalled.

"Shit, you don't have to tie me up. Why can't you trust me?"

"Put your right hand over that pipe. Do it!"

Graddis swore crudely but did as he was told, ramming the torch into the nearest pile of bat droppings. Quickly and expertly Detroyd tied him to the pipe. Graddis winced and moaned about loss of circulation, but Detroyd ignored him. Satisfied that both the guide's hands were incapable of undoing the tight knots, Detroyd sat back. "Wouldn't you do the same?"

Graddis snorted. "Yeah, yeah. But I told you I'd get you out. At first light."

They sat in silence for a while. Detroyd found the eerie lack of sound disturbing. "So what is out there?" he said.

"Forest. Hundreds of miles of it."

"Many people?"

"Not that you'd find. They keep to themselves. I deal with two groups. They're like tribes. Simple sort of life. Just want to be left to their own devices. Trade a bit. They do okay for food. The hunting is brilliant. So you going to join them?"

Detroyd made no reply so Graddis rolled onto the pipe to make himself comfortable. "I'm knackered. I'm going to sleep. But I reckon you want to put that torch out. If they come after us, they'll see the glow."

Detroyd nodded, taking the torch from its mucky resting place. With a final glance at Graddis, he plunged its head into the muck and heard it sputter out. The darkness closed in on them like a black wave, engulfing them utterly. Detroyd suppressed a gasp and sat back uncomfortably. And waited.

· ✳ ·

"This is appalling!" Sunderman gasped. "I never dreamt that the Historical Society would stoop to murder! But it is them, isn't it? That knife— and now the flight of their principal members. It has to be them."

"We'll soon have the truth," said Deadspike with a smile that set Sunderman's nerves on edge. "Tannerton, Moddack, and Marlmaster are all being detained."

"You've apprehended them?"

"I thought it best. I've had them all under observation for some time."

Sunderman's thoughts churned, the implications of what Deadspike was saying not fully registering. He'd seen Canderville earlier and been told to keep well out of the affair. Canderville had been livid about the murder. So was Deadspike in charge of the situation? What was going on here?

"I was concerned about specific members of the Society," said Deadspike. "They have all been removed to where they can do no harm. One, regrettably, appears to have slipped his custodians."

Sunderman's face was ashen. "Who?"

"Erroll Detroyd. He fled to the north-western boundary shortly after I interviewed him. I had a message a short while ago to say that he was making a break for the outside."

"*What?* Where is he now?"

"Those who watch over the escape routes are well armed, sir."

"You mean with *guns*?"

"We police their activity quite strictly. The Greywalls thugs are only too glad to cooperate with us. Executing one runaway is well within their capabilities."

"Is it necessary to kill him?"

"Not if you're prepared to let him escape the city, sir. We have no idea yet what information he is carrying. If it gets outside—"

Canderville would crucify me, Sunderman thought, slumping back. *And I am now relying totally on Deadspike to get me out of this mess.*

· ✳ ·

Detroyd snapped awake, pulled out of sleep by the sharp, low call of Graddis. But it was the strange sound high overhead that snared Detroyd's attention, rather than the urgent voice of his companion.

"The bats. Dawn's just about up. Come on, let me loose. Time to get moving."

Detroyd rubbed at his eyes, unable to focus at all at first, but then the vaguest of light filtered in from somewhere. By its pale glow he could just discern the slumped shape of Graddis. He went to him and used his knife to slit the bonds that held him. Graddis swore profusely, rubbing circulation back into his wrists.

"Don't light the torch," said Detroyd softly.

Graddis grunted, setting the torch down. Detroyd swung his bag onto his back and let Graddis lead off down the narrow alley of pipes. Gradually the seeping dawn light strengthened. The bats swarmed like bees far overhead, wings thrumming the air. There must have been thousands of them: the high vaults heaved with their movement.

The guide came to a great gash in the wall, some five feet wide, the stones thrust apart by the staggering power of the vegetation and its slow but inexorable force, which had widened the tall crack. Graddis turned to Detroyd. "Keep close to me. It's about twenty to thirty feet thick, this wall. Once we're through, there's a slope made up of leaves and rotted branches and the like that starts right from the exit point. Soft underfoot, but we go down to its base. There's about thirty feet of grass before we hit the trees. Once we're out, move fast and don't stop until we're in them."

Graddis turned, worming his way into the crack. Detroyd followed, just about managing to get his bag through with him. They were in the dark for a moment, but up ahead the dawn brightened second by second. Detroyd thought he was going to get snared by the crumbling brickwork and knuckles of thick ivy, but he got through. Graddis was at the exit.

"Ready? Get down the slope. Over on our right there's a gate into the city. It should be closed. There's a bridge running out into the forest. Ignore it and just run."

They exchanged a final nod and then Graddis was out, sliding down the slope he had described. Detroyd followed, dropping onto the spongy bed and immediately sliding downward towards the tall grass expanse that bordered the forest. Graddis stumbled at the bottom, tumbling forward but rolling as if he had done it a hundred times. Detroyd kept his feet, passing the guide as he reached the bottom. Then he was up and sprinting through grass half his height. It was slow progress but Graddis was close, breath rasping with effort. Halfway to the trees, they heard a sharp crack of sound from what must have been the bridge and then several more.

"Shit!" snarled Graddis. "The bastards have got guns. Get to the trees!" There was panic in his voice now and Detroyd barely resisted the urge to look across to where the stone bridge loomed over them.

They've been waiting for us, he thought. *That's why they didn't bother to come down into the pipe chamber. They knew we'd have to come out. And when.*

But he made it to the trees, just as the air around him zipped and buzzed as if with a dozen furious hornets. He heard the *whump* of the earth as what must have been bullets struck impotently but terrifyingly close. Once into the trees, dragging in huge lungfuls of air, he paused, waiting for Graddis. There was a heart-stopping delay before the guide came limping out of the grass, face ghastly with pain.

"My fucking leg!" he moaned. "They've hit me in the leg." He reached out as if to pull himself into the trees, but his back gave a sudden lurch and he twisted sideways as if he had been buffeted by an invisible fist, dropping down to his knees, sprawling in the grass. He was still yards from the first of the trees.

"Graddis!" Detroyd cried. For a moment he was about to rush out to the stricken man, but the crack of gunfire and the

thud of bullets into the tree bolls sent him back. They were
on to him now. He dared not show himself. Graddis's head
appeared from the grass, a smear of crimson running down
his chin, soaking his shirtfront. He was spitting blood. "Fuck,
fuck! You go on. I'm done for." He sank down like a man going
under waves. Another swarm of bullets zipped around him,
confirmation that rescue was out of the question.

Detroyd swore but he had no alternative. He swung back
into the trees. Thirty feet further on, he saw the path. It ran
back to the bridge in one direction and off to the west in
the other. He ducked down and loped along it, wishing he
could jettison his bag, but knowing that was the last thing
he should do. Voices shouted out from behind him and more
bullets hummed overhead. But they were far too close. He
needed cover, veering into the long grass again. Exhausted,
he dropped down and fumbled the bag open. With practiced
speed, he pulled out the bow and several arrows. Jamming
the arrows into the soil, he strung the bow and fitted a first
arrow to it. He heard footfalls on the path, heralding several
pursuers. They were off the bridge now, near at hand, hom-
ing in on him like the dogs he and Graddis had sought to
avoid last night.

Gun versus bow. No time to think ahead. Just act.

XX

PETRA / LONDONBOROUGH

FATHER MADDING HAD rehearsed his words for his meeting with Chad Mundy carefully. Mundy was still an unknown quantity. Madding had quizzed Wilkinson gently last night about Mundy's movements, but the youngster had revealed nothing about the teacher that suggested he was a threat. Wilkinson had seen him with Goldsworthy's crowd, but Mundy had not been back to Overwater or made contact with people like Anna Vasillius. The Brethren, also shadowing Mundy, had confirmed this.

"Chad, I take it you got my message?"

"Yes, Andrew Wilkinson passed it on. How can I help you, Father?"

"Well, you'll recall our last conversation— drink, by the way?"

"Thanks." Mundy accepted the glass of cold well water. Even though it was early morning, already the air was heavy, almost leaden.

"It's just that the festivities will be underway soon. I wondered what sort of involvement you are likely to have."

"I've been invited to attend a few events. Some of them in preparation for the festival in the town." Mundy had gone over this carefully with Wroxton. He was clear on what to say and what to avoid.

Madding's eyes betrayed his greed for knowledge. He was trying to appear relaxed, but Mundy sensed the tension in the man.

"I understand that during the main festival, there are various processions and dances. A celebration of nature," said Mundy.

"We encourage everyone to treat it as a recognition of all creation, all God's bounty. But I fear that the pagan element drives it, Chad. It's an excuse to flaunt their crude beliefs, a return to primitivism. It's not healthy."

"Well, apparently these things have to be rehearsed. And some of these events take place away from the town, so that the dances, the costumes, and all the other displays are only unveiled during the parades on the appointed days. Part of the mysticism, I guess."

"Yes and you can imagine the potential for disaster!" The priest snorted. "The people get very excitable. The pagan rites and rituals are, in my view, partly used as an excuse for, well, let's be blunt, Chad, the excesses of the flesh. I'm sure a young man like you would find that sort of comment risible, but in my experience, it's the sort of behavior that can all too easily lead to moral decay - the undermining of all we are trying to build. Oh, I don't begrudge people their fun and the genuine celebrations of the good things about us, but this goes much deeper than that. If the people can't control themselves, we have to do it for them. It's a vital role for the church. But I'm preaching, Chad."

Mundy smiled. "No, I understand, Father." *Only too well. The Authority has trained you thoroughly.*

"You said there were to be certain activities across the river?"

Mundy nodded. "Rehearsals. I've agreed to join one of the dance teams in a tribute to the forest and its annual cycle of growth and re-generation. That sort of thing. It sounds harmless enough."

"It should be. And it would be wrong to suppress it. As long as it conforms to decency and aspires to the true growth of the community, then embrace it. Everything out there, all that immense wilderness, is God's creation, Chad. The cycle turns through His grace, not ours."

Mundy nodded solemnly.

"I'm not asking you to betray your friends, Chad. Or to reject all the ideals inherent in their thinking. But idolatry, blasphemy and sin in general— such things have led to the fall of our world. I just need to know what they are doing. Sometimes foresight can be invaluable. To avert, if not di-saster, well, at least, painful circumstances. In many ways these pagans are like children! Who knows better than you that they need to be protected from themselves."

Mundy grinned. "Quite."

"We have had our dark days, even here. Things could have been worse. The dissident elements have not conducted themselves well. Your own arrival here comes on the back of a very sad incident. You know about it, of course?"

"Drew Vasillius? Yes. A tragedy."

Madding nodded. "And a warning for us all. We're all subject to pressures. How much do you know about it, Chad?"

"I didn't like to pry, Father. Obviously everyone's still sensitive about it."

"Naturally. Well, it is true that he was under pressure. He had his fair share of responsibility at the Academy: during the time before and during the inspection, he was undoubtedly leaned on. The Enforcers demand high standards and so does the Prime. But Drew Vasillius was a strong character. Pressure of work alone would not have been enough to push him to suicide."

Mundy nodded slowly. *What is behind this? Madding knows exactly what happened to Vasillius. He was part of it.*

"It's not something that people like to talk about, Chad. I know you must be wondering why I've brought it up. Talking about the pagan rituals put me in mind of Drew. He and I got on, but he wanted as little to do with the church as possible. He was very involved with the dissidents. And I believe it was that involvement that cost him his life."

Mundy managed to make himself look surprised.

"The Prime and Drew had several very tough interviews. He was told to rein in his pagan leanings. If the Prime thought he was having a dubious influence on the students, she would have given Drew an ultimatum. Possibly dismissal. But Drew wouldn't have taken that lightly. He certainly wouldn't have put aside his pagan beliefs."

"So you think that was as much to do with his suicide?"

"Yes, that and one more thing. I shouldn't say anything, but I am concerned about what you are getting into, Chad."

The lies slip so easily from his tongue. "I appreciate that, Father."

"Drew's involvement with the foresters, the true pagans, led him down a volatile path. I think there was a time, maybe twenty years ago, when he had to make a difficult choice. Remain at the Academy and develop what was a promising career here. Or go into the wild lands and join the people out there. The choice was made even more difficult by the scandal."

Mundy said nothing, but this was something new. *Another red herring?*

"I told you that the pagan rituals encourage a type of behavior which can bear difficult consequences, Chad. They certainly did for Drew. Putting it simply and, I regret, a little crudely, he had a woman out there. A young girl, no doubt impressed by his charisma— he had plenty of that."

"Was he married at the time— to Anna, isn't it? Did she know about this?"

"I don't think so. There were only a few of us that did know. Brin Goldsworthy, as Drew's firmest friend here in Petra, knew. I suspect that Sebastian Wroxton knew, too. Carl Trencher, necessarily, through professional involvement. People were appropriately discreet. Drew was not, however: the affair produced a child. Sadly, Drew and Anna had tried to have children of their own but were unable to. Drew blamed himself. Perhaps his affair was a way of proving himself— who knows? Men do strange things, especially where issues of manhood are involved."

Mundy listened to the almost casual revelations, momentarily taken off-guard, though he managed to feign indifference. "How old would the child be now? Twenty?"

"A little less. It was a son. But who he is and where he is, no one here knows. The mother and the boy stayed across the river and there has been no mention of them in Petra since. I'm sure some people know, but they are all understandably discreet."

Mundy's mind was racing. If this were true, if this really had happened, then how did it sit with what Anna had told him? About genetic inheritance?

"So Drew Vasillius suffered other pressures. After this, he spent less and less time with the pagans. He held firm to his beliefs, but remained with his wife and applied himself at the Academy. You can imagine the strain he was under. It must all have become too much for him. It's a treacherous path, Chad. Our world is not a stable one. The slightest rebellion or deviation from the things we have set in place to protect ourselves can cause grief, pain, and, in the case of poor Drew, disaster. Now, I do want you to be my ears and eyes out there. But I ask you to be very careful. Don't take risks. Don't give anyone, especially the dissidents, a hold over you. Put your faith in God. He won't disappoint you."

Mundy rose. He met the priest's level gaze. "You've been very patient, Father."

"I try to be. Come and talk to me again soon."

So what you really want, Father, is the name of Drew's illegitimate son. So that you can have him erased, just as you erased Drew? Close the bloodline.

· ✳ ·

Detroyd instinctively called upon the rigorous training he had undertaken, forcing himself to behave mechanically, coldly, to maximize his body's potential under attack. Fear, panic, uncertainty— all these would, he knew, work against him. He had to flatten them all out, control his reactions and act quickly and decisively. He had never killed anyone and he had to thrust the thought that here and now he may have to do so to the back of his mind. Disciplined accordingly, he reared up, took in at one glance the view along the path and the men coming down it towards him, fixed on the first of them, and released an arrow.

He was ducking down and fitting another arrow before he could even see the flight of the first. Then he was up again, unleashing the second arrow before dropping back down. He moved his position, keeping the arrows in the ground near at hand.

On the path, two men from the city were knocked clean off their feet by the power of those first two arrows and the astonishing speed of their flight. Both arrows had pierced the men's throats, the arrowheads bursting from the back of their heads. Detroyd's precision was immaculate. The other men immediately scattered into the long grass, firing off bursts of ammunition aimlessly, as if the noise alone would frighten off any ambushers.

Detroyd rose up quickly, saw that his pursuers had taken cover, and ducked back down again. Time to move away. The path was the easiest and quickest route to freedom, but it would be too easy for them to pick him off in the open. He hunched down, took his arrows, and ran in an awkward crouch for the trees. When he reached their shade, he skirted their edge. The tight undergrowth made progress difficult.

He heard shouts behind him and knew that the men were following, getting closer. In the brief moments that he had stood up and fired, he had seen about a dozen of them. Unless he outran them or found a bolt-hole soon, they would recapture him, possibly even shoot him. If Deadspike was behind this, he would rather have him dead than escaped.

"You in the trees!" shouted a voice from no more than twenty feet away in the grass. "Chuck your bow down and come out. Otherwise we'll fuckingwell blow you apart! You've got no fucking chance of getting away from us."

It would be difficult to pick them off one at a time. They were wiser now, trying to encircle him for sure. As soon as he showed himself, even for an instant, they would send a swarm of bullets his way. If he gave himself up, there was nothing to say they wouldn't just carry out their threat and kill him. And going back to Deadspike as a prisoner was not an option.

A sound behind him, the soft snap of a twig, made him swing round, another arrow fixed and aimed. He was facing a pointed shaft, a makeshift javelin. It was inches from his heart. The man wielding it was crouched down, like him, hidden in the grass. His face was bronzed and bearded and the eyes regarded him keenly. Even if Detroyd released the arrow, the spear would gut him.

"Don't move," the man said, barely above a whisper.

From another direction, Detroyd heard the unmistakable drumming of hooves. With his free hand, the spearman put a finger to his lips and it was only then that Detroyd realized, with something of a shock, that this man was not here to kill him.

The riders were coming from the west, thundering down the path. Detroyd heard them pull up close by. Someone whistled and the man with the spear gestured with the weapon for Detroyd to drop down. "Get flat to your belly," he said, doing so himself.

"They've got guns," Detroyd told him, obeying the instruction.

"We heard them. Come on, get behind me and weave towards the track. Quickly!"

Detroyd crouched and rescued his arrows. He tossed them into the bag and slung it over his shoulder, clutching his bow as he ducked and weaved his way to the track behind the bearded man. More bullets zinged through the air, inches above them. As they came to the track, Detroyd saw a score of horsemen, all dressed in skins and pelts, some carrying spears, others with bows, their arrows fixed on the path to the city. One of the men, who was at their head and who appeared to be their leader, made a gesture and moments later a hail of arrows tore into the long grass on either side of the path where the pursuit lay hidden. The cries and curses made it clear that the arrows had wreaked a degree of havoc.

One of the men at the rear of the group beckoned Detroyd over and reached down a burly arm. "Get up behind me," he called. Detroyd didn't hesitate. He gripped the arm and swung up in a flowing movement, clamping his thighs to the horse with practiced ease. The rider twisted the horse around and raced back up the trackway, a group of the forest riders breaking off from the main body and following. The overhanging trees closed in like massive green fists, sheltering the fleeing riders, the shadows of the forest claiming them.

Behind them, Detroyd heard the rattle of gunfire, spasmodic and uncoordinated, quickly diminishing. He thought he heard cries, harsh and feral. But soon there was silence, broken only by the immediate thudding of hooves and the snort of the horses as they drove on at breakneck speed into the embracing wall of foliage.

· ✳ ·

Deadspike used an ornate paperknife to slit open the envelope and pulled out a note given to him by Eversley. The Enforcer's face betrayed no shred of emotion as he read the words.

To Nightingale —

> *Mundy is to attend some preparations for the festivities. He has been primed to observe, learn, and report. We believe that he will not disappoint.*

> *Your Father.*

Deadspike read the message twice before filing it in one of his drawers. *So, you still think Mundy is inclining towards us, do you, Father?* He finally glanced up at Eversley. "No reply, Eversley. By the way, any news about the detainees?"

"They're still undergoing questioning by Mr. Karswell and the Interrogation Section. I am expecting Mr. Karswell's man later this morning, with full reports," said his assistant.

Deadspike nodded, barely managing not to grimace.
Karswell was one of the few associates who made him feel
truly uncomfortable. But then, that was Karswell's job, making people feel that the end of the world was imminent. And
he was very good at it.

· ✳ ·

Norrisall stared in open-mouthed horror at the chaotic scene.
The room, a cold, bare storage chamber, where a number of
old tables were pulled up in a central heap, was choked with
discarded boxes and papers. But it was not these that had
caused Norrisall to rant and swear effusively.

Tossed almost contemptuously across the tables like sacks
of grain were the bodies of two of his men. Their upper torsos
were smeared with dried blood, both their throats dark with
it. The cause of this mess was only too evident: each man had
been shot through the neck with an arrow. Both offending
items remained grotesquely embedded in the dead men.

Dougal stood to one side, his expression mortified. Beside
him, another guard waited in silence, like a disgraced child.

Norrisall walked around the corpses, his feet abruptly
kicking up against something else on the floor. He looked
down to see a third corpse, its face hidden in the darkness.
"Is this another one of ours?"

"No, sir," said the guard. "It's Graddis, sir."

"Graddis? The fucking guide who betrayed us?" snarled
Norrisall.

"Yes, sir. We shot him."

Norrisall gave the body a vicious kick. The cadaver was
stiff and unyielding. "But you didn't shoot Detroyd? He got
away? Is that it?"

"He had help, sir. A bunch of outsiders. Must have been
at least fifty of them, sir. Pinned us down and got Detroyd
out on horseback before we could stop them."

"How many of them did you shoot?"

The guard shuffled his feet, staring at them disconsolately.
"None, sir."

"I gave you *guns*, you arsehole! How many guns did *they*
have? Well?"

"None, sir."

"Bows and arrows. Against guns. Fuck me, you're brilliant!
Two dead men and my prisoner escaped. The Roach is going

to raise hell about this. You want to tell him? You want to explain to him how a bunch of men armed with guns were made to look like a lot of wanking idiots by *savages with bows and arrows?* Get the fuck out of here! Go on! Before I blow your fucking brains out."

The man was about to make good his escape, relieved to have got away with no more than a tongue-lashing, when Norrisall called him back.

"Wait! What about the guns? These two men here had guns. Did you recover them?"

The gaping mouth of the guard was answer enough.

"No. You didn't. So we just lost two brand new guns. The Roach is going to love us. We can afford to lose two twats like these. Ten a fucking penny. But the guns! Have you any idea what it costs me to get us guns?"

Norrisall kicked at Graddis's corpse, the sound like someone beating a hunk of beef with a paddle.

XXI

NOVA CALLEVA / PETRA

THE RIDERS POUNDED through the forest for two hours: to Detroyd time seemed condensed, so swift was the journey. These men knew the terrain intimately, keeping in the main to the trackway, but eventually branching off it to ride alongside a stream that had almost dried up in the fierce summer heat wave. They rose up through endless pine trees, the going easier as there was little sunlight penetrating the overhead cover and none of the strangling undergrowth of the main forest. Throughout the journey the men were mostly silent. They seemed very confident, very much adapted to their surroundings, but Detroyd noticed how alert they were, their ears evidently attuned to any sound that was alien to the terrain.

At the crest of the rise, they left the trees for an open valley that curved upwards to higher uplands and a cloudless sky. They rode more leisurely through the long grass. Presently Detroyd saw a line of tall wooden fencing running across the valley, a palisade that blended into the natural V of the valley, invisible from a distance. It was a settlement, fortified against any potential attack and he could see that it would be easily defended. The leading riders waved to the figures up in the two watchtowers that looked imposingly down on them.

After a brief pause, the company rode on and two wide gates swung open to admit it. Detroyd was stunned by the settlement. It was like something from the far past— a hill fort from the Iron Age. Numerous huts and buildings had been set out around a series of streets and there were corrals for horses, what looked like a mill, and more than one farrier's workshop. Scores of men, women, and children hurried about, working and playing, deeply immersed in what they were doing. Some paused briefly to call out to the riders. There was an extraordinary sense of *busyness* about the place— an amazing contrast to the long silences of Londonborough and the discreet movements of its inhabitants, as well as the almost overpowering quiet of the endless forest. Detroyd felt an immediate response to this hive-like retreat, as though something within him that had been shut away was stirring.

He was taken to a central part of the settlement, built on a rise above the stream that bisected the place. It had its own palisade and a long house with a beautifully crafted thatched roof. The men dismounted, and the horses were taken directly to water, and drank eagerly.

Detroyd was escorted by two of the men, both the one who had first discovered him and the one on whose horse he had been brought here, to the door of the long hut. Neither man had spoken to him on the journey: he wondered if he were a guest or a prisoner. But these people were renegades, fugitives. Or so the Authority would have viewed them. They were bound to be cautious.

It was mercifully cool within the hut and it took a few moments for Detroyd's eyes to accustom to its shade. A tall, muscular man was seated on an elaborate, carved chair. Again Detroyd was reminded of something from a long lost age. The man rose and came over to offer his hand.

"I am Allan Barrows," he said simply. "And this settlement is Nova Calleva." His grip was very firm, his whole bearing confident but not aggressive. "And you are?"

Detroyd explained who he was and how he came to be fleeing Londonborough. As far as he knew, none of his colleagues had ever had dealings with these people or even knew about them. For sure Barrows would know nothing of the Historical Society, so he was circumspect about what he told him.

"Well, Erroll," said Barrows, making no attempt to sit down. "If you are a runaway, you're welcome. We need to grow. Each year, more and more people flee the city and its dictates. We've established a strong counter-culture and we're trying to rebuild an organized system that allows our people to develop freely. We're necessarily secretive— or, at least, well concealed. I imagine the Central Authority sees us as outlaws."

"I'm sure it would," said Detroyd.

"People who wish to join us and become integrated into our community — and I assume you are one such person — have to undergo certain tests. We need to be certain that they are not spies or agents of the Authority," Barrows added bluntly.

Detroyd nodded. The steely gaze of the tall man never wavered.

"We have had to deal with such characters," Barrows added, with the hint of a smile. "We're not very merciful." He let the words hover between them, their meaning clear.

"I understand," said Detroyd. "I would be only too glad to try and prove my loyalty. I have left friends behind and I fear for their safety. And there is another one I need to contact. He was posted to the fortress port of Petra Dumnoniorum, as a teacher in the Academy."

"You're a long way from Dumnonia."

"My friend is almost certainly in grave danger. We're not Authority men."

"When you escaped, what were your intentions?"

"To get to Petra."

"Alone? You were going to travel two hundred miles through the forest? How? The only way you could do it would be along the Great Western Way."

"I had no time to plan. I was lucky to get out alive."

"Yes, my men saw what happened. Your former captors could have killed you, as they killed Graddis. We'd had dealings with him. Norrisall's thugs evidently thought he was expendable. He was a double-dealing bugger, but it's a shame we've lost him. Small consolation that we've gained a few more guns."

"So what happens to me now?"

"Well, Erroll, you probably appreciate my position. I have to look at the worst case scenario. For all we know, you could be an agent, your escape a set-up. They let you out, shoot at you, but not too closely. They even sacrifice Graddis to make it look like the real thing."

Detroyd shook his head, trying to contain his frustration.

"We need time to satisfy ourselves about you. Consider this, Erroll, *if* you were an agent of the Authority, look at the damage you could do to us, once we absorbed you. The information you'd have about our strengths, our distribution, and so on. Right now, you're a high risk."

"Then let me go. I have to get to Petra, to warn my friend."

"If I let you go, you wouldn't last a day. Alone in the forest, you'd be eaten alive, one way or the other. Travel along the Great Western Way and the military will get you. They have guns all along that route."

"Have you men who could get me through the forest?"

"Sure, but I can't spare them. Not for one man's quest."

Detroyd pursed his lips in annoyance. He was no better off! "Look, if I was an agent and the Authority wanted to send me to Petra, they'd have sent me there by the usual route. Protected. Why go to the elaborate lengths of staging a bogus escape?"

Barrows studied him for a moment. "I understand your frustration. Be patient. I promise you, you'll get a chance to demonstrate your loyalty. When I can be sure of you, we'll talk again. Oh, and one other thing. If you try to leave Nova Calleva without my express authority, you'll be killed without question. You do need to understand that."

Detroyd nodded reluctantly. *And in the meantime, I'm powerless to help Chad.*

· ✳ ·

Andrew Wilkinson loved working in the herb garden more than anything. Of all the tasks set for him by Father Emmanuel, or even Mr. Trencher, those jobs that required him to work in this little sanctuary, tucked away in a quiet part of the church grounds, kept the youth most contented. Father had told him that he had a natural way with plants and that they responded to him. It was true, Wilkinson knew it. Even this summer, the hottest anyone had ever known, the herbs thrived. A lot of it was due to the constant watering.

This evening, with the air finally cooling down, Wilkinson was halfway through his chores when he found the last of the outdoor rain barrels had run dry. There had been no proper rain for weeks to replenish the barrels, which collected from all areas of the church roofs and normally provided plenty of water all summer. But there was more water inside, where, in one of the small storerooms, a big steel trough was fed by a tap that Mr. Skellbow had fixed some time ago to take water from some other tanks. Reserve tanks, he had called them. Mr. Skellbow was brilliant with pipes.

Wilkinson was filling his watering can from this tap when he heard voices so close that he nearly dropped the can in shock. But he realized that the men who were talking were in a room next door. There was a mesh in the wall. Cautiously he sidled up to it, and by getting close he could see into the room without being seen. He knew this because he had done it before. He could hear what was being said very clearly.

Several of the Brethren were in there, a small room in which they sometimes sat around a table and played cards or had a drink— and Wilkinson knew it wasn't just water they were drinking. Their leader was there, Jarrold, a horrible man, always quick to curse Andrew, usually for no good reason. Opposite him were Worsley and Batch. The one Andrew hated most, Zennet, wasn't there.

"I don't suppose you'll miss this place," Jarrold said to Worsley.

"Too bloody true, mate. To be honest, the knife wound's healing up fine, but if it's my ticket back to Londonborough, so much the better," Worsley growled, touching a bandaged area around his midriff.

"Zennet's not recovering so well," said Jarrold.

"No. Dunno if he'll ever be any good in a scrap again," said Batch. "He's like fuck about it, too. He don't mind going back to Londonborough, but he knows it'll be to a shit posting where he won't get much action."

Worsley cleared his throat and spat. Wilkinson drew back instinctively. He hated these men for many reasons and *spitting* was only one of them.

"If he'd stayed on, he would have wanted to have sliced that Mundy guy up into fillets," Batch said.

"Say the word," Worsley told Jarrold. "Me and Zennet'll do it before we go."

"Nah," said Jarrold. "Father just wants him watched. Not touched. Anyway, you and Zennet will be off as soon as the new boys get here. Couple of days."

"Who are they?" said Batch. "Anyone we know?"

"Names of Dean Munk and Silas Spragg."

Worsley snorted. "I know Spragg! Right hard bastard. Any of those fucking trawlermen try to jump him, he'll rip the bastards up."

"Yeah? Then I look forward to meeting him." Batch laughed.

Wilkinson could stand to hear no more. He shrank away, carefully taking the two filled cans and returning to the herb garden, where no one would notice him.

Soldiers! They're soldiers. Father said not, but they are, they are!

And they didn't like Chad Mundy. They had talked about... doing something terrible. Wilkinson's hands shook as he splashed water on the plants. He must warn Mr. Mundy. Mr. Trencher said to watch him, make sure he was safe. But Wilkinson was too terrified to say anything to Mr. Trencher. If he told the Brethren off, they would take it out on him. Maybe even do those horrible things.

What do I do? He kept asking himself, tears welling in his eyes.

· ✳ ·

Time crawled painfully for Detroyd in New Calleva. Barrows put him in the hands of his two principal rescuers, Smithing and Gunnett, and although they seemed to soften towards him a little, they were generally tight-lipped. They showed him around the settlement, making sure he knew where all the palisade boundaries were and how well they were patrolled day and night, just to underline Barrows' warning about not trying to escape. The town was evidently on a war alert, just as the Authority always insisted on its own counter-Invasion plans. Certainly anyone attacking New Calleva would find themselves up against a formidable defence.

In the following days, Detroyd was given ample opportunity to train and demonstrate his own prowess, particularly with his own bow. There were archers here, many of them excellent, but it soon became apparent that in this newcomer, they had a master. Detroyd learned that all new recruits were treated with caution, but his remarkable skill quickly earned him the respect of those he exercised with. Gradually he began to pick up more detail about this place and the iron-willed man who ran it.

"You're well prepared for any invasion," Detroyd said one morning out on the archery field, where a dozen of them were training some young lads.

Gunnett, the bearded man who had been his first contact in his run for freedom outside Greywalls, nodded. "We are that. You've seen our strength, Erroll."

"There must be a thousand men here. And as many women and children."

Gunnett nodded. He knew it was no secret now, as Detroyd had seen most of the settlement. It didn't do any harm to show your strength. Besides, this Detroyd had come across as honest enough. Gunnett for one didn't think he was a spy.

"Do you think there'll be an invasion?" Detroyd asked him. "Not everyone in Londonborough is sure about it. They think it's something the Authority has embellished in order to control the fortress ports."

"There'll be an invasion, all right," Gunnett grinned.

Detroyd masked his surprise. *Is he saying that Barrows means to attack Londonborough? But that would be courting disaster.* The city was ill-prepared for an attack from the forests, but even so...

While the group got on with their continuous daily regime, a small band of watchers overlooked them from a discreet vantage point higher up the valley. Among them Barrows was studying Detroyd keenly.

Detroyd had mounted a feisty young stallion, handling it with the same consummate skill that he did with the bow. He nudged it down to the beginning of a row of targets set up at the field's edge. This was to be a demonstration to some of the new youngsters.

Detroyd gripped the stallion's flanks with his knees and thighs and gently lifted his bow, an arrow nocked, ready for flight. Over his shoulder he carried his quiver with a dozen more arrows in it. At a command from the nearby Gunnett, Detroyd urged the horse forward, quickly breaking into a full gallop. Amazingly he did not need his hands to control it, using only his knees. He remained perfectly balanced. As he passed the first target, some twenty yards away, he unleashed the arrow, slickly lifted another from the quiver, notched it, and released it. On the run past the targets, he let five arrows fly in blurring succession. Every one of them pierced the straw effigies of men in the fatal area of the heart.

Barrows let out a small gasp.

Behind him another man stepped forward. "That's the kind of man you want fighting for you," he said, equally as admiring of Detroyd's work.

Barrows turned to him. "Danton! They said you were on your way." The two men clapped each other on the back. "Before we sit down and talk, I'd like you to see something," he said, turning back to the archery field. He pointed out Detroyd. "Latest escapee from Londonborough." Barrows repeated the story Detroyd had given upon his arrival.

"How did you come to pick him up? Were you tipped off?"

"No, we've got scouts posted all around the northern boundary of the city. We're slowly covering all the outlets. Greywalls has been a regular hideout for runaways, so we always have a strong troop there. But I just feel uneasy about this one. May be nothing. So for now, we're keeping him under strict control. If he is an agent of the Authority, he's very well disguised. He's also a very frustrated man, more so than most that come to us. He makes no bones about the fact that he is desperate to get to Petra."

Barrow's companion's eyes narrowed and he studied Detroyd's distant figure with renewed interest. "Is that so? Does he say why?"

"He has a friend there. A teacher, newly appointed to the Academy."

"And does this friend have a name?"

"Mundy. Chad Mundy."

"That's very interesting, Allan."

"You know this man?"

"I do."

"Detroyd swears he's in some kind of danger. He wants to get to him to warn him. He won't elaborate. Who is this Mundy?"

"He's important to us, Allan. Very much so. I don't think he needs your Mr. Detroyd to protect him. We're doing that already. There've been one or two attempts to ruffle Mundy's feathers, but we've contained any threats. But there is another possibility. If all this is a cover, Detroyd could be an assassin and Mundy his target."

Barrows nodded slowly. "In which case, Nova Calleva can be his home for a long time."

"How are you prepared for the Midsummer Solstice?"

Barrows broke his concentration on Detroyd and smiled. "It'll be quite a gathering this year. And you?"

"The High Lord goes from strength to strength. This man Chad Mundy is to play a part in the celebrations. The usual secrecy surrounds it all. The High Lord was never one to risk loose talk."

Barrows laughed. "It's a good policy, Danton."

"Sure. So whatever conclusions you draw about Mr. Detroyd, you keep him here until after the Solstice."

"Then what?"

"I'll be coming to meet you. The best thing may be for me to take him back to Petra with me. Put him to the test. One way or another, we'll find out who he serves."

Barrows nodded. "Good." He turned to Smithing, who had diplomatically withdrawn a little while the two men had been talking. "Smithing, would you show Mr. Connell to his quarters. I expect he'd like a good soak after his journey."

XXII

PETRA / LONDONBOROUGH

FATHER MADDING WATCHED the class of youths going through their paces around the field, driven on by the relatively youthful teacher, Guy Lurrell. *God, they seem to get younger and younger. Children leading children*, Madding thought. *They really do need a guiding hand.*

"Come on, Warson, pick your feet up, boy! That's it. One last effort. It's only pain," the teacher called out to a straggler.

"I'm knackered, sir," grinned the red-faced lad, sweat streaming off him.

"You haven't done anything to get knackered!" Lurrell snorted. The youths all laughed. "Okay, okay. The bell's not far off. Go on in and get scrubbed down. Slowly! No pushing and shoving. That's the fastest you lot have moved all day."

Lurrell had seen the priest, who he knew from time to time patrolled the school and grounds, taking in the activities of the students. He must be dedicated, out in this ferocious heat. It was a wonder he didn't get heatstroke. Lurrell walked over to him, one eye on the youngsters as they left the field and went back into the Academy.

"You'll have to excuse the language, Father."

Madding chuckled. "My dear Guy— it is Guy, isn't it? One can't live in a school environment without getting used to the crudities and profanities."

Lurrell ran his hands through his thick blond hair and mopped sweat from his own forehead on the back of his wrist. "This heat doesn't help."

"It's very oppressive this year. But I always enjoy seeing the youngsters making progress. One day we will be relying on them, I'm sure. I did wonder about you, Guy. You've not been to church for some time."

The young teacher looked slightly awkward. "I've not been a very good follower of the faith, I admit. I've let other things sidetrack me. The Academy has been through a tough time these last few months."

"I perfectly understand. And with the summer break upon us, not to mention the festivities, we'll be tested even more thoroughly. I know the town enjoys a degree of liberation, as it should. But the lure of the pagan path can be a dubious distraction."

"Yes, Father, *distracted* is right."

"Have you been through some uncomfortable personal experience?"

Lurrell was reluctant to open up. "All this messing about with old religions and ceremonies from pre-history— it's primitive and archaic. An excuse for something else entirely."

"Well, Guy, you're not alone in reaching that conclusion. It's a movement that, more and more, is reaching out to the young. When I see these fine lads here, it concerns me that they are at an age when they could so easily be seduced by these outside elements. The pagan way appeals to the sensual side of human nature. Instant gratification, moral ambiguity. Youngsters are not equipped to deal with temptation."

"It's not just the kids," the teacher grunted.

"No, I'm sure you are right. But it's heartening to know your views are clear. Does your young lady share them? I used to see you in church together—"

"I don't think she does, Father. Penn and I don't share the same views any more." *And at the moment, we don't share the same bed.* "It's something I'm coming to terms with. Penn's no troublemaker or revolutionary, but she's a free spirit. She never dismisses anything out of hand."

"That's an impression I had of her, yes."

"So she's entitled to discuss whatever she wants with whomever she likes. But these dissidents are far more..." He groped for an appropriate word. "Persistent. And subtle with it. Once Penn was as indifferent about the festivities as I am. Live and let live. But now— something's changed her." His face clouded. "She spends a lot of time with Brin Goldsworthy's lot. They're all sympathetic to the pagan stuff. And a new teacher's joined their little clique. Chad Mundy. Replaced Drew Vasillius."

Ah, thought Madding. *Herein lies a raw nerve. Jealousy festers. This man's loathing of Mundy is an open wound. This is useful knowledge indeed.*

"No disrespect," Lurrell was saying. "But Vasillius was a notorious dissident."

"Yes, it was a sad situation, Guy. And you see what it led to. It's just the sort of thing I am so anxious to avoid. Things must be kept in perspective."

"Well, I don't want anything to do with them. And if Penn insists on being part of their culture, then there won't be any reconciliation."

Madding smiled understandingly. "I see that, Guy. Yet sometimes it's better to confront adversity. You're right to want nothing to do with the festivities, on the face of it, but the church needs support. I need eyes and ears everywhere, especially now. I need to know what's going on. Your help could be invaluable."

Lurrell looked slightly contemptuous. "You want a spy, Father?"

"I wouldn't ask you to betray anyone's confidences, Guy. Carl Trencher and I work hard together to divert people away from paganism. Penn almost certainly has no idea what she's getting into."

"She's not naïve. But I don't know what she wants."

"I have a group of companions, the Brethren. They're not simply servants, Guy. They're highly trained and I choose them very carefully. As guardians of the whole of my flock, they have to be of a certain calibre. And they have been educated in the military arts to a very high level, more so than most."

Their slow walk had brought them to the doors of the Academy. Lurrell weighed this hint of an offer carefully. "I'm a teacher, Father. My days are very full."

"The Brethren are both dedicated and highly effective. But, like me, their vision is limited. I've been thinking of extending my— understanding of life in Petra. There's no reason why someone as able as you could not be a teacher *and* a member of the Brethren. In terms of your own advancement, Guy, well, it would be assured. Carl Trencher and I, as I said, work together. You would enjoy many benefits."

· ✳ ·

Deadspike thumbed through the great wad of papers. All were covered in an untidy scrawl, which the Enforcer immediately recognized as the hand of the Interrogator, Karswell. They were written in ink, not pencil. More permanent: Karswell rarely missed an opportunity to express his power, no matter how small. The only thing that surprised Deadspike was that the work had not been etched in blood, which would have been in keeping with the Interrogator's nature.

There were individual reports in literally gory detail. Deadspike grimaced as he picked out a sentence or two. But he fixed on the summary sheet, certain details about the Historical Society standing out.

> *These subjects were detained in isolation from each other and questioned comprehensively by the Interrogation Section ... each subject remains in isolated detention, awaiting further deployment ... a specific line of questioning followed any knowledge that members of the Society might have had of a coded subject, not named within the report, but known verbally only to those persons authorized to read this report.*

Deadspike smiled grimly to himself. Karswell was never one to leave himself open to criticism. In the highly unlikely event that his report got into the wrong hands, no one was about to see the name "Daybreak" written into it.

> *...each of the subjects displayed a varying degree of resistance. However, their tolerance levels were limited and the required information was accordingly extracted from them...*
>
> *The Interrogation was exhaustive and it is a firm conclusion that there remains no more information available that would be of relevance to the Central Authority...*
>
> *While all of the subjects clearly recognize the coded subject, they are equally as clearly lacking in an understanding of what it means. Part of their function has been to attempt to ascertain this. This was tested using various serums... tests confirmed that the detainees know the name, but not the meaning of the coded subject...*
>
> *There was one common source of reference the detainees used, but it was apparent that their own interpretation of it was vague and did nothing to illuminate the coded subject...*

Subsequent Interrogation revealed that although there may be a small number of other members of the Society, or peripheral contacts, none of these have any understanding of the coded subject. Within the Society itself, members are apparently encouraged to minimize any discussion about it.

The Interrogation concluded, therefore, that the nature of the coded subject and its implications remain uncompromised.

And that, thought Deadspike, *is really all we need to know. That and the whereabouts of Detroyd. This report, however, suggests that he almost certainly knows no more about Daybreak than his colleagues in the Society. Is he really worth worrying about?*

· ✳ ·

Later, Deadspike visited an insalubrious public house that he and his more dubious contacts frequented. Slake entered the twilight surroundings, his face a sheen of perspiration. He mopped at his brow and cheeks with a huge white handkerchief and grumbled something about the freakish heat, slumping into a creaking chair, his expression slightly wretched. He crumpled his hat as if he would screw it into ruin and toss it aside. Deadspike said nothing, waiting like impending doom.

"Things have not gone well, Mr. Deadspike. Not well at all. Very badly, in fact. My contacts at Greywalls have three dead men on their hands. One of them a guide. A very unpleasant business."

Deadspike kept his reactions under control. "Someone has been busy."

"Like I say, three dead. Two killed by Mr. Detroyd. The guide, who helped him, by Mr. Norrisall's men."

"So you're telling me that Detroyd has *escaped*?"

"I am, Mr. Deadspike. We think he jumped the guide, forced him to help him get to the outside, then made a break for it. I have to say, Mr. Detroyd was very good."

A damn sight better than Norrisall's goons, that's for sure! "So where is he?"

"Like I say, Mr. Deadspike, he's outside. Gone into the forest. He had help."

"*Outside* help?"

"A bunch of riders came out of the forest and scooped him up. Very slick."

Deadspike grunted. *So we've lost him for good. Once the woodsmen got him, that was it.* But he thought again of Karswell's report. Limited knowledge. Detroyd knew nothing damaging about Daybreak. So let him run free. He was as good as dead.

Slake explained in some detail the nature of Detroyd's escape and the consequences, including the loss of the guns.

"A complete cockup, then?" Deadspike was enjoying Slake's discomfort immensely, though his face remained cold and unforgiving. Slake looked mortified, again dabbing at his dripping features.

"You owe me for this, Slake."

"I can't argue with that, sir."

"So what are we going to do about it?"

"I don't have any reliable contact with the outside, sir."

"No, I can only treat Detroyd as lost. But there is other work you can do for me. In recompense. That's only fair, wouldn't you say?"

"You have only to name it, Mr. Deadspike. Like I say, I am in your debt. My whole operation is at your service."

"The people in the Historical Society that you had watched for me, they'll be sent to you shortly. They need special attention."

"You want me to have them discreetly shut away?"

"No, Slake, I want you to have them discreetly *eliminated*. I would not normally place such a burden on you, though I know your capabilities. But like *you* say, you do owe me for the fiasco at Greywalls."

"Only too glad to make some kind of restitution, Mr. Deadspike."

"No slipups. That would be unforgivable. Am I clear?"

Slake's face contorted itself into something vaguely resembling a smile. He was a beacon of relief. "I do, sir. Indeed. I will attend to the disposals personally."

· ✳ ·

Even later in the day, Deadspike mulled over his messages and reports. The more he thought about the Historical Society and Detroyd, the more he convinced himself that they posed no substantial threat to the Authority. They knew nothing of import.

He had looked at the appendix in Karswell's report that referred to the "common source of reference" to Daybreak that the Society members had used. It was a rhyme in the Old Tongue. Karswell had had it translated into modern English:

> *Speak to me of coded subject*
> *One midsummer's morning.*
> *Whisper all its secrets*
> *Cry their fearful warning.*

The Old Tongue. It put him in mind of his one niggling doubt. Chad Mundy. He was well versed in the Old Tongue—and something else. Yes, dialects. Something about all this made Deadspike uneasy.

But the priest had suggested that Mundy was prepared to work for him.

I'd like to talk to you, Mr. Mundy. Just to satisfy myself that you, too, know nothing about Daybreak. It would be good to be reassured.

Deadspike turned it over in his mind. *Bring him back here during the summer break? But if he is a dissident, that would alert him and, like Detroyd, he'd probably run for the trees. Go to him? I'm not due in Petra until October. But a pre-Inspection visit would be nothing out of the ordinary. The Prime knows only too well that we are not happy with the Academy as it stands. She could hardly object to my turning up.*

· ✳ ·

Sunderman had been nodding through most of the report Deadspike had just delivered. Even the news about Detroyd's escape seemed less important now that the Historical Society was clearly a dog without teeth.

"Karswell is, as one would expect, very thorough in his work," Deadspike went on. "He appended a list of names to the report, names of various contacts of the main players in the Society that the detainees divulged to him. Given that they knew nothing specific about Daybreak, it is safe to assume that their contacts are no wiser. The one anxiety we had about a leak of information relating to Daybreak was centred on the teacher, Drew Vasillius."

"An issue that has been resolved."

"But Vasillius's name was not alone on the list of contacts. Another named contact of the Society in Petra is Sebastian Wroxton, a Senior Magister."

Sunderman frowned in thought. "Wroxton? Yes, I recall him. He was strongly placed to become Prime. *He* is a member of this infernal brigade? As I recall, Cora Vine was considered to be better Authority material. Wroxton was perceived to be a little too sympathetic to the local community. Too liberal minded. Whereas Cora Vine is far more direct in her approach."

Deadspike smiled coldly. "It may be purely academic now. The Society no longer has any credence here in Londonborough. But Petra— I would just like to know that we really did nip the problem in the bud when we had Vasillius removed."

"You think Wroxton could be a problem?"

"He's powerless while Cora Vine holds sway."

"What do you propose?"

"A visit. Pre-Inspection. Once Wroxton knows the Society has been discontinued, I'm sure he'll feel less inclined to compromise his own safety. Our grip on Petra is tightening. I understand they have some kind of festivities down there. Pagan rituals or some such nonsense, to do with Midsummer." He let the word hang in the air for a moment, but Sunderman did not react.

"I think these people need to know that the Authority is very aware of them and is quite prepared to be as firm with them as it needs to be," Deadspike went on.

If Sunderman were insulted, he did not show it. "Very well, I'll make the arrangements for you."

XXIII

PETRA AND BEYOND

THE CANTEEN WAS even fuller and noisier than usual on a Friday evening as people began preparing for the festivities in earnest. Mundy somehow managed to single out Brin Goldsworthy from the throng, but they were squeezed together, private conversation impossible. It was hard work prizing Goldsworthy away from the excitement, but Mundy eventually persuaded him to go somewhere quieter. He followed Goldsworthy out through the heaving aisles into the corridor beyond. Goldsworthy unlocked a small classroom. Its sudden silence seemed stifling. Mundy saw a flicker of unease in Goldsworthy's eyes.

Mundy hesitated, but then spoke bluntly. "It's about Drew. Did he have an affair, about twenty years ago?"

Goldsworthy nodded uncomfortably. "It's not well known, but yes, he did."

"With someone outside the town?"

"Keep all this to yourself. Yes. A girl from across the river. He spent more time than most of us over there. We were all a lot younger then. A bit wilder."

"Was there a child?"

Goldsworthy drew in a long, almost painful breath. "Who told you this?"

"Father Emmanuel."

Goldsworthy nodded. "Trencher knew, of course. Too much to expect him to have been discreet. And he's as thick as thieves with the priest these days. Madding is always quick to put the knife in. Yes. Drew had a son."

"Do many people know about it?"

It was as if all the energy had been slowly pulled out of Goldsworthy. His face was suddenly lined, his years weighing on him more heavily. "No. At the time, only a small group. Not all of us are still here. We don't talk about it much, for obvious reasons. Why do you bring it up, Chad? It's not something I really want to talk about. It can't achieve anything."

"I'm sure it has a bearing on Drew's death."

Goldsworthy looked horrified. "I don't see how—"

"Drew and Anna had no children of their own."

"No." Goldsworthy was looking more and more uncomfortable. "You can't imagine how unhappy it made them both. Ironically, if anything it brought them closer together. I know that must sound odd. Drew having had an affair. And a son by another woman. But he loved Anna. More than anything. If she ever found out about it, it would break her heart. That's why I'd rather not go back over this."

"Brin, believe me, I'm not here to point the finger. What you've told me won't go any further. Anna will never hear it from me. Listen, we know that Drew was killed to silence him."

"Yes."

"And Drew's son— is he still across the river?"

"Yes."

"Does Penn know about him?"

Goldsworthy shook his head. "No. Long before her time. I'd rather you didn't say anything to her."

Behind them there was a commotion as a group of staff barged along the corridor. Someone shouted, "Come on, Brin! Time to get the preliminaries started."

"Coming," Goldsworthy boomed back. He patted Mundy on the shoulder. "We'll talk about this later." He relocked the classroom door behind them and led the way back to the canteen.

Mundy's thoughts were mixed. The promise of the evening's rituals was an exciting one. But the shadow that hung over Petra had deepened. Whatever these old secrets were that he was unveiling, he wondered if they may be better left hidden.

· ❋ ·

Mundy took to horse as easily and comfortably as he had done in his days at Wellington Military Academy and established an immediate rapport with his steed. It responded to his skill as a rider and settled into an empathy with him that both Penn and Brin recognized. They were expert riders, and as they headed out of the gates of Petra, along with two score more colleagues from the Academy, they felt the rush of pleasure that always came with a ride into the woodlands. Mundy's mood of earlier rapidly changed as he began to rediscover the experience of riding.

Penn had told Mundy that tonight was not quite what the Academy — or more particularly, the Authority — thought. It was to be a real festival, a ritual marking the summer solstice itself. In the pagan calendar, Penn told Mundy, it was very significant. Although there were only forty or so riders in this party, Penn had said that there would be far more groups attending and, most interestingly to Mundy, all of the pagan clans from the neighbouring forests. He had been spoken for, otherwise he would never have been allowed near the place that they were going to: the old quarry, disguised as a plague pit.

Curious, Mundy thought. *Where is the actual plague pit?* No one had mentioned any. But then, they were not the kind of place that anyone wanted reminding about. From what little accounts he had read of such places, they contained an unimaginable number of victims. Time would have rendered them down by now. Back to the earth, fodder for new growth. Part of a regenerative process that the pagans would have appreciated.

Across the bridge southwards along an old trackway they rode, ducking to avoid the low branches that created a long, green tunnel. In places it was unusually straight for as much as a mile. Mundy marvelled at the path, which must have an interesting history. Perhaps it predated the Plague Wars, one of the few things that had survived. It was well worn, though enclosed. He mentioned it to Penn as the party had to slow its pace and ride in twos, dropping to a slow trot.

"So much of it seems to be amazingly straight," he said. "I assume it was quite a sophisticated road once. I've heard stories about vehicles that were self-powered long ago. Can you believe that?"

"There's a legend about this trackway to do with a fire-breathing vehicle. It was said to eat stones. But Brin reckons it was like a version of the boiler at the Academy. So maybe it needed coal."

Mundy grinned. "The Authority may encourage us to leave the past well alone, but it's not in our nature, is it? I know it's not in mine. Whatever travelled up and down this trackway will do it again. Maybe not in our time."

She smiled. "I can't imagine anything nicer than a horse, though." Her mood changed slightly. "Can you tell me what you were talking to Brin about?"

Mundy leaned up in the saddle to see where Goldsworthy was, but he was several couples ahead of them, well out of earshot. "Yes. It was to do with the death of Drew Vasillius," he said softly. "I've been a bit cautious. I wouldn't want to be responsible for leaving anyone open to reprisals. Even Anna didn't know what Drew carried in his head. He refused to tell her, or anyone, for fear of endangering them. Even Brin, and I know how close they were."

"Yes. When they were our age, they were inseparable. They shared everything, except that. Brin never complained. He knew there was a reason for Drew's silence."

"Drew may not have known what he was carrying."

She looked puzzled. "What do you mean, Chad?"

"I wonder if it was encoded, you know?"

She looked across at him, eyes widening. "Have you found something?"

He nodded, lowering his voice even more. The forest folded them in, muffling their words. Although there were riders close ahead and behind them, they felt as though they were alone in the grip of the wild lands. "I think Drew did pass the secrets on. But he could only have done it one way."

She said nothing, but he could feel her burning desire to question him. He wanted more than anything to share what he knew with her. If he didn't, he would be slipping a barrier between them, the last thing he wanted. He was on the point of saying something when Brin, a few paces ahead, turned around and indicated the stretch of forest to their left. They were nearing the unauthorized area.

"Let's talk later," he said. "Would it surprise you to know that I'm incredibly nervous about tonight?"

She laughed, and the momentary shadow had passed.

"Sebastian has tasked me with trying to find out exactly what Drew knew. I'm beginning to ask myself, do I really want to find out? Is it best left well alone?"

"There aren't many people I would trust, Chad. But Sebastian is certainly one of them. And he is well respected. So many people at the Academy — and outside it — wish he were running things. I think he genuinely cares about the people."

"I know people in Londonborough who feel the same way about him."

"I trust you, too, Chad." She laughed.

"Me? How do you know I'm not a spy?"

She grimaced. "Hey, don't even joke about it!"

"Your friend, the priest, thinks I might be. He wants me to work for him."

"Creep. He's the last person we'd want to get hold of any secrets. He'd have everyone hanging from the walls of Petra if he had his way— or burned alive."

"He'll get nothing useful from me. He wants a report on tonight's proceedings, but it won't necessarily mirror what really happens. And when, exactly, are you going to tell me what that is?"

"You'll have to wait and see. It's a secret." She tried to keep a straight face but found it impossible not to laugh. The hush of evening closed in, punctuated by the late, harsh croaking of rooks settling in their resting places. Penn and Mundy had fallen silent as the procession filed off the trackway and along an even narrower path, its sides thick with bracken, the scent rising from them powerful on the air. Mundy noticed the ancient, weather-worn signs on either side that proclaimed this area out of bounds. DANGER! was splotched in thick paint, now flaking, above other grim warnings, such as: PLAGUE AREA, KEEP OUT and NO ADMITTANCE BEYOND THIS POINT and HAZARDOUS TO HEALTH. Skull motifs were dotted threateningly in the corners of all the signs, and as the party moved further down the green gullet of the track, there were gorier reminders that this was an area unsafe for human visitation. Bones, obviously human, and actual skulls on poles decorated the trees and branches.

Deep in the forest now, embraced by the rampant verdure, the riders could see watchers up on the banks, where the people of the forest monitored their progress. Mundy saw them wave, most of them armed with spears and what looked like swords. Their faces were painted brightly, their arms and lower legs decorated with feathers. In spite of their slightly fearful aspect, they were welcoming the riders. The path itself abruptly widened out into a cleared space that ran on ahead between two rocky bluffs.

Goldsworthy nudged his horse back to join Penn and Mundy. "Quarry up ahead," he said, for Mundy's benefit. "Keep close to us and everything will fall into place. In a moment we can dismount. The forest people will look after the horses."

Mundy felt as though he was approaching a cathedral, only one whose vaults were sculpted by huge branches. The scent of the forest was almost overpowering and the humans seemed minute in the scale of things. At the edge of the clearing they did as Goldsworthy had said and dismounted, forest people gently leading the horses away. Beyond was the edge of the ancient quarry. Mundy could see its shape and dimensions, chopped neatly out of the stone of the forest's heart. Grey walls rose up from both sides, stepped upwards in a manmade amphitheatre that was about five hundred feet across. The far side was over seventy feet tall, its chiselled edges overhung with bramble, bracken, and other thick tresses of plant life.

But it was not the geometric beauty of the quarry that drew Mundy's attention, it was the mass of people within the space. There were a number of huge square-cut blocks of stone scattered about, some jumbled at the perimeter of the quarry, but others had been deliberately dragged and positioned within it, to make a natural stage for the ceremonies. Upon a number of these blocks, which themselves had been painted with bright sigils and glyphs, stood what Mundy took to be the equivalent of the forest priesthood: men and women who wore long robes, mainly green, laced with leaves and feathers, their faces, arms and legs painted in bright forest hues.

In front of these impressive figures the congregation had gathered. It consisted of at least a hundred of the forest dwellers in their simple garb, camouflaged against the leafy background, as well as the party from Petra. The latter began to mingle, and each person was welcomed openly by the natives. Mundy could see that with many of them it was a case of old acquaintances meeting new. He could also see, silhouetted up on the rising skyline, what he took to be guards: men bearing weapons, mainly long spears, who ringed the amphitheatre. The evening sunlight from the west fell on their faces and chests, daubing them in bright russets and gold, giving them the appearance of carved statues.

As the gathering settled itself, Mundy turned to Goldsworthy, who stood beside him as if in silent prayer. "Which is the Green Man?" he asked softly.

Goldsworthy frowned at him, surprised. "Not here till the ceremonies begin," he replied, his voice equally low.

"Anna said I need to speak to him."

Goldsworthy's frown deepened. "Anna told you to speak to the Green Man?"

"Yes."

"But why? Why him?"

"She said he might be able to shed some light on Drew's knowledge. She seemed to think it was fairly important."

Goldsworthy was suddenly concerned. "*Anna* told you that?"

"Yes. Why, what's wrong?"

"But the Green Man... this year it's Uther."

Mundy looked across at Penn as if for guidance. She could see that Goldsworthy was agitated about something, but she hadn't heard the conversation. They were almost whispering.

"Uther," repeated Goldsworthy, keeping his voice low, with some difficulty. "He will be this year's Green Man." Mundy realized that he was quite shaken.

"But what does that mean?"

Goldsworthy spoke slowly and painfully. "It means that Anna must *know*. She's directed you to Uther. The one person that Drew must have confided in. His *son*."

Mundy was nodding, realizing. "Yes. He will have inherited his father's knowledge. Whatever secrets Drew carried, his son will automatically inherit. Drew would not necessarily have had to tell him."

Goldsworthy's looked perplexed. "I don't understand, Chad. Why automatically?"

"It's to do with the bloodline. It must be a genetic process. Started back in Londonborough with Drew's father and grandfather. The knowledge is passed on genetically. So it would follow that Uther will have been implanted with the knowledge that everyone is so keen to have. Or repress."

"My God," said Penn softly, having moved closer beside them. "Did I hear that right? Uther is Drew's *son*?" The two men had forgotten her in the intensity of their exchange.

Goldsworthy looked distraught, putting a finger to his lips. He nodded.

"Does he know?" said Penn.

"He does," said Goldsworthy. "I thought Anna had been spared all this. But it turns out that she knows too, from what Chad has said."

"What Uther may not know," said Chad, "is that he carries the information."

"But Anna knew," said Goldsworthy and the understanding seemed to have hit him like a sword stroke. "Why else would she have told you to speak to Uther?"

"She said the Green Man."

"She wouldn't have directed you to the Green Man unless she knew it was to be Uther," Goldsworthy insisted. "She must have known that he was the one with the inherited information. Drew's secrets. All this time." Goldsworthy took a deep breath. "All this time she *knew* Drew had a son by another woman. Never said a word to any of us. Never showed any anger, any pain." His face clouded.

Penn put her arm around his shoulders. "It's okay, Brin. She didn't want us to know. She preferred to keep it all inside herself."

To Mundy's surprise, there were tears springing from Goldsworthy's eyes. He shook his head, evidently horrified by what he had learned. "Anna." For a moment he looked diminished, a shadow of himself. But suddenly he straightened, as if annoyed with his reaction, the old bluster returning. "I'd better try and see Uther. I've already set up a meeting with him for you, Chad. You two enjoy the ceremony. I'll catch up with you both later."

Moments later the crowd, indifferent to their quiet drama, had absorbed him.

"He's taken this badly," said Mundy, moved by Goldsworthy's concern.

"Poor old Brin," she said. "He's in love with her. I've known it for a long time. And if Uther is Drew's son, Brin knows how much it must have hurt her. It's just a mess."

"What do I do, Penn?"

She looked mildly infuriated. "Do? You can't do anything. Oh, speak to Uther. Find out what these bloody secrets are, I suppose."

"That's assuming he'll want to tell me."

She frowned at him. He could see that her mood had been completely soured by what had happened.

"We've never met," he said. "He doesn't know me. If he's kept the information to himself all this time, like his father and others before him, why should he say anything to a complete stranger? One from Londonborough at that?"

XXIV

THE FOREST

PENN AND MUNDY mingled with the crowd of watchers at the opening to the quarry. The cut of the stone meant they were able to sit in a stepped area at its front end, an ideal vantage point as events unfolded.

"Guy didn't want to come, then?" Mundy said hesitantly, but the look on her face made him immediately wish he hadn't.

She shook her head, eyes fixed ahead. She muttered something he didn't hear. He wanted to put his arm around her, but it was the last thing he dared do. She looked very beautiful. *She's annoyed with me for not telling her before that the Green Man is Drew's son. That must be it. Or she may be angry with Guy. She doesn't say much about him.*

In the natural theatre, the ceremonies began. Several men and women, clearly the equivalent of priests, called for silence. It dropped like a cloak over the whole proceedings. Everyone automatically fell into a complete stillness, relaxed and totally calm. Mundy felt it too, as if a current of warm air had passed through them, removing for a few moments all their anxieties and frustrations. It was an extraordinary feeling, this ebbing of stress, this total serenity. He glanced at Penn and she had, like many others, closed her eyes, her hands lying motionless in her lap.

But Mundy wanted to drink in the scene. It was like something outside of time, or, at least, from a time long before now. In a few slow moments the gathering had become an integral part of the forest, as if each person there were like a tree or stone, linked through the earth to the bedrock. He felt something stir deep within him, a primitive longing, an emotion hitherto buried, immersed by the trauma of the life he was used to. Like strong wine it coursed through him, heady and intoxicating: he gripped the edge of the natural stone seat to steady himself.

Eventually the priests murmured something that was lost in the cool evening air, sitting on top of the huge stone blocks. One of them, wearing a beautifully carved wooden mask and a garland of oak leaves around his neck, stepped forward and opened his arms in a gesture of welcome, his chest rising and falling as he took deep breaths and exhalations. Mundy sensed the entire congregation, including himself, breathing in time with the priest— a voluntary, natural response. And somehow he felt that these people were all tuning themselves to the forest's rhythms, as though it, too, breathed.

They've tapped into some organic force, he told himself. *It's as irresistible as the air. And it's amazing. I feel as if I want to get up and fly!* He desperately wanted to say something to Penn, but she was as still as stone, eyes closed, though a warm smile played on her lips.

The strong voice of the priest gently broke the spell. Nothing here was hurried. "This evening sees a special change of day. As the sun subsides into the west, it readies itself to bring us the dawn of the solstice. The birth of a new season, a renewed celebration of life. The forest is enriched."

"The forest is enriched," replied the gathering and, surprised, Mundy realized that he had automatically repeated the words himself.

"The earth is enriched," said the priest, his words ringing out clearly now, echoing back from the stone walls. Again the crowd spoke his words.

"We are enriched."

This repetition ended with a loud cheer that reverberated around the quarry. Several birds, startled by the volume of sound, clattered up into the twilight sky.

Mundy had not been one for religious ceremony in his life. His beliefs owed more to lip service and general obedience to the rules than to a true faith in God. Had he been in a church now, he would have been uncomfortable, struggling to participate in the true spirit of proceedings, but here, at this moment, it seemed the most natural thing in the world to release himself into the ritual. He could feel his heart beating, his blood flowing, the rhythm of something under him as the earth pulsed in harmony. It was slightly unnerving, as if he had been drugged, or hypnotised, but he was sure he had not been— at least, not by any devious means. He had reacted instinctively, prepared for this moment by an inner desire that the forest had drawn from him.

The ceremonies became celebrations and the crowd revelled in the dances, songs, and words of the priests and priestesses as they paid tribute to life, the earth and the endurance of its spirit. Mundy watched Penn from time to time: her face was flushed, her eyes bright with excitement. She glanced at him and smiled as if to say, *This is the truth of how things are. This is life shed of all the secrets and lies and deceits you are so used to.* He nodded, suddenly laughing in response to her own unfettered joy, and singing as best he could.

When it all ceased, long afterwards, when the sun was down below the tree line and the first torches had been lit, huge trays of food appeared. The smell of roasted meat was overpowering and Mundy suddenly felt ravenous.

Penn took his arm. "You okay?" She could see the ceremonies had meant something to him, something he could not hide. He could not fake indifference. His delight beamed from him. It was what she had expected of him, even if he hadn't realized himself what was deeper within him.

"Come and eat— and drink!" She laughed again. "But be careful, Mr. Mundy! If you drink the mead, you'll find yourself flat on your back very quickly. It is very, very strong. And the wine is pretty heady, too!"

"I wouldn't want anyone to take advantage of me." He grinned.

Her eyes were sparkling. "Well, if you drink too much, you wouldn't appreciate it anyway."

In the arena the priests, dancers, foresters, and everyone else were all mingled, eagerly toasting each other with flagons and smaller wooden cups and chewing on great slivers of cooked deer, boar, and wild chicken.

Penn said, in a more serious tone, "You'll need a clear head when you meet the Green Man."

"I thought he would be part of this ceremony."

"Not until we parade through Petra later in the month. But he is here."

"Hello, you two!" boomed a voice beside them. It was Goldsworthy and Mundy snorted with amusement when he saw the huge wooden platter he was holding, heaped with meat and steaming vegetables. "Did you enjoy it?"

"I feel renewed," said Penn. "It makes you understand how quickly you get clogged up, working back in the Academy." She realized she was still arm in arm with Mundy and diplomatically extracted herself, indicating a nearby table.

"Come on, get stuck in," Goldsworthy encouraged them. He seemed to Mundy to be in better spirits than when he had left them.

When they had all eaten their fill and even the vast appetite of Goldsworthy had been satisfied, they eased themselves to the edge of the gathering. Evidently the revelries had only just begun. There were groups of people spontaneously forming to sing and dance, and others had begun to toast each other repeatedly. It was going to be a long night, Mundy could see. Everyone would be here to greet the dawn, whatever state they were in.

Mundy was on the point of asking Penn to join in with one of the dances. It looked exhilarating. But Goldsworthy gently tugged him aside.

"I've told Uther you're here. He's uneasy, Chad. Uther is a bit of a hard case. Not very trusting. Especially of someone —"

"From Londonborough, yes, I get the picture."

Mundy turned to Penn. Until now he hadn't thought about her role, but from her expression it was obvious that she intended to go with him to meet Uther. They followed Goldsworthy through the crowds, exchanging greetings with several people they knew. Mundy saw one or two of the staff from the Academy and they waved cheerily. He thought he recognized other faces in that mass. *Trawlermen?* The men who had saved him from the attack on the quayside? But the faces were gone in a moment.

Goldsworthy led them back to the woods, to where a narrow path threaded through the lush press of ferns. They gradually worked their way upwards, above the quarry, moving further into the forest. The trees and tall undergrowth muffled the sounds of singing until silence enclosed them. Mundy was conscious of occasional movement among the trees, where he could sense rather than see the forest guardians. Goldsworthy said that no one expected anyone from the Authority, or their spies, to be out here, but there was never a moment when the forest folk were not vigilant.

As they neared the crest of the path, Mundy could see through the thickening shadows the open ground beyond the wood, a long curve of matted grass that formed a tor. Occasional boulders punctuated its slope, like frozen animals, silent guardians of the hill. Near the summit, some distance away, there were torches, their smoke curling slowly up into the descending gloom.

The three of them ascended the slope, Goldsworthy's breathing laboured. He mumbled something about eating too much, but otherwise they were silent, caught up in the atmosphere. Overhead the immeasurable dome of the sky was a blue-black, crystal clear, with the first stars blinking into view. The climbers were above the tree line now, and far across the forest in the remote west, the last aura of sunlight was dimming down, its final reds and oranges merging into the purple of night.

Mundy paused to look at the view, savoring the moment. The endless forest below throbbed with power, hidden energy that he could almost reach out and touch. There was movement at his arm. Penn studied him, a strange expression on her face.

"Magnificent, isn't it?" he said softly as they prepared to climb the last of the long path up to the tor.

When they eventually reached the huge stones that topped it, two figures moved into view, lone spearmen. They looked stern but unthreatening, recognizing Goldsworthy and nodding for them all to pass beyond the huge stones.

Goldsworthy said softly, "Morgana is here. She is what you might call the high priestess. And Uther."

Mundy felt uneasy. Only the experiences of the evening, the eerie powers he had tasted, gave him any confidence. He wanted to grip Penn's hand, but she was behind him now, as if preparing to take a minor role in all this. They went through a natural declivity and into the grassed area beyond. By the glow of torch flames, Mundy could see two figures, one sitting on a slab of stone, the other standing beside him. She must be Morgana.

"This is Chad Mundy," Goldsworthy said to her.

She came forward, looking vaguely formal in her white robe and garlands of flowers around her neck and wrists, but she offered her hand and smiled. Mundy guessed her to be in her late thirties. He took and shook her hand. Her grip was firm and assured. Mundy was struck by her remarkable beauty. She had deeply tanned skin and long, black hair, into which even more flowers had been woven.

"Welcome, Chad Mundy," she said in a melodious voice, her stare riveting.

"I am honoured to have been brought to the ceremonies," he said. And then, a sudden thought striking him, adding in the Old Tongue, "and it is a deep pleasure to have been allowed to experience them."

It brought a smile to those brilliant eyes. "Brin did not tell me you spoke the tongue of the elder folk. And so well."

"It is like beautiful music," he said, again in the Old Tongue.

If her reactions and her delight at hearing it spoken as if by a native were encouraging, Mundy was less at ease with the seated figure of Uther. He declined to rise but appraised Mundy with undisguised suspicion.

"What do you want with us?" Uther said, but not in the Old Tongue. He was a muscular youth, his bare arms an even darker tan than Morgana's, tattoos running from elbow to shoulder. Even though he sat, Mundy could tell that he was taller than most. There was a slightly wild look to him.

"This is my son, Uther," said Morgana. "He's not yet learned how to be patient with folks from beyond the forest."

"Why should I be patient?" Uther snorted. "What has my family got to thank the city dwellers for?"

Goldsworthy, who had been standing behind Mundy, eased himself forward. "Your father was a city dweller, Uther. We're not all to be despised."

Uther stood up and he was indeed tall. He now seemed even burlier, the true product of a life of concentrated exercise. "No, Brin. I'm sorry," he said after a moment's reflection. "You're right to remind me."

To Mundy's surprise and great relief, Uther offered him his hand and he took it, trying not to wince at the unusual power of the grip.

"You are welcome," Uther said. He turned to Penn, a slightly puzzled look on his face. "Do I know you?"

She seemed very small, looking directly at him. "I'm Penn Ranzer."

Uther didn't offer her his hand, but nodded. "Brin tells me you need to speak to me, Chad. About my father and why he was murdered." He used the word clinically and almost viciously. His bitterness glowed like heated embers.

"That's right." *But I'm not sure how to begin this.*

"Come with us," said Morgana, indicating to Chad that he should follow her and Uther further into the stacks. Goldsworthy simply nodded for him to go and a moment later Mundy was on his own with the two forest people.

Behind him, Penn gripped Goldsworthy's arm. "Is he safe?"

Goldsworthy's eyes flickered and Penn saw what he was looking at. More guards up on the rocks. "Uther is a moody devil. But Morgana will take it from here. Chad is safe with her."

Penn watched Mundy go. She half-expected him to turn to her, to acknowledge her, but he didn't. A brief pulse of disappointment throbbed inside her, but she suppressed it. *Suit yourself, Mr. Mundy.*

Mundy found himself on the highest point of the tor, the dark stone sloping slightly away on all sides as if there was a deep drop into darkness beyond. Stretching away all around him below the tor was the forest, silent and even more immense in the fading light. The sun had been replaced by the moon, a huge ball, its vivid light washing everything. In that unique stillness, the world seemed to have stopped, the air, still thick and humid from yet another torrid day, devoid of even a suggestion of a breeze.

Uther stood, arms folded like some ancient demigod, his face set, stern, his thoughts apparently far away.

Morgana called Mundy to her side. "What's brought you here, Chad?"

"I know about Uther's bloodline. You and Drew Vasillius are his parents."

She nodded, but her expression gave nothing of her emotions away.

"Drew was the keeper of certain knowledge. It was first passed on in Londonborough, I don't know how many years ago. It came here with Drew's grandfather, passed to his father and then to him."

"I know about it," she breathed. Uther may have heard, but he remained as fixed as a statue.

"Do you know that the knowledge was passed down in a subliminal way?"

"Yes, I understand. Drew told me that he was a carrier, but he didn't really know what it was he was carrying. He described it as like having a room inside himself, a room filled with information. But he didn't have the key to its door. He had very strange visions from time to time. Fragments of truth."

"It will be the same for Uther."

Again she nodded, looking across at her son, a deep pride in her gaze. "It's passed to him. He's more... troubled than his father. It's more than just a difficult childhood. It was hard for us both. This knowledge comes at a cost."

"It cost Drew his life," said Mundy.

"As with his father and back down his line. The Authority has always tried to eradicate this knowledge. It probably thinks it has done so, with Drew's murder."

Uther abruptly tore his gaze from the forest and walked across to them. His eyes, a deep brown, fixed on Mundy like those of a hawk detecting movement below it in the landscape. "What is it you want to ask me?"

Mundy was conscious that there were at least three guards very close at hand, as if they expected him to present a threat or that he might even be an assassin. "I don't know," he stammered, suddenly frozen by doubt.

"What do you mean, you don't know?" snapped Uther, and for the first time Mundy realized the forester was gripping the haft of some kind of sheathed weapon.

"The knowledge locked inside you, Uther, is vital to all of us. I mean, to all of us who would resist the Authority. It is very afraid of it. The knowledge would harm it. I've no idea what it is. But we— you, and the dissidents, need to know."

"Since it's been handed down for generations," said Morgana softly, "why should it be revealed now? Is there something significant about the present?"

Mundy was groping in the dark for answers, guided by blind instinct. "I think there must be. Londonborough is growing in power, year on year. It's doing all it can to control Petra, which is one of its remotest stations. If the Authority does take full control, everything you stand for could be lost. Our world is at a crossroads."

"We need to unlock the door to that inner room. In Uther," Morgana said.

"Yes," said Mundy. "But I don't know how you do it."

"Oh, I think I do." She smiled. To Mundy's amazement, she stroked his face. He felt mesmerized. "Every locked door has a key, Chad. Drew told me that one would be sent. By the old Society that he belonged to."

Her words stunned him. "The Society sent me. You mean...
I'm the key?"

Uther was glowering at him, but still remained silent, as
if disapproving.

"But what do I do?"

"Did the Society offer any kind of clue?" said Morgana.

Mundy concentrated on the deep forest, which was now
completely dressed in darkness. In that moment of utter calm,
the obvious surfaced as if from a pool.

"They told me to listen out for anything connected to
something called Daybreak. But I know absolutely nothing
about it—"

His words were cut short by an abrupt, unexpected movement from Uther, who dropped to his knees as if hamstrung.
He put his hands over his ears, rocking to and fro as if a
sudden, blinding headache had hit him like a fist. Chad's
immediate reaction was to go to him and offer a hand, but
Morgana drew him back.

"Wait!"

"What's wrong? Is he okay?"

"Yes. The word you spoke has begun this."

Mundy gaped at Uther. The big man took his hands from
his head and looked up at the night sky, tears rolling down
his cheeks. But they were not tears of pain or sorrow: they
seemed to be part of some superhuman effort, as if he were
wresting something from within himself, like tearing an embedded stone from the earth. His eyes turned from the stars
and locked with Mundy's. He spoke and now his words were
in the Old Tongue.

"Speak to me of daybreak," he said, and the words rolled
gently around the hilltop, as though the very stones themselves
amplified them. Uther was clearly waiting for a response
from Mundy.

"One midsummer's morning," said Mundy, also in the
Old Tongue.

"Whisper all its secrets."

"Cry their fearful warning," finished Mundy, the words
reverberating in all their heads. There came an echoing vibra-
tion in the ground, a stirring of something vast and primeval.
Mundy dropped to one knee as if a tremor had rocked the tor.

Uther, in contrast, got to his feet, drawing on reserves of
resolve, spreading his arms as if in supplication to the night.

He closed his eyes for several moments. The three guards edged closer, anxious about their priest, but Morgana stilled them with a brief gesture.

Uther opened his eyes, but only their whites showed.

"My God," gasped Mundy, "he's fitting!"

"No! Leave him!" said Morgana, her arm restraining him.

Uther began mouthing something, words that were meaningless to the watchers. His head turned from side to side and those terrible eyes seemed to be watching something in the skies, as if scenes, visions, were whirling and dancing above him.

"The knowledge," Mundy said softly. "He's seeing it, *reading it.*"

Morgana's face clouded with fear. Uther's great frame shook as whatever powers had been unlocked flooded into him. Sweat poured off him, his hands in spasm, and he looked as if at any moment he would simply break apart. But the inner door had been flung wide: whatever had been locked away came out now in a torrent, cascade after cascade.

PART FOUR
A LAPSE OF REASON

XXV

PETRA: THE NIGHT BEFORE THE SOLSTICE

GUY LURRELL HAD spent an exhausting afternoon on the river with a group of students who were the best rowers that Petra had. The young teacher ignored the sultry, cloying heat, driving the kids on remorselessly. They complained and cursed but pushed themselves. They liked Lurrell because he got them to deliver their best, and they gained a sense of achievement. Today, they sensed he was in a bit of a mood — enough of one for all the smartarses to avoid making crass comments about Miss Ranzer, who they knew was Lurrell's girlfriend. The rowing went on beyond the school day, but even though it was a Friday, few of the kids minded.

Afterwards, Lurrell went down into the town, making for the Feathers. Penn was sure to be there. Friday after school in the Feathers was almost compulsory for staff. On his way to the pub, Lurrell rehearsed what he would say to Penn. First off, he would apologize. He had behaved like an idiot. He didn't like to admit it, but she had a point. He didn't own her, although he didn't think he was being unreasonable expecting her to put him first. Okay, he wasn't going to argue. Apology. Then see about this bloody festival. If it meant that much to her then he ought to make some kind of effort and join her. And if things did get out of hand, he could let Father Madding know about it. That was too good a card not to play.

But the Feathers proved abnormally quiet. It should have been overcrowded and noisy, and as he went in, Lurrell knew something was out of order. There were few staff about, nowhere near as many as usual. He could see at once that Penn wasn't here. Maybe the crowd she was hanging about with had gone across the river to the Anvil.

He exchanged a few words with some colleagues and they confirmed that Penn had gone with her crowd to the Anvil.

"Thought you'd have gone, too," someone said with a knowing leer.

"Yeah, I meant to. Got held up. I'll catch up with them."

Lurrell left the pub, ignoring their smirks. They knew what this was about. He went further into the town, towards the barracks: the teachers would have gone to the stables and taken to horse. When he got there, the main doors were shut and bolted. He went through a side entry, calling out for the ostler who was in charge of things.

The man, a scrawny specimen with bad teeth and clothes that looked as if they belonged on a scarecrow, answered his shouts, wiping his nose on his sleeve.

"What's up, boy?" he growled.

"Did the teachers go out earlier, a big crowd of them?"

"Yeah, they did. 'Bout forty of 'em. Hardly a horse left."

"I meant to go out with them. Is it too late?"

"Yeah, only got a coupla lame ones left, boy. Your best bet would be in the barracks. If they'll let you borrow one."

Lurrell cursed. He could see the ostler was in no mood to open up the stables and get him a horse. He was shutting down and heading for the pub, that was obvious.

"What time are they coming back? Did they say?"

"Yeah. It's an all night do. Sunrise tomorrow is special. Longest day, boy. I reckon they'll all be out on the piss. Sun'll wake 'em up and they won't be back here till midmorning. Don't bother me none. Do the horses good to have a run."

All night. Lurrell fumed inwardly. Penn had gone off to the pagan ceremonies without saying anything to him. No doubt with Mundy.

He started back up the street, ignoring the farewell of the ostler, whose wave turned into a *V* salute as he went back inside.

I must have been an idiot if I thought I was just going to make up with her and carry on as before. She's dumped me. Simple as that. I must be soft, thinking I would apologize and it would be fine. Well, screw her.

He thought about trying to get a horse and crossing the river into the forest. It wouldn't be hard to find that mob and all the grubby band they'd be with. But if he did ride in on them, they'd probably have lookouts posted and some brawny pagan with a spear would be looking to play the hard man.

There was no guarantee that he'd be let in to join the party at this late stage. They'd just assume he was a spy.

What am I going to tell Madding? The priest would be disappointed that he hadn't gone along with the revelers. *He'll be expecting some kind of report, after our last conversation.*

As he climbed back up through the streets, he chewed it over. *Maybe I'll talk to Penn tomorrow, when she gets back. Be all reasonable and understanding. Tell her I'm sorry that I missed out— make her think I did want to go and be part of it all. That way she'll get carried away with her own enthusiasm and tell me what the rituals were about. What went on. I'll just pretend that I'm not interested in Mundy. Maybe she'll buy enough to let me join whatever they get up to next.*

Meanwhile he'd go back to the Feathers and look up his mates.

· ✳ ·

Dunstan Fullacombe was high up in one of the old towers of the Academy, in a large store area stuffed with crates, most of which had been nailed shut. He knew these had been here for many years, but he'd never asked what they contained. He assumed they were old records and possibly half a ton of redundant schoolwork, but it was of no importance to him.

At the back of the store, piped into what he knew to be a chimney flue, was a wide sink, an ancient model that had been here for ages. Its taps were dusty, their coating flaking. Fullacombe had never attempted to turn them on: the grime and muck in the sink suggested that no water had passed into it for decades. But if his calculations were accurate, the rusting pipes going into the wall linked up with the system he was trying to revive. He gripped one of the taps and attempted to turn it.

Jammed solid. Thought as much. But we'll see.

He slipped from his long back pocket a steel tool, a relic from past ages that he had learned how to use. Carefully he fitted it around the tap, tightened it up until it gripped as firmly as he could get it and then turned. Fullacombe was a strong man, but it took a whole lot of exertion to gain any movement. However, once he had made the first tiny turn, the rest followed. The tap belched, discharging brown water that slapped into the sink. It shook, spitting air and droplets and then released a gush. Behind the wall the pipes shook and protested, but the water continued to flow. It was coloured with the rust and muck of years of neglect.

Fullacombe put his hand under the flow. "Got you," he murmured. The water was warm, warmer than if it had been simply standing still in the hot June air. This water was picking up heat from the old system that he had been trying to repair. From the boiler down in the basement, through its fires, heated water was being pumped up into the highest part of the buildings.

"Success," he mouthed to himself. "Barry, you can moan all you like, mate, but I told you I'd make it work."

He switched off the tap and watched the half-filled sink empty itself down its waste pipe. It was a slow process: there was more work to be done, clearing out the pipes, unblocking the whole system. But it would work.

Fullacombe mopped sweat from his face and neck, realizing just how warm he was. He leaned on the sink to get his breath back, chest heaving with effort. It had been harder work than he'd thought.

As he paused, he heard something in the pipes. A kind of roaring. He reached for the tap but knew at once that it was too hot to touch.

"Shit!" Something was wrong. The pipes were overheating— ominously. "Barry, you pillock, if you've left the bloody boiler door open—"

Fullacombe took up the tool and made for the door, rushing out of the storeroom and into the stairwell, taking the stairs a bunch at a time. It was a long trip back to the basement, but he needed to get there very fast. He almost broke his neck in doing so.

· ✳ ·

Down in the old boiler room Barry Skellbow stood for a moment in shock, gaping at the open boiler and the blazing fire within its maw. He had done a round of rubbish collection from up in the Academy, a regular Friday evening chore. Most of what he brought here was from classrooms, the discarded paper of the students, but among the sacks that he'd collected for incineration was one from Chad Mundy's room.

Skellbow had been heaving as much waste as he could burn into the boiler. When he opened Mundy's sack, he'd found a small pile of papers and some old files, together with the clothes that Mundy had secreted in the sack after the incident on the quayside. As the papers and clothes went into the fire, the blood-soaked shirt landed uppermost, unfolding to reveal its stains. Skellbow stared in horror, fixed on them and nothing else.

Blood. Everything in the boiler was turning to blood! It was another warning. *They won't leave me alone.* He couldn't bring himself to move, transfixed by the vision. His hands gripped the crucifix, willing the blood to evaporate, but it was all he could see, a widening crimson tide.

After what had seemed an endless descent to Fullacombe, he burst into the boiler room. At its far end the old boiler loomed like some hellish demon, its furnace torches lighting the scene. Barry Skellbow was standing like an idiot, gaze fixed on the open door, where the fire roared dangerously.

"Fuck me, Barry, what the hell are you playing at! Shut that fucking door!"

Fullacombe raced over to the boiler, kicking the door shut with a clang that abruptly cut off the thunderous sound of the furnace. He used a chunk of wood to knock a lever in place, securing the door.

"I told you, once the furnace gets blazing away, keep the door shut. Don't have it roaring away like hell itself! The whole fucking lot will blow!"

Hell itself, that's a good one, Skellbow thought, barely shaken out of his stupor. But he said nothing about the blood.

God, has the idiot been drinking? Fullacombe wondered.

"Sorry, Dunstan. I was watching," Skellbow muttered unconvincingly. "Did it work?"

The Master of the Watch was drawing in air like a beached porpoise, his whole body drenched in sweat. He dropped the wood and nodded. "Hot water, pumped up to the very top, Barry. I mean, *hot* water. Once it's refined, it will be steaming. This old bugger is going to be busy in the winter."

"You said you'd do it." But Skellbow was still watching the furnace door as if something unspeakable was going to come oozing out of it.

Fullacombe grunted. "But you've *got* to be careful with it, Barry. If you use it, don't let the furnace roar on with that door open. Got me?"

Skellbow seemed to have woken up. "Yeah. I'll be more careful." He hid something inside his shirt and Fullerton realised it was a crucifix. Creech had been right: Barry's terror of the supernatural had become obsessive.

· ✳ ·

Carl Trencher left the Academy early that evening, reflecting on the meeting he'd just had with the Prime and senior colleagues. She was even more tense than usual, now that word had come that there was to be an imminent visit from some of Sunderman's Enforcer team. If Wroxton had felt any qualms about it, he'd masked them with his usual aplomb. It would be no coincidence, Trencher mused, that this visit would coincide with the festivities. Well, Londonborough needed to see what the Academy was up against. Time these bloody troublemakers were put in their place.

Trencher lived in the town and his walk took him not far from the Feathers, a pub he only occasionally visited. As he was crossing a street, he noticed someone walking up the slight incline in his direction, hands deep in his pockets, a disgruntled expression on his familiar face. He recognized Guy Lurrell.

"Evening, Guy," he called when the young teacher was closer.

Lurrell's head snapped up. He caught sight of Trencher and attempted a smile. "Hello, Carl. I was miles away." There was a slight slur to his words, suggesting that he'd been in the Feathers for a few drinks.

"Thought you'd be out with the pack tonight! Catching the solstice."

Lurrell grunted. "Missed the boat."

"I hope you didn't let your girlfriend loose," Trencher chuckled, trying to make it sound like a bit of easy banter. "God knows what those forest folk get up to."

Lurrell gritted his teeth. "No, I should have gone."

"Still, you'll hear all about it tomorrow, I expect."

Lurrell looked at him as if he had been caught doing something irresponsible.

"It's okay," said Trencher, moving closer. "I gather you've spoken to Father Emmanuel. Keep your eyes and ears open, eh? Times are tough at the moment, Guy. The last thing we want is any nonsense from the pagans. We need our staff very much with us. No stray lambs."

Lurrell nodded. The priest and Trencher must have discussed him.

Trencher nodded. "Keep me posted, eh? Or Father Emmanuel. I understand he's rather impressed with you and your work here. There are always opportunities for someone like you here in Petra."

· ❋ ·

As darkness smothered the world, deep, deep into Midsummer's Eve, a lone horseman rode through the streets of Petra, down to its locked main gates. The steed was jet black, its harness studded with what looked like silver. The rider wore a voluminous black cloak and a thick hood. If this appearance had been designed for dramatic effect, it had been completely successful, for very few of the inhabitants of the town (if they were awake at all) wanted to look out on such a figure, which was almost supernatural in its aspect. The hooves of the great steed, a particularly large creature, were muffled with light cloth, so that its progress to the gates was almost silent, adding to the spectral nature of its passing. At the gates, primed to watch for the rider, a single figure slipped from the gatehouse, barely glancing at the shape that seemed to fill the gatekeeper's vision, and undid the huge bolts and locking beam. In a moment the rider passed through and into the night, disappearing like mist. Behind the rider the gates creaked shut, the bolts slid home. *Duty done, as promised,* the gatekeeper mused, with a final shudder.

Over the bridge and out into the bright moonlight the figure rode, the only sound that of the steed's breathing, its eyes wide with excitement as it began to pick up speed. Somewhere nearby, across the river, a handful of soldiers who were on little more than a token night watch, saw the horseman, but drew back into the darkness, preferring not to interfere. Traditions and superstitions died hard in these parts of their world, and while they would have laughed scornfully at any suggestion that a spirit was amongst them, they preferred not to put it to the test, not on Midsummer's Eve.

Once across the bridge, the horseman rode fast along the old trackway, out into the immensity of the silent forest.

XXVI

MIDSUMMER'S EVE

DEEP IN THE forest, at the summit of a tor that broke through its thick verdure, several figures faced each other in the pale wash of moonlight. It was a long time before Uther, rocked by his inner visions, became still, statuesque. His eyes closed, his breathing becoming normal again. Morgana held up her hand for continued silence. Beyond her, moving in around them, were three guards, all carrying spears, their faces clearly indicating their unease, their readiness to act. But Morgana's gesture was for them as much as Mundy. They stood still, like hounds poised to strike.

Morgana was about to say something when Uther's eyes opened wide, as if mesmerized by one last apocalyptic vision. No one had time to react as he drew his weapon — a short, stabbing sword — and swung round, murder on his face. He flew at Mundy with a deep roar of fury. The blade came whistling down through the still air.

Mundy's reactions saved him from what would have been a quick death. If the blade had landed, it would have split his skull. But his years of training paid off. At the last moment he swerved, raised his right arm to block Uther's, and released a punch with his left fist that landed firmly in the big man's solar plexus. The sword spun from Uther's fingers, harmlessly dropping to the ground, while Uther grunted in pain and started to gasp for breath. He fell to one knee and within seconds Mundy was behind him, locking an arm about his upper chest and throat, the other securing it in an unbreakable grip.

The three guards were horrified, wanting to rush in and stab Mundy with their spears, but afraid to injure their leader.

"It's okay! It's okay!" Mundy told them.

Morgana, slightly unsure, raised her hand again. "He means Uther no harm," she told the men. "Wait."

They hung back, no more than a few feet from Mundy. He knew the odds were highly in favour of one of them gutting him if they pressed their attack. But Uther was not struggling, gradually getting his breath. He slowly sagged in Mundy's arms.

"Uther," Mundy said in his ear. "Can you hear me? Can you speak?"

The big man nodded. "Release me." He breathed, dragging in gulps of air.

Mundy did so, slowly, standing back. Gradually Uther got to his feet. He rubbed at his face and eyes, as if clearing them of pain and whatever else had taken hold of him. "I have seen," he said eventually, again looking out over the moonlit forest.

Morgana went to him, putting her hand lightly on his arm. He turned to her and nodded. Mundy glanced at the three guards. They had withdrawn a little, but continued to watch the scene like hawks.

"What have you seen?" Morgana asked her son.

Uther looked up at the stars. "My father's father's father spoke to me and showed me things. As clearly as if he had been standing here, alive, before me. He spoke of the secrets that have been locked away for so long."

To Mundy's relief, Uther appeared to be himself, whatever traumas he had endured.

"This man brought the key," said Uther, indicating Mundy, "to the knowledge that must be shared."

"The High Lord is coming," said Morgana. "He'll be here long before dawn."

"Then we'll wait for him. Call as many of the chiefs as you can from below. Chad, you stay with us."

"What about Brin and Penn?" he said, suddenly remembering they were near.

Uther shook his head. "They'll have to wait a little longer. Everyone will be told in the fullness of time."

Morgana spoke to one of the guards and within moments he had left the hilltop. "Let me look at you," she said to Uther, her maternal concern overriding everything else.

He grunted. "I'm fine, Mother. Apart from an ache in my gut. That was some punch, Chad."

Mundy was grateful to see the big man smile. "Sorry. It was instinctive. I think you'd have cut me in half if I hadn't reacted."

"You're pretty handy for someone without a weapon."
Uther grinned.

"What caused the attack?" Morgana said. "Why Chad?"

Uther shook his head. "He was just there. I felt this explosion of anger. Against the terrible visions. It's not good. Chad
was the first thing I saw and I just struck out. I'm sorry." He
held out his hand and Mundy took it.

· ✻ ·

Through the forest, the single horseman rode, never slacken-
ing his pace for a second, on towards the quarry where the
earlier celebrations had now dimmed down like the flames of
a fire to its embers. Many of the gathered people were awake,
few singing now, while others were snatching at sleep, all
eager for the first rays of dawn. At the entrance to the path
that led to the quarry, the lone rider was met by forest guards
who saluted stiffly, as if a general had appeared among them.

The rider dismounted, throwing back its hood, smiling
at them. "Look after my horse," he said. "Give him a good
drink, mind. He's earned it."

The men did not bow, but from their attitude they held
the cloaked man in reverence. He patted the steed a last time,
spoke into its ear as if to a confidant, and then strode up the
path to the gathering.

· ✻ ·

On the tor, Mundy was introduced to four men who looked
disturbingly like warriors from a remote past. Their dress
was partly ceremonial, but he guessed that, as foresters, their
whole way of life was very different than that of the citizens
of Petra. They were all armed with the same type of short
sword that Uther had carried, and from their physiques he
could tell that they were as thoroughly trained and exercised
as any military man from the barracks. They were unsure of
him, but Morgana's reassurances did a lot to set their minds
at ease. She spent a little time explaining what his part had
been in the drama that had unfolded up here. To Mundy's
relief she said nothing about Uther's attack on him.

One of the men, Carston, Mundy took to be the overall
leader, or at least the one to whom they all deferred, including Uther. He had a beard and a thick, drooping moustache
that added to the aura of a distant age. "I hope you haven't

dragged us up here on a bloody wild goose chase," he said bluntly to Uther.

"He hasn't," said Morgana, always the calming influence.

"It's okay, Mother," said Uther. "Carston's right to question me. I know I must seem like a bit of a freak when these ... things ... hit me."

"The ceremonies and rituals are fine," said Carston. "But we're not primitive savages. We don't want to start regaling our people with mumbo-jumbo, Uther. I mean no harm by that, but you know what I'm saying. They're not fools."

A voice spoke behind him and he swung round, lithe as a cat, one hand on his sword hilt.

Mundy gasped when he saw who was there. It was Sebastian Wroxton who had spoken. The huge man, looking double his normal size in a thick black cloak, strode forward, hand outstretched.

"Carston!" He beamed, shaking the man's hand before the other could do anything but return the handshake. "Good to see you! And Turner, Mithel, Brooks. And you, Uther. And of course, Morgana." He turned his gaze at last on Mundy. "Chad. You got here. Is it all becoming clearer?"

Mundy simply nodded.

"You were saying, Carston? No mumbo-jumbo. No witchcraft. At least, not that kind." Wroxton smiled. Even amongst these powerful figures, he was a giant.

Carston nodded, but his face still looked more than a little grave.

"There's no need," Wroxton went on. "What Uther knows is not dressed up in mythology and mystery. Am I right?"

Uther stiffened, as though glimpsing again some of the things that he had seen. "Yes. What I saw was simply the past."

"Actual events?" said Wroxton.

"Yes. You need to know the truth. So does everyone."

Wroxton looked around and indicated a place where several large stones flanked part of the hill. "Then let's sit here and listen."

They did so in patient silence as the last of the night began to seep away.

"My great grandfather," said Uther, "was a Londonborough man. A scientist who worked with others of his profession. They were based in a part of the city that was shielded from everywhere else. They had a secret mission."

"Was this before the Plague Wars?" said one of the chiefs, Mithel.

Uther snorted. "There will be a few myths exploded when I get through this," he said. "For a start, there were no Plague Wars."

He paused to let this sink in. All gathered around him were shocked by his words, although Wroxton nodded slowly as if the revelation was less of a surprise to him. Mundy stared at Uther in utter amazement.

"The Plague Wars were an invention of the scientists to cover up what really happened. Make no mistake, the world suffered appallingly, and who knows how many millions — yes, *millions* — died. Can you even imagine what a million people looks like? Ten million, twenty, — more? A billion?"

They all remained silent, trying to comprehend the incomprehensible.

"The scientists didn't even know *how* they died. But it was not through plague. Almost all those who perished disappeared."

Wroxton frowned. "Disappeared? Can you expand on that?"

"It's to do with the project. It was called Daybreak. The scientists, driven by the government of the time, now the Authority, were working on the Daybreak project, deep in a shielded area. It went wrong. And it was the consequences of that which led to disaster."

"So what was this project?" said Carston.

"I don't understand it," said Uther. "It's not mumbo-jumbo, Carston, but it may as well be."

"Try me."

"It's to do with something they called alternative space. Or, to be more precise, alternative *worlds*. This world of ours, they thought, was just one of a number. They thought these worlds run in some kind of sequence. Linked like a chain."

"Sounds ridiculous," said the taciturn Brooks. "If the Plague Wars really were a front, this sounds even more stupid. Surely it's just another cover-up."

"I don't think so," said Uther patiently. He was far calmer than he had been, as though the spirits of his bloodline were speaking through him. "Because they were certain that these other worlds existed, close to us, but normally unreachable, they tried to create a gate to the first of them. That's what my great grandfather was working on, this Daybreak project.

The technology available to those scientists then was vastly superior to anything we know. I couldn't begin to describe it."

"There is plenty of evidence for superior technology in Londonborough's wastes," said Wroxton. "There's no doubt it was very sophisticated by our standards."

"I agree," said Mundy. "The city is full of very strange machinery and derelict factories. The Authority is very precious about them. No one is allowed near them."

"Avoided like the plague," said Wroxton with a wry grin. "Part of the grand deceit."

"Exactly, Sebastian," said Uther. "The grand deceit. A perfect name for it."

"So this project," Carston said, "went belly up."

"In a big way," agreed Uther. "It must have been like opening the door to Hell. I've only been shown a fraction of its consequences, but I got an impression of something immeasurable, a force beyond anything we can imagine. Like a dam bursting, but one the size of a world. They realized far too late that the gate between alternatives was never meant to be created, so my great grandfather said. Instead of simply stepping through, everything was swept aside. It was, literally, the end of the world, or pretty close to it."

"So how did your great grandfather survive?" said Brooks skeptically.

"On the day the gate was opened, he was in the center of the city, meeting with officials. They were monitoring Daybreak from a distance, in case it went wrong. No one has any idea what powers were unleashed. It was shown to me as a kind of extreme rupture of the earth. Even time may have been twisted."

"I don't buy it," said Brooks.

"So what happened to the people? The millions?" said Wroxton.

"I can't give you a clear answer. The scientists were obviously confused: they had lost control. The shock waves of the disaster were beyond imagination. They spread across the entire world, in something they called a domino effect. One thing knocking another down and another and so on. When things had settled, long afterwards, the result was that a mere fraction of the population had survived. The rest were just— gone, as if they never existed. Perhaps they fell through the rent between worlds. Technology collapsed into ruin and the world quickly plummeted into a kind of vacuum."

For a while the whole group sifted their own reactions, lost in confusion or doubt. Then Uther spoke again.

"The government reformed as the Central Authority and started to organize the city. It clamped down on everything and ensured that any survivors were subject to their new, rigorous laws. For the benefit of mankind. To cover up this disaster, they invented a reason for it: attempted invasion from Evropa. They quickly spread the word about the Plague Wars and fear of them. What they had apparently wrought held the people in thrall."

"And this invasion was an invention?" said Wroxton. "Another fabrication?"

Uther nodded. "Yes. Another form of control. Evropa was as badly hit as Grand Britannia. Everywhere was. There will be few survivors across the sea and they'll be far too busy to invade us. Maybe in time they'll visit. But so far, no one has." Uther fell silent, as if he had finally finished purging himself.

"The Society," said Mundy. "All this time it has been seeking the truth."

"A truth that has been rigorously suppressed," said Wroxton. "And the signs are that the Authority is moving towards even firmer control. Over the last year, more and more soldiers have been sent into our barracks in Petra from the city. Half the men are from Londonborough."

"How long before they run Petra completely?" said Carston. "Another year and you know what'll happen. They'll be out here, hunting us down."

Wroxton was nodding. "It's the reason why they're bringing in more guns."

Uther swore, in spite of his mother's presence, but if she was offended by his language, she made no show of it. "There is more surviving technology than we could dream of," Uther said. "Again, the Authority control it and its release, where they see fit. They do have guns. And a lot worse than that. They have teams of people working at restoration projects all the time. In the buildings they call plague pits. And we... we are mere peasants."

"Little better than slaves," said Carston. "Is that the idea?"

"It's all about control," said Wroxton. "Conformity. And as to that, well, I've some news." He had their complete attention at once. "The Authority will re-inspect the Academy in a few months' time. But they're sending someone down very soon."

"Who?" said Uther.

"His name is Michel Deadspike."

"You know this man?" said Carston.

"By reputation. My sources tell me he is a hardliner. He answers to the inner circle of the Authority. So he's coming for a reason. I believe it's the thin end of the wedge. We all know that Drew was murdered." He glanced at Morgana.

"There's no doubt of that in my mind," she said, her jaw tightening.

"Nor mine," Uther said coldly.

"I don't think they will stop at one man," said Wroxton. "I think there will be more than a few deaths in Petra, if the Authority has its way." He bent down and picked up the sword that Uther had dropped in his tussle with Mundy. Turning its blade, he offered the handle to Uther, as if he had known of the incident.

Uther accepted it and looked at it. "Then we must take Petra," he said, holding the sword up so that the moonlight caught its edge. "And soon."

Mundy felt the nape hairs on his neck rising. *Take Petra. What does he mean, take Petra? By force?*

Wroxton did not argue. "In a week's time, the first of the processions will take place in the town. The festival will begin in earnest. Will that be soon enough for you, gentlemen?"

There was a unified cry of assent and again Mundy found himself chilling at the prospect of whatever they had in mind. *Surely they don't mean to take on the military powers at Petra?* But Wroxton's grim smile suggested that was precisely what they had in mind.

"Dawn will be upon us soon," said the big man. "Let's go down and share it with everyone. Let's treasure the day."

"When will we tell them?" said Carston. "Everyone must hear the truth."

"They must indeed. But initially we must handle this very carefully. I think the time to reveal the details of what Uther has shown us will come later. We have to impress upon people that the knowledge we have uncovered is powerful. Soon we will be able to use it to undo the Authority's grip on Petra and beyond."

"Will you address them, Sebastian?" said Morgana. "They will listen to you."

"You're our High Lord," said Carston. "None of us would dispute it. You tell us when to move, when to say nothing, when to take up arms."

Wroxton's huge frame seemed to shudder for a moment. "It's not a responsibility I'm very comfortable with. We curse the Authority for its abuse of power."

"Not you, Sebastian," said Morgana. "We know you better than that."

Wroxton laughed then, a deep, warm sound that brought smiles to all of them. "I'll choose my words carefully, then. Let's go down. For one thing I could do with something to eat, even if the roast boar must be cold by now."

As they began to file back down the tor, Wroxton came to Mundy's side. "I can't tell you how vital your role has been, Chad. You've been incredibly patient."

"Sebastian," Mundy replied anxiously, "these guys don't mean to *attack* Petra, do they?"

Wroxton clapped an arm across his shoulders. "No, not exactly. But we have to move before the Authority does. This man Deadspike means no good. I'm sure he is the one behind Drew's death. And who knows how many others?"

"What do you want me to do?"

"After the dawn ceremonies are over, you and I and any of our staff and others from Petra must ride back. I'll need to slip in quietly. Wouldn't do for our good friends Trencher and the priest to know that I'm a pagan dissident, much less their leader."

"High Lord."

"I would have preferred something less pompous," Wroxton grinned. "Never mind that. I do have work for you. We need to concoct a suitable 'report' for you to give to those two scheming little rats. Are you on for that?"

Finally Mundy found something he could smile about. "Oh, yes. That's the least of my worries."

XXVII

SOLSTICE

BELOW THE TOR, Penn and Goldsworthy waited quietly. His mood had become very sombre.

"You okay, Brin?" said Penn.

"Me? Yes. Just a bit concerned about Anna. Knowing about Uther, but never saying a word."

"You care about her a lot, don't you?"

Goldsworthy brushed his emotions aside with a typical gust of laughter. "Sure, but Mara and I are very happy. Never been any question of my leaving her for Anna. I love Mara. I suppose I love Anna, too. I guess you can love more than one person."

Penn said nothing, watching his face and his conflicting emotions.

"I'm quite happy as I am. But I can't help feeling concerned. I can't imagine how hurt she must be to know that she couldn't bear Drew a child, but—"

"Love is a complicated business." Penn looked sullen.

Goldsworthy sensed her own mood at once. "You and Guy," he said. "Is everything okay? You seemed to be pretty much settled. But now—"

Penn saw his eyes look towards the rocks where Chad had disappeared. She shrugged. "Guy's too quick tempered for his own good. And I resent his dumb accusations."

"Men get jealous. Maybe Guy's just anxious about you and Chad. It's pretty obvious that you're drawn to him, Penn. None of my business—"

"I *am* drawn to Chad, but he's very distant. Just now, when he went with them, I may as well not have existed."

"If you love Guy, don't throw it away and then regret it."

"I'm just a bit confused. I don't really know how I feel about Chad."

"Maybe you should talk to Guy when you get back."

She nodded. "Yes, I will."

"Let's join in with whatever's going on below. Cheer us both up. Chad's perfectly capable of looking after himself. He can catch up with us later."

· ✳ ·

As Mundy and Wroxton emerged from the rocks at the top of the tor, they saw that the entire company of forest people and inhabitants of Petra that had come were all now gathered on its slope. There must have been a thousand people there, standing quietly like a huge congregation in an open-air version of Father Emmanuel's church. As they saw Wroxton, a murmur ran through the crowd.

Mundy was straining his eyes to try and catch a glimpse of Penn and Goldsworthy, but in that sea of moonlit faces, it was impossible. They could have been anywhere.

"Dawn," said Wroxton, glancing across the vastness of the forest to its eastern horizon. The faintest glow edged it. The moon was still high, but seemed to have shrunk to half its size as if in respect of what was about to rise from the world's rim.

"Stand with me, Chad," said Wroxton. "I want everyone to know you and your part in what has happened. They must be told something about that other Daybreak."

"The grand deceit, as you put it."

"Afterwards, ride back to Petra with me. There'll be plenty of work for us all."

Mundy nodded, but felt a stab of guilt at not being able to see or contact Penn. *She must think I've abandoned her and Brin. But that's daft. She knows I've had to see Uther.* And while Wroxton and the leaders, Uther included, prepared to address their people, Mundy fretted on, becoming more and more frustrated.

Wroxton was well versed in dramatic presentation. He judged the timing of the dawn perfectly, waiting in absolute silence for the last few moments before its arrival, raising both arms in supplication to the new light. Beside him, the leaders raised their swords and Morgana held up a garland of many forest flowers. As the curve of the sun's blazing disc edged upwards, there was a deep-throated cheer from the gathering, growing louder as the sunlight intensified.

Mundy forgot his frustration, bathed in the sheer exultation of the moment. He could feel the power of the sun and a waking emotion responding to it. *As it must have been since the beginning of men,* he thought, *when it was worshipped as a god.*

· ❋ ·

It was gone noon when the company rode back into Petra. Penn and Goldsworthy parted company and she watched him walk off toward the Feathers. He gave her a cheery wave, as though there was nothing wrong with the world at all.

Where would Guy be? Certainly not back at her place, waiting for her. Too unmanly. He'd probably be kicking a ball about in the gym or on one of the sports fields. They would be as good a place as any to start.

Penn made her way up the hill and in through the gates of the Academy. She glared up at its windowed front, as if she would see Trencher or one of the Prime's other cronies staring down at her reproachfully. But the windows were blank. Her face was damp with perspiration. There was just no letup in the June heat.

She went to the section of the buildings that housed the gymnasia and washing facilities and sat in a corridor outside the showers. She didn't have long to wait. Soon Guy emerged, towel around his shoulders, his hair still drying.

He frowned at her for a moment, but then put on what was evidently a brave face. "Didn't expect to see you," he said. "Where's your big buddy?"

She shook her head patiently. "I didn't come here to have a row, Guy."

"You've been with him, though, haven't you?"

"There were scores of us. You know where we were."

"All fucking night."

"I'm not going to start arguing."

He glared at her for a moment, but then tried to soften. "How do you expect me to react? You're out all night with another guy. So there was a big crowd of you."

"Chad Mundy just happened to be there. Something important happened last night, Guy. You need to know about it."

"Go on then, amaze me."

"Not here." She looked around, although the place seemed to be empty.

"I did look for you last night, but I missed the boat."

"You would have come?"

He shrugged. "I know it means a lot to you. I was angry. You know why."

"There are more important things going on than Chad Mundy," she said. It was easier to say it when she reminded herself that Chad had been so dismissive of her and Brin last night. And neither she nor Brin had seen him since.

"Do you want to have something to eat? Anywhere but the fucking Feathers."

"I'm still full from last night. But a drink would be nice."

They went back into the blazing heat of Midsummer Day. They didn't link arms, the tension between them as taut as a wire.

At least we've stopped swearing at each other, she thought.

"Things aren't right, Guy. Not just here in Petra, but in Londonborough as well. Sebastian spoke to us all last night and —"

"Wroxton? He was there? Didn't think he was a pagan."

"You shouldn't think of them as wild men of the woods or primitives, Guy. In their way — in *our* way — we believe in the same things as the priest. The power of the earth, regeneration. It's not evil or corrupt. Surely you don't believe that."

He shrugged, but couldn't meet her steady gaze. He was thinking of Madding and their conversation, the clear promise of advancement.

"But there is evil in the world. And corruption beyond belief. Some of it is here, festering away like a sore. The Authority. The things it's done to control us all. It's all bullshit. If you'd been there, hearing the truth, you'd know how they've manipulated us."

They had reached a small pub, one rarely used by the staff of the Academy. It was half-full, but they didn't see anyone they knew well enough other than to nod briefly to. Once Guy had collected some drinks, he and Penn found a quiet corner.

"I need you to trust me," she said "I'm not just spinning a line of crap. Sebastian is no fool. He has access to so much information and knowledge. He's uncovered something about the past. It will change life here in Petra, probably across the whole of Grand Britannia."

"About the Authority?"

"It'll do anything to hold on to control. It's written history to suit itself. Its own twisted version. Guy, the Authority *kills* to protect itself."

"Penn, do you have any idea what the Enforcers would do if they heard you?"

"Aren't you listening? Of course I do! I said, the Authority *kills* people. But it can't kill scores of us, hundreds of us. It can't kill the whole town!"

"If the Prime or Trencher heard you, they wouldn't need to kill you. They'd just sack you. Is that what you want?"

"They and all their sycophantic followers are on borrowed time, Guy."

"For Christ's sake!" he fumed, one eye on the nearest people in the pub. "Listen to yourself! What is this, a bloody revolution? Your wild men of the woods are going to topple the Academy?"

She held her anger in check, her eyes narrowing. Coldly, quietly, she told him, "Yes, Guy. It's coming. And soon."

"It's fucking mad!" he said, trying to keep his voice down. "Penn, don't get mixed up in this. There's a barracks full of the military at the bottom of the hill. One sign of trouble and they'll be out here. They won't take any prisoners. There must be a hundred or more very hard cases from Londonborough among them. And the word is that they've got *guns*."

"Yes, we know all that. More killing to protect their lies."

"You're scaring me, Penn. I don't want you hurt. I've been a twat, but I'm sorry and I don't want to mess up anymore," he blurted.

She gripped his arm. "It's okay," she said. "It doesn't matter. But we can't go on as we have been. I mean all of us. Conned by the Authority. Brainwashed by it."

"But you're not serious about *attacking* them?"

"It doesn't have to be like that. There are such things as bloodless *coups*. There are enough of us to force the issue here in Petra without having to resort to violence. With what we know, the Authority will have to see reason."

"And what is it, exactly, that you do know?"

She stared at him, as if trying to read something behind his eyes, something that would enable her to trust him. She'd sworn a vow of secrecy, but if she broke that vow and shared what she knew with him, how could she be sure that he would keep the secret too?

"They kill people?" he said when she didn't answer straight away. "You can prove it? You have undisputed evidence that the Authority kills people?"

"I know you don't care for Chad, and that's my fault. But he's found something out. I don't know what, but it's to do with Drew Vasillius. He didn't commit suicide, he was murdered. Chad knows who was responsible. It will all come out in time, probably at the festival."

"If he knows something, people should be told."

She shook her head. "The wrong people are in charge."

"Look, I've got work to do this afternoon. Can I meet you later?" he said.

"Sure. I need to go home and clean up. Will you call for me around tea time?"

He stood up, nodding, but again his eyes did not meet hers. "Yes. I'll do that."

As she watched him go, she began to get the feeling that this had been a mistake. She should have said nothing. There was more she could have said, but not now, not later, not ever. She could not trust him. With it came the realization that it really was over between them. And with that came a sudden feeling of relief.

· ✳ ·

Madding sat in his office, fanning himself in a desperate attempt to cool down. The church was like an oven, even with some of its doors open. Any movement was like a struggle underwater, although it had been a long time since the priest had indulged in anything as active as swimming. His boyhood belonged to a different world, another age. It had not been a happy time. He shut off any thoughts of it, relieved when he heard a voice out in the church calling for him.

He dragged himself up, and as he reached the door he almost bumped into Guy Lurrell who was coming in at that very moment. "Guy! How are you, my boy?"

"Fine, Father. Can I see you for a moment?"

"Come in. Have a seat." Madding closed the door, forgetting the stifling heat.

"I thought I ought to tell you, I've seen Penn Ranzer. She was out at the festivities last night."

Madding nodded, sitting again, the perspiration already dribbling down either side of his neck. His clothes were sticking to his back. "You didn't go yourself?"

"No, but something's about to break. Penn really has got herself mixed up with the wrong people. I tried to reason with her, but it's no use. Nothing I can say will dissuade her from whatever it is she wants to do."

"And what, exactly is that?"

"Their leader is Sebastian Wroxton. He's the one running the show."

Madding felt something stir across his chest, a pang of excitement. "*Wroxton* is behind this? We had our suspicions, but he is their *leader* you say?"

"Apparently he's learned something about the Authority. She says…"

Madding could scarcely contain his eagerness. "Go on."

"She said it kills people to get its way."

"*Kills* people?" repeated Madding, as if revolted by the idea. "What does the girl mean? The Authority doesn't kill people!"

"I asked her if she had proof—"

"And what did she say?" Madding was trying not to be too pressing, but his pulse had started hammering.

"Chad Mundy thinks Drew Vasillius was murdered by the Authority."

"That's ludicrous! Who does he think did it?"

Lurrell looked at him for a moment and Madding sat back, realizing he was going to have to be very careful how he phrased his questions.

The youth shook his head. "She didn't say. But it's all going to come out during the festival next weekend. That and a whole lot of other stuff from Wroxton. He's the one with all the information. Something is going to kick off next weekend."

Madding again looked horrified. "Whatever do you mean?"

"Penn said it won't be violent. Bloodless, she said. And Chad Mundy is part of it." Lurrell's face clouded, his bitter resentment transparent. "I wouldn't trust him any further than I could spit, Father."

Madding studied Lurrell for a moment. "That's interesting, Guy. Mundy's supposed to be watching things for me."

Lurrell snorted with derision. "If you've put your trust in him, Father, you'll be sadly disappointed. He's playing games with you. Mocking you."

Madding's deep unease was obvious, his racing thoughts almost visible. At last, with a sudden great sigh, he said, "This utter nonsense about Vasillius being murdered could do a lot of damage to the Authority. I can see what Wroxton's plan is:

to cause chaos when the Enforcer arrives. Perhaps Mundy needs to be taught a lesson."

Lurrell nodded. *I'd teach him a fucking lesson, all right.*

"Perhaps you'll be the one to do it," Madding added, with a wry grin.

"He's too well protected by his new friends."

Madding leaned forward. "Well, not all the time, Guy. In a short while he'll be here, out in the gardens. Reporting back to me, pretending to be helpful, but in reality, as it now transpires, deceiving me. The only others here are the Brethren."

Lurrell sat very still, his mind spinning. *Is he telling me to tackle Mundy? Physically?*

Madding sighed. "He's very self-assured. Arrogant, in fact. I told him to be careful, but he sat in that very chair and laughed. There was no one, he said, that he couldn't snap in two with his bare hands. So, I wouldn't want you to bite off more than you could chew. These lies cannot be allowed to surface. Mundy must be put in his place. I can't say more than that, in my position."

"We'll see," said Lurrell softly, and it was obvious to Madding that he had probed a nerve. The young man was seething, so eager to unleash his fury.

"Wait for me here a moment, Guy. I'll go and put the Brethren in the picture. Should you, by chance, happen upon Mundy while he's here, well..." He let the comment hang for a moment.

Lurrell looked uncomfortable.

"Don't worry, my boy. The Brethren will keep an eye on things. A blind eye, if you like," he laughed.

XXVIII

MIDSUMMER'S DAY

MUNDY'S FRUSTRATION AT not being able to meet up with Penn renewed itself on the return to Petra. By the time he got back, his head was splitting. A combination of the sun's ferocity and his maddening inability to find Penn seemed to be driving spikes into his brain. Shortly after midday he was sitting outside the Feathers with others who had been at the festivities. Most of them dropped off to sleep in the blazing sunlight, while a few, like him, were content to sip cold well water. To Mundy it was the best beverage the pub served. Overhead the sky was a curving blue cauldron, the air shimmering. Somewhere in the distance there was a low rumble, as if a huge beast was stirring. The promised storm would not be long in coming.

Mundy was thinking about renewing his search for Penn when he saw a familiar figure twisting towards him through the benches. It was Wilkinson, looking thinner and, in spite of the endless sun, paler than ever.

"Andrew. Do you want a drink?"

Wilkinson shook his head. He leaned over, dropping his voice. "Father Emmanuel wants to see you. He's up at the church. He said it's very important," he added nervously. Mundy could see that his hands were shaking. Something had evidently upset him, more so than normal.

"I'd better come with you, then." Mundy rose and stretched. "Andrew, you don't look too well. Is everything all right?"

Wilkinson was like a cat on hot bricks. "Yes. No. Yes, Mr. Mundy."

"Which is it?" Mundy grinned. "Something's bothering you." Someone may have been bullying the lad again. He was constantly being bated.

"Be… be careful, Mr. Mundy," Wilkinson eventually blurted, as if he had been trying desperately not to let the words slip out.

Mundy rose and stretched. "Come on, then, let's go." Perhaps the young man would open up a little as they walked.

By the time they were climbing the last of the slope to the church gates, Wilkinson had still said nothing more. Mundy paused, easing them into the shade, out of the blistering sun. "What's this all about, Andrew? What do I need to be careful of?"

Wilkinson glanced in fear at the gates. There was no one else about, the air thick, the silence comprehensive. "The Brethren. They're like soldiers. I've seen them when they've been fighting. Two of them have bad wounds. Cuts."

Mundy feigned calmness. But there was something about this that brought him up with a start. Who, exactly, were these Brethren? What sort of business did they carry out on the priest's behalf? "Fighting, Andrew? Where?"

"They train in the gardens. But I know they fight in the town, at night. You mustn't tell them — or Father Emmanuel — that I said. You mustn't! They'll hurt me."

"I won't let that happen." *In the town! So it could have been them who tried to bully me. And Skellbow? That must have been them, too. But why him?* Something else struck him then, like a slap. *Vasillius. Murdered. By— these Brethren?*

"Andrew, go and get on with your duties. I'll see the Father. Where is he?"

"He said to meet him in the gardens. But sometimes the Brethren are there. I heard them talking." Wilkinson had gone even paler, as if he might gag. "They said— they would *slice* you." He waved an arm as if he was doing something with a knife. "They wanted to kill you."

Mundy patted him on the shoulder, trying to calm him down. "Are they in there now, waiting to attack me?"

"The Father doesn't want you hurt. They said."

"Okay, Andrew. Thank you for being so brave. You go on now. Go on. I'll be fine." He ushered the lad out into the sunlight and, spurred by his evident terror, Wilkinson hurried through the gates and out of sight. When he was gone Mundy went quietly through the church gates himself, turning towards the gardens. Surely Madding would not be such a fool as to risk having Mundy attacked by the Brethren, least of all here, on church property. He would never be able to justify that kind of violence.

Mundy decided to play this out. His bluff was obviously blown. But if the Brethren were behind Vasillius's murder, he had to know. So he opened the small garden gate and entered, his body taut. He shielded his approach to the gardens using the taller shrubs, peering between them. The place seemed deserted. No sign of the priest. Perhaps he was somewhere among the cloisters beyond. Mundy waited, silent as stone, for long minutes. Nothing. No movement.

He shifted positions, checking his back. Satisfied that he had an escape route if he needed it, he moved across the path to the lawn. He would approach the cloisters with as much open space around him as possible, affording himself good vision. He was used to fighting without a weapon, but he was beginning to wonder if he should have brought one.

At last something moved in the shadows beyond the lawn. A figure emerged into the sunlight, and leaned casually on the wall, studying Mundy's approach with apparent indifference. It was, unexpectedly, Guy Lurrell.

"Is the priest in?" Mundy said, deliberately keeping the sun behind him.

"No one is going to bother us, Mundy," Lurrell sneered.

"So what's the problem?"

"You are. You and those primitives out in the woods. Bunch of fucking monkeys, the lot of them."

"This is about Penn, isn't it?"

"What's she to you?" Lurrell almost snarled.

"A friend, that's all. A working colleague. I thought she was your girl."

"She was. But not last night, you bastard. Last night she was out in the woods with you and those other cavemen." He'd rolled his sleeves up. Mundy could see that he was a wiry, well-muscled man, no doubt as well trained as he was. And he was spoiling for a fight. But why here? Was this Madding's doing?

"This isn't the time or place to be arguing about it," he said.

"You're wrong there, sunshine," said a voice from deeper back in the cloisters. The man, Jarrold, stepped into the light, and near at hand, another, Batch, followed. Mundy sensed movement now at the back of the lawn, where at least two more men had emerged from shadows. The Brethren.

"I'm here to see Father Madding," said Mundy.

"He's not here, mate. There's just you and us. No one to interrupt."

Mundy recognized him. He was one of the men who had attacked Skellbow outside the Feathers. And the other man had been at the quayside scuffle broken up by the trawlermen. Were they armed? Clearly Madding was prepared to allow an affray here. There was no way out of this.

"Go on, Mr. Lurrell," said Jarrold. "We'd all like to see you beat the crap out of this interfering bastard. And if you don't, by fuck, we will."

· ✳ ·

After giving instructions to the Brethren, Father Madding went to Carl Trencher's office, where he blurted out what he'd learned from Guy Lurrell. His panic and his hastily conceived solution did little to reassure Trencher.

"Dammit, Emmanuel, isn't that risky?" he said anxiously.

"Actually, it's rather neat," said the priest. "Lurrell gets badly injured. Enough to have him shipped out later. Mundy is barely prevented from killing him by the Brethren. Unfortunately, in the melee, he is killed. No one is to blame. Four men will swear to that before God."

"A row over a girl."

"Yes. I'm sure your colleagues are aware that there's been a bit of rivalry developing between these two young bucks. A fight would seem inevitable."

Trencher was pacing his office restlessly. "It's vital that the Brethren's credibility is unshakable. Everything hinges upon that. What about Barry Skellbow? Are we sure of his silence? What if he blabs, in spite of our warnings?"

"I don't think so, Carl. He's terrified. He knows you hold his son's future in your hands. He has nothing to gain by saying anything. He can't implicate us."

"And you say the girl told Lurrell that Wroxton is the *leader* of these dissidents? He actually ran the ceremonies last night?"

"Is it so surprising?"

Trencher shook his head. "We must tell Nightingale at once."

"I agree," said Madding, trying to look calm, but Trencher could smell the priest's fear, as if it was oozing out of his pores along with that endless sweat.

"If the dissidents do something stupid, it would be good for Deadspike to see it firsthand. Then he can bring down retribution on a grand scale if it suits him."

"We will have fulfilled our obligations admirably," said Madding, taking a deep gulp of water, frowning at the glass as he set it down. The water was distastefully lukewarm.

"Yes, I'll contact him before I go and see Gunnerson. He'll need priming."

· ✳ ·

Mundy watched Lurrell as he slowly moved towards him, eyes locked on his. He had been taught to judge an opponent's caliber by his eyes. What he read in Lurrell's was anger, but also a hint of uncertainty. He would be very good, Mundy was sure. But beatable. The Brethren, also closing their circle, were harder to judge. From what he had seen of them previously, they were hardened men, no doubt vicious opponents. There was no doubt in his mind, however, that they would also bring a high level of skill to the contest.

Lurrell moved to within a few yards from Mundy, feet slightly spread, body well balanced. Part of him was hesitant, knowing this was an inappropriate way to settle things. But Mundy was a thorn in everyone's side.

Batch laughed mockingly. "Don't hold back, Guy. This piece of shit has been screwing your woman. He's laughing at you."

It was enough to push aside any doubts Lurrell had. He closed in on Mundy, aiming to grip his right arm and throw him. But Mundy was unusually fast. As soon as Lurrell drove forward, he countered, content to sidestep and simply twist away. He was trying to keep the movements of the four Brethren in view. For the moment they were holding back, letting Lurrell do the work. Mundy had no desire to hurt Lurrell, but he would have to disable him somehow.

Lurrell stepped in and this time Mundy let him grip his arm and shirt, from which buttons flew. They wrestled for a moment, legs twisting. Lurrell felt Mundy going limp, saw an advantage and went for the throw that would give him the advantage. But as he got Mundy's legs off the ground, Mundy rolled his body over Lurrell's back, landed solidly, and swung him into the air. Lurrell knew that if he resisted the throw, he'd have a broken arm to show for it. He had no alternative but to let himself fall. He hit the ground awkwardly, the breath smashed out of him. Mundy had him at his mercy and could have ended the fight with ease, but he held back, watching the Brethren. At least one of them, Jarrold, had pulled out a long knife. But they kept their distance, goading Lurrell on.

Slightly dazed, his back wracked with pain, Lurrell again tried to close. But he knew the edge had been taken off his speed. Mundy easily avoided another strike and this time used his balled fist to hit Lurrell over the kidneys. It felt like being knifed and Lurrell dropped, gasping. He knew that if he persisted in this madness, Mundy would end up seriously damaging him. Mundy was in a different league.

The Brethren had also seen this. Lurrell had no chance. They nodded to each other and began to close up their circle. One knife had become four.

· ✳ ·

Trencher wasted no time in visiting the military barracks at the foot of the town. His trips here were infrequent. He disliked the world within a world, the microcosm that was made up of men in uniform, exercising and parading endlessly, the air of male *toughness*, the mechanical rigidity of the system here. The irony of it did not fail to impress itself on him. Control and obedience, watchwords of the very Authority he supported. Nowhere were such measures more apparent than here. But it was all necessary and would be more so than ever in the coming week.

Gunnerson emerged from an annex and strode into the room, shaking the Senior Magister's hand. Commander Gunnerson was a thickset man with thinning reddish hair and a blotchy complexion, not helped by exposure to the present June sunlight. In his fifties, he stood with a ramrod straight back, hands gnarled as though constantly pummelling something. Raw recruits, if the rumours had it right. "Plonk yourself down, man. Drink?"

"Water would be fine."

The Commander filled two glasses and handed one over. "So, why are you here?" He sat, still upright, eyes glittering, fixed unblinkingly on Trencher's face.

"You may know by now that we're having a visit from another Enforcer."

Gunnerson snatched up a sheet of paper, holding it slightly away from him. "A Mr. Deadspike," he said. "From Londonborough. What kind of a name is that?"

Trencher smiled thinly. "You met Mr. Sunderman during the inspection."

"I did. Good chap. Liked him. No bull, straight to the point."

"Mr. Deadspike is his, shall we say, strong right arm. He's here to prepare for the revisit in October. He'll be running that."

"Fair enough. What d'you want from me?"

"Saturday's festival, Storm. In my time in Petra, I've grown long ears. I've picked up a few things. Things that are a bit disturbing."

Gunnerson downed his cold water in several noisy gulps and pushed the glass aside. It slid obediently to the edge of the table, but did not dare topple over. "Care to elaborate?"

"These wretched dissidents. The word is that they intend something — I don't know what — on Saturday, probably during the procession of the Green Man."

"Are we talking violence?" Gunnerson leaned forward, hands clamped together on the surface of the desk.

"Possibly. But with Mr. Deadspike here, we can't take any risks. I'm sure Sebastian will talk it all through with you, if he hasn't already."

"Usually see him on Saturday mornings. Missed him today."

Trencher thought better of saying why. "I just wanted to pass on my own feelings in the matter. As I see it, Storm, we must be absolutely certain that the pagan elements don't get out of hand next week. You need to police them thoroughly. More so than normal."

"Seems reasonable."

"And I know you've got arms, Commander. By which I mean, guns," Trencher added, clearly uncomfortable.

"Sounds like heresy. What would Mr. Enforcer say to that?"

It was Trencher's turn to smile. "Well, given that he or his colleagues were unquestionably the ones who supplied them, I'm sure he would be only too glad to see you putting them to good use. You may not have to do more than *display* them."

"Of course. So you think these bog people are going to run amok?"

"Sooner or later they'll make a move of some kind. Everything points to it."

"Can't have the peace upset. My boys could do with a bit of exercise."

"Use your discretion, Storm. We're in your hands. We don't want any bloodshed. But then again, if things get out of hand—"

Gunnerson tapped the side of his sharp beak of a nose with a finger. "We'll do our job, Carl. Rest easy on that one."

· ✳ ·

Mundy singled out one of the Brethren who seemed to him to be most edgy. He feinted to make a break away from the one he had selected, then turned and closed quickly with him. The man swore, deceived by the move, and stepped back as Mundy had thought he would. Mundy timed his attack to the split second, his right foot kicking out and landing with a sickening crunch just under the left knee of his opponent. The man went down with a scream of agony, rolling over. Before the others could react, Mundy bent and scooped up the fallen knife. He swung round to face the others and their amazement. But they pulled themselves together quickly, knowing that three of them should still be too much for him. Now that they had seen his methods, they would be much more wary. Slowly they closed again.

Lurrell had staggered to his feet, though almost doubled up. This had to stop. Someone was going to get killed. That wasn't right, no matter how much of a problem Mundy was. Murdering him was not the answer. Lurrell reached out to Jarrold, who made a sudden grab for him, taking him easily, knife held at his throat.

"Keep still, Mundy, you fucker. Toss that knife well away, or I'll open this boy's gizzard from end to end. And you can carry the can for it."

Mundy knew then that this had been their plan from the start. To have them *both* killed. And for him to be cited as the killer of Guy Lurrell. He had no doubt that the man would do exactly what he said. He dropped the knife.

Mundy exchanged the briefest of glances with Lurrell, and in those eyes Mundy read more than a gleam of determination. Lurrell sagged, as if the pain from Mundy's kidney punch had taken every last ounce of defiance out of him. Mundy was praying now that it hadn't. If Lurrell was going to avoid a cut throat, he was going to have to find something extra. As he drooped forward, Jarrold eased his grip a little, eyes fixed on Mundy.

The three others closed in on him, one of them weaving his knife to and fro in a pattern that was intended to confuse him. Mundy was not distracted by the movement, fully aware of the others. The man was no fool and almost certainly an expert. Mundy had to do two things: avoid the knife and get his assailant between him and the other two. Ducking and twisting, he managed to do it. Everything depended on speed; there was no margin for error in timing or in the cramped space. As the blade tore past Mundy's shoulder, he shifted his weight from one foot to the other as a second opponent, partially blocked by the first, dodged to avoid what he thought would be another vicious kick from Mundy. Instead Mundy used his hand like a piston and drove it under the man's heart. He gasped, dropping to his knees, his face ashen. Agony coursed through his chest.

Mundy followed up the punch by swiveling around and ducking again, thus avoiding the wild sweep of the remaining assailant, Batch, whose knife came within an inch of slashing off Mundy's ear. Lurrell and the man holding him watched in stupefaction as Mundy moved with unbelievable speed. He swung round and faced the three standing men, the other trying vainly to rise from his knees.

Lurrell chose his moment well, capitalizing on Jarrold's momentary relaxation of his grip. He rammed his elbow backwards into Jarrold's nose and felt it crack. The man flew backwards, spurting crimson. But he rolled over and came up, still gripping his knife. Blood poured from his smashed nose, but it very clearly served to do no more than make him hell-bent on reprisal.

Mundy glanced briefly at Lurrell. He was still feeling the effects of Mundy's earlier blow, not quite doubled up, facing one of the standing Brethren. It was a bad match, with an inevitable result. Mundy called to him. "Here. Take the knife."

Lurrell reacted quickly as Mundy flipped it end over end to him and caught it by the handle, amazed that Mundy had given it to him. Jarrold tried to laugh, but his shirtfront was drenched in blood and his nose showed no sign of stopping its flow.

"Use it on *him*, Guy," he said, spitting more blood. "Finish what you started."

But Lurrell had no intention of attacking Mundy again. Instead he continued to face the priest's servants. They had been ready to carve both of them up.

Mundy moved suddenly and was between two of the men before they could react. His hand chopped out sideways,

landing like the blade of a sword against the neck of one of
the men, while he ducked and kicked out at Jarrold. Both men
went down. Jarrold fell awkwardly, trying to roll aside and
cover his ruined face, in no state to continue. The other was
about to get up, but Mundy followed up his lightning attack
with a punch that smacked into his temple. For a moment the
man rocked on his legs, then dropped like a sack of stones.

Lurrell found himself fending off a fierce knife attack from
the last of the men and he drew back, desperately trying to
avoid several sweeping slashes of the blade. In so doing he
fell over and Mundy watched in horror as Lurrell's assailant
stepped in, straddled him, and raised his arm to deliver what
would be a fatal downward stab.

There was a scream from the cloisters just behind them,
enough to divert the man's attention for a few precious moments. Startled, Lurrell's assailant looked up, the knife strike
frozen midair. It was Andrew Wilkinson, horrified by what
he saw on the lawn. The youth was powerless to help, standing rigidly, transfixed with terror, hands to his mouth. But
it bought Mundy time to intervene. He hurled himself at
Lurrell's attacker, taking him just above the knees, sending
him crashing to the ground, the knife tumbling from his grip.

Mundy moved fast, one arm locking around the man's
neck, as he bent him backwards using his knee. "Which of
you killed Vasillius?" he said, his breath hot on the man's ear.

The man could hardly breathe, his eyes bulging. He shook
his head.

Lurrell was shocked at the change in Mundy, who, whatever
else he had thought of him until today, had seemed relatively
mild natured. But here, in control of this nightmare, Mundy
was almost demonic, his eyes filled with something very cold
and hostile. He meant business.

"*Which of you?*" he hissed again, tightening his grip. Tears
sprang from the man's eyes.

"Not us," he finally spat out. "They've gone. Back to
Londonborough."

Mundy rolled him aside and got up, grabbing the fallen
knife. He looked over at Lurrell, who was on his feet, but
clearly still in pain. "You okay?"

Lurrell massaged his side, but nodded.

Mundy turned to the last of the Brethren to have fallen and said dismissively, "You'd better get your friend some medical treatment before he bleeds to death."

Jarrold was on his knees, trying to staunch the flow of blood from his nose. Two others were stretched out on the lawn, only partly conscious. Wilkinson stood, still gaping at the mayhem Mundy had wrought.

"Let's get out of here," Mundy said, indicating the path to the gate. He gestured, first to Lurrell to join him, then Wilkinson. "Come with me, Andrew. Come on, you can't stay here."

Once they were by the gate to the garden, they heard a shout, and turned to see more of the Brethren emerging from the cloisters. But they were out through the gate and away across the front of the church before the other Brethren had made it to the garden. They reached the Academy without being pursued.

Lurrell was exhausted, badly shaken by the incident.

"Go and get yourself off to the nurse," Mundy told him as they entered the main porch. "Get patched up. And watch your back. Don't get caught on your own. Keep near to Brin and the others. We're all potential targets. This whole mess is coming to a head."

"We should report this—"

"No," said Mundy, shaking his head. "Not yet. Don't say anything about this to anyone except Brin. You can trust him. But we must wait until the festival before we say or do anything. Andrew?"

Wilkinson was watching the road beyond the main gates, still terrified.

"Not a word to anyone, you promise? This is very important. You help Guy get to the nurse. Then stay with Mr. Goldsworthy."

Wilkinson could only nod in abject misery, but at least he was with friends.

"Guy, will you take Andrew with you? Don't let him go back there."

"Sure. And look, Mundy—"

"I know. Let's talk later."

XXIX

PETRA

MUNDY WAS SOAKING in the mercifully hot bath when he heard the knock on his apartment door. It could be Penn, who he still hadn't seen since their return from the forest earlier in the day. Wrapping a towel around himself, he lurched out of the bathroom and pulled the door open.

Brin Goldsworthy was standing there, looking slightly apprehensive. Mundy ushered him in, briefly looking up and down the outside hallway himself, but it was clear. Mundy was about to apologize for having missed him and Penn after the dawn ceremony, but Goldsworthy gave him no time.

"I've just arranged to keep Guy and Andrew out of harm's way. Are you okay? They said there was a fight. Guy said the Brethren had *knives*. That they were going to use them. Is that right?"

"They wanted to shut me up, just as they did with Drew Vasillius."

"We're going to have to be even more discreet until the festival. We better split up. Be less obvious. Disband the so-called Goldsworthy group. We'll meet with Sebastian at some time, to firm up what's happening."

"I haven't seen Penn since we got back. I really felt awkward about not seeing either of you after I went to Uther and Morgana. I tried to find you for the dawn ceremony, but Sebastian took me under his wing and..." Mundy was starting to babble.

"That's okay, Chad. We understood that. Things are moving fast now and they're going to speed up even more."

"Penn must think I'm a real prat."

"Look, I don't want to interfere, Chad. I know you like Penn—"

"What you mean is, she's spoken for."

"Well," said Goldsworthy uncomfortably, "she's been together with Guy for a long time. They've had a few ups and downs."

"I know, Brin. I don't want to make a fool of myself. I just—"

"None of my business. But maybe this week would be a good time to let her sort things out with him. He's had a hell of a shock up there with you, but at least he knows now who his real friends are. I don't know where he and Penn are heading. We just need to be careful, discreet. It would look a bit odd if we didn't speak to each other at all, but we ought to avoid huddling together like conspirators."

"Yes, sure, but look after Andrew. And— can you just let Penn know that I'm sorry that I didn't get back to you and her?"

"I'll tell her. Just give her time, eh?"

"Okay. I appreciate this, Brin. I—"

"I better go. Take it easy."

Mundy would have said more, but Goldsworthy patted his arm, opened the door, and was gone before Mundy could phrase whatever it was he was going to say.

· ✳ ·

"I've had a note from Nightingale," Trencher told Manning, who was still flapping about the abortive attempt to subdue Mundy. "It simply says to take no further action until he arrives. He will deal with Mundy personally."

"The Brethren will keep a low profile. But where is that wretched boy?"

"I've seen him with the staff. He'll be far too afraid to say anything to anyone. Let's just wait until the weekend. I'm sure matters will be resolved then."

· ✳ ·

In the days that followed, those who were part of the perceived Goldsworthy group were every bit as diplomatic and discreet as they were told to be. Mundy dealt with his own frustrating situation by throwing himself into his work, especially the physical side of it, spending extra hours either pushing his students or working out in the gymnasium, to the extent that some of his colleagues asked him if he was trying to give himself a coronary. People in the group still met in the Feathers, but they mingled far more than usual with other colleagues and always in the open, where they could be seen by anyone who might be taking notes for Trencher and his followers.

Penn did see Guy Lurrell, but their conversations were brief, as though both of them were dancing around whatever it was they really wanted to say to each other. Penn found it hard to feed him anything that would in any way retract what she had told him on Midsummer's Day. He deliberately avoided saying anything about Chad Mundy, and she sensed that whatever else, he had decided that he no longer wanted anything to do with her. He was making Chad an excuse to free himself of any further obligations to her. It wasn't real jealousy, she told herself. Just convenient. But she was becoming comfortable with the idea herself.

She saw Chad at a distance more than once, but he never gave her the opportunity to speak to him: he seemed to be taking full advantage of Sebastian's decree that everyone should keep to themselves. If she had wanted to speak to Chad, it would have been very difficult. *Surely if he had thought anything of me*, she told herself, *he would have said something when we were out in the forest. Only an idiot wouldn't have seen that I was waiting for him to put his arm around me or hold my hand or something. Why didn't he? It must be that I'm not that important to him, that's all. But then, why should I assume that I should be?*

· ✳ ·

By Friday the storm, amazingly, still had not broken, but the rumblings from across the forest grew more threatening as it closed in. Clouds appeared, piling up on the eastern horizon, swollen with the promise of a deluge. Mundy watched them morosely. The fight and his efforts in the week had exhausted him: he had not slept properly for several nights.

It was late afternoon. Tonight would see the final meetings and the last of the secret planning for tomorrow and the festival. Goldsworthy's group were going to have to get together and prepare.

There was a knock on his door. He still hadn't given up hope that Penn might suddenly appear, even if it was only to berate him, but he suspected it would be Brin, giving him a last minute instruction about tonight.

It was neither. Carl Trencher stood there, the materialization of Mundy's deepest misgivings. Mundy stared at him slightly dumbly for a moment.

"Chad," said Trencher stiffly. "I know this is an off time for me to come calling, but I have a message for you." He entered uneasily.

"Anything wrong?"

"No. We're all a bit on edge, that's all. The Enforcers have arrived. The man in charge is a chap called Deadspike. He doesn't waste any time. He's been with the Prime already and drawn up a list of people he'd like to see. As our latest recruit, you're on it, I'm afraid. I hope you haven't got anything too exciting planned for tonight." Trencher avoided eye contact with Mundy.

"He wants to see me tonight? In my time?"

Trencher smiled with mock sympathy. "I'm afraid your time and my time belong to the Authority, Chad. You'll be sent for. Would you mind waiting here?"

"Any idea how long?"

Trencher shrugged. "Can't say, I'm afraid. These chaps don't work a normal timetable. Maybe half an hour, maybe three hours. Just be prepared." He smiled thinly and left.

Mundy closed the door after him with a bang. It was all he could do not to kick it off its hinges.

An hour went by sluggishly. Mundy attempted to focus on some marking but his attention kept straying. His eyelids were leaden and he caught himself dropping off. But he knew that if he slept now, even briefly, he would feel like shit when he was called. He went into the bathroom and splashed cold water over his face. But his anger remained.

Fuck it. He decided to go and get some tea. If they wanted him, they could damn well have him fetched from the canteen. The man would need feeding himself, so there was a chance that Mundy could get away for at least half an hour.

In the canteen, there were a few scattered staff. Most of the usual crowd were in the town, readying for the weekend. The Feathers would be stuffed to the gunnels. Mrs. Bazeley had far fewer to feed this evening and she grinned resignedly at Mundy.

"Double portion?" she said. "Plenty to spare tonight."

Mundy nodded, though he knew he wouldn't finish it. He was half-done when Carl Trencher appeared in front of him like an unwanted spirit.

"Chad! For heaven's sake! I told you that Deadspike wanted to see you."

"That's fine, Carl. I've finished."

"It's not a good idea to keep someone like him waiting."

Every eye in the place watched them as they left, conversations freezing for an instant. Once they were out of the room, a noisy hubbub resumed.

"The Prime wants a word first," said Trencher, the anxiety apparent in his voice.

"Am I in trouble?" Mundy said flippantly.

Trencher scowled, but it was all the admonition he was going to dish out.

Up inside the building, the Senior Magister led them along a corridor to an office. He knocked, listened, and then nodded to Mundy. "She's in here."

Mundy pushed past him brusquely and went in. It was an annex to the Prime's usual office area, an empty shell of a room. The Prime was standing with her back to him, staring out of a full-length window that overlooked one of the inner courtyards. She turned as he closed the door, her mouth a thin, hard line. "What do you think you're playing at?" she snapped.

"I beg your pardon?"

"You were told to be ready for an interview. To wait in your room. When Carl went to fetch you, you weren't there. Is there an explanation?"

Mundy made no attempt to hide his surprise at her tone. "Yes, I was having my tea. I had no idea how long I was going to be kept waiting."

"An Enforcer is here! A senior official from Londonborough. You're new here, Chad, but you know well enough how vital the Inspections are to us. We *cannot* afford to offend these people. Surely you know that!"

"I meant no offense," Mundy said, as patiently as he could manage.

"He hasn't commented, but he won't be pleased. And *I'm* certainly not." She stared at him for a moment as though preparing to launch into a real tirade, but then shook her head. "Go and see him now. He's in my office. You and I will discuss this later. Before you go back, if it's not *too* inconvenient."

Mundy nodded, closing the door behind him. He walked down the corridor and knocked on the Prime's office door.

A man in a dark suit opened it. "Can I help you?" he said blandly.

"Mr. Deadspike?"

"No, I'm Eversley, his assistant."

"I'm Chad Mundy. To see Mr. Deadspike."

"A moment, please. Would you mind taking a seat?" He nodded to the wooden bench across the corridor.

Mundy went over to it, dropping down, suddenly feeling even more tired. After half an hour of not being called in, he knew that it was going to be a long wait.

· ✳ ·

Penn nursed a frothy pint of beer, sitting with some of her less familiar colleagues in a corner of the Feathers. Her week had been a frustrating one. There was no point in speaking to Guy anymore, other than to exchange brief greetings. It was as though they had now accepted the reality of the situation. No point pretending otherwise. The bottom line was that if he didn't get his own way, he didn't want to know. *I know I'm a stubborn cow,* she told herself, *but I'm not totally inflexible. Well, he can go to hell.*

She became more determined to make one last effort to speak to Chad. Brin had said she mustn't think too ill of him for ignoring them.

"Sebastian commandeered him after the ceremony," Brin said.

"That was several days ago, Brin."

"Yes, but Chad's game of double bluff didn't work. Madding tried to have him killed! So I told him to keep his head down until the festival. It'll be safer for him. He knows he'll be grilled. He doesn't want you — or any of us — dragged into the same net. Chad's just trying to protect us. You in particular."

She nodded, but it didn't make her feel a lot better.

"Once the festival starts, it'll be different," he said. "And when it's over, well, there will be a whole lot of changes."

She went over Brin's words several times, before her moody thoughts were interrupted by the sight of a thin figure, squeezing through the crowd. It was Andrew Wilkinson, the creepy youngster who always seemed to keep himself on the edge of everything, as though he wasn't sure if he wanted to be part of the Academy community at all. For the last few days he was never far from Brin's side, as if afraid to be anywhere else.

She got up and found a way to intercept him. "Andrew, hi."

His eyes widened in surprise. "Hello," he said, his whole frame shaking.

"Andrew, you know Chad Mundy, don't you?"

"Yes, I do."

"I've got to be off in a minute. Loads of stuff to do for the festival tomorrow. I was expecting to see Chad in here. He's helping some of us with one of the floats."

"Floats?" Wilkinson looked bemused. Talking to Penn Ranzer here, in the middle of the crowded pub made him feel almost unbearably self-conscious.

"You know, Andrew. Horse-driven carts, with straw figures, statues, tons of flowers. Don't say you weren't here last summer!"

"Oh, yes! Of course! I help with those."

"That's great. Look, Chad's helping too. I've got some notes for him. Things he needs to prepare. I'm not going to get time to see him tonight. Could you pop this up to his room for me? Even if he's not there, just slip it under his door? I really, *really* would appreciate it." She handed him a sealed envelope.

"Okay," he said, slipping it into his jacket pocket, anxious to ensure that no one would see.

"Don't say anything to anyone. Just deliver it. No one needs to know. I'm really pushed for time and even if I wasn't, it might look a bit, you know, odd, me being up there. My chap gets very jealous."

Wilkinson coloured, recalling only too well the horrors of the church garden. "Yes, Guy helped me—" He was going to say 'get away from Father Emmanuel' but thought better of it, clamming up.

"Guy's got a fiery temper, Andrew! I don't want to upset him. Be a sport."

He nodded as she started to slip away before he could object.

As she sat down, she watched him briefly. He looked a little bemused, his face writhing with uncertainty. But she knew he'd deliver the note. He was so desperate to be liked. And Chad had been kind to him. It was a risk, she knew, but a small one. If Chad ignored the note, then she'd know where she stood.

XXX

PETRA

AN HOUR LATER Mundy was finally called to the Prime's office. Eversley showed him in, melting into the background. The Enforcer sat behind the Prime's desk, scrutinizing several papers as though unaware of anyone else. If it was an attitude calculated to make Mundy feel intimidated, it only served to make him scornful. He recognized the embodiment of everything he had come to loathe about the Authority.

Deadspike looked up, his cold grey eyes fixing Mundy dispassionately. He saw a young man in his early twenties, slightly disheveled, signs of strain in the darkness around his eyes. "Mr. Mundy," he said, not getting up. "I apologize for the delay. Please. Do sit down."

Mundy did so, trying not to slump. He suddenly felt even more tired.

"I'm Michel Deadspike, Enforcer for the Authority. Here to do a little preliminary work before the final Inspection later in the year."

Mundy nodded.

"How are you finding the natives?" Deadspike asked him.

Mundy was wary about his answers. This was the enemy. No mistake about it. There would be no compassion, no mercy here. But he had to draw on whatever reserves he had if he were to see this game through. "Dumnonia is very remote. It could be overpowering, but people seem to get on with life."

"Not too uncivilized?" The smile was reptilian.

"No more so than they are in the city."

"You speak their language, I gather."

Again Mundy paused. "You mean the Old Tongue? I've not actually encountered it here yet. Modern English is still the universal language."

"I read your thesis on dialects," Deadspike said casually. "Fascinating. What drew you to such a topic? Oh, of course — you're a historian."

Mundy nodded. He knew exactly where this was going.

Again Deadspike smiled. "The Authority has firm views on historical research. I expect you're fully aware of them. We're inevitably called upon to rein in the occasional over-enthusiastic student of the past. Now that I mention it, we had cause to do so very recently, back in Londonborough."

Mundy felt as if something cold were sliding down the back of his neck.

"To do with a group called the Historical Society. Mean anything to you?"

Mundy shook his head.

Deadspike grinned. "Nothing, really. Just a group of crack-pots. Don't suppose you'd know them. Hewitt Marlmaster, Harrald Moddack, and some woman, Amelia something or other. Tannerton? Yes, that was it."

Mundy shook his head again, but each name was like a body blow.

"But wasn't Moddack a tutor of yours?"

"Harrald? Harrald Moddack? Yes, of course. I'd forgotten his surname."

"He never mentioned this Society to you?"

Mundy shrugged. "He may have, in passing."

"Well, it's of no consequence now. They've all been dealt with."

He wants me to ask, Mundy thought. He said nothing.

"We have to be ruthless sometimes. Forgive me for per-sisting with this rather depressing topic, Mundy, but there was one other associated with the Society. Someone you did know— and were quite close to."

Erroll. God, have they got him, too? What have they done, executed them? Surely they wouldn't have gone that far.

"Erroll Detroyd. You roomed with him."

Mundy hardly moved. "Yes, we spent a lot of time together. But— are you saying he was a member of this Society? I can't believe that. I would have known."

"I'm sure you would have."

"No, you must have the wrong man."

"I don't think so. We were interrogating him and he rather gave the game away. When we turned up the heat, so to speak, he made a break for it."

"I'm sorry— made a break for it? What does that mean?"

"He knew the game was up, so he tried to flee the city. Rather stupid of him."

"I don't know what to say. Whatever possessed him?"

"We'll never know. The northern boundary is very well policed. He was shot. Ideally we would have recovered him alive and brought him back, but the guards are very enthusiastic. Detroyd's body was brought in. At least it was quick and clean."

Mundy tensed. A few strides and he could be over the desk and snapping Deadspike's neck before the man knew what was happening.

The Enforcer must have read his mind: he stood up nonchalantly and eased the lapel of his jacket to one side. Mundy saw the holster there, the protruding black grip of the handgun. "We avoid such weapons as much as we can," Deadspike said. "But some of us have to bear arms. Not everyone appreciates our work."

"Did you call me in for any particular reason, Mr. Deadspike?"

"As a matter of fact, I did. To be blunt, I think your talents are wasted in Petra. I think the Authority could put you to far better use in Londonborough."

"I've not been here that long," Mundy said with a forced smile.

"You can easily be replaced. I won't beat about the bush. Once my party goes back, in a few days' time, you'll be traveling with us."

So that's it. Back to face what— execution? Just like the others. Poor Harrald and Amelia. And Marlmaster. Erroll. Simply wiped out. He felt flooded with a mixture of anguish, fury, and remorse, and yet he knew he must remain deadpan. If there was to be a moment for retribution, it was not here, not yet.

"I see," Mundy said. "Well, if that's how it is, I'll start packing up."

"Yes, you do that, Mr. Mundy. Oh, on your way out, could you ask the Prime to pop in and see me? Thanks." Deadspike turned to the window behind him, as if inviting Mundy to attack him.

No, it would be very convenient for Deadspike to shoot me here. Self-defense. Enemy of the state. The one thing Mundy needed was time. At the moment Deadspike was calling the tune, utterly confident.

Mundy closed the door behind him before the phantom shape of Eversley could appear from his corner of the room to do it for him.

Deadspike called his assistant to him. "Make sure Mr. Mundy does not leave this building. Tonight or tomorrow. I want him confined until we are ready to go back to the city. I'm sure he'll resist, so be wary."

Along the corridor Mundy knocked and opened the Prime's door. She was still at the desk, scribbling across more papers.

"Chad, come in. I want to finish our—"

"Sorry to interrupt, Prime, but Mr. Deadspike wants to see you."

She looked at him, her face slightly flushed.

"He's not a man who likes to be kept waiting," Mundy added pointedly.

Her flush deepened, the irony not lost on her. He held the door open for her.

"Perhaps we can talk tomorrow morning," she said coldly as she swept past.

He went back to his own rooms, his mind churning. He wondered now if Deadspike had been bluffing. Had the Authority really disposed of the main members of the Society? Given the coldblooded way that the Brethren had been prepared to have him and Guy Lurrell cut down, he could believe the worst. And that gaunt monster, Deadspike, would have had no qualms about eradicating insurgents.

· ✳ ·

Andrew Wilkinson spent the evening wrapped in fear and confusion. Mr. Goldsworthy had looked after him since that horrible, horrible fight in the church gardens. But Mr. Goldsworthy had said, stay close to the staff and his friends all the time. Don't go back to the church. Keep away from Father Madding. And don't go to the Academy, unless it was with Mr. Goldsworthy or some of the others. That was okay, but now he had this note for Chad. He had to give it to him. Penn Ranzer said Guy Lurrell would be angry if he found out. But it was important.

But where was Chad? He hadn't come to the Feathers all week. Had the Brethren tried to get him again? Wilkinson didn't want to think about it.

In the spare bed he had been given in the house of one of Mr. Goldsworthy's friends, Wilkinson tossed and turned all night, the note for Chad burning a hole in his shirt pocket. *What do I do? What do I do?*

· ✳ ·

Bellona Haveris had come to the naval base at the north-western edge of Petra early the following morning to have her weekly meeting with the Naval Commander, Wesley Tithe-combe. They normally shared a conversation for barely an hour: Wesley was a no-nonsense character who rattled off his duties promptly and explicitly, and thus expected the same high standard of all the seamen he commanded. Although it was the first day of the festival, Miss Haveris had no reason to suppose it would be any less efficient and expedient a meeting than usual. This suited her fine: she needed to get back to the Academy to get on with the real work of the day.

Upon her arrival, instead of being smartly escorted to Wesley's spotless office, she was taken up three flights of stairs to another, almost empty room.

"Commander Tithecombe's apologies, ma'am, but he will be a little late. Please could you make yourself comfortable. Would you like any refreshment?"

She shook her head at the young recruit, who saluted stiffly and left her alone.

She went to the window and stared out at the view beyond. The air was still thick, the distant rumbles of thunder sometimes seeming to come tantalizingly closer. *Maybe it'll pass us by altogether.*

Outside, stretching up towards the estuary north of the town, the river shimmered like the iridescent skin of an immense serpent. Her attention was immediately snared. *I can't be seeing this!* her mind cried. Between the walls and the estuary mouth, no more than two miles downstream, a small fleet of sailing ships was moving slowly but assuredly up towards the town. She pressed her face against the glass, squinting to try and see details.

But the sails told her all she needed to know. They were white, belling out to display their emblems fully. Green, four-leaved clovers.

"My God," she breathed. "They're from High Burnam!" Her heart pounded. There must be at least a dozen ships.

She knew from conversations with the Commander, who had tangled with them out at sea, that each ship could carry a hundred men or more. *Men?* They would be warriors. Erish warriors! Real fighting men, who had literally carved out their own base on the mainland of High Burnam, across the western sea.

She turned back to the door, wrenching at the handle, but to her shock the door would not budge. She pulled, twisted, and tugged, and her dismay turned to confusion. It was locked. *Locked? Why on earth —?* She banged on it with her palm.

"Open this door!"

She was further amazed to hear a voice through the door. Someone stationed outside on guard duty. "Sorry, ma'am, Commander's orders. I'm to detain you until he returns."

"There are *ships* coming up the river! Erish ships! For God's sake, do you know what that means? This could be the Invasion! Do you hear me? *The Invasion!* They could well be part of it. You've got to let the Commander know."

But there was no reply.

She banged on the door several times more, but it was futile. She prayed that the guard had gone off to alert his chief. She went back to the window and watched in horror as the fleet of ships came closer, then pulled up to the far bank, anchoring them insouciantly, less than a mile from the walls. Movement among their crews was minimal. Whatever game they were playing, it was a waiting one.

· ✳ ·

Mundy had slept poorly again, drifting in and out of slumber, his mind whirling, taunted by images of Deadspike, the Prime, and Penn. His friends in Londonborough had been murdered. It was almost a certainty. The thought pounded and pounded at him, like a fist. He was soaked in sweat, his single sheet twisted and discarded. He had finally dropped into a deeper sleep just before dawn and now heaved himself out of its suffocating embrace. Half the morning had already gone. At this rate he would be late getting started on Wroxton's detailed plans. Everyone needed to adhere to them, if chaos were to be avoided.

He sluiced himself with cold water, rubbing at his eyes. Instead of feeling refreshed, he felt more exhausted. He threw on his clothes and went to the door. Twisting the key, he tried to pull it open, but it was immovable. The key normally worked. He tried it this way and that, cursing crudely.

It dawned on him then that he was locked in. Bolts on the outside? He stared at the door, trying one last time to get it open. But last night's conversation with Deadspike came back to him.

...far better use in Londonborough. Deadspike was going to take him back. *And he has no intention of letting me slip from his grasp. He said that Erroll made a break for it. This is his work. He's not going to let me do the same. Or if he does, it'll only be to have me cut down somewhere remote.*

Swearing, he paced the room. This was the only door from these rooms out into the corridor. *The window?* He rushed to it. It was narrow and had not been opened in a long time. But this floor was high up. The wall outside was sheer, with nothing to grip. Even if he opened the window, there was nowhere to go. Too long a drop, and onto hard stone. He'd break his legs, if not his neck.

It has to be the door. He went to it, listening. There was no sound outside. As far as he knew, no one else occupied any of the rooms nearest his. One thing was certain: he dared not remain in captivity. If Deadspike did haul him back to Londonborough, he was a dead man. Deadspike had said Erroll had been shot while trying to escape. Mundy would get the same treatment and the Authority would simply applaud the Enforcer.

He steeled himself, breathing deeply. Then, crouching down and measuring the distance carefully, he gently extended his right leg, touching the door lock with its heel. He did this three times in slow motion, familiarizing himself with the precise distance. His eyes fixed on the lock. It became the center of his universe.

When he finally unleashed the kick, it concentrated every last dreg of energy in him. His right heel hit the lock full on and there was a splintering sound like the snapping of a thick beam. The whole door and its frame shook. But the door remained firmly in place. Mundy examined the damage.

Again he went through the process, ignoring the pain in his heel. There was more snapping and creaking of wood. After a brief pause to listen for any sounds from outside — no one seemed to be out there — he kicked three times in rapid succession and the door swung out on its hinges, its own substantial weight ripping at them and buckling them sideways. One last violent kick smashed the door back, and he was outside in the corridor.

He turned left and hobbled along it as quickly as he could. Still he could hear no voices or any suggestion of pursuit. If it came, it would likely be from the opposite end of the corridor, where stairs led into the main body of the Academy. He came to a narrow stairway, pausing to listen yet again. Nothing. More slowly he eased downwards. No telling if Deadspike had stationed guards around. But having bolted his door so thoroughly, they probably didn't think there would have been any need.

Upstairs, behind him, someone did now emerge along the main corridor. A single nervous-looking young man was approaching Mundy's smashed door. It was Andrew Wilkinson. He had resolved his dilemma. His desire to help Chad had overcome his terror of being caught by the Father or those horrible Brethren. *Soldiers.* So, eventually overcoming his fears, the youth had snuck up to the Academy, choosing his moment to slip inside the main doors and up the stairs.

He reached the door to Mundy's room, without anyone being aware of his presence. He was used to anonymity.

Yet when he saw the shattered door, he gasped. What had happened here? Where was Mundy? Inside?

Wilkinson was too frightened to find out. All he wanted to do now was get out of there. He turned and ran back down the corridor, rushing headlong down the stairs and finally, relieved, out of the main entrance to the Academy. He thought he heard someone call his name as he pelted across the playground, but he did not stop running until he got to the Feathers. And he would just have to burn the letter and pretend he had delivered it.

· ✳ ·

Mundy worked his way through the maze of smaller corridors and stairs at this far end of the Academy, unsure where he was exactly, but convinced he could find a way outside. At the head of one narrow corridor, he could see down to a door through which sunlight made a rough rectangle. He went silently along the passage, which was dusty and presumably not well used. He paused at the door. He tried the handle, but as he feared it was locked. There was a frosted glass pane at the top of the door; he recognized it as old-fashioned fire glass.

Hard to smash. The wood of the door was even thicker than the door he had broken upstairs.

He swore again. If he had to kick this one down it would not be easy. His right heel was already badly bruised.

"I think you'll find that door's locked," said a voice from the shadows.

Stunned, he swung round, hands flattening in a posture of defence. If anyone tried to stop him getting out now, they would have to take the consequences.

The man who had spoken stepped forward. It was Dunstan Fullacombe. "Mr. Mundy," he said. "What would you be doing down here?"

Mundy relaxed, his attitude less threatening. "Dunstan. I'm in a bit of a jam. I need to get to the festival. I'm already late and the others will be wondering where I am. I took a wrong turn somewhere—"

Fullacombe nodded. "No problem," he said, pulling a bunch of keys from his belt. "Is everything all right?"

The teacher looked to be in a bit of a state, his hair unkempt, his eyes ringed, his whole body taut as a bowstring. Mundy nodded, unconvincingly.

"I'll cover your back. Is anyone following you?" he said softly.

"No, but if the Enforcer knows I'm here—"

"He won't hear it from me." Fullacombe unlocked the door and pushed it gently open. "I work for Mr. Wroxton. Stay here a minute." He was outside before Mundy could reply.

Mundy waited, still expecting someone else to step from the darkness of the corridor, but no one did.

Fullacombe's head poked around the door. "It's clear. Come on, I'll get you to a side gate. You'll be outside in no time."

Mundy went out and they slipped along the side of the building into more shadows and went on until they came to the huge wall that enclosed the Academy. True to his word, Fullacombe found them a gate, unlocked it, and pushed Mundy through into the cool tunnel.

"You look after yourself, Mr. Mundy."

"You, too, Dunstan. Things are going to start boiling over soon."

Fullacombe grinned. "That's not such a bad thing, boy." *But you really don't look too good*, he thought. *Not too good at all.*

XXXI

PETRA: THE FESTIVAL

COMMANDER GUNNERSON WALKED up and down the stiff-backed lines of soldiers on parade, examining each with an experienced eye. Word had it Storm Gunnerson was nothing like the tough man he'd been in younger days, but those who knew him well had a better understanding of the iron will that still shaped his character. As he studied these particular men, all of them recruited from Londonborough and not one of them a native of Petra or even Dumnonia, he knew they were a hard-boiled lot. No doubt the War Ministry in Londonborough had selected them specifically for this reason. The Ministry liked durable, reliable soldiers who obeyed whatever harsh commands were given to them. And these boys were about to get some very harsh commands.

Gunnerson's other charges, the bulk of his garrison, were made up of local youths. Most had spent time in the city, being trained, but they were of a different persuasion to this mob. They were tough, he knew that; but they had a special allegiance to Petra and Dumnonia. This lot before him knew only one boss: the War Ministry. They were its whores.

Their sergeant, Crammon, walked alongside Gunnerson, chiseled and finished as dressed stone, his eyes unemotional. Gunnerson knew he only had to lift a finger and Crammon would take action, dispassionate and remorseless. These men were willing to die for him if orders required it; today, if the anticipated trouble came, some of them would.

"Very good, Sergeant," Gunnerson said, turning to Crammon. "Excellent turnout. They look well prepared. Dismiss them but have them on standby. We'll all be taking up our posts in the town shortly. Come to my office as soon as you are done."

A few minutes later they met alone in the cooler air of Gunnerson's office.

"I understand that Mr. Deadspike's company brought a few more arms with them. Were they all stored in the armory when they arrived?" said Gunnerson.

"Indeed they were, sir. Regulations are very strict about that. No weapons are allowed in the barracks at any time without your express approval. All new ones were decommissioned and locked away as instructed. They have been there since."

"Very well. Today, arms will be issued. I am not convinced that our men should be armed for events like this festival. Personally I think the pagans are capable of no more than a bit of horseplay. We should be organized enough to deal with any problems without the use of weapons, particularly guns."

"If you say so, sir."

"However, both Mr. Wroxton and Mr. Trencher tell me they are a little concerned about today. Feelings are running high among the dissidents. There may be disorder. So I am instructing you to arm some of your men. That troop I've just seen. It now numbers one hundred and fifty men. Correct?"

Crammon knew that Gunnerson would have not only known the exact number, but probably the names of all the men, too. "That is correct, sir, yes."

"With the Enforcers here I want any trouble dealt with immediately. Issue guns to one man in three of your company. Fifty should be deterrent enough."

"Very good, sir. Do you want to issue any weapons to the local troops, sir?"

"No. I'm sure they are all good soldiers and obedient. But many of them have families out there in the town. God forbid that we have to actually use the guns, but if we do, I don't want anyone having to shoot his own kin. For one thing, they may not feel inclined to pull the trigger."

Crammon nodded, as though he had been given an every-day task. *We'll deal with the bastards, don't you worry your arse about that, Commander.*

"I have issued orders to Sergeant Bazeley in supplies. He should already have the guns prepared for you. Tested and inspected, oiled and primed."

Crammon nodded again.

"And Crammon, do everything in your power to avoid use of the guns. But if you do use them, it will be sanctioned by me."

· ❋ ·

People emerged into the streets of Petra from early morning, many to apply their energy to dressing up the town in its festival finery. Flowers festooned the main highways, either in large tubs or hanging baskets, some particularly grand displays in rowing boats dragged up from the river for the occasion. Evergreen branches had been cut from the edges of the forest and brought in to make the main road up to the town square almost a tunnel of greenery. Willow had been cut and worked into all manner of sculptures: animal and human figures, birds with outspread wings, and basketry of every conceivable fantasy. The town square itself was not only decked out in magnificent floral displays but had at one end a dais where speeches would be made. Around the square's three other sides, banks of seating had been set out. Masks of the Green Man proliferated.

The inns and pubs were soon busy, mainly preparing food: the smell of roasting venison and other meats hung thick upon the air. Overhead, the sky remained cloudless and that deep blue azure, but now there were the occasional front runners of cloud from the east, where huge grey banks were piling up. Inland the sounds of remote thunder continued, growing ever louder and closer, as though some immense beast prowled there, padding step by step over the forest, inexorably bound for Petra and its environs. Everyone prayed that the storm would hold off, at least until night. Meanwhile the air, already as palpable as smoke, shimmered, each minute closer to midday an ordeal for the workers.

Along the road, from across the bridge, a steady stream of people moved into the town, as they had been doing from first light. The inhabitants of the forest were welcome this day. They came in droves, all dressed in festival costumes, wreathed in flower chains, faces masked. Up on the high wall around the town, guards watched them uneasily, but they could hear the jollity, the sense of fun that the outsiders brought with them.

· ✳ ·

Satisfied that he had slipped out of the Academy unobserved, Mundy reached the Feathers to find the entire place heaving with activity. Apart from many of the regular crowd, there had been a steady influx of forest people during the morning. He had to shoulder his way through them to get to the back of the pub, where it had previously been arranged for him to meet with Goldsworthy and others. Even this area was congested, everyone in high spirits, voices raised, laughter breaking in constant waves. In a side room, Dane Elland and Zak Miler were busily distributing the last of the costumes and masks to Goldsworthy's group. They shouted to Mundy to join them as he squeezed through a packed press of bodies.

"Thought we'd missed you," said Zak, holding out a full-length green garment. "Here, get this on."

"Is Brin about? And Penn?"

"Somewhere. The town's crammed." Zak helped Mundy get the green shift over his head and followed up by hanging chains of pine cones around his neck. He topped it off by giving him a mask cut from some kind of dyed sacking. It covered his whole head, tying at the back, with only gaps for his eyes and mouth. Mundy found it almost stifling and unbearably hot, but he knew that during the festival and all that was planned, anonymity would be vital.

How does anyone move or get into position in this throng? It's a wonder no one is crushed to death. But he wormed his way through the crowd and up towards the town square. Hopefully Brin and Penn would be there, if he could find them. Surely they had not contemplated such vast hordes?

It was gone noon when Mundy reached the square. The sun still baked everything in its pitiless glare. More than a few people passed out, keeping the medics busy. Mundy took shelter under an awning, close to a huge barrel of water that had been placed there. He queued for what seemed an age to get a drink. He had no sooner had it and gone back to waiting before he felt his thirst raging again. His head throbbed, hammered by a migraine or something akin to one, and he fought off nausea.

A procession, led by the fabulous Green Man, at long last reached the end of its march through the town and burst into the square. The crowd had become more orderly, pulling back on all sides to allow the dancing figures room. Up on the dais, a number of dignitaries, including Deadspike, sat beneath another awning, watching proceedings with deep interest. Mundy was vaguely aware of them through the haze.

The Green Man was dressed in a magnificent cloak composed entirely of leaves, a huge, artificial head strapped to his shoulders, its mask garish, the wooden features carved

intricately into an expression of almost insane joy. It was the
face Mundy had seen around the town on doors and over
lintels, and repeatedly in his dreams. Capering around the
figure were a dozen men and women, bedecked in flowers and long fronds. Behind came row upon row of people,
resplendent in similar garb, tossing bunches of flowers into
the crowds. The noise was deafening, almost drowning out
the sound of pipes and other instruments as the music of the
forest was brought into the town.

Mundy realized for the first time that there were two lines
of soldiers across the front of the dais, at least a hundred of
them. He recognized Sergeant Crammon from his final trip
here from Londonborough. Wroxton had said the soldiers
would be there. And he had predicted that many of them
would be armed. Mundy studied those soldiers and realized
with gut-wrenching discomfort that Wroxton had been right.
Not all were armed, but every other one had a gun. Mundy
knew little about guns, not having trained on any, but these
looked like *machine* guns. Weapons that could spray out a
murderous hail of death.

*The Authority is not prepared to allow any kind of rebellion
here*, he thought. *Surely Wroxton does not expect us to attempt
to overwhelm those men, no matter how superior our numbers are?
It would be a massacre.*

He studied the dais. Apart from Deadspike, who sat calmly
on his seat as if completely unaffected by either the heat or the
proceedings, the Prime was there, her own face slightly drawn.
Carl Trencher and Father Emmanuel Madding sat, diplomatically apart, at either end of the dais. The two Commanders,
Gunnerson and Tithecombe, sat impassively. And Wroxton
himself, calm as a statue, eyes taking in everything. Mundy
admired his confidence. To look at him, no one would have
thought that the huge man was orchestrating a rebellion,
about to light a bonfire, a potential conflagration. It was a
gamble. If it went wrong, the consequences were going to
be horrendous.

But here in Petra, enough was enough. Drew Vasillius had
been murdered and God alone knew how many others. They
would all be avenged this day.

Mundy despaired of trying to find Brin or Penn. They
would be somewhere here, but while the dancing and singing
went on, followed by the rituals, it would be impossible to

move through the crowd. He waited, fighting exhaustion and his gruelling headache. Not far away he could hear rumbles of thunder, closing in. The timing of the storm, something which even the resourceful Wroxton could not manipulate, was going to be critical. If it burst too soon, everything could go belly up.

A few more clouds, no longer puffs of white, underbellies daubed in grey, drifted by. A deep hush fell across the multitude. Mundy saw the Green Man raise his staff, its streamers whipping out in a breeze that had suddenly stiffened. He pointed it at the dais and the soldiers lined before it. The huge, iconic figure spoke in the Old Tongue. The Green Man delivered his address for some time, extolling the virtues of the forest, its regeneration and the relationship his people enjoyed with the land. His speech was interrupted by cheers and cries of approval from the many voices of the gathering, but those on the dais waited patiently, only Wroxton understanding the words. After a long pause, which was impressively silent, Uther spoke in a new tone.

"The time of the Forest has come. The invaders have had their day! The Forest will expunge them!"

This slightly shocking cry was taken up by the people of the town, all Wroxton's followers and the huge influx of forest folk from outside. Up on the dais, Deadspike's calmness was at last stirred, like the rippling surface of a pool. He looked at Wroxton, realizing that this blasphemous Green Man creature from the forest had spoken aloud its planned heresy. The priest looked uncomfortable, mouth opening.

Down below them, Sergeant Crammon turned to Gunnerson for a command, final confirmation of what was required. Those that were close to Crammon were probably the only ones who saw what happened next. At first they didn't understand it. Crammon jerked stiffly, hands flapping at his neck. His neck— where a slender shaft had appeared as if from nowhere. Crammon staggered into the man next to him, clawing at the arrow, for arrow it was, trickles of blood showing at the entry and exit points. With a gasp of acute pain, Crammon dropped.

Panic ran amok. Panic and raw fear. It was only a matter of a few moments before the obvious reaction set in. The soldiers who had guns raised them, and without waiting for a command, they fired. Exactly as Wroxton had said they would. The noise was deafening, as though the thunder in the distance had suddenly broken right here in the square. Fifty machine guns roared into life.

And every gun exploded, blowing itself and the man holding it into bloody oblivion. The men standing beside those with guns and the dancers and forest folk at the forefront of their ranks were drenched in gore and human meat as a consequence of the horrific blasts.

It had taken a huge leap of faith for the foresters to hold their line, knowing, as they had, that they would be fired at. Now, pulling back their smocks, tabards, and other ceremonial robes, they drew out their own weapons, steel swords, and rushed forward, shrieking like demons. The combined effect on the remaining soldiers of seeing their companions blown apart and the oncoming mass of swordsmen shattered any unified resistance. What happened next was ferocious to the point of ghoulishness. Most of the front line soldiers were cut to pieces. Up on the dais, the watchers gaped in stupefaction at the slaughter. Wroxton alone seemed impassive, unmoving in his seat. Deadspike leapt up, two of his closest aides, including Eversley, immediately beside him, offering their bodies as shields. Trencher, to his credit, similarly shielded the Prime, while Madding slumped in his own seat, practically in tears, his whole body shuddering.

Mundy, like most of the people around him, was appalled by the unfolding events. He had been told about the plan, but he'd never thought the soldiers would be coldblooded enough to fire. "They will, trust me," Wroxton had said. "Storm Gunnerson is sure that the men he arms will use the guns. He will have had them doctored. Anyone firing one will be executing himself." But surely even he could never have guessed how vile the consequences would be.

Mundy knew that now, around the city, especially on the walls, foresters would be swarming like ants into the planned positions. Wroxton and Gunnerson had been coordinating this for weeks. And there was more. Tithecombe, the Naval Commander, had been holding secret meetings with the Erish from across the western sea, with whom he had been collaborating for a long time. At this very moment a fleet of their ships, anchored far up the river, would have disgorged a swarm of Erish seamen, and they would be through the barracks and up into the town. From the deep forests far to the northeast, a contingent of warriors from Nova Calleva would also be riding in to complete the circle. The Authority's soldiers would be outnumbered.

Mundy saw frantic movement up on the dais. Everyone there, with the exception of the two Commanders and Wroxton, was leaving, intent on getting to the only sanctuary available, the Academy. Deadspike was among them: he was now Mundy's target. Whatever plans were in place, whatever was expected of Mundy, he thrust from his mind. There was room there for one thing and one thing only. The Enforcer. *That murdering bastard.*

Mundy pushed on through the crowd, across the square. It was easier as the crowd began to draw back. The deaths up ahead were not something people wanted to be part of. As Mundy elbowed his way to the dais, a detonation of thunder sounded almost over his shoulder. The storm had decided it could wait no longer. As if condoning — or condemning — the dreadful acts by the dais, it burst in all its dreadful fury. Moments after the heavenly crash, rain pelted down. More thunder, directly overhead and all around, followed, and with it the continuation of the deluge. Pandemonium broke loose in the square.

There was resistance to the merciless onslaught of the forest warriors, led by the Green Man, now seen to be Uther in all his terrifying armoured aspect, for he had discarded his costume to reveal himself. Mundy briefly glimpsed him leaping up onto the dais, partially shielded from the driving rain, exhorting his men to action. The soldiers, those who were not local men but Authority vassals, surrendered, dropping their own swords, still totally bewildered by what had taken place so swiftly. Mundy stepped through the ripped and mangled corpses of the dead, choking back his disgust, and forged along what was immediately becoming a very muddy street towards the Academy. As he went, he flung aside his mask and the trappings of the ceremony.

When at last, after a strength-sapping struggle with the battering rain, he got to the steps, he heard a shout behind him. He turned to peer through a wall of water that almost totally impaired visibility. Lightning crackled and danced across the sky like the embodiment of madness, and more thunder rolled and boomed from everywhere. Mundy's head was splitting, fit to burst, and he just barely discerned the hunched form of Brin Goldsworthy, striving to cross the play-ground to get to him. Brin waved, but Mundy ignored him, charging into the Academy.

Goldsworthy was a few steps short of the Academy when he felt something like a length of cold steel slide into and under the center of his rib cage. The sheer pain knocked him to his knees, the weight of his drenched clothes almost drag-ging him to the ground. On his hands and knees he crawled towards the steps, breath now coming in great, sobbing gasps.

"Chad!" he tried to shout, but his voice was gone. More thunder mocked him. He reached the steps, and lurched up them. His left arm was numb, the nerves jangling right down into his fingers as if he had ripped a ligament. He tried to get through the doorway, using its frame to steady himself. Another terrible stab of pain tore at him and he dropped to one knee.

"Mr. Goldsworthy!" He was barely conscious of someone shouting in his ear, though they seemed to be miles away.

"Chad," Goldsworthy gasped, desperate for air. "Don't do it! Leave him. Let us—"

It was Dunstan Fullacombe. He gripped Goldsworthy and got him to his feet. "Brin, what is it?"

"Arm— chest— can't breathe—" A third shaft of agony speared him and he slumped into Fullacombe's arms. His eyes were open, but the Master of the Watch knew then what it meant. Heart attack. A bad one at that. He lowered him gently.

"Don't move. I'll get help." Fullacombe looked about in sheer desperation. In a few moments someone would be here from the town. Not necessarily friendly. The Academy must be secured. God knew what the rebels would do now. These things, however necessary, had a habit of going bad. The Academy would almost certainly be a target for one bunch of hotheads or another, high on the smell of blood. Fullacombe sensed movement at his shoulder. He swung round.

"What's up?" It was Barry Skellbow. "Is Mr. Goldsworthy okay?"

Fullacombe shook his head. "I'm going for help. Look, Barry, you're in charge here. Secure the Academy, understand? There's going to be trouble. Help me get Mr. Goldsworthy inside and wait for me. But *secure* this place!"

Skellbow nodded. "Security," he said. Mechanically he helped Fullacombe manhandle Goldsworthy into the Academy's foyer. They looked at each other, both knowing the truth. Then Fullacombe got up and raced out into the storm, rushing back towards Petra through the chaos of the elements.

"Security," Skellbow muttered, reaching for a huge bunch of keys at his waistband. He looked down at Goldsworthy, who was as white and as motionless as marble, his eyes closed. With no further thought for him, the caretaker went into the building. He'd foreseen this. That's what the blood in the fire had meant. It had been an omen.

XXXII

THE WALL

UP IN THE main tower, in her office, the Prime shook herself like a huge dog, shedding a cloud of raindrops. She used a thick towel to dry her hair and face. Madding, completely shocked by events, folded up into a chair, head in hands, as if somehow he could reverse time. Trencher was more composed, but like his companions, utterly stunned. His chest heaved as he leaned on the desk, his saturated clothes dripping onto the carpet.

"What in God's name *happened*?" the Prime said, barely above a whisper.

Madding stirred at last. "Not in God's name, Cora. This is the work of Satan and all his unholy devils." The priest was almost in tears.

Trencher shook his head. "I heard the guns. They must have been defective. God, it was unbelievable! The soldiers were torn to shreds. And then the foresters—"

"Murdering bastards!" Madding snarled, his fists beating the air impotently.

"Okay, calm down," said the Prime, throwing aside the towel. "We're safe enough here. I'm sure Gunnerson will regain control. He's got enough soldiers to contain those damned pagans. It needs a bit of time, that's all."

"I hope so," said Trencher, amazed by the Prime's remarkable composure.

"Where's Mr. Deadspike?" she said, staring at the open door.

Trencher turned, as if expecting to see the Enforcer. "He was just behind us."

Madding collapsed deeper into the chair, face covered.

"We'd better find him," said the Prime. "This is a complete disaster! When the Authority hears about this, we'll be finished, Carl. You know that, don't you?"

Trencher shook his head. "No. Deadspike will see how well Petra responds to this attack. Once order is restored, he'll praise Gunnerson for putting things right. The pagans cannot possibly expect to overthrow us. It's madness even to try."

"Find him," she said, unconvinced. But as she went towards the door, it swung shut and they both heard the sound of keys being turned. What they did not hear was the sound of Barry Skellbow's voice, repeating the word "security" over and over to himself, his private mantra.

"What the hell is going on now?" snapped Trencher. "Who's locked us in?" He thumped on the door, but to no avail.

"It's okay," said the Prime. "I've got keys." She rummaged around in a desk, producing a key ring with two long keys on it. She put one in the door. It turned with a loud click, but when she attempted to open the door, it would not move.

"There are bolts on the outside," she said breathlessly. "We're locked in."

Trencher swore crudely. The bile of panic rose in him.

"Let's not overreact," said the Prime, although a deep sense of unease was stealing over her. "This may be the safest place to be for the moment."

· ✳ ·

Fullacombe's progress through the town was impeded by the continuing ferocity of the downpour and the unprecedented amount of water flooding down the sloping streets: the drains could not cope and there was a danger of the streets themselves becoming rivers. But Fullacombe got to the town square, where he knew there should be medical help. His eyes fell upon complete horror when he got there. For a moment he stood, utterly numbed by the carnage. There were bodies everywhere before the dais, mostly of dead soldiers, but there were as many wounded. The mud that drained off from the square like farm slurry was deep red, curdling with the blood of so many victims. Whatever medical help existed in Petra was here, trying to mop up the aftermath of what had been some dreadful event. *What was it, an explosion?* he asked himself.

He rushed over to one of the rain-soaked medics, who was desperately trying to stem the blood flow of a maimed young soldier. "I need help!" Fullacombe shouted above the din of the storm.

The medic shook his head, pointing, and whatever he said in reply was lost in another crash of thunder. Fullacombe went further into the square. He stared about him in bewilderment. So many dead! How was he going to get a medic up to Goldsworthy? None of them could be spared.

"Dunstan!" someone cried, his name barely audible. He swung round.

It was the young teacher, Penn Ranzer, soaked to the skin, her hair plastered to her head as if she'd just emerged from a pool.

"Miss Ranzer! I need help. It's Mr. Goldsworthy."

"Where is he? What's wrong?"

"He's had a heart attack. Up at the Academy."

Her face turned ashen. "I'll come." She started forward at once. "I'm not a medic, but I can do first aid, maybe I can help Brin. You won't get anyone else."

They made their difficult way back up through the square. "What happened, Miss Ranzer? What happened?" Fullacombe repeated, voice choking.

She shook her head. "Madness, Dunstan. Complete lunacy. They had guns. They were going to use them on us. But they blew up in their faces."

He shook his head in disbelief. They fell silent, concentrating on the effort needed to get up the flooding street to the Academy. It was exhausting. Halfway there, Fullacombe stopped in his tracks.

My God. The boilers. Barry—

Penn paused reluctantly, but saw the sudden shock in the big man's face.

He started forward again. "We're putting on a demonstration for the Enforcers. The boilers. I left Barry in charge. The main boiler needs shutting down." He was speaking now through huge gulps of air. "If he forgets to do it again, the whole thing will blow."

"What does that mean?"

Fullacombe looked mortified. "Half the building will be torn apart."

· ✳ ·

Deadspike and his two aides had reached the Academy a few moments after the Prime and her companions. Once inside the main entrance, they conferred briefly.

"Stay close by," Deadspike told them. "I'm afraid you two will have to cover my back until this wretched business is sorted out. I must not be detained."

Eversley nodded. "You go on, sir. Lock yourself in with the Prime."

Deadspike turned into the building along the corridor ahead of him as quickly as he could. The brief delay with his colleagues had separated him from the Prime and the others. He paused briefly at a wide stairway, listening for the sound of retreating footsteps. He thought he heard something, so went on up. By the time he reached the top, he realized he had taken a wrong turn somewhere. The Academy's labyrinthine passages and corridors had confused him. He had no idea where he was.

· ✳ ·

When Mundy reached the Academy, not far behind Deadspike and his aides, there was murder in his heart. He shook himself, his drenched clothes dripping puddles onto the tiles of the foyer. He paused only briefly to listen. The building was silent; then someone moved in the corridor to his left. A moment later he was facing Deadspike's two aides. He recognized Eversley's face. His once immaculate suit was stained with blood, as sodden now as Mundy's clothes.

"Where's Deadspike?" Mundy said.

Eversley knew by Mundy's expression what was in his mind. "*Mr.* Deadspike doesn't want to be disturbed at present."

Mundy ignored him and made to brush past. Eversley reached out an arm, intending to grip Mundy's shoulder and pull him back, but Mundy moved with extraordinary speed, ducking down, taking Eversley's arm in both of his own, and swiveling around. The aide was caught completely unawares and off-balance. He was whipped over, landing with a loud smack on the tiles, his back taking the weight of the fall. As he sprawled there, mouth working for breath, Waites swore and made a lunge for Mundy.

Mundy leaned back and kicked out, his right foot landing a ferocious blow just below Waites's knee. With a scream of pain, the aide went down, clutching his wrecked joint, rolling over in agony. Neither of the aides would be on their feet again for some while.

Dismissing them, Mundy raced on into the building, assuming correctly that the two men had been protecting this
passage because it was the one Deadspike had taken.

· ✳ ·

Wroxton had allowed for the mayhem in the square in his
planning. This was no time to be squeamish. He gathered
around him a score of his own fighting men, including the
bowman who had so expertly taken out Sergeant Crammon.
He also called on a captain from Gunnerson's home troops,
one from Tithecombe's naval troops, and one from the Erish
sailors who had linked up with the rebels. At a word from
Wroxton, all now mounted, they spurred up towards the
Academy.

When they arrived outside the doors, dismounting as one
in the continuing downpour, it was to find Fullacombe and
Penn Ranzer on the steps. The girl was bent over a fallen
figure. Wroxton saw at once that it was Brin Goldsworthy.

Penn's face was streaked with tears. She held Goldsworthy's
head in her lap.

"Brin?" said Wroxton, dropping to one knee.

"He's gone," she said. "His heart. He's gone."

Wroxton shook his head slowly, reaching out and touching
the face of his friend. "Not now, Brin. This shouldn't have
happened."

Penn gently laid Goldsworthy back against the pillar.

Abruptly Wroxton remembered where he was and the
circumstances enfolding them all. "Where's the Prime? And
the others?"

"Chad was chasing them. And the Enforcer."

Wroxton nodded grimly. He waved his men into the building and they split up, beginning their own search. Fullacombe
muttered something about boilers and rushed off as if suddenly scalded.

Wroxton took the left corridor and within minutes heard
sounds from a small adjacent room. He pushed open its door
to find Deadspike's two aides, one trying to administer to the
other, whose leg seemed to be badly damaged.

"Where's your boss?" said Wroxton, ignoring their dilemma.
"With the Prime?"

Eversley felt as if his spine had been crushed. He pointed
dejectedly to the corridor that Deadspike had taken. "Mundy

went after them. He's lost his mind." Wroxton ignored them and led his group of men along the corridor and up stairs. He needed to snare the last of this vermin.

· ❋ ·

Deadspike swore as he wound through the endless corridors of this accursed old building. There was little light outside, the skies almost black as night. The storm dragged on, as if battalion after battalion of clouds were crashing past, throwing endless bolts of lightning onto the buildings below. It was as if all those long, long days of blistering heat were being atoned for. The Enforcer peered through a window. Outside he could barely discern a huge length of wall, beyond which was a high tower. There were lights up there. It must be where the Prime and her companions had gone. Possible safety.

Ahead was a door he assumed led to the wall across to the tower. He tried it and thankfully it was not locked. He opened it and it smashed back, buffeted by the force of the wind, narrowly missing him. Ducking his head, he went out into the furore of the elements: he was on the wall. For a moment he almost turned back, seeing the size of the drop on the other side of the low parapet. The sea raged far down below, flinging up long white tails that almost reached the wall's lip.

Inside the building, Mundy was racing along corridors, searching every room, certain that Deadspike was here somewhere. A vivid flash illuminated the scene outside and Mundy saw the massive silhouette of the outer wall. He was sure that someone was up there, limned for a moment in that garish white light. He ran for the nearest outer door, flung it open, and went out into a courtyard. There were stone steps leading from it up to the wall. He ran through the torrents, almost slipping, but climbed the steps two at a time. When he got to their top he paused. There was someone here, crossing the wall, battered by the snarling wind and rain.

Mundy waited. Thirty feet away, the figure paused, sensing it was not alone. It looked up and Mundy found himself staring into the cold grey eyes of the one man he wanted to meet.

Deadspike saw that he was not alone and stiffened.

· ❋ ·

Fullacombe burst into the boiler room, deep below the buildings. One glance told him all he needed to know. Mercifully

Barry had shut and bolted tight the boiler's steel door, containing that raging furnace. *Barry, you're a bloody hero,* he said to himself. Hugely relieved, he headed back for the stairs.

Skellbow himself was wandering higher up in the sprawling edifice, waving his huge bunch of keys and his crucifix about like a shaman dispensing magic spells. "Security, security," he muttered repeatedly, as though it was an incantation to ward off the devils and evil spirits which were undoubtedly here now, just as promised. He knew none of the staff were here, but he had heard those malefic entities and meant to trap them all. He locked every door and swung bolts across them where he found them, sealing them with a touch of the cross. He was unshaven, his eyes dark-ringed, a strong smell of alcohol pervading him.

"No more mistakes. Can't point their fucking fingers at Barry Skellbow! Lock it all up. Make it secure!"

In the foyer, men were taking Brin Goldsworthy into the building, to a classroom where they could lay him out and cover him. Penn knew there was no more she could do. She had to find Chad. God knew what he would do up here. The thought terrified her.

· ✱ ·

They met halfway across the wall, no more than ten feet apart. The rain suddenly eased, as if whatever dark forces coiled about these ancient buildings subsided, listening in on this ultimate drama.

"Mr. Mundy," said Deadspike above the wind and sea. The teacher was haggard, a hint of madness in his glare. "I presume you are part of this monstrous conspiracy?"

Mundy indicated the wall. "Fitting that we should meet here, you bastard," he said. "The first of your murders happened here."

Deadspike frowned for a moment. Then those eyes lit up. "Ah, yes. The untimely death of Drew Vasillius. Is this where he fell?"

"You were responsible. They *called* it suicide. But we all know better now. Just as we know all there is to know about Daybreak. Soon everyone in Petra and beyond it will know the truth."

Deadspike's mocking grin dissolved. For a moment he had no answer. But then that grin returned, made more unpleasant by the flickering light around them. He pulled back his saturated jacket to reveal the holster slung over his shoulder and the gun within it.

"I hope you don't think you're going to throw *me* over the edge, Mr. Mundy."

· ✳ ·

The Prime cursed as she tried the last of the doors to her suite of offices. Every one of them was locked and bolted. "It must be," she said, though not with any real conviction, "that we've been locked in for our own safety. Until order is restored."

Trencher and Madding had been around the rooms with her. Madding was shivering uncontrollably. He kept wiping frantically at his robes, trying to scrape off the blood with his fingernails.

Trencher was about to comment when there came another detonation of thunder directly overhead. Almost simultaneously there was an extraordinarily loud sound of something being ground up, an avalanche of noise. The entire tower shook so badly that they all lurched to one side, Madding actually falling to his knees.

"We've been hit," said Trencher. "Lightning. It's hit the tower above us."

"Oh God, oh God, oh God," Madding cried, staying on the floor, hands over his ears like a child.

The Prime glared at him in disgust. There was nothing they could do but wait.

"It's retribution," Madding moaned.

"What do you mean?" snapped the Prime.

"For Vasillius."

"He's babbling," said Trencher. "Pull yourself together, Father."

"*What do you mean?*" the Prime demanded icily of Madding. "We shouldn't have done it. We knew it was wrong."

The Prime swung round on Trencher, face aghast. "Is he saying what I think he's saying? Carl? *Well?*" It was only now that the truth struck her.

"We can't be blamed for Vasillius's death. He was ill, dammit." Trencher glared at the priest, but Madding rocked from side to side, helplessly.

They waited in silence. The results of the lightning strike took fast and furious root. Tons of masonry had been hurled aside as if by a maniac storm god. A number of wooden beams, dried out over the years, burst into flame. Flame that gorged itself avidly, uninhibited by the rain. Down into the tower it plunged with volcanic force, splitting more of the walls asunder, digging out more timber, floors, walls, doors, gorging itself.

The Prime was the first to understand. It was the smoke. A few tendrils drifted under one of the doors.

Madding, still prone, lifted his head. He saw smoke lapping towards him across the floor like an incoming grey tide. He shuffled into a sitting position, pointing.

"My God," said Trencher. "The tower's on fire! We must get out!" He rushed to the nearest light chair and picked it up. "The windows! It's the only way."

"*No!*" shouted the Prime as he swung the chair. But it was too late to stop him. He hurled the chair at the nearest window, smashing it. Cold air and rain rushed in. But behind them the door to the room shuddered, as though something huge and incalculably angry were battering at it with iron fists. Something that would not be contained.

· ✻ ·

Mundy and Deadspike's attention was arrested by the sudden bolt of lightning that speared down, bringing havoc to the tower behind them. They both instinctively ducked as chunks of masonry flew asunder in the massive explosion. Already they could see a sheet of flame up there as fire took instant hold.

When Mundy turned back to face Deadspike, the Enforcer had drawn his gun.

"It's all over for you, Deadspike," Mundy told him. "And the Authority. You may have had my friends back in Londonborough murdered, but you can't kill us all. Daybreak will expose you for what you are. You've lost Petra."

Deadspike pointed the gun at Mundy's chest. "Pity you won't live to celebrate."

Mundy laughed emptily. "Shooting me won't save you. And anyway, you won't do it."

Deadspike aimed the gun skywards, pulling the trigger. The sound of the shot was only partly muffled by the cacophony of the storm. "It *is* loaded."

"Petra has beaten you, not me. Petra and all it stands for."

"I don't think so, Mr. Mundy. I'm just a good citizen protecting myself. From a man who is seriously disturbed. You mean nothing to the Authority. I don't need to *kill* you. I can just as easily maim you." The gun dropped a fraction, now aimed at Mundy's lower body, a wisp of smoke from its muzzle sucked away by the wind.

To Deadspike's surprise, Mundy edged closer to the rim of the wall and stepped up onto its low parapet. Beyond that was a drop of over a hundred feet. What was the idiot doing?

"You claim Vasillius committed suicide,"' Mundy said. "Imagine what it would mean if you were to claim that there was yet *another* suicide up here. Who would believe a coincidence like that?"

Deadspike's attention was briefly distracted by something up in the blazing tower. It sounded as if there were people up there *screaming.*

Behind Mundy, on the steps, figures were emerging from the darkness below, climbing up the steps to the wall. In a moment they would be level with them.

Mundy stood on the very lip. It had all become quite clear to him now. There was a way to destroy not only Deadspike but all that he stood for. The world had become deathly still, as if the very storm had drawn its breath. He felt a sudden sense of peace. The wild madness that had consumed him — indeed, all of them — was passing. "Well, Mr. Deadspike? Who would believe you?" he said.

And he dropped.

Penn Ranzer was the first to reach the wall. She screamed in denial at what she saw. She had heard a single gunshot and Mundy was gone! Deadspike had shot him! She came racing across the wall so quickly that the Enforcer swung the gun and almost opened fire. But, impossibly, an arrow appeared in his bicep, ripping through flesh and jarring bone. He was flung back by the impact, gasping in pain, the gun spinning away across the wall.

Penn dropped to her knees on the parapet, craning her neck. Somewhere below her, Mundy had disappeared into that foaming maelstrom.

Wroxton and his companions quickly joined her. Among them were Danton Connell and the bowman. The latter knelt down beside the distraught girl, his own face, like hers, glistening with tears. It was Erroll Detroyd.

EPILOGUE

THE ANTEROOM TO the luxurious office suite of Lionel Canderville was cold, its walls bare. Surprisingly, Luther Sunderman thought, it did nothing to underline the ambition of his superior. Perhaps, though, that was part of the political game.

Eventually the door to Canderville's office opened and Sunderman was called in. He found himself alone with the man whose job he craved, once Canderville had secured his own promotion. With any luck, it's what this interview was all about.

"Luther," said Canderville with something approximating a smile. "I'll be brief. How long have you been in your current post?"

This is it. He is *moving on.* "A little over three years."

"Time for a change, I think."

"Well, I believe I am ready for a new challenge."

"Good. Something very interesting has cropped up." Canderville looked across at him and suddenly Sunderman felt cold. His intuition told him that something was wrong.

"Byron Hoarsely, the Prime at Northcastle, has retired," said Canderville, leaving the statement to hang in the air for a moment.

"He's been an invaluable servant," said Sunderman, completely thrown.

"Yes. And we have an excellent replacement for him in Garth Mowley, his current Senior Magister. In fact, Mowley is taking up the post of Prime as we speak."

"I met him on my last Inspection up there. Seems sound."

"Indeed. I'm glad to hear that you approve."

How does all this affect me? Sunderman wanted to snap.

"Your new challenge, Luther. Time to get away from the city and its trials and tribulations. Your current role here is changing. It needs a new breed of incumbent. Someone more ruthless, less patient. And you need something more proactive, somewhere less volatile. I want you to take on the Senior Magister role at Northcastle."

In that godforsaken northern wilderness? This must be a joke.

"In the fullness of time, I would expect you to take over from Mowley. You yourself could become its Prime."

Mowley is no more than forty! He'll be Prime for decades. What is this?

"You deserve a good posting, Luther. I've already started making the arrangements." Canderville walked around the desk and offered his hand.

Sunderman, barely concealing his horror, shook it, and moments later found himself back outside, staring at the blank walls. Northcastle! Promotion? This was a catastrophe, nothing less than banishment. But why?

Deadspike had handled the potential problems with the Society. Even now he was in Petra, tidying up the mess. But Sunderman realised in that moment how naïve he had been. *Someone more ruthless. He* means *Deadspike! When he comes back from Petra, he'll take the credit. So it's betrayal.* And, of course, it was far too late to do a thing about it now.

· ✷ ·

In Petra, the day after the festival, an old building in the heart of the town that occasionally served as a meeting place for local dignitaries was opened up and used for a unique gathering. The storm had died away, but the skies were still dark grey and showers passed across the Dumnonian landscape periodically. Most people had gone back to their daily routines.

Seats ringed the auditorium on three sides, facing a small stage, the focal point of the hall. A handful of Petrans sat for the most part in the front rows, watching the stage. Occupying a central position up there was the huge figure of Sebastian Wroxton, the High Lord, his face impassive. On his right, sat the two Commanders, Gunnerson and Tithecombe. To his left sat Uther Vasillius, Erroll Detroyd, Danton Connell, and Rannick Carston, now dressed in simple garb, weapons no longer at their sides. With them was another huge figure, Kruach O'Branner, the leader of the Erish war party so effective in securing the town. It had been the final act in cementing an alliance whose seeds stretched back to that distant day when Dunstan Fullerton and his father had saved Kruach from oblivion as a youth.

To one side of the stage, a single chair had been placed. It was empty, but the Petrans watched it as though someone would materialize there. There was a long pause while thoughts turned to those who had fallen and with them a murmuring of remembrance. Eventually Wroxton stood and held up a hand for silence. It fell almost instantly.

"Today is the first day of Petra's independence," he said in a voice that carried effortlessly to the back of the hall.

A spontaneous cheer of approval went up from the small gathering.

"Today is the first day of a new truth, the day that the Authority and its many sins are laid bare before you. A new doctrine will go forward from here. You've been chosen carefully from among the people of Petra, the forests, New Calleva, and High Burnam. Chosen to hear the truth. It is a more powerful weapon in our defense than anything the Authority could use against us." He turned to someone in the wings.

Two of Gunnerson's loyal men brought in Deadspike and ushered him gently to the lone seat. The Enforcer sat there stoically. His right arm had been dressed in a sling and any movement of it brought a twitch of pain to his face. His eyes fixed unwaveringly on Wroxton.

"For those of you who do not know him," Wroxton told the gathering, "this is Mr. Michel Deadspike. He is an Enforcer, a servant of the Central Authority. He is here today to witness our seal on what will be a new charter for Petra." Wroxton faced Deadspike as though inviting a comment, but the Enforcer said nothing.

Wroxton went on, "The events of yesterday were not without tragic consequences. You all know the price that we have had to pay for our rebellion. We regret that lives were lost. You may know that, during the height of the storm, the central tower at the Academy was struck by lightning. Three people died in the resulting fire: the Prime, Miss Cora Vine, my senior colleague, Mr. Carl Trencher and our priest, Father Emmanuel Madding."

There was a renewed murmuring amongst the audience and Wroxton waited for it to subside.

"We also lost a very valued colleague, Mr. Brin Goldsworthy, not to the fire, but to a fatal heart attack. And one other member of the Academy staff died. Not all of you will have known him as he was relatively new to us. His name was

Chad Mundy." Wroxton turned to face Deadspike. "Chad Mundy was murdered, up on the Academy sea wall. Just as his predecessor, Drew Vasillius, was murdered."

Deadspike remained unmoved.

"The Central Authority has been protecting its interests and its many secrets for decades," Wroxton continued. "It is a history of lies and deceit, going back to the time of the Plague Wars and something you shall hear about more thoroughly. Something called Daybreak. To protect the truth about Daybreak, the Authority has gone to great lengths, even resorting to murder. Those in Londonborough who tried to expose the truth were eliminated. The lucky ones escaped."

Wroxton turned to Erroll Detroyd, who inclined his head, his own eyes fixed on Deadspike. The Enforcer appeared indifferent.

"Drew Vasillius carried the truth and was murdered because of it. Mr. Deadspike may not have undertaken the killing personally, but his servants, Father Madding's Brethren, were responsible. Mr. Deadspike, however, was responsible for the killing of Chad Mundy. Do you wish to comment, Mr. Deadspike?"

Deadspike remained in his seat. But he turned to the hostile faces before him. "It would be a pity if you attempted to set yourselves up as an independent state and based your constitution on inaccuracies and misinformation."

There were more than a few shouts of disapproval and several voices called for Deadspike's execution.

He ignored them, face a bland mask. His voice was thick with contempt when he spoke. "Drew Vasillius committed suicide. A *truth* that no one here is prepared to acknowledge. Suicide is obviously a contagious disease in Petra. I watched Chad Mundy end his own life. He went off the wall last night in a pathetic attempt to implicate me in his death."

Again the voices rose, some snarling their fury.

But Deadspike had the stage and his own voice grew in power. "I assure you all that the Authority will not countenance any rebellion, declaration of independence, or the ratification of any charter! Whether you intend to execute me or not is of *no consequence!* Unless you undo your own murderous actions, you'll find *an army* at your gates. You have no idea of the power that the Authority can bring down upon you.

In view of the wholesale *murder* committed in this town, you can expect little mercy."

This time a number of the audience stood up, shouting angrily, but Deadspike simply leaned back in his chair, smiling with derision.

Wroxton finally quelled his colleagues. He, like Deadspike, was perfectly calm. "Mr. Deadspike has not grasped the reality of the situation," the High Lord said. "I promised you the truth. It is simply this. Years ago, scientists undertook an abortive experiment that changed our world, almost destroying it. They covered up their disaster with a false history, centered around the lie that was the Plague Wars, and a potential Invasion from Evropa. You will hear it all and you will pass it on to your friends, families and colleagues, when the time is right. Word will eventually spread throughout the forests, both here in Dumnonia and across Grand Britannia.

"We will teach a new curriculum in our Academy and in our military bases. We will teach the truth about Daybreak and all its consequences. The Authority can send as many armies as it likes, but it cannot destroy us all. Murder is not the answer. Murder, Mr. Deadspike, is redundant.

"We have no intention of executing you. We have a much better use for you. You will carry our demands to the Authority in Londonborough for us."

Deadspike spoke softly, but even so, everyone in the hall heard him clearly. "The Authority will crush you, Wroxton. It will never accede to your demands."

"It will have to. It will have no alternative."

· ✳ ·

After people had dispersed, Deadspike was alone with Wroxton's principal colleagues, one of who was Erroll Detroyd.

"You're lucky that I only sent an arrow into your arm," said the latter.

Deadspike smiled. "Mr. Detroyd. You may have slipped your leash back in Londonborough. Your partners in the Society were less fortunate."

But Detroyd refused to be intimidated. "Even so, you owe your present predicament to them."

"And what is my predicament?"

"We have a job for you, Deadspike," said Wroxton. "Mr. Detroyd here will be delighted to assist you in it. He will escort you back to the gates of Londonborough. We would like you to deliver our charter to your superiors."

"Your naivety surprises me," said Deadspike. "But do go on."

"And our terms. Petra will become a free state, self-governing and altogether independent of the Authority or any other external power."

"What could you possibly have that could win you their agreement? They'll come in numbers, Wroxton, and this time the guns will not be spiked."

"We have something they would kill for. Who knows that better than you?"

Deadspike frowned, genuinely puzzled.

"The truth. It can stay in Petra. Oh, we'll teach it. But part of that teaching will be its sacred nature. It needn't go out into the world. Not yet, anyway. But if the Authority's response to our demands is refusal and reprisals, the Islands will be ablaze with an understanding of Daybreak and its consequences. The entire Islands would be up in arms and the Authority would have no power to repress them. It's what it has been afraid of for decades. Without our discretion, the Authority will lose all credibility."

"Not only that," said Detroyd with a grin, "but word will infiltrate the city itself. I got out, Deadspike, I can get in again. And so can others."

"And of course," said Wroxton casually, "there is the small matter of murder. I would imagine that the Authority would find it intensely embarrassing were it to become known throughout Londonborough that it has been responsible for sanctioning the deaths of several scholars. And you, sent here as an executioner."

"That's absurd."

"Really? We've a witness to your shooting Mundy. And we have another who saw enough of the murder of Drew Vasillius to put the verdict beyond doubt."

Deadspike suddenly let out a harsh bark of laughter. "Well, this is rich! So *you* will have a secret to keep and *you* will have to ensure its safekeeping! And how far will *you* go to achieve that? Would you kill?"

Wroxton towered over him. "Well, that's no longer your problem, Mr. Deadspike. It's for us to decide."

· ✳ ·

The following day, Brin Goldsworthy was cremated out in the forest. It was a pagan ceremony, attended by a large crowd. Once the pyre had died down, with evening drawing on, the ashes were taken and spread out in the glades. A multitude of flowers were placed around the scene of the pyre. There was a ceremony, too, for Chad Mundy, though his body had never been recovered from the sea. Like Drew Vasillius before him, he had been swept away, though never far from the thoughts of those that had lost him.

Goldsworthy's wife, Mara, stood in silence, watching the last tendrils of smoke drifting on the light breeze. Beside her stood Anna Vasillius, Penn Ranzer, and Morgana. Without a word between them, they took each other's hands, bowed their heads, and prayed silently to their forest deities. After that there was only the deep silence of the endless trees.

· ✳ ·

A month had gone by since the fall of Petra.

Deep in the empty canyons of Londonborough, in a run-down pub, the candle lights flickered. In a solitary booth, a figure slumped on the smoke-stained seat, eyes drooping. A cracked cup on the table contained a powerful alcoholic drink, manufactured privately in some backstreet still. The effects of the drink had blurred the man's thoughts as well as his vision.

When a figure appeared before him, he glanced up momentarily.

"Well, now. If it isn't Mr. Deadspike," said the newcomer, clutching his hat tightly as if afraid it would escape him.

"Slake?"

"At your service, Mr. Deadspike. I should say, at Mr. *Sunderman's* service."

"Sunderman?" Deadspike slurred the word. "He's long gone, Slake. Thrown out. The Authority has sent him far away."

"So I gather, sir. But before he went, he bought my services, for a last time. Seems he was a very wealthy man."

Deadspike frowned and picked up his cup to cover his momentary confusion. He emptied it, setting it down unsteadily, and wiping his mouth with a soiled sleeve. "He's gone and so has his boss, the ambitious Lionel Canderville. A victim of the Dumnonian fiasco. You know Dumnonia, Slake?"

"Not my neck of the woods, Mr. Deadspike. But I do hear as how it's become an independent state. No longer under the Authority's jurisdiction."

"No. Well, it's done for Canderville." *And I did for Sunderman. He can't help me now. One cock-up after another. And the Authority's days are numbered. Dumnonia is just the first. All a matter of time.*

"Would you like another, Mr. Deadspike? My credit's good here."

"Why not?"

Slake picked up the cup, smiled, and made his way to the bar. He stood beside a man who was dressed even more shabbily than he was. "Got a little job for you," Slake said softly. "Something needs to be got rid of."

Rick the Razor nodded very slowly.

"What do you need?" said Slake, catching the barman's eye.

Rick the Razor carefully opened the front of his coat, displaying a dozen or more sharp, steel blades. "Could always do with some more of these, Ottomas. What's the job?"

"It's a who, not a what."

Rick the Razor grinned. 'Who's were much more fun than 'what's. He specialized in 'who's.

"Like I say, it's a who. I'm getting a drink for the geezer sitting in the booth behind me." The barman passed the refilled cup across the counter to Slake.

Rick the Razor glanced casually in Deadspike's direction, but the man was oblivious. "Is he the one?"

"He is. Let him finish his drink, eh?" said Slake, tapping the cup.

Rick the Razor looked down at it. Whatever the drink was, it looked to be unusually cloudy. "Sure, Ottomas. You want me to have him discreetly shut away?"

"A bit more than that, Ricky. This one's a disposal."

· ✳ ·

Acknowledgements

The author would like to express special gratitude to his agent, Richard Curtis, for his invaluable help in helping to mould the novel into its final form and would also like to thank his copy editor at EDGE, Robyn Read for her tireless patience in beating the book into a fit state for publication.